Luke

A.S. ROBERTS

Version 1P
ISBN: 9798487513397

Edited by Karen J.
Proofreading by Freda Smith.
Beta read by The Fireball Fillies.
Cover art by J M Walker @justwritecreations
Formatting by J M Walker

Playlist

All songs, song titles mentioned in this novel are the property of the respective song writers and copyright holders.

https://open.spotify.com/playlist/4UdYMjCzvl0mweb5T6WHbZ?si=IDmRwg-jQtOopXoOl2MArA

Emma.
Sometimes even your wildest dreams come true.

Dedication

To everyone who has ever been abandoned
and to all of those who wish to be found.

I see you; I feel you and I send you love.

And, as always, it's dedicated to my husband.
Thank you for finding me, for loving me and for walking hand in hand
by my side.

Prologue

LUKE

Thirty-four years ago

FATHER MCKENZIE HAD BEEN asleep for possibly two and a half to three hours, when the phone downstairs in the hallway started to ring out its shrill and incessantly annoying tone. The phone's volume was always at the absolute maximum, to ensure any cry for help could be heard all through the clergy house. The sound it made reverberated around the silent building. The noise was one he'd heard too many times to count since arriving at St Columba Roman Catholic Church in New York City only nine years previously, from the much quieter city of Dublin in Ireland. He could have sworn on many an occasion that it was enough to wake the dead. If, of course, he swore.

Coming to with a start, he realised that the noise would soon be rousing everyone else from their slumber too and he needed to make a move to answer it.

It might be the twenty-first century, but he knew that even with all the do-gooders and charitable organisations available, there would always be the "haves" and the "have nots" in this world. It was his mission to console and help the latter. He let out a sigh of acceptance that circumstances were unlikely to change in his lifetime and that perhaps they were worse now than at any other point in history. Muttering a quick prayer, he roused himself to move his frame off the warm and comfortable mattress beneath him.

Operating on automatic pilot, he opened his eyes, swung back the covers as he always did and jumped out of bed, propelling himself towards the dark-stained wooden door. Then he pulled it open quickly and winced as the cry for help hit his ears again.

He stopped only once, to retrieve his bathrobe from the chair beside the door, then thrusting his arms into it he hurried out of his bedroom. The several inches of snow on the ground around the clergy house had turned the world white. Thankfully, this reflected through the bare, stained-glass window and lit his path.

He shivered as the cooler air hit him and his stomach turned over in apprehension of what he may have to deal with in the small hours of the morning.

As he made his way down the large staircase, Father McKenzie silently prayed for the strength he needed to help the poor soul on the other end of the line. Although the sound of the phone was always the same to the untrained ear, he had realised, a long time ago, that he was very often aware of what the person on the other end needed before they'd even spoken.

And this person, he could feel in his heart, was desperate and possibly at breaking point.

Without a shadow of a doubt, he recognised that the ring he could hear, in the early hours of Christmas morning, was the pain-filled cries of help from yet another frantic and weary soul.

Luckily, Father McKenzie was still young enough to run down the stairs two at a time. He stretched out his arm as he rushed towards the old black phone, desperate to offer words of comfort, as the receiver renewed its attempts to vibrate itself off its cradle.

Finally, he grabbed it in his large hand.

'St Columba, clergy house. Father McKenzie speaking.'

The shaky sound of someone trying to draw breath came through to him.

'It's okay, we're here to help. Tell me how I can help you?' he tried again, making sure his voice was encouraging in its tone.

An emotion-filled sob reached his ears and his heart broke a little bit more, the same as it always did when he absorbed the pain of another.

'Please tell me how we can help you, my child?' he gently pleaded into the phone.

Father McKenzie gripped the receiver even tighter in his hand. It was his only connection with the troubled soul on the other end and he willed them to feel the strength of the love he was trying to send them. He willed them to carry on, to not put the phone down, and to connect with him in some way, so that he could help them.

'My baby...' the young woman on the other end whispered to him, in between the sobs that were now wracking through her body. 'Please.'

'Your baby?' he questioned, making it loud enough so that with a raise of his eyebrows and a nod of his head the clergy housekeeper, Francis, and one of the younger priests who had also answered the loud cries of the antique phone, automatically sprung into a routine that was far too well practised for his liking.

'How can we help your baby, my child?'

'Steps,' she whispered back to him.

With an over pronounced wave of his arm, he sent the two people who were looking expectantly at him for information, outside their warm house to the church next door, where he knew, in his heart, they would find what she was gifting to them.

Within minutes, Francis and Father Heyward appeared back at the open front door. Francis held a small, tightly wrapped up bundle in her arms. Father Heywood disappeared back outside and into the snow to look around for anyone watching nearby, as they all knew that the baby's mother was bound to be close, making sure her child was taken inside.

'It's okay, my child. Help is on its way,' he spoke back to the desperate woman on the other end of the line.

'Thank you,' the young voice whispered back to him.

'I can help you too, please stay and talk to me. We can come and get you, wherever you are.'

Francis removed the dirty looking blankets from the baby and silently showed him the obviously new-born child.

He could sense that the girl on the other end of the line was getting ready to leave. 'Your son is beautiful. You've done such a good job, my child. We can help you look after him. Please tell us how to find you.'

Father Heywood appeared back at the front door, sadly shaking his head after not finding what he was looking for.

'I can't see her anywhere nearby. Any footprints in the snow have disappeared,' he whispered, as he shivered in his nightclothes. 'The normal call and diversion tactic,' he carried on, making sure his voice was no more than a whisper and couldn't be heard by the caller.

Just then the baby boy scrunched up his fists and let out a strong wail of indignation. Father McKenzie knew that whilst he might have been newly born and left out in the snow by his mother, he was strong and apparently very hungry.

The young woman's voice found a certain strength after hearing her baby boy's cry and it spurred her on to speak. 'Tell him I love him; tell him I'll always love him... it's just better this way.'

A click sounded in his ear. With tears pricking the back of his eyes and a loud sigh of resignation, Father McKenzie replaced the receiver and held out his arms for the newborn child. He held him tightly to his body and willed his warmth into the tiny infant.

'Father Heyward, please dial nine-one-one.'

He looked down at the boy in his arms.

'Welcome...' Then he looked back up expectantly at Francis. 'Now, where did we get to, Francis?' he sighed.

'Let me see, Father.' She stopped talking momentarily and used her fingers to work out the answer to what he'd asked her. 'Matthew, Mark. That's right... we got to Luke.'

Using his forefinger, he gently drew the sign of the cross on the baby's forehead.

'Welcome to the world, Luke McKenzie.'

One

LUKE

Two and a half years ago

'SO, WHAT DO YOU think?' I suppressed the urge to laugh out loud at Raff's accent. It was fucking weird how, although we'd only been in the U.K. for a couple of days, he was already sounding like the Brit he was by birth.

When no one answered immediately, Raff pulled away from the group, to move in between us and the huge, red brick building in front of us. He opened his arms out wide and turned around on the spot, looking strangely like that woman from the sound of music.

'Just look at it,' he spoke again.

His enthusiasm was obvious, and a wide smile took over his face. Somewhere inside, I knew I was happy for him. He was home, for the first time in fifteen years or thereabouts and it was exactly where he needed to be.

But where the fuck do I belong?

The same haunting question I'd been asking myself since I was a small child reared its unwelcome voice inside my head. It had been silenced while Cherise had been in my life, because the two of us had belonged together, but now she was gone it had returned with a vengeance that I couldn't, or didn't want to, extinguish.

I no longer had the answers to anything. Questions flooded my head constantly, until I guiltily craved the same oblivion Cherise had found nearly three months before, when she'd taken the ultimate way out. At the same time, she'd shown me that my love for her and our love for our daughter and the family we'd both always craved, wasn't strong enough, or just simply enough, for her to choose to stay with us.

And she never confided in me why.

I wasn't even sure what I thought or felt anymore. Her death had made me question if what I had thought I understood about love and life, was way off the fucking mark.

So, I took a few minutes and hoped Brody and Cade would answer him, instead of me.

I wish I'd died instead of her.

I squeezed my eyes together tightly, trying to rid myself of everything flying around inside my head.

The pain I constantly felt was temporarily side swiped away by guilt, as for what must have been the millionth time in the eighty-two days she'd been gone, I wished myself dead and our daughter alone.

Just what sort of fucking dad are you?

SHUT UP! I felt myself screw my eyes tightly shut as I tried to extinguish the broken man I was inside. As the pain and questions began to ebb away, I nervously opened my eyes again to face the bright sunshine of the day.

And this was the way grief seemed to go for me. Round and fucking round I went with it, until I was almost too exhausted to function.

But, however exhausted and emotionally wrung I was, it was nothing compared to the doubts in my mind about who I really was.

Am I a good enough dad?

I certainly hadn't been a good enough husband.

But the one thing I was now, was clean. And for now, I hoped it was enough.

I sighed out loud, trying to release the pent-up pain from my body and into the open air. My body shuddered with the exertion and catching myself as I disturbed the sleeping form of my young daughter, I stopped breathing briefly, until I was sure I could exhale without waking her.

Needing to feel her strength, I pushed my forefinger into Brielle's pudgy hand. The same one she always put on my chest as she fell asleep in the only place she would now sleep, without whimpering her loneliness, and I felt her fingers instinctively take a firm grip on to it and me.

Fuck.

Yet again, the feeling of panic at being her sole parent rushed through me, followed by the calmness that she brought with her. She was so very young, but so damn fucking knowing at the same time. Her hold on me, her love for me, was ninety percent of the reason I was still here, living and breathing. The other ten percent was down to the men around me, my brothers, in every sense of the word, except name.

Life, I'd discovered, was never to be taken for granted. All those worries that I'd had about the future, when I was a kid growing up in the church orphanage, seemed completely redundant. As I'd found out, tomorrow wasn't a given for anybody. The plans that Cherise and me had made together years before, lying on the roof of our shared duplex back in Vegas, had been ripped into shreds the moment I'd found her collapsed on our bathroom floor, with the syringe still hanging from her vein.

And love? I'd only ever experienced any kind of love, with Cherise. But the night she'd made the decision that she'd couldn't cope with life anymore and had driven that loaded syringe into her arm, choosing death over the three of us being together, would be forever seared onto my brain. That one night had taught me that even love was a selfish fucker.

I knew I'd love her in my own way for the rest of my life, but what about the cold hard hatred I had for my once vibrant but now dead wife? The one that I hadn't admitted to anyone but myself. Would that also stay with me until I took my final breath? The same had to be asked of the gut-wrenching pain that had ripped out my insides and shattered my heart into a billion tiny fucking pieces.

Because, if so, I wasn't sure I was strong enough to survive them.

Up until three months ago, I'd always been the loudest, most in your face of the four of us. The one who was willing to try anything and everything life had to offer, with a passion the other three in DD seemed to sometimes struggle to keep up with. But now she was gone, and I was empty, void of passion and feeling, and it appeared even life itself.

I was the stupid fucker who, with his own need for the next adventure, had introduced us all to the smack that had subsequently given me the comeuppance I knew I deserved, and ultimately my moronic choices had taken my wife. I'm not saying the fuckers wouldn't have found it on their own anyway, but it was a decision I knew I'd always have to live with.

I closed my eyes, dipped my head forward and buried my face into the sleeping form of my little girl, Brielle. And I breathed her in, while I listened to her gentle snores and the banter around me.

'It's fucking immense... beautiful even... and everything you described it as,' Brody put in. After he stopped speaking, I heard him inhale a deep lungful of the fresh air around us, as if to prove the point he was trying to make.

'You're talking about it like it's a woman, dude.' I knew without looking up that Cade would have rested his arm around Brody's shoulders while he teased him. 'Raff, can it definitely be done in the timescale and budget we want?' questioned Cade, who was forever our numbers man.

'I've shown you all the plans,' Raff replied.

'Yeah, I know, but I don't understand the English... you and they speak. It's like a different fucking language.' Cade started laughing. 'Fuck... Fuck off!' Cade's voice sounded out in surprise and warning. I imagined, by his reaction and the change in direction of his voice, that Raff had sent him sprawling to the ground next to me.

'They've assured me it can,' Raff answered with an amused tone.

'That's good enough for me,' Brody muttered under his breath next to me, apparently now lost in thought. Then he cleared his throat and carried on. 'We agreed about needing the new focus, about putting down some roots and here is as good a place as any I've seen.'

'There's just under a hundred acres of land around the place... so it can be a flagship hotel, and at the same time we can build ourselves homes here deep in the English countryside,' Raff carried on. 'If we want to, of course.'

'Fresh air and shit,' Cade added. 'And away from the media,' he groaned.

I heard them all starting to mutually agree that it was exactly what they felt we all needed.

The new start, that God knows we all wanted, to get our lives back on track. The new start we needed to save us all.

Their voices drifted away on the breeze, as I tried to dig down fucking deep inside myself to try to work out what Cherise would have wanted me to do. She'd been in my life from the second I'd first saw her, moved in with me that same night and had stayed right there beside me like no one else ever had, until she'd abruptly left my life and taken everything I ever thought I was, with her.

Emotion was a painful fucker. You'd think all these weeks later, I'd be able to control how it swept through me and took over every single piece of me, but I couldn't, and I knew I was no longer strong enough to want to even try.

I sank down to the warm, soft grass beneath my feet and changed my hold on our daughter, so I could look at her properly while she slept soundly. With her still gripping on to my finger, I gently stroked Brielle's face with the rest of my fingertips as I remembered doing the same to her mom's only a short time ago. A couple of weeks before, tears would have poured down my face right about then. But they were another thing that had left me, it appeared I wasn't even worthy of the cathartic release they would offer. Instead, some weird fucking almost primitive noise left my slightly open mouth and in response I clamped my mouth tight. Because deep down inside me, I knew I didn't even deserve the comfort of letting the world hear my pain.

It was mine and mine alone. I'd dug the fucking hole I was in, and I was resigned to living in it.

I felt them sit down around me in solidarity, as they let me have the few minutes that they knew by experience I needed.

I loved them all the more for their silent understanding.

For a few minutes, in a large green covered field in England, with the sun beating down on my face, I tried to remember who I even was.

Sure, I'd been an orphaned child back in NYC, but I'd never let that affect me in any way. I'd always had an inbuilt self confidence that Father McKenzie said was way beyond my years and circumstances. I saw it as nature not nurture. When I grew old enough to understand, Father McKenzie had taken me to one side, as I knew he would, having watched him for years with the kids older than me. He'd explained what little they knew about my arrival into the world. The phone call in the early hours of the morning, and my birth mom's disappearance once she'd known I was safe. He explained that it was how so many of us had come into the church orphanage and how it was a "default distraction" technique that so many desperate mothers used.

Inadvertently, my birth mother had not only given birth to me that night, but with her actions she had also given me our band name and my future family.

Some things, I'd taken upon myself to figure out. With my reddish-brown hair and bright green eyes, I'd decided I was from Irish descent. And as the Irish always made their own luck, I'd taken life by the balls early on and charmed my way into situations that didn't normally fall into the laps of deserted children.

My motto had always been "Life is what you make of it" and I knew that subsequently, it was with that drive and my self-taught talent on the bass guitar and violin, that I'd risen to great heights in the music industry with the brothers that now silently surrounded me and my daughter. Followed closely by the peace that this little piece of the world seemed to have in abundance.

No more. Stop thinking. Stop remembering.

'What do you think Cherise would have thought of the place?' I lifted my head slightly to question them all.

'She'd have fucking loved it,' Brody answered, without even taking a second to think. 'And, Bro… she'd want this for the two of you. Hell, she'd want it for all of us.'

His enthusiasm and conviction caused me to look up from my daughter and take in The Manor once again.

'She could have had it with us,' I whispered, feeling my throat tighten.

'She's here with us, I can feel her around us,' Raff observed as he lifted a hand to gently stroke Brielle's bare arm.

'Imagine the kids having this place to grow up in, to grow strong in and to make their own way in life from,' Cade added.

'Kids?' Raff questioned, laughing and trying to lift the atmosphere. 'We've only got the two.'

'At the moment… Don't ask me why, but I see this place fucking full of them,' Cade reflected.

'All your wild oats coming out of the woodwork then, Morello?' Brody questioned, laughing.

Normally, I'd have joined in with their fucking around, but for some reason I couldn't take my eyes off The Manor.

'This, well… is this…' I shrugged my shoulders as I tried hard to find the words, 'is this what a home feels like?' I quietly questioned.

One by one they turned their heads towards mine. I didn't meet their eyes, but continued to stare at the Victorian structure taking up most of the distant horizon. I could see it needed completely renovating to stop it eventually disintegrating away to nothing.

It was then that the realisation took hold of me and I understood that the building and I were alike.

'Yes, Mac,' Raff replied. 'It's exactly what a home feels like. It's solid and strong, like us four. It'll protect the family that's inside it. Because, like the four of us, it has four very separate and different corners holding it altogether.'

For a few seconds, silence wrapped around us as we contemplated our past and our future. The only thing that I was sure about right in that second, was my love for my young daughter and the three men that were gathered around me.

I knew this move was the stepping stone I needed.

'Fuck me!' Brody shouted out to Raff, having obviously just let Rafferty's words sink in. 'Who the fuck are you? William fucking Shakespeare?'

Cathartic laughter abruptly started drowning out the sound of the countryside around us, and I watched with a fleeting smile on my mouth as they pushed each other around on the grass beside me, like a bunch of teenagers.

Yeah, it felt like I thought a proper home should.

With the three of them still fucking about around me, I lifted my face to look up to the few clouds in the otherwise blue sky.

I knew then that Brielle would one day be part of a family. The family that neither Cherise nor I had growing up.

Cherise might have gone, but my promise to her still remained.

Two

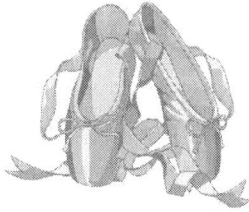

Nikki

Present day

'MUM'S MADE SOME CHEESE on toast.' My sister Louise tapped on the door gently, with what I presumed was her fingernail, as she spoke.

I pulled my head out from under my pillows, turned myself over and stared straight up at the ceiling. Fleetingly, I allowed my eyes to look around my very dated bedroom, decorated in the pinks and yellows of childhood. Then I brought my eyes back into focus as I homed in on the tattered edges of one of the many posters next to my headboard. At one point, my room had been covered with all the bands I loved to listen to, but this one had been more special than the others. I picked at a piece of the old poster with a fingernail and then let out a slow, hopefully not audible sigh.

'Would it work if I said I wasn't hungry?' I called out to my sister, who was concealed behind my closed door.

'Come on, Nik. What do you think?' She groaned and I could almost hear her rolling her eyes from the other side of the door. 'You rushed in the house giving us a quick hello, had a shower and shut yourself away in your room.'

'Okay,' I sighed again, but resigned myself to the knowledge that I'd run out of time. Picking up my spare pillow at the side of me, I clutched it to my chest like a life preserver.

Mum and Louise had already been good enough to let me have two hours, since my unexpected arrival back home and it must have killed them to not come questioning me earlier. 'Give me fifteen minutes and I'll be down.'

I watched as the white glossed door to my bedroom slowly opened and my sister poked her head around the wood.

'I'd make it more like five. Mum's pacing the small space between the units in the kitchen, and she's been cleaning the same things for at least the last two hours while we "give you some space."' She used two fingers either side of her head to air quote our mum's words.

I scrunched the fabric of the well-worn pillowcase tighter beneath my fingers, hugged it closer to my chest and breathed in the familiar smell of the lavender fabric conditioner my mum had used for as long as I could remember.

The lavender was supposed to calm and relax, but today it just wasn't working.

I knew it was inevitable that I was going to have to explain why her supposedly successful and independent daughter was back in the Kent countryside.

'It's really no big deal,' I sat up, shaking my head at her as I attempted to add conviction to the sentence.

'Really? You know that Mum loves seeing you and so do I. But you were due home in a couple of weeks' time for your Christmas break, so why on earth would you have turned up earlier?' Her expression questioned me, before she carried on talking. 'I think if that hadn't already made alarm bells ring, the fact that Angela Wooten from the nannying agency has already been on the phone this morning to speak to you, might have.'

'Really?' I sighed heavily and felt my body sag as I fell back onto the mattress. 'She just couldn't wait to sink her claws in, could she?'

'What's happened, Nikki? She didn't really tell us anything, but she does want you to call her back, and she said she wanted that to happen today.' She overly dramatized the last word and rolled her eyes skyward.

Lou sat down on the bed and took my hand in hers.

'It can't be that bad,' she offered.

'I've left my job, under a cloud as far as the agency will be concerned. I won't get a reference from the Millars… So, in short, I now have no job, probably no prospects and that means more importantly no income.'

'Oh no. What on earth happened?' she grimaced and then questioned, as with a sweep of her right hand she flicked my long hair away from my face, so she had a clearer view to look into my eyes.

'Come on let's go downstairs. I'll explain to you both together.' Resigned to my fate and knowing I couldn't protect them from the truth and the complications it brought with it, I grabbed a tight hold on the hand she had already offered me and made to stand up around her.

Being the eldest and taking the role as seriously as I had always done, I inhaled deeply, took the step I needed and pulled her up from the bed behind me. We walked out of the small bedroom hand in hand and down the stairs to find our mum. Our family home was compact, so within a few seconds, we arrived at the doorway to the back room of our neat terraced housed. I peered tentatively around the doorframe and began to take in our mum. It had been a couple of months since I'd last been home and I remembered in those all too short seconds, how just her presence could reassure and centre me.

In the background, as always, I could hear the radio playing on low and sure enough she was spinning around in the tight confines of our small kitchen, while she tried to busy herself to feed us and attempted to shelve her concerns over her eldest child.

My mum Tina was only just fifty, but life had left its scars on her. Today, with her long hair tied back tightly in a scrunchy, her worries were showing, and I knew me arriving unannounced had taken her back to the edge of the precipice she seemed to constantly exist on. The same one our dad had left her on when he'd walked out, leaving her with three small children, never to be seen or heard from again. We'd heard he'd left the country to get away from us, but I had resigned myself to the fact we might never know why he'd left, nor where he'd gone to and truthfully, I knew I was stronger for gaining that acceptance.

But my mum, well that was another story.

They say that people are only given the stress they're strong enough to cope with. Well, my mum was a strong, hard-working lady, but I wished whoever it was that had decided she could cope with everything life had thrown at her, would give her a bloody break.

She turned suddenly, as if she caught me in her peripheral vision.

'Mum.' I attempted to offer her a smile.

'There you are, Nikki. I knew the promise of cheese on toast would tempt you down.'

Truthfully, even the smell of my favourite comfort food was turning my stomach.

She watched me wince and her expression immediately softened as her arms opened wide for me to walk into her hold.

So, walk I did. Then I wrapped my arms around her tightly and did the very thing I'd sworn to myself I wouldn't do.

I burst into tears.

'Louise, bring the food and the mugs of tea through into the living room, will you please.'

'Will do,' Lou replied.

Throughout the few minutes of my ridiculous outburst of self-pity, I clutched on to my mum like a small child and allowed her to lead me through to the living room, where we both sank down heavily into the burgundy coloured, settee.

For a short while, I let the tears I'd been fighting to keep under wraps fall, as I remembered just what I'd been through last night.

The chink of the mugs and plates, on the tray Louise carried into the room behind us both, brought me out of my stupor, and I lifted my head off my mum's shoulder to see her offering me a small smile and a tissue.

'You know what they say, Nikki. A problem shared.'

'I'm sorry, Mum, I've lost my job.' I blurted it out fast and held my breath as I watched the understanding wash over her.

My eyes focussed on her through my tears, and I watched as she nodded just the once and swallowed deeply with resignation.

'I thought as much.'

'I'm sorry,' I offered.

'Was it your fault?' she gently questioned.

'No.'

'Then what on earth have you to be sorry for?' Mum moved her hands to rub them comfortingly up and down my arms. 'What happened, Nikki? The fact that Angela has already been on the phone, to remind you that you signed a privacy agreement with the Millars, has been worrying me.'

'Unbelievable.' I knew the woman was all business, but her lack of concern for her employees was hurtful. But of course, she would take the side of the people who paid a hefty monthly sum to her agency.

'You needn't worry any longer, you're home now and we'll sort it out together, like we've always done,' Louise added, trying to reassure me as she sat down on the one and only chair in the small room.

'Agreed,' my mum put into the conversation. 'And just for the record, I've never liked that woman, from just the few things you've told us over the years. She phoned just after you arrived home this morning.' I watched my mum's shoulders lift as she shrugged. 'You were in the shower, and I sent her away with a flea in her ear and told her she could keep her condescending tone and veiled threats to herself.'

'You did?' My voice lifted in disbelief and with an element of pride in my mum defending one of her own.

'Yes, I did, and I'd do it again too. I'd protect all of you with my life, if necessary. I'm sure you both know that?'

Louise and I nodded in unison as she turned her head to look at us one by one.

'So, now all you need to do, is to tell us what happened?' Mum carried on.

'Well… there's no easy way to say it.'

'Then just say the words, Nikita,' she encouraged.

We always knew our mum meant business when she called us by our full names. I inhaled a deep breath, and on the exhale, I let the words, that hadn't stopped flying around my head in disbelief since the incident, fall from my lips.

'Mr. Millar tried to…' I stopped as a feeling of violation ran over my skin. 'Well, what I'm trying to say is… he tried to rape me last night.' The actual words were harder to say than I could ever have imagined. Because it made it more real, if that were even possible. But I knew the words would hurt her, more than he'd hurt me. Suddenly, I could smell him again and taste his expensive cologne on the air around us. His hands were right there pulling at my clothes and ripping through the only protection I had, that would stop his eyes seeing my skin… my bare body.

Anger flashed through me, and more adrenalin released into my bloodstream, as I remembered fighting him off for all I was worth.

'He did what?' My mum's hands moved, and she unexpectedly gripped on to my upper arms. I jumped instinctively as I got ready to run, until I took in the kind eyes of the woman who had always loved and protected me for as long as I could remember, and my body sagged with relief.

'But you're his nanny, you look after his children.' She shook her head slowly from side to side, mirroring mine and realising how tight her hold on me was, she relaxed her fingers while she voiced her disbelief.

'Fucking hell, what an arsehole,' Louise released into the room. I heard her stand up and instinctively move herself closer to the two of us.

'He didn't manage it. Emily heard me screaming and came running in to help me.' In my mind, I could still see Emily, the junior nanny, standing frozen at the open door for a few seconds, with her mouth wide open as she watched the scene unravel in front of her.

'Thank goodness she was there.' My mum exhaled with relief.

'Did he hurt you, Nik? Did... well, did he touch you?' my sister suddenly questioned.

'He flung himself at me. His hands were all over me.' I stopped speaking for a few seconds as revulsion washed over me. The depraved look in his eyes and the smell of the sickly-sweet Champagne he always drunk, invaded all my senses. 'No, I'm not hurt, although he managed to rip off my pyjama top.' I stuttered when I spoke, which was something I hadn't done since our dad had walked out when Lou and I were in primary school, as I attempted to tell my mum and sister just what had happened.

But I was determined that he wasn't going to get the better of me after his attack and I made myself carry on. I was going to release it to the world, so I wouldn't be carrying it around like some shame-filled secret. 'He groped my breasts. I haven't looked, but when I had a shower earlier today, I'm sore just above my left one. I think his head must have bruised me. He fell heavily onto me as Emily arrived and tried to move him.'

'I'll bloody kill him... what right does he think he has, to do that to you?' I was shocked at my mum's use of language as she swore so rarely.

'He was strong,' I carried on, feeling annoyingly shaken reliving the moment, 'he managed to pin me down with one arm, while he pushed his hand into my bottoms to touch me.' I stopped speaking and grimaced, as I swallowed down the sickening feeling that had released inside of me once again. The same feeling that had tried to suffocate me when his manicured fingers had pushed their way in between my legs. 'Then Emily arrived after hearing something was wrong and between us, we eventually got him off me.' I virtually spat out the last sentence as I attempted to pull myself together.

'He's a huge man, how on earth did the two of you manage to get him off?'

'He was drunk,' I answered without having to think.

'That's no fucking excuse,' Louise spoke again and mum twisted her head around to fix her with a look that we both knew meant to watch her language.

A few seconds passed, with the three of us lost in our own thoughts.

'How long had you been feeling uncomfortable there?' my mum finally questioned.

I found her eyes with my own and knew that even after having lived away from home for several years, she still read me so well.

I blinked slowly and sighed out loud.

'A while…' I swallowed, hoping to relieve the dryness trapped inside my throat, 'he was always just that little bit too handsy. It's my fault. I should have walked away earlier, but I loved… no, I love the children and it was the well-paid job we, as a family, needed me to have.'

'It's not *your* fault. Now, get that into your head. I know my daughters and you would have never led him on.' Her face was etched with anger and emotion. 'We'll manage, we always have done before. Maybe Stephen will have to come home for now… I don't know, I'll think on it.' Worry took over her features, making her appear older than her years.

'I've got some money saved, Mum,' I tried hard to reassure her. 'At least enough to cover everything for the next two months.'

She nodded and sat up straighter as concern for us all ran through her, 'Oh, I've just thought… please tell me Emily has left that place, too?'

'Yes, we left together in the same taxi,' I nodded at her, knowing we'd done the right thing for ourselves, but also knowing I was going to miss the Millar children terribly.

'Good, she wouldn't have been safe there.' Still standing next to where we were sitting, I watched as Lou crossed her arms over her chest and shook her head.

'No, she wouldn't have. It's a shame, she was turning into a great nanny, but I expect she won't have any references to use for another job now, like me.'

'Did you call the police?' Lou questioned.

'No, I didn't… According to the media, he and Chelsea are the perfect couple.'

'So?' Lou's voice rose in strength, and I knew she was about to mount her soapbox.

'I'm okay and Emily is okay and it's just not worth it,' I implored with her not to start. I was my sister's greatest supporter, but knew I couldn't listen to her, not right then.

'I beg to differ,' my sister answered, clearly getting angrier by the second. Louise had been standing up for what was right since we were infants and didn't suffer injustice easily. Especially not now she was in her final year of studying law at university.

'I think we should let Nikki handle this how she wants to,' our mum added with a firm nod of her head at Louise, who rolled her lips inwards, to bite down on them to shut herself up, I assumed. 'But it just goes to show that you never know what goes on behind closed doors, doesn't it?'

'No, you don't,' I replied, as I slowly began to relax a little into the settee underneath me, having finally voiced what I'd been dreading telling them.

'Now, do you want me to call the doctor?'

'No. I'm fine… I think I could eat the cheese on toast though, now.'

I smiled at them both and attempted to put them at ease.

Three

Nikki

'N	O, MY CLIENT WON'T be talking to you again and I must insist you make no further attempts to contact her, either personally or through The Park Nanny Agency.'

I was leaning against the magnolia-coloured wall in our hallway with my hand clamped over my mouth.

I'd never in my life felt admiration like I had at that moment for my younger sister. Luckily, the admiration and love I had for her, had overtaken the churning, nauseous feeling that had threatened to engulf me when I'd first heard Hayden Millar's voice reverberating around the small area, we were stood in.

'So, my client wishes to make you an offer. You provide her and Emily Trent with the glowing references they both deserve, and they won't contact the police about your... well, what shall we call it? Oh yes... about your unwanted advances.'

I heard Hayden raise his voice and the words, 'They wouldn't fucking dare...'

'Mr. Millar!' Louise's voice strengthened in force as she assertively stamped all over his attitude. 'I would like to remind you that we have photographic evidence of your teeth marks on my client's upper body and Emily Trent as a witness to what occurred in your residence in Holland Park last night. Due to the high profile "Me too" campaign, I am absolutely certain your clients would dispense with your services the minute we press charges.'

Earlier on, our mum had found the bite mark just below my collarbone, after I'd winced in front of her. Although his teeth hadn't broken my skin and violated me further, Lou had vowed to make him pay for what he'd attempted. Knowing what was at risk for all of my family, I'd agreed to let her do her thing.

I heard him grumble his complaints into the phone and lifted my eyes up to my sister, instead of the trailing telephone wire I'd been following with my eyes as I nervously waited beside her. She raised her eyebrows at me, winked and gave me a thumbs up, and I knew we'd got him by the bollocks, the same ones I'd managed to not very effectively knee him in only the previous day.

'So, we're in agreement then? You've come to the right decision, Mr Millar... yes, uh huh. My client and Emily Trent will expect their references from you within the next twenty-four hours... Goodbye.'

I waited momentarily as she replaced the phone onto its cradle and grabbing hold of her tightly, I pulled her into me, wincing only slightly as she met the bruising on my upper body.

'You are bloody amazing!' I offered, but the statement seemed so ridiculously inadequate. 'In one more year the courts in England are going to get such a boot up their stuffy arses with your arrival in front of them.' I was speaking of her dream to become a barrister and to defend the "little" people.

I felt her pull away from my hold. I looked into her grinning face as I watched her nod back at me.

'I'm convinced he'll comply with our demands,' she agreed.

'Comply? He sounded terrified that this would be all over the media. I can almost picture him typing up those references right this very minute, with his own two fingers.' I released the words with a small laugh.

'He'd better be, else I'll be gunning for his sorry arse. How very fucking dare he think he can do that to any woman. Let alone my sister.' She shook her head as she spoke.

'Love you, Lou,' I whispered, as I leant back onto the wall beside the phone and let a long sigh release from my mouth.

'Love you, too, big sis,' she answered, rubbing her hand up and down my arm. 'Now, with the reference, you can get another well-paid job in London.' She nodded encouragingly at me.

I turned my head sideways to fully look at her and pulled a tight-lipped smile. 'Getting that reference will be fantastic, Lou. But I'm not sure I'll be able to walk into another job just like that, and especially not in London.'

In truth, I knew it wasn't going to happen. I was going to have to come up with another plan to keep our disabled brother, Stephen, in the place where he was living and to help Louise finish her last year on placement and at university, if I could.

'What?' Her body stood momentarily taller and her body language showed that she was taken aback by what I was saying. 'Why?' she almost pleaded.

'Angela would have spread some rumours by now, and even with that reference, I seriously doubt I'll be taken on by another agency in London.'

'That's a load of fucking bullshit!' my younger sister exclaimed.

'It is what it is.' I spoke calmly to her, trying to quell the tense situation that was rapidly developing in our cramped hallway without alerting our mum, who I knew had all her hopes riding on me getting the reference she felt I deserved. 'It's okay… I can go elsewhere. Maybe even out of the country if I have to. With my qualifications and the Millars' reference, well… that gives me no obvious break in employment and ultimately that will help me get the well-paid job I need for us all.'

'So, what you're saying is, that it doesn't matter how hard the under-dog fights, we still can't win?'

'I'm not saying that at all.' I stepped back into her and gathered her up in my arms to hold her closely to me, and took a few seconds to appreciate just what a marvellous human being my sister had grown up to be. Eventually, I let her go and after taking a gentle hold of both of her cheeks, I stared pointedly into her eyes. 'Don't you, of all people, ever believe that. I'm just saying that I might have to move further away to get the job we all need me to have.'

'Do you want to move abroad?'

My mum's voice sounded from behind me, and I stood frozen into place by her question.

'I'd be fine, Mum,' I answered her, with my eyes opening wide at my sister in alarm that our conversation had been heard and she mirrored my reaction. I had hoped that I'd have time to prepare myself to tell her that I might have to move further away, and with that careful preparation, she wouldn't be able to see right through me.

Shit.

Silence met my answer and on instinct I turned around to face her.

'Try again, Nikki,' she persuaded.

'I've lived away from home for years now, Mum, I'd be fine abroad.' I opened my arms out wide, as wide as the narrow hallway would allow, in a bid to convince her with my body language.

'You're a very competent young woman, Nikki, and I'm certain you would be fine, but that's not what I asked.' She nodded at me, taking in my posture. 'So, I'll ask you again… do you want to move away and live abroad?'

I felt my shoulders drop in resignation and my arms fell to my sides. 'Not really, but I'll do what I have to do.'

'No, you won't. Don't think I don't appreciate everything you've done for our family, Nikki, but it can't carry on. Stephen needs to stay at Finchley Hall and as his only parent I will do what needs doing. So, I've come to a decision. With you girls spreading your wings, I've decided to sell the house.'

'What?' Lou questioned, with a rising sense of panic wound around her tone. 'But where would you live?'

'I'd find somewhere, maybe as a live-in housekeeper or something.'

'You can't!' My tone sounded more accusing than I meant it to, and I reached out to touch our mum's arm with my silent apology.

Mum shook her head at us both and a ghost of smile tugged at the corners of her mouth. 'I already work in social care. I know there are positions out there that I would be very suitable for.'

'I didn't mean it like that.' I offered.

'But this is your home. You remember, Mum? The one place we can come to shut out the world and just be us,' Lou added.

'I know, but you girls should know by now that a house doesn't a family make, it's a family that makes it a home and we can live anywhere.' She nodded as she spoke to us, trying to convince us of her decision, but she forgot to remove the pain that was so evidently showing on her face.

For a few seconds, the three of us looked at each other, all stood in the cramped entryway to the only home we'd ever had, and all I knew was, that without a doubt I was going to have to find us a way out of the shitty situation Haydon Millar had put us in.

Four

LUKE

'WHATDAYA THINK… DO YOU like it, Brie?' I'd watched my young daughter walk slowly and methodically around the room for at least ten minutes. She touched each piece of the off-white coloured furniture and fingered all the different pieces of fabric, in the pinks, pale greens and creams I'd chosen for her with the interior designer's help.

'It's so pretty,' she exclaimed, with her eyes opening wide as she spun around on the ball of her foot to face me. 'Is this *my* bedroom?'

'Yes, Shorty, it's all yours.'

'So, is this our house? It's very big, Daddy.'

I had to catch myself from laughing out loud at the happy but puzzled look on her face, as she shared her joy, but virtually reprimanded me at the same time.

'It's a hotel,' I answered as I nodded at her, trying to encourage her to be happy about where we were going to be living for the foreseeable future.

'Oh,' she replied and as the word left her, so did her earlier enthusiasm.

I crossed the floor between us and after taking hold of her hands in my own, I fell to my knees, so we were now eye to eye.

'It's not any old hotel, Brie. It's our hotel. Ours, Uncle Brody's, Uncle Cade's, Uncle Raff's and Flint's. That's why this bedroom has been decorated especially for you.'

'All of us are going to live here?' I knew she was talking about all of DD, as we'd become a family unit over the past few years.

'Most of the time, yes.' I picked her up quickly before she asked another question and stood her on the wide ledge of the large window in her room. 'Until we explore outside there, for the perfect spot to build a house that will be just for the two of us.'

Her hands took hold of my forearms which were around her waist, and she squeezed them in her excitement. 'It looks like a magical forest, Daddy.'

'Where else would I build a house for us, Shorty?'

'And Flint?'

'What about Flint.'

'He can live with us too, can't he?'

'Well, Flint can stay with us sometimes if he wants to, but all your uncles are going to have a home near here somewhere, so I expect he'll probably stay with Uncle Raff most of the time.'

I let her take in my words and the view around us, while I waited for her to pass judgement, and I hoped it would be in my favour. God knows she'd been witness to a couple of my poor decisions in the past couple of years. Since Cherise had gone, ninety-nine percent of the time everything I'd done had been to ensure Brie's happiness, but occasionally I'd fallen down the hole to get what I desperately needed.

Since Cherise's death, I'd had a few warm and willing women in my life, but they were just someone that for a one-time fuck or more, I could bury myself balls deep inside and try to forget. I'd never taken them to my bed as that was a hard and fast rule of mine, but I'd keep them in my life for a few days or even for a couple of weeks until their pussy was no longer creating the illusion I needed. When Brie had come across a couple of them, it was laughable just how quickly and easily she would pass judgement on them. As a rule, she was a good and kind kid who would befriend anyone, and surprisingly she remained generally unspoilt by all the things I'd lavished her with. But the few times it had happened, and she'd come across me with someone in a room full of people, even though I'd never touched them in front of her, somehow she'd known they were there because of me. Her left eye would narrow on them, and her hands would curl into fists at her sides, as she wordlessly told me they weren't good enough for her nor me.

Silently, I'd always agreed with her, and made sure she never saw the same women again.

'I like it, Daddy,' she whispered, after taking in the view of the miles and miles of green fields, woods and hills that the view from her room had to offer.

My heart jump started as I absorbed the joy that radiated off her.

'You see that hill over there?' I released one arm from around her and leant us both closer to the glass so we could see far off to the right.

'Yes,' she replied, with her cheek pushed hard against mine.

'That's where you and I first saw this place, you were only a baby then.' I knew I was probably saying too much to a kid that wasn't yet five, but I carried on anyway, feeling the need to explain to her. 'But it felt like home.'

'Me and you, we'll be happy here.'

'I'm pleased, Brie.' I moved us both upright again. 'You've been going on about how much you want to learn to dance like Mom, and settling down here, I'll make sure you can do that.'

'Really?' Her voice sounded full of childish excitement as she turned around in my arms and flung herself at me, wrapping her arms around my neck. Nose to nose her bright green eyes stared deep into mine as she over exuberantly Eskimo kissed me.

This kid. She never ceased to amaze me. I laughed with her as she carried on far longer than necessary.

Eskimo kisses and ballerina wishes. I could hear Cherise's excited voice in my head.

'Really, Brie… and there's more.'

'Yeah?' With her hands still holding on to my cheeks, she pulled her face about an inch away from mine while she waited impatiently for the answer.

'Guess?' I lifted my eyebrows at her.

'Nancy is back.'

Fuck.

I had to stop myself from sighing out loud. Just when I thought it was going so well, I could virtually hear it crashing down round my ears.

'No, Brie … Nancy has had her own baby.' I thought hard how I could explain in a different way to the previous hundred times I'd tried. 'Nancy doesn't look after any children other than her baby now.'

'I know.' Her eyes filled with tears momentarily and then she blinked them away. 'But, if I can't have Nancy, can I have a different Nancy?'

'I look after you, don't I, Brie?'

'Yes, Daddy, always… but I'd like another Nancy too.'

Stupid fucker.

It was all so clear to me now. Nancy had been gone from our lives for the past four months. I swallowed deeply at the understanding that swept through me. I'd hoped that me and the rest of DD were enough for her, since Nancy had left to start her own family with her wife. But thinking on it now, I could see that my little girl needed another female influence in her life.

'Sure, I can look for another Nancy here in England. How does that sound?'

'That sounds good, Daddy.' And just to show me how good, her hands clasped my cheeks tightly while she placed a wet kiss on my mouth. 'How soon?' she questioned as she pulled away and looked at me with such a serious expression that her forehead crinkled under the pressure.

'I'll look into it in the next couple of days.'

'Promise?'

'Yeah, I promise.'

'Good.' Her body sagged in my arms as if she been wanting to ask me to replace Nancy for some time but wasn't sure how to.

'I want her to be able to dance like Nancy, and she must like to read to me and play at the park.' Her head shot around to look out of the window again. 'Are there any play parks here?'

'If there isn't one close by, Brie, I'll get one put in.'

'Thank you,' she whispered as she turned her head to smile at me again.

'Anything else on this list for your perfect nanny?' I asked half-heartedly with her full attention now on me.

'She needs to be pretty like Mary Poppins, not warty like Nanny McPhee.'

'Pretty,' I repeated, feeling more and more amused. 'Can I ask why?' I questioned.

'She needs to be pretty for you, Daddy.'

I heard Cade, Brody and Raff's laughter sound outside of the doorway, before I had the chance to question my daughter any further on her motives.

'Can we come in yet?' Cade shouted in, knowing they'd given themselves away.

'Brie, as we've agreed to make this our home for now, we've got a surprise for you,' I offered her, as a look of further excitement spread rapidly over her face.

The sound of a puppy yapping his greeting outside the door, as he realised that was his moment, made my daughter squirm in my hold to be put down.

I reluctantly released my hold on her and watched as her feet hit the floor and she took off as fast as she could towards the open doorway, squealing as the yapping increased. The guys moved into Brie's room, with Cade holding a struggling puppy who appeared overly eager to meet his new companion, so eager he was washing Cade's face in between yapping, as he begged to be put down.

No sooner than he was given his own way, my daughter and the bundle of fluff collided, and their two lives became entwined on the pink, fluffy rug, in a mess of licks, squeals and most importantly requited and instant love.

'You're the colour of my favourite cookie,' Brie exclaimed, as the puppy took several licks of her grinning face.

'They call them biscuits here in England,' Brody offered, as he crossed his arms over his chest to protect himself from the lovefest.

'Cookies are biscuits?' Brie questioned, as she attempted to prise her face away from her overly enthusiastic new friend. With an expression of complete happiness and a love shining out from her eyes, she looked over at me.

'I love him, Daddy… can I call him Biscuit. He needs an English cookie name, doesn't he?'

'Yes, Brie. Call him whatever you like, he's yours to love and to name.'

Who fucking knew.

So, just maybe I understood love after all?

Now all I had to do was to find Brie a new nanny, who fit her very demanding wish list.

Five

Nikki

'I'M PLEASED YOU PHONED her; I knew it was exactly the right thing to do when I contacted her yesterday.'

I smiled into the phone I was holding and wrapped the coiled lead around my index finger.

'Thanks, Mum. I'm sure I'll be fine once I get back to the barre, although I have to admit I'm a bit nervous at the thought of helping to teach again.'

'Betty was really happy to hear that you're back for a while. And even if it's only for a few hours each week for a few weeks, I know she'll be pleased of the help. It'll also give you something to do until you find a job where the family appreciate you.'

'Mum… thanks. Thanks for always being my greatest cheerleader.'

'Always… are you ready to show those kiddies just why you could have been a prima ballerina?'

I laughed at her and felt the weight of the last forty-eight hours roll away just a little bit more. 'I'm already dressed and ready to go.' I laughed a little nervously as I cast my eyes down myself. 'I'm nowhere near that good Mum and you know it, but I love the fact you think I could have been.'

I heard her blow me a kiss down the line.

'Oh, that's good you're ready early, because also...' By the way she said the last two words I knew she had something else to say to me, but she'd been waiting for what she thought was the appropriate moment to drop it in. 'Dr. Carpenter has a few bits and pieces he could do with you helping him with please.' I could feel myself exhaling as I waited to be told exactly what he needed.

'Does he?' Even I could hear the trepidation in my tone.

'Now don't say it like that, Nikki,' she whispered into the phone, and I knew without a doubt he was still in the room with her. 'I told him you were around for a little while and he was desperate for me to ask you. Now, if you've got a couple of hours before you need to be at Betty's ballet school, would you like to pop over here and get the details of the jobs? I thought you might be able to do a couple this morning?'

I could picture the two of them at the local retirement home, where I knew Mum had met the doctor to discuss a mutual patient earlier this morning. She'd probably told him exactly what had happened to me and between the two of them they would have decided that I needed to keep busy. Then he would have declared that he had a few things I could do to help him. It was the way small villages around here worked and most of the time I was grateful.

'Care in the community?' I questioned.

'Exactly... people who need errands running etc.'

'Errands?'

'Yes,' she replied.

'I'd be happy to.' I smiled as I heard her relay what I'd said to Dr. Carpenter. I was only too happy to run errands, it was the care for the elderly I just couldn't handle. I took my hat off to the carers who looked after the old-aged pensioners, and those in the nursing homes. I just couldn't handle it. With children I could do anything. including wiping their bums and clearing up sick. But with grown adults, I couldn't. I knew it sounded heartless and it hadn't been my proudest moment when I'd acknowledged the fact, but it was what it was.

'Wonderful, come to the care home as soon as you can.'

'I will… love you.'

'Love you more.'

The line went dead and I hastily picked up my keys and mobile from the small shelf in the hall and dropped them safely into my rucksack, which I'd discarded on the floor when our home phone had rung. The last thing I needed was to lose my phone, when all of the very expensive adverts I'd placed in all the *right* magazines had it as my contact number for enquiries.

What if there are no enquiries?

I shook my head at myself because it wasn't an option. I knew I would do just about anything to give my siblings what they needed and to keep my mum's home over her head. The pressure of it all meant I'd had a tension headache and a stiff neck since I'd woken up that morning and the only relief had been when the postman had arrived earlier with a recorded delivery letter which I'd found contained the reference I'd been waiting for. The Millars had also included another non-disclosure agreement in the same envelope, which Lou and I had decided he could wait forever for and had set light to with the matches from our kitchen drawer.

I grabbed my leather jacket and after thrusting my arms into the sleeves, I picked up my rucksack and swung it over one shoulder. My dirty looking, pink ballet pumps swung from my rucksack, tied on by their thick ribbons. I glanced at them and grabbing hold of one, I took a couple of seconds to run my fingertips over the soft, pink silk. Joy filled me inside and I recognised in that minute, that helping the local dance teacher was precisely what I needed to get out of my own head.

With a wide smile stretched over my face, I reached out to take hold of the door latch and swung it open wide. There was a chill in the air that hadn't been there when I'd arrived home a couple of days before. I knew that snow wasn't forecast, but having grown up here I could smell it on the cold east wind that had been blowing in since late yesterday. I closed my eyes and took in a deep lungful of the fresh, cleansing air and allowed it to reawaken me. This situation was merely a blip on my horizon, and I wasn't going to let it dictate the way my life was going to go in the future

'I was wondering when you were going to make an appearance.'

My eyes opened at my sister's voice and I raised my eyebrows at her in question.

'Mum just called me and told me I would find you outside.'

I shrugged at what she'd just told me, still trying to understand what she was actually doing outside. She was standing shivering on the path that led to our front door, with a blue racing bike in her clutches. And not just any old racing bike, but mine from years ago.

'Crying out loud, where the hell did you find that thing?' I questioned as I stepped off our threshold and pulled the door shut behind me using the knocker.

'It's your old bike.'

'What you meant to say was, it's Gladys,' I corrected her.

'Oh yeah, I'd forgotten you'd named her,' she replied with a laugh.

'How could you have forgotten?' I questioned her, with a smile on my lips and shaking my head at her, as I walked nearer. 'I can't believe we've still got the thing.'

'You can't believe we've still got "Gladys,"' she corrected, laughing back at me. 'She hates being called "thing."'

'Touché.'

'Nikki, you know Mum, she keeps everything. When I remembered seeing her a while back, well... I thought it would be better for you than walking everywhere while you're here.'

'Yeah?' my eyes opened wider, not entirely sure if I agreed with her or not. 'Does she even work?' I questioned. 'You know... do her wheels go round etc?' I laughed at her look that said, "I'm not stupid."

'Oh, ye of very little faith,' she accused, grinning back at me. 'Fred next door took a look at it for you yesterday, he oiled all the metal stuff, changed the tyres and brake thingamajigs. And now, apparently, she's good to go.'

Our eyes met in mutual understanding; both knowing that we had no idea how to maintain anything. Louise released her hold on the handlebars slightly and leant the bike towards me. I took it from her and grinned back at her thoughtfulness. Running my fingers over the scruffy silver bar tape, I reminisced about all the places Gladys and I had been together.

'She'll do great.'

I stood onto my tiptoes that were encased in Chelsea boot style Dr. Martens and placing my arm around Louise's neck, pulled her towards me and placed a quick peck on her cheek.

'Thank you. I don't know what I'd do without you and Mum.' Then releasing her a little I stared at her longer than necessary, making sure she'd understood exactly what I was trying to say.

'Yeah, yeah.' She blushed a little as my words hit home.

'You're cold,' I added.

'Don't worry, I'm going back inside… It's just that I need to see you ride "Gladys" before I leave.'

'Needing a laugh today?'

'Maybe. It's just I've never seen anyone ride a racing bike wearing a pair of Docs, rugby socks, ballet pink tights, a tutu and leather biker jacket before. You look like a one-woman carnival.' It was an old joke between the two of us. I had a few tattoos, she had none. I had several piercings, Lou only had her ears done and just the once. She wore conservative clothing, and I wore whatever the hell I liked. She was made to be standing up in court, I on the other hand was made for… truthfully, I hadn't a clue. But I knew I was true to myself and that was all that mattered. Then it dawned on me, I was made to look after children, as in their innocence they were still non-judgemental.

'I aim to please.' I offered her a quick wink and after wheeling the bike out to the road, I swung my leg over it quickly before I gave anyone else watching an eyeful of just what a ballerina wears under her tutu, and placed my right boot on the peddle.

Out of the corner of my eye I watched her walking towards me.

'One last thing,' she said, holding out her hand with a white envelope captured between her fingers. 'I've made these.'

I took the envelope from her and after curiosity got the better of me, I peeked inside. 'What are these?'

'I made them for you. I know you've put the fancy adverts in the media, but they won't go live until after Christmas. I just thought that as we live in the heart of the English countryside and we're surrounded by large estates and houses, there just might be someone around here requiring a wonderfully caring nanny, like you.'

I heard her words, but my eyes were already running over the A5 pieces of card that she had thoughtfully laminated against the weather. The cream card inside the plastic contained the carefully worded advert that Lou, Mum, and I had devised together.

'I only made up six, as I run out of ink for the printer, and the laminator didn't work as well as I'd have liked… But they are what they are.' She grimaced as she explained herself. 'Anyway, I thought that you could place them on all the local village noticeboards around here, as you travel around.'

I lifted my eyes up to hers. 'Thank you. I'm now wondering if you slept at all last night.' I knew she'd been getting together a personal statement for a placement she was after and along with organising the resurrection of my antique bike, she'd taken the time to create these for me.

'I did get some. I just want to help. You've always helped me and I'm just trying my best to reciprocate.'

Honestly, I wasn't sure that anyone read anything on those noticeboards these days. Social media had all but taken over everything. But I knew that we had one in each and every village within a twenty-mile radius, so I nodded at her enthusiastically, before I tucked them in the side pocket of my rucksack.

Then, blowing her a kiss goodbye, I pulled shakily away from our home.

Six

LUKE

'I LIKE IT HERE, Daddy.'

'Yeah, Brielle?' I lifted my eyes up briefly to catch hers in the child mirror I'd had insisted was installed in the new car and grinned at her.

'It's so sparkly and pretty, and green.'

'And green?' I questioned in amusement.

'Yeah,' came the reply as I watched her refocus on the fields going past us.

Green. She'd grown up in the dry heat and reddish browns of Vegas, so I could understand how England looked so green to her, even in winter.

I fleetingly glanced at her again. I could see the look of wonderment on her face as she looked out of the window beside her and, not for the first time, the sense that as long as I could keep her world magical, I *might* just be able to wing this parenting shit after all, came over me. All I had was the love I had felt for her the second she'd entered our lives, but although I found solo parenting to be a fucking rollercoaster, mostly… so far, I thought, so good. It was the moments like this that made me appreciate just what Rafferty was going through with his son Flint. He was no longer the small boy who loved to be around his dad and the band. In fact, he did what he could to avoid us, apart from Brie, and of course Cade, when Cade gave him a couple of hours as he taught him to play the drums. He was closed off most days and completely unreadable and I knew how much it pained Raff when he felt he could no longer reach him.

I could hear Father McKenzie inside my head declaring it was "just a stage" he was going through, just as I'd heard him say that phrase about most of us kids in the orphanage at one time or another.

It appeared that I'd been given a daughter who wore her heart on her sleeve for the moment, and it was a stage I was fully ready to embrace before the teenage years kicked me up the ass. Brielle had accepted everything that had been thrown at her in her short life, the constant touring, when I spent weeks locked in the recording studios and me on occasion losing my shit. Now, we were at last putting down roots and I intended to make sure she had everything she needed to fly.

And to fly fucking high, if that's what she wanted.

I looked into the mirror again and smiled as I watched her twiddle with a piece of her long red hair, as she used it to tickle the inside of her palm and briefly my heart stopped. An ache filled the void where I knew the beat should have been. I knew she didn't remember much about Cherise, as much as I talked about her, showed her pictures and smelt her favourite perfume with her, and it hurt like hell; not for me, but for Cherise and Brie. My one consolation was that Brie had Cherise's mannerisms. And she always insisted on using the same coconut shampoo that Cherise had used for as long as I could remember, in her words "to smell like Mommy."

I hoped I'd always be able to see parts of Cherise right there, enclosed inside our daughter. Because, although my wife hadn't been able to see it within herself, I'd always thought she was one of the kindest people I'd ever met. In a world where I had been surrounded by fake celebrity wannabees the minute Default Distraction had started making any money, she'd grounded me. The instant we'd met, we'd quickly comprehended that we needed each other to survive. I didn't think ours had been a conventional sort of love. Instead, to begin with we'd stayed together out of necessity, a necessity and a will to survive. Eventually, I'd stopped sleeping with every willing, wet pussy that came my way, when I'd understood how fucking much it hurt her to stand by and watch.

Our relationship had developed organically and by the time she'd discovered she was carrying Brie, our hearts were so intrinsically entangled, I didn't know where she ended and I began.

But she had demons within her, demons that I hated with everything I was. However, I had understood a long fucking time ago that I had fallen for her because of them and not in spite of them. They made her someone I fully understood, and they made her real in a sea of fucking imitation. But the same demons that I embraced and loved, had eventually become toxic within our marriage and had started to tear us apart. Until they'd become too strong for me and her to fight any longer and they'd stolen her away from us both, ripping my fucking heart out in the process.

I'd never forgive myself for not fighting harder, but it was almost impossible to fight for two, when you were the only one in the battle.

Shutting down my thoughts, I shook my head sharply to one side as I attempted to dislodge everything that had collected there for me to dredge over.

Then I looked at Brie in the mirror and allowed the pure love I felt for her to ground my emotions.

Our daughter, as always, took my breath away. The sun was low in the sky as the time of year dictated and although the rear windows were made of privacy glass, the sun coming through the windscreen caught her hair. The vibrant copper strands sparkled like a precious metal. She was still young and developing her own likes and opinions, but her personality was already dazzling, and I was proud to say I'd fathered her. I might be a member of one of the planet's biggest rock bands, but her creation had definitely been my finest moment so far.

'I like it here, too,' I finally replied, more to myself than her, as I tore my eyes away from her and brought them back towards the road ahead. I lowered myself down further onto the steering wheel, to allow myself a better look at the country lane we were travelling on.

'YAP.' Biscuit added his own agreement.

'Louder!' Brielle demanded, as her favourite song appeared once again on her playlist, which she'd insisted we had to play as we drove.

Inwardly I cringed, knowing I was going to have to deal with another burst of "Let it go" from my daughter.

'What do you say?' I gently reminded her of her manners.

'Pleeeaasse,' she overly pronounced the word I'd been asking for.

I turned up the volume, hoping it would be enough to placate her, but low enough for me to ignore and I smiled as she once again started to sing all the words.

It was just over a week before Christmas and the weather meant the scenery around us was everything I'd ever remembered seeing in pictures of the English countryside in Winter. The trees sitting either side of the lane were now mainly devoid of leaves. Weirdly, they had grown towards each other in many places and had created the illusion of travelling through a tunnel. The gaps in between them showed us that the fields either side of the road were covered in a heavy frost. It was a frost that even the winter sun didn't seem to penetrate, even though it was only an hour away from midday.

The lane stretched out in front of the black Mercedes GLA that I'd bought especially for ferrying my small family around. I'd thought it would be a safe drive and it was. I'd also thought it would be a good fit for the smaller roads here in England, but the truth was I was so fucking wrong it was laughable. The Merc under my fingertips would be great on the motorways, but here in the Kent countryside most of the so called "roads" were only just passable for two-way traffic. The beast I was behind the wheel of dominated the small space and meant that either I had to wait in a passing spot for someone to pass me or vice versa.

It had taken me much longer than I expected to get from one village to another. I made a mental note for next time I was under a time constraint, that doing one mile here could take as long as five miles back home.

Finally, we arrived at the T-junction I'd been looking out for and, casting my eyes over the white wooden sign, I read the word Marsham on the arrow that pointed off to the right. I looked around quickly and pulled out for the final part of our journey.

Our change of direction meant that the sun was now shining directly at my face and behind the sunglasses I was wearing, I squinted as I tried hard to focus on the road ahead.

'Fuck.' I tried hard to whisper the expletive as the sun momentarily blinded me, before my pupils attempted to resize themselves.

'We're nearly at the village, Brie,' I called out, desperate to cover up the fact I'd sworn once again in front of my daughter. I needn't have worried as she was too busy singing along to her favourite song.

My eyes had just about refocussed, when I caught sight of a strange looking cyclist not ten feet in front of me. Instinctively, my foot hit the brake and although my new vehicle was a four-wheel drive, I felt the back end of the car slip on some of the ice I'd seen in the places where the sun never seemed to penetrate.

'FUCK!' I shouted out as the heel of my hand came down heavily on the centre of the wheel to sound the horn, as I angrily tried to make them get out of my way.

'Daddy!' Brie reprimanded me and then went straight back to singing.

The only indication I had that the cyclist in front of me had even heard my horn, was that they moved out of the centre of the lane they'd been blocking and over to the left-hand side. I began to shake my head, as still not being able to pass them and then intrigued at the sight in front of me, I started to examine them.

The man's cycle being ridden had seen better days, the frame was rusty, and bits of tape were peeling off the handlebars, but the tyres at least looked road worthy. Although it was its rider that interested me more than the possible death trap in front of me, the death trap I was reluctant to force any further into the side of the road, in case its rider had an accident in the drainage gulley that ran along the side of each lane.

Slowly, amused by the sight, I crept the vehicle closer.

Even though I was getting more and more irate at the thought of being late for our appointment, I couldn't help the twitch that was starting at the corners of my mouth.

There was no doubt that the rider was female.

Whoa!

No doubt whatsoever, when she pushed her ass out of the saddle to attempt to pull further away from me. My dick twitched in response as I saw the fucking perfect sight in front of me.

'No way,' I muttered under my breath. 'She has to know what she's showing.'

Blinking quickly, I took another look.

I watched as the well-toned legs that were only encased in sheer pink tights and striped socks, used the heavy looking boots on her feet to push down harder onto the pedals to pick up speed. But my eyes remained fixated on the shapely ass she'd revealed as she rose out of the saddle. I might be a widowed dad in his thirties, but the college kid in me demanded I got a better view of just what I thought I must be imagining in front of me.

I pushed my foot gently down on the accelerator and urged the car quietly forward as I leant my chest further onto the top of the wheel.

The net skirt thing she had going on, had blown up in the wind and whatever she was wearing underneath her black leather jacket and translucent tights had disappeared in between her butt cheeks, leaving the beautifully sculpted globes of her ass on show.

My dick twitched in appreciation. The fine view in front of me reminded me of when, as a youngster, I'd get my rocks off watching the girls in the orphanage trying in vain to follow the old keep fit videos every Thursday night, shut away in a room behind glass partition doors that were meant to be a barrier to us boys.

The sudden insight into my life hit me and I couldn't help but laugh out loud at my situation.

I was trapped in a car that normally I wouldn't have been seen dead in, with a small child who was singing her head off to the inanest shit I'd ever heard under the disguise of music. To top that, Biscuit, who was riding with us clipped into his harness, was attempting to howl every single time my daughter struggled to hit a high note. And yet my dick was twitching at the sight of the finest ass I'd seen since I'd watched Jane Fonda in her leg warmers.

Warmth spread through me as my laughter grew.

I'd grasped that Brie had now stopped singing and was laughing along with me.

'What's the lady doing, Daddy? Her legs must be very cold.'

I was trying to choose my words carefully to answer my daughter, when the woman I couldn't tear my eyes off stopped unexpectedly, not ten feet from the front of my hood.

'Jesus fucking H!' I managed to brake in time and instinctively operated the handbrake. Muttering under my breath, 'Stupid woman,' I linked my fingers together on top of the steering wheel and leant even closer to the glass in front of me. My eyes opened wider, and I lifted an eyebrow at her in question. Wearing Aviators and a trapper hat, I knew she wouldn't be able to see my expression, but I hoped she'd fucking feel it when she turned around to face me. I grabbed hold of my beard with my right hand as I slowly contemplated the confusing vision in front of me.

Go on, fucking turn.

It was fucking unreal just how much I needed the woman with the fine ass to turn around to look at me.

I stared harder at her, willing her to and let out a long exhale as she finally put her left foot to the floor underneath her. She leant to the same side in one movement, and I watched transfixed as she looked over her right shoulder and stared straight at me, accusingly.

Oh no, you fucking don't, lady.

Through the lenses of my sunglasses, our eyes met and for the second time that day, my heart jolted and missed a fucking beat. But instead of the beat being replaced with a dull ache, it was filled with a sudden burst of need.

In my head I was saying all the words I stupidly wanted her to hear.

What the fuck are you doing? Do you want to kill yourself?

And then a question for myself. *Mac, why the fuck do you even care?*

But knowing she was nothing to me, and swallowing down my weird compulsion to get out of the car to demand she got back in with me, so I could look after her, I forced myself to stay seated. Instead, needing to show her how annoyed I was with her, for risking herself on the road, I lifted my left hand. Then I pointed at her and touched my finger to my temple, as I silently indicated that I thought she was mental. I'd already gauged she wasn't wearing a helmet when I'd caught sight of her brightly coloured hair. Her pink hair certainly seemed to compliment the whole look she had going on.

For at least a minute or more, and for some reason that I couldn't manage to work out, I couldn't drive away. Instead, I sat there blocking the road, with my eyes lingering on hers. I watched as very slowly she lifted her right hand up. Mesmerised, I stared as she turned over the end of the child-like pink mitten she was wearing and with her fingers now exposed, she effectively flipped me the bird with a beautifully painted, black coloured fingernail.

'That's so naughty! That lady's just like Uncle Cade, Daddy,' came a voice from behind me, which brought me back to earth with a very loud resonating bump.

Laughter ripped through me as I listened to Brie, and I carried on laughing as the stranger stared back at me like I was a madman. Eventually, I stopped myself and lifted a tentative hand to my accuser in acceptance, and reluctantly I watched her break eye contact as she pulled her gaze away and looked forward again.

'Enough, Mac.' I spoke low and hoped the shit music my daughter was listening to had covered up me reprimanding myself. Then I accepted quickly that I needed to stop gawping at the girl in front and I turned the wheel slightly to the right to steer around her and to try to avoid the puddle in the middle of the road, which had been created where the ice on the ground had melted from the sun.

I heard the tyres hit the puddle that I'd tried hard to avoid and sighing, I shook my head at myself.

Shit!

I knew without a doubt I'd hit her with some of the water, but our encounter had been so goddamn weird I knew I couldn't stop the car again to go to her aid, without her getting worried I was a serial killer out looking for his next victim.

As I continued slowly down the lane, I couldn't stop my eyes wandering to the figure that was now behind me, when she paused for a second and threw her arms up high in the air. I could see the air fill with condensation as she let rip into the cold air and, I guessed, let me have every expletive she knew.

'Sorry,' I spoke under my breath.

At last, she resumed her journey.

I entered Marsham still shaking my head and smiling at the weird encounter.

It was going to be a good day; I could feel it. Another smirk formed on my mouth as I comprehended that I hadn't felt that in a very long time.

Seven

Nikki

'GO ON, TELL THEM what happened to you today,' Lou encouraged. 'It could only happen to you, after all.'

I looked up from the beer bottle in my hand, to glance at a couple of our friends who were sat around the table and grinned at them.

'It really wasn't that interesting.' I shook my head at her.

I watched as Emma and her husband Tom stopped drinking and rested the weight of their expectant gazes on me.

'Nikki... You haven't been gone from around here for that long you can't remember how staid and bloody samey our lives are, have you?'

In response, I lifted my bottle again and took a quick sip of the cold liquid inside and offered Emma a smile.

'Well, I went into "A Stitch in Time" today and bought myself some pink mittens and a matching snood,' I offered, looking straight at Lou and lifting my eyebrows at her as I smirked.

'Not that,' Lou exclaimed as she put her wine glass onto the stained, round table, just so she could use her empty hand to shove my shoulder.

'What do you want me to say?' I asked, as I regained my balance on the small stool beneath me, laughing.

'Evening all,' came a voice from the doorway as it opened, interrupting our conversation, and a draft of cold air enveloped us all. I shivered, having only just got warm, hours after being soaked through by *that* car earlier today.

Lewis, the boy I'd dated after secondary school, had walked in. We'd only got the one public house within our few neighbouring villages, so I knew I was bound to bump into him some time or another. But with what little thought I'd given it, I'd hoped it wouldn't happen anytime soon. I watched as he raised his hand in greeting to the few people in the room. His eyes worked their way around the tables and then finally fell on the table we were sitting at and connected with mine. A wave of sickness washed through me.

'Hello, Nik. I'd heard you were back home.' Just the way he said it raised the hackles on my back, as I thought back to the last conversation we'd had, about me not being strong enough to be able to live away from home for very long.

I caught Emma's look of disgust before I spoke. 'Hi, Lewis, nice to see you.'

I almost rolled my eyes at myself at my absurd English politeness as he was the last person I wanted to see now I was home. *What the hell is wrong with me?* 'Great, just what I needed,' I whispered, ducking my shoulders slightly and hoping that only those sitting with me heard the last sentence.

'I saw on the Falham noticeboard that you're now advertising your services, Nikki.' Lewis laughed as he walked up to the bar to order. 'You know I'd happily give you money.'

'Ignore the fucker,' Tom offered, shaking his head.

'Don't worry, I was going to.' Out of habit and for something to do, I lifted my beer bottle to my mouth again. After taking a sip, I placed it back down on the table and spoke again, in a bid to show the immature arsehole I used to date that his arrival and crass comment meant nothing to me.

'Tell me there has been someone else since that scrotum?' Emma questioned quietly.

I lifted my eyes to hers and sucking in the side of my cheek, I clamped my teeth down onto the soft flesh, as I shook my head gingerly from side to side.

'Fuck getting a job being your next priority.' Tom leant nearer and grabbing hold of my hand, he casually ran his thumb over my knuckles in concern. 'Your biggest priority is getting someone to erase the memory of where that arsehole was the last one to be.'

The four of us laughed and the strange atmosphere that had surrounded us with Lewis's arrival dissipated.

'I'll drink to that.' Lou raised her wine glass and the four of us saluted each other in agreement. I agreed with them all, but in my job, a job that I wholeheartedly loved, meeting a man wasn't easy, especially when you lived in with the family you worked for.

I knew I needed to erase Lewis and I also wanted to wipe away the feeling of having Haydon Millar's slimy hands all over my body, but I just wasn't sure how the hell to go about it.

I felt a shudder run down my spine and I masked it with a shiver, pretending I was cold in front of my sister and friends.

'Anyway, where were we?' I started, and waited until they were all with me. 'Today, I ran a few errands for Dr. Carpenter.' I fleetingly looked up towards the bar where I knew Lewis would be leaning, drinking his pint of Guinness and straining to listen to what we were talking about. 'And although I'm more than happy to be back for a few weeks, I'm too invested in my career to be around for long, so as you've just heard from Lewis, I posted up a couple of cards on the village noticeboards, in case anyone nearby is looking for a qualified nanny.'

A laugh fell deliberately from Lewis's mouth, and I watched as Tom sat up straighter and turned to fix Lewis with a stare. Emma lifted her hand and placed it down on his forearm, effectively holding him gently in place next to her.

'That's a great idea,' Emma answered. 'Personally, we'd love it if you stayed nearby to work, as we'd get to see more of you.' Her voice was intentionally louder than normal. 'But either way, I'm sure some grateful family will snap you up soon.'

Over the top of Tom's head, I watched as Lewis moved away from our side of the bar to greet another farmer who had just entered the pub. I wasn't sure the farmer wanted to talk to him, but at least it meant he was further away from me.

'Thank God, he's moved away,' I whispered and felt myself relax a little.

'Forget he's here and carry on talking. Tell us what happened today,' Emma probed.

'Where was I? Oh, yeah, I ran the errands and then put up a couple of the cards Louise had made me, before I went to see Mrs. Brown in Marsham. And it's all decided, after I helped her today with a new pupil, she's going to let me help her teach a couple of classes a week.' I smiled at them and added, 'Just while I'm here, anyway.'

'That's all positive,' Tom replied and grabbing hold of my hand, he gave it a quick squeeze of reassurance.

'Only a couple of cards… I thought you made Nikki a few more?' Emma questioned, directing that at my sister.

Once again, Louise put her wine down. 'That's what I wanted her to tell you about. It's been amusing me since I saw the state of her earlier, and she told me what had happened.'

I felt four pair of eyes resting on me and knowing that only three lots could hear me talking, I leant in closer to my sister, her best friend and her husband, knowing they would copy my body language.

'Okay, you two can have a laugh on my behalf, too…'

I explained about my ride between Falham to Marsham this lunchtime. How I'd stupidly thought, when I'd dressed myself in my dance attire this morning, that I would be getting on the bus to travel between our village and the next. Then how Lou had presented me with "Gladys" and I'd thought I could travel around on the bike, working my way through Dr. Carpenter's list of errands and then to my original destination without anyone really seeing me.

'But, oh God, I was so wrong!' I added, as I saw their eyes getting wider and mouths beginning to twitch in amusement.

'I was very nearly at the T-junction at the end of Station Road, when I could feel a car creeping along behind me.'

'Picture it… Doc's, Kent rugby socks, ballet tights, tutu and leather jacket,' Lou pushed into the conversation.

'With baby pink mittens and snood from Mrs. Harper's shop,' I added, nodding and grinning at them all.

I carried on telling them what a mistake I'd made, as a man driving a large black Mercedes had nearly run me off the road, and then soaked me with what had to be the only puddle to be found amongst all the ice in between the two villages. I could see Emma's look of horror as I explained then, how I'd arrived at Betty's dance school in my pink ballet attire covered with clumps of mud and dripping wet from the filthy, dirty, smelly puddle water he'd covered me with.

'The puddle must have been huge… because even the laminate didn't hold up on the cards I'd made her. They *were* in an outside pocket of her rucksack, though,' Lou pushed in, laughing and acting like she was resigned to the fact that I hadn't taken better care of the cards she'd made.

'So, it's lucky I got the two cards up,' I nodded, grinning at them all as finally the beer I'd been drinking began to take the edge off the anxiety I'd been carrying around for a few days.

'That's good, at least,' Tom offered with a smile and shaking his head slowly side to side, as Emma slapped a hand over her mouth to stop the spray of wine that threatened to hit Lou and me square in the face. 'But I can't imagine old Mrs. Brown was very happy.'

'No, she wasn't impressed. You'll remember what she was like when she used to teach us R.E in secondary school. "Everything has a place, let's make it the right place."' I mimicked Betty's voice, and everyone laughed again. 'Well, I certainly didn't look like I was in the right place. I was made to redo my hair and to put on some spare tights she had before she would even let me out of the bathroom and into the hall with the children. Luckily, my ballet shoes remained fairly unscathed.'

Their laughter sounded and it made me feel warmer than I had all day.

'Honestly, I'm surprised she let you in, let alone invite you to actually help her,' Louise interjected.

'Well, I had to promise to come on the bus next time.' I turned over the yellow and blue beer mat I'd been fiddling with since Lewis's arrival.

'Just to give you both a visual. I watched Nikki pull away on Gladys this morning… here, look.'

Suddenly, I was aware my supposed lovely little sister was offering her phone to our companions.

'So, imagine that picture and cover her with mud and you'll get the image in your head that I was greeted with when she arrived home this afternoon.'

'Christ, Nikki… did you know your Tutu was that short?' Tom's eyes opened wider as he grabbed the phone off my sister and using two fingers, he expanded the photo. 'You can see what you ate last night.'

'Fuck off, all of you.' I raised my voice, but a smile had spread over my face.

'It's a wonder the poor fucking bloke driving the Merc didn't kill himself,' Tom carried on.

I shook my head at them all, and pondered just how pleased I was that the laughter and friendship between the four of us had managed to effectively shut out my ex.

Then stupidly, I thought back to the only part of my story that I'd shared with no one else. The Merc may have nearly forced me off the road, and its driver had gesticulated that he thought I was tuppence short of a ha'penny, but as his eyes took me in, for those all too short seconds before I'd allowed my temper to flare up; I'd felt discovered.

Eight

LUKE

'OH, SHIT… NOT THIS again.'

I turned my head to find Raff, who had appeared at Brie's open bedroom door, and looking straight at him I put a finger to my mouth as I signalled that he needed to be quiet. He nodded just the once in understanding and almost as if he knew I needed some adult company, stood firmly in place.

I carefully shifted my body to the side and with the utmost care, I took my arm away from around Brie's body. Gratefully, I took in the fact that me pulling away from her hadn't even made her stir. Then, standing up next to her pink couch, I stretched my aching body and pulled up her unicorn covered throw, tucking her and Biscuit in. I prayed they would carry on sleeping.

'You got a minute?' I questioned, after realising I hadn't disturbed either of them.

'For you man, always,' Raff offered.

I walked behind him and out into the hallway, before following him into the room at Falham Manor that he'd made his own. As he walked inside his room, he grabbed two bottles of water off the side and knowing exactly where to find me, he threw me a bottle by twisting his arm back behind him.

'Thanks.'

I wasn't even thirsty, but as I sat down on the large leather couch, which Raff had placed deliberately to take in the view outside, I unscrewed the metal top and took a quick glug on the water to moisten my throat, which had felt tight and constricted with emotion since Brie had finished her first ballet lesson earlier that day.

'How am I doing?' I put my bare feet up on the glass topped, low table in front of me and looked to the side as Raff sat down next to me.

'What?' he questioned, shaking his head.

'This dad stuff... how am I doing? And be fucking truthful.'

'You're asking me, dude,' he countered, amused.

Yeah, I'm asking you... fuck.' I shrugged my shoulders at him. "You're one of only three dads I know, and you're without a doubt the only fucking one I like.'

I could see him frowning in thought as he tried to work out who the hell I was talking about.

'Lawson, our manager, your ex-father-in-law.' I nodded at him, trying to drive my words home. 'And your step-dad.'

'Well, fuck... God help you, man, if we're the only ones you know.' He laughed out loud as he smacked his hand down hard on the seat between us.

When I didn't laugh with him, I saw the minute he understood that the question I'd asked was as serious as a goddamn heart attack.

'Come on, Mac... in all honesty you must know you're doing alright?'

I shrugged at him again.

'It's fucking hard, you know.' I moved my feet off the table with the admission and shelving my sudden need to pace up and down in front of the main window in his room, I leant forward and fixed my eyes on the cold day outside. 'When you've got *nothing* to go on... absolutely fucking nothing... not even a distant memory of what a parent would do... well, it's hard to know whether I'm doing right or wrong.'

I heard him sigh at my admission, then the leather creaked underneath him as he shifted himself enough to put an arm around my shoulders.

'Let me tell ya, I know exactly how a parent should fucking parent, but I question my own abilities every day.'

I looked to the side at him and then away to the window again, not able to keep eye contact. Because even now, having been outside the orphanage for nearly nineteen years and having known him, Cade and Brody for the best part of that time, I still found it fucking hard to accept the emotional connection I had with them all.

'I know it.' I admitted. 'It's just, I know it's fucking needy, but… well, sometimes I need someone else to validate that what I'm doing is okay.'

'What you're doing as a parent is way more than okay, Mac.'

I nodded at his answer and let it sink in.

'Look at us… we're here aren't we? This place has to be the best decision we've ever made for Flint, Brie and ourselves.'

Raff stood up and went to look out of the window himself. I watched as he shoved his hands into his pockets and then as he released a long exhale as he mulled over his own shit.

'I spoke to Lawson earlier, Flint got on the plane to come over.'

'That's great news,' I added, smiling and knowing Brielle would be made up when I told her.

'Yeah, you'd think, wouldn't ya. But this parenting shit gets no fucking easier. I know he doesn't want to be within spitting distance of me since my marriage to Ashley broke up.'

'He'll get over it.'

Just like that the tide had turned between us.

Raff spun around quickly in front of me.

'What I'm trying to say, Mac, is you can only parent with love and hindsight, and you have to hope that's enough.' He shrugged his shoulders and ran both of his hands through his hair, before parking his ass on the stone ledge of the windowsill. 'Some days it'll feel like you're doing the most amazing job in the world, and you'll be riding so fucking high on it you'll wonder why the hell we ever inhaled so much fucking charlie, because there is no way it ever made you feel as good as you do when you know you've made a good parenting decision…' His eyes opened wider as he carried on. 'Then others you'll feel like you're fucking drowning in the guilt of getting it wrong… but inside there's always the love and hope that tomorrow is a brand new fucking day, and we get to try all over again… and sometimes that just has to be enough.'

Raff turned back to the window after finishing his speech and crossed his arms over his chest. I swallowed down my earlier emotional pity-fest and walked over to join him. I knew he had so much more going on than just Flint's arrival. But having nothing to bring to the party by way of advice to him, about being back in the village where his first love, Lauren still lived, I stood next to him in silent solidarity and hoped he could feel what I was trying to offer him.

The weather changed as we stood there. Floating down in the wind, I could see the soft flakes of the snow the weathermen had been predicting since we'd flown in. Apparently, I'd heard that it wasn't going to lie just yet as the ground was too wet. But I hoped it would soon, because I had a little girl who was desperate to see and experience it.

The thought of Brie's happiness, as I imagined her playing with Biscuit in the white fields around us, filled me with hope. I could see me and her flying down nearby Summerhouse Hill, the first place I'd ever seen The Manor from, on a sledge as we played together.

'So, what brought this on?' Raff asked.

I widened my stance and crossed my arms over my chest as I tried to think of where to start.

'You know, the usual… trying to be both parents, when I'm not really fucking certain I'm equipped enough to even be one.'

'I get that… But look at this place, you're here to make her a permanent home. She's finally got the puppy she's wanted for at least the last year and having the dance lessons you promised her.'

'Yeah,' I replied, nodding my head as I tried to convince myself. 'Yeah, I know… you're right.'

'How did her dance lesson go?' Raff questioned as the atmosphere around us began to lift.

'She loved it… me, not so much,' I admitted. 'All I heard on the way home and until I put *that* film on yet again was about her new dance teacher. Then I mulled over just how much Cherise should have been here to experience Brie's first dance lesson with her.'

'She should have been here for it, Luke… but she's not and somehow you will find a way through without her. You've done it for the last three years and that beautiful, happy, smiling girl is a credit to you, and to you only.'

'With a little help from her uncles,' I added.

'Well, of course.' Raff laughed. 'I, for one, was always happy to help… not sure about the other two fuckups in the band, but I loved helping.'

I let a gentle laugh leave my body, knowing the other two fuckups, as Raff called them, also loved my daughter like their own. I knew I couldn't have wished for a more supportive set-up than what they'd all offered over the past few years. They looked after Brie willingly and gave me the alone time I needed to function.

Once upon a time, in the land of rock 'n' roll, we'd existed as separate entities. After living together in a cramped duplex for well into two years, as soon as fame had come calling and we'd begun to make money, it had pulled us in very different directions. We'd always found our way back to each other for writing, recording, and touring, but we'd enjoyed our very separate spaces. I knew we hadn't grown apart, and we definitely hadn't grown up, but we enjoyed all the entrapments fame brought us, the all-time highs and serious fucking lows. Instead of always getting high and shitfaced with each other, we'd been fucking generous and like the millionaires we'd become, we'd dutifully shared that shit around.

But the minute Cherise left, they'd appeared, like the family we'd become all those years ago in Vegas, and hadn't left my side since.

I looked at him sideways on, before clearing my throat and admitting what I now knew to be true. 'After her lesson today and understanding how happy she was to have been around females for an hour… well, I think I need to get some proper help going forward with Brie,' I finally admitted.

'I agree. Nancy has been a loss and as we're putting down some roots, employing a new nanny here would be a great idea.'

'However bad it feels admitting it… I know it's not just gonna be for her… I need some time and space too.'

'Yeah, ya do.' Raff lifted his tone as he replied and slapped my back in reassurance. '*Fuck*, I think you might actually be in the right place for one of us to say something.'

'The right place?' I muttered sarcastically, shaking my head.

'It takes one fuckup to know another, asshat.' I hadn't comprehended until I heard Brody's voice that he'd entered the room and was now standing on the other side of me.

I removed my gaze from the window to look at Brody, who was still wearing his running gear and then back at Raff. My earlier emotion had lifted, and I felt comfortable listening as the words he wanted to say fell from his mouth.

'Daniels,' Raff offered, leaning around me to look at Brody standing beside me. 'Great timing as always.' Then he carried on with what he wanted to say. 'Look, hear us out, Luke... Brody, Cade and I have been waiting for you to get to the right head space for us to be able to say something. You're very much still alive, Mac.' He was nodding vehemently to get his point across, 'And you need to stop acting like you died along with Cherise, not only for Brie's sake, but for your own too.'

'And fuck, man... for ours too. You're hell to fucking live with and we're sick of babysitting ya,' Brody added, laughing as he tried to inject some humour in between the seriousness. I nodded at them both, slowly at first and then with more effective movement.

'You know we're right,' he insisted.

I carried on nodding at them both and then on an exhale I voiced what had been going around my head since this morning.

'I met a woman today,' I admitted and standing there sandwiched between two men who had been voted "World's Sexiest Men" at least twice each, I told them about the strange encounter I'd had with the fiery-tempered, pink-haired girl riding the bike.

I could feel their eyes on me as I raised up onto the balls of my feet. I shoved my hands into the back pockets of my jeans and used the backward rocking motion as my heels met the floor again, to carry on speaking and to tell them about my weird day.

'So, let's get this straight. You nearly ran her off the road, she gave you the bird and then you drove away soaking her in the process?' Brody questioned, laughing as he slapped me on the back.

'Yep,' I admitted.

'Then later, you realised she was Brie's new dance teacher, and you didn't even apologise.' I could feel Brody giving me his "stupid fucker" look.

'Also, yes. And I know it wasn't my finest fucking hour when I made sure she never caught sight of me.'

'Ain't that the fucking truth,' Raff added.

'I needed to get my head back on straight... But when Brie goes again this week, I'm gonna apologise to her and maybe ask her out for something to eat... Whatdaya both think?'

I wasn't good at working myself out, but I could work out others. Growing up in the orphanage, it was a skill you learnt early, to protect yourself. I'd spent years watching Cade and Brody fuck up with the opposite sex, while I lived in the relative comfort of having Cherise by my side. She'd often remarked how she thought they'd have better luck with women if they tried the old-fashioned way of getting a woman and actually took them out.

I knew why they didn't, simply because there was no fucking need to. Wet and willing pussy fell open and available everywhere we went. They, like me, knew it wasn't a long-term thing, but who gives a fuck when you're not after anything long term anyway. When all you need is someone warm and willing to chase away the devil off your shoulder, it worked well, until one day we got clean and sober enough to work out it no longer worked for any of us.

'I'm fucked if I know, I haven't dated in years,' Raff added laughing. 'But it sounds like a plan.'

'I hear those sorts of weird almost fatalistic meetings, are the best ones,' Brody thoughtfully put in.

Thoughtfully?

I caught Raff's amused expression at Brody's statement and knew it had to match my own. In a well-practised routine, we both turned on Brody. Shit had got far too fucking real in those few minutes, and we all understood that we'd dug up enough solemnity for one day.

I moved quickly and wrapped my arm around Brody's neck, and knowing I'd caught him off guard, I held onto it with my other hand. Raff kicked the back of his calf and took him down to the floor with me following.

I rubbed my knuckles quickly over his scalp.

'Yeah, man, and how the fuck would you know?' We tormented him over and over.

'Fuck right off,' he shouted out and I covered over his mouth hoping that Brie would sleep on a bit longer.

The three of us messing about on the floor was exactly what I needed. Eventually, we moved apart still laughing at each other. I dragged myself backwards to lean on the couch behind me and swept a hand through the longer strands of my hair that were now covering my eyes and grinned at them both. I knew it was the right time to show them what I'd come across outside the village hall, as I waited for Brie to finish her first lesson.

I rolled to the side, pulled out the cream, plastic-covered piece of card from the back pocket of my jeans and offered it to them both.

Brody's hand reached out, and he snatched the card from me so he could read over the advert first, then he handed over to Raff.

'What do you both think?'

I watched as Raff read over the words a few times, the same ones I now knew off by heart.

Qualified, Wentworth House trained Nanny
Miss Nikita Osbourne seeks a private situation.
References and employment history available on request.
Please contact 07923565721

'Wentworth Nannies are the ones who wear the uniforms.' Raff imparted his knowledge with an added nod of his head, 'The royal family use them too, I think.'

'Uniform, huh? I'm fucking sold.' Brody raised his eyebrows and smirked.

Raff dug into the back pocket of his jeans for his cell. 'I think you need to make that call, Mac.'

Nine

Nikki

'YOU GOT EVERYTHING?' TOM questioned as he turned right, went under the red brick archway and pulled into a parking space.

I let out a long exhale as I turned my head towards him and nodded.

'I think so.' I patted my bag and felt my wallet inside.

'You don't have to get the bus home, I can wait.'

'Tom, I'm really grateful for the lift in, as I would have hated to have been late, but I can get home after, thanks anyway... Now, how do I look?'

'Very nice.' He nodded back at me.

It had been hard choosing something that looked smart enough, and would be warm enough to be out in the snow our little part of country was enveloped in. I'd wanted to look smart, even though the prospective parents I was about to meet had decided "The Fairy

Garden" was a suitable choice for a more casual and comfortable meeting.

I cast my eyes down myself. Long over-the-knee, black leather boots, the only solid colour pair of jeans I owned and a borrowed long-line, V-neck, silver coloured jumper. I'd worn my new baby pink snood, which hung loosely around my neck and added the colour I felt the outfit needed. For the first time in as long as I could remember, I'd put on some make-up; silver eyeshadow to make my eyes pop, and I'd brushed my long, dark hair until it shone, before winding it up into a charcoal coloured bobble hat.

'Have you not got any paperwork to give them today?'

'No. After the phone call on Friday night, I emailed my references, qualifications and DBS check to them yesterday. They obviously must have gone through them and arranged this for today.'

'Well then, you're good to go, Nik.'

'Yes.' I said the single word like I needed it to sound convincing to myself.

'Break a leg,' Tom spoke and laughed out loud.

'Don't tempt bloody fate in this weather!' I raised my voice as I replied, thinking how that would probably be just my luck, now that a more local job seemed to have fallen in my lap and so quickly.

Shaking my head at him, I opened his car door and tentatively put a step to the ground. Luckily, the car park appeared to have been salted and I stood up, then after offering Tom a wave of my hand, I slammed his car door shut and made my way towards the tearooms.

I hadn't ever been here and after taking a couple of steps towards the door and hearing Tom sound the car horn as he departed the area, I stopped walking momentarily to take in the beautiful, converted building. It had been a former coach house, I thought I remembered being told by my mum when it had opened a few years back. All the windows were arched and the frames were black in colour, which contrasted fantastically against the red brick of the old Manor outbuildings. I let my eyes wander over the glass, hoping I could spot anyone inside who appeared to be waiting for someone. But, although I could make out the many shapes of people inside, it was so busy the windows had almost completely steamed up.

The wind suddenly gusted, blurring my vision completely with the snow flurry that came with it, and I pulled my heavy coat around myself. Then sighing, I gathered my thoughts and nervousness at being interviewed for a new position. Trying to rally myself, I focussed on the soft and friendly twinkle of the many fairy lights that had been placed against the windows.

A bell tinkled above my head as I entered the building and knowing I was letting in the cold air behind me, I stepped backwards quickly to make sure I'd closed the glass door firmly behind me.

I occupied myself momentarily, to stop my eyes frantically looking around to search out my prospective new employers, by shrugging my shoulders to rid myself of the heavy coat I'd worn. The heat from the log burner in the centre of the room had hit me instantly the door had shut behind me. Then I began to lightly bang my feet on the coir matting beneath me, as I attempted to rid my sister's best boots of the snow that had collected on them in the few steps I'd taken from the car. As soon as I'd finished, I'd found a waitress standing near to me and smiling.

'Good morning,' I offered her. 'I'm meeting a Mr. McKenzie.'

I vaguely recognised her face, probably from secondary school I thought, although I had a feeling that she might be a few years older than I was.

'Oh yes, follow me. He's waiting for you.' At the same time, she wordlessly offered to take my coat to hang it on the row of pegs beside the door.

I followed her as she made her way through the various chairs, settees and low tables. All of which seemed to be full with people, eager to start their Christmas festivities a week early. I followed behind, pulling off my gloves, loosening the snood around my neck and lastly, I carefully pulled off the bobble hat on my head. With the waitress still blocking my view of the table she was leading me to, I ran my fingers carefully through my long, thick hair and felt its weight fall to the middle of my back.

'Mr. McKenzie… your guest is here.'

Slowly, I lifted my gaze up from the varnished floorboards and saw a man stand up from the armchair he'd been sitting in, placing down the saltshaker he'd been playing with. I watched on as he shook his legs to make his ripped jeans fall into place over the Timberland boots he was wearing. My eyes jumped up to see him extending a heavily tattooed, bare forearm for me to shake his large hand.

Well, he's a surprise.

'Miss Osbourne.' An unexpected accent bled into my ears just as our hands touched for the first time.

American? And by himself?

I had been expecting a Mrs. McKenzie, but then when I thought about it, perhaps I'd been wrong in my assumption.

I remembered that all our correspondence over the past couple of days had only been between the two of us and he had only mentioned that he had the one child, a four-year-old daughter. Never had he given me any indication that there was a Mrs. McKenzie. I was a young, tolerant twenty-six-year-old and would accept any type of family, but however open-minded I was, it surprised me that I automatically assumed a family included a mum and a dad, which of course wasn't always the case.

I wondered how I'd feel about working for him if it turned out he was single, after my run in with Mr. Millar? Well, that remained to be seen.

My hand instinctively met his and as his hand held firmly but gently onto mine, an awareness hit me. An awareness that I knew I hadn't ever felt before. My forehead creased immediately into a frown as I tried hard to understand what on earth was going on. Our hands moved gently up and down in greeting a couple of times as I tried to recover my equilibrium and I remained transfixed at the sight of his hand enveloping mine. All around us, the sound of other people's conversation fell away and became a dull background noise. All I could see and feel, was the two of us trapped within this moment. But the one thing I could work out, was that after only a few seconds in his company, I trusted him. The fact that he was interviewing me for a position to look after his daughter and was by himself, was completely and utterly irrelevant.

Totally too soon for my liking, his hand released mine and my arm fell, like a dead weight, stupidly back to my side.

'What can I get you?' It wasn't until the waitress spoke again that I realised she was still standing to the side of the table she'd brought me to.

Trying to recover from what I was sure must look like my very weird behaviour as he met me for the first time, I dropped my gloves, hat and bag to the chair next to me and smiling broadly I replied, 'A hot chocolate please.'

I smiled over to her, eager to attempt to normalise and to replace the strange feelings that were unfurling themselves around my body. Mr. McKenzie was a tall and, from the small glances I'd allowed myself in my peripheral view, lean but muscular man. He dominated the small space around our table, and I was certain that if I could freeze time to take a quick peek around us, I was bound to see that many of the other ladies in the room would be equally aware of the man's presence.

I still hadn't summoned up the courage to look at him properly yet and wished he'd sit down, just to give me a minute to compose the strange reaction he had awoken inside of me.

Enough, Nik. You're just nervous.

'With marshmallows and whipped cream?' our waitress questioned.

'You must try the whipped cream, Miss. Osbourne.' His deep, soulful voice washed over me, as did the edge of teasing he'd wrapped around the sentence.

'Yes, please.' The words left my mouth not even a millisecond after his.

My eyes left the waitress as she moved away and then darted straight towards the owner of the voice that had captivated me.

It took me mere seconds to take in the man standing not two feet away from me. I'd already worked out his build, but as my eyes took in his medium brown coloured hair, which occasionally glinted red in the lights around us and his bright green, very amused eyes, I felt the back of my knees begin to twitch in reaction.

No, it can't be!

My brain was screaming at me. *It is!*

The man stood only feet away from me was *the* Luke McKenzie. *The actual fucking Luke McKenzie.* The bass guitarist and occasional violin player from the *only* rock band I needed to be in existence. In seconds, my eyelids began blinking rapidly at him in complete and utter disbelief, as I took in the man I'd crushed over since I was thirteen years old.

A flush of embarrassment hit my cheeks and in reaction my hand felt for the back of the armchair next to me, as I tried not to make a complete fool out of myself and to remain standing. The flush on my cheeks grew hotter as with his eyes completely and utterly claiming mine, I recollected that I had just a few days before, masturbated as I stared into the same mischievous green eyes that peered down from a poster to the side of my childhood bed.

'Luke!... Luke McKenzie?' I tried hard not to raise my voice as I questioned him, but as the dull noise of people chatting around us fell quiet, I knew I hadn't managed what I was trying so hard for.

'The one and only... Sit down.' The last two words fell from his mouth as an order and my now shaking body complied immediately.

I felt the air evaporate from around me.

I wasn't sure which of the two of us looked more shocked, but I felt sure the expression on my face was worse than his.

'I'm sorry, I'm not normally so starstruck,' I offered, as I cursed my own infatuated reaction to our meeting. 'I've worked for other famous people before… it's just, you're Luke McKenzie from Default Distraction.'

'That, I am,' he acknowledged, beginning to look less and less amused by my crazy need to keep telling him his name.

'I'm not normally like this,' I insisted, shaking my head from side to side at him as I silently hoped he'd believe me.

'Miss Osbourne,' he leant nearer to me as he whispered, 'people in the tearoom are beginning to watch us. If it's a problem, the possibility of working for me, you need to tell me now, then we can have a drink here and go our separate ways.'

'I'm fine.'

I screamed at myself in my head, to compose myself as the situation began to piece itself together. I was sure I remembered my mum telling me at some time or another about my favourite rock band having bought The Manor a few years back, but never did I dream that we'd ever see them actually here.

A memory flashed through my mind of reading how his wife had died a few years back, leaving him with one daughter to raise, and everything fell into place with a loud crash.

'Yeah, 'cause after going beet red, you're now looking as white as a sheet, darlin',' he offered, with the start of a smile crinkling the corner of his mouth.

'There we are. Two hot chocolates.' A third person's voice entered the conversation to the side of us.

Unable to tear my eyes away from Luke… Mr. McKenzie's face, I watched as his eyes left mine to politely thank our waitress.

'Thanks very much. Can I ask if you've got any of those cinnamon… something that Lauren used to make?' His face creased up and he began to shake his head, as if he was trying to recollect the word he was looking for and his right hand came up to stroke through his beard, the same beard I had for years imagined I could feel on my lips and down lower, in between my legs. 'I think one of us here has had a shock and needs some sugar.'

Bloody hell.

Realisation hit me.

'It was you!' I accused and I stood up abruptly as I remembered how two days previously, I'd been soaked and left dripping wet in the lanes by a man in a black car who stroked through his beard as he thought.

Ten

LUKE

TO GIVE OUR WAITRESS her due, she didn't even flinch when the far too attractive woman, who was here hoping to become Brie's new nanny, stood suddenly and pointed her finger accusingly at me.

'I thought we'd already established who I was?' Amused, I looked up at her and wondered just whose fucking idea it was for me to phone a number on a card, left on what was labelled as a parish council noticeboard, instead of calling an agency to do all the vetting for me.

Asshat, it was all yours.

I tore my eyes reluctantly away from the woman who was once again stood across the other side of the low table and pulled myself the fuck together. I looked between her and the waitress at the side of us, trying to rein in my growing attraction to her. I'd seen, and had, many attractive women, but this one was beautiful on a whole new fucking level. Each time I glanced over, her deep mercury-filled, grey eyes magnetised me and for a couple of seconds each time I knew she'd rendered me near speechless, unable to remember who the fuck I was, nor just what the hell I was supposed to be doing. I had to fight to look away, just to breathe. From those all-seeing and consuming eyes, to the long, dark hair that seemed to nearly touch the top of what I could tell would be a voluptuous ass, she was fucking stunning.

'Amy made some cinnamon whirls today… is that what you wanted?'

I snapped the fingers on my right hand together, making Miss Osbourne and the waitress next to me jump. 'Yes!' Turning back to her standing at the side of the table, I answered, 'Thank you, that's it. Lauren used to make those for us all back in Vegas.' I nodded, knowing they both probably hadn't a fucking clue what I was on about.

'One or… two?' Our waitress questioned as her eyes flicked between the two of us. Me still sitting, as I tried to send over a sense of calm to my guest as she continued to stand over me glowering.

Why, I had no fucking idea. I got her surprise and the initial reaction of working out who the fuck I was, but her reaction was completely over the top and I knew that if she continued to behave like this, the deal I wanted to offer her would be over before I'd even laid it out on the table.

But fuck.

That was the last thing I wanted, as she was everything I already knew I was looking for in a new nanny for Brie. Her resume spoke for itself. I'd seen her qualifications and as I'd run my eyes down her list of likes and hobbies, the minute my eyes had fallen on music and dance, I was sold.

She was young and quite obviously fit, and I knew she'd be able to keep up with my daughter and her new puppy and thinking back to Brie's requirements, I knew she'd love her.

Like Mary Poppins, Daddy, not Nanny McPhee.

I knew she was a great fit for Brie.

And pretty for you.

By the way my dick was twitching inside my jeans, despite her ability to make the whole fucking tearoom look over at us in amusement, I knew she'd equally be a great fucking fit for me, if I was going to go there, which I wasn't.

I allowed my eyes to sweep up and down her quickly and fought with the urge to grab her and lay her out over the table while I devoured and consumed every single fucking part of her. Bringing myself to heel, I allowed my eyes to roam back up the beautiful figure of Nikita Osbourne and watched as her hands, tipped with black fingernails, twisted around each other as she attempted to either warm them or fight off the nervousness that I could tell was threatening to consume her.

Then it dawned on me, black fingernails and those deep filled eyes. *Well fuck.*

I inhaled slowly as it dawned on me that we'd pretty much met before.

'Miss Osbourne, or should I call you Nikita?' I made the pretence of thinking about what I'd asked her, when I knew exactly what I wanted to call her. 'Are you staying to hear about mine and my daughter's requirements for a nanny, or going?' I knew the answer I wanted to hear, but I wanted her to speak the words herself.

'It was you on Friday, wasn't it?' she whispered, refusing to answer my question.

'Yes.'

'What the hell, just because you're who you are... I mean, do you normally run people off the road?' I exhaled loudly and smiled at her retort. Finally, it appeared that she'd thrown off the mantle of starstruck teenager and I liked the fiery woman she was showing herself to be, even more.

I was trapped in between amusement and annoyance at her question.

'Only women dressed in next to nothing, who are quite happy to flash their ass at me.'

Her mercurial eyes swirled, and I watched as she rolled her plump lips into her mouth as she tried to stop the laugh I could sense was threatening to escape at my come back.

'Look, I didn't know it was you on the road on Friday and I *was,* in my defence, going to apologise when I took my daughter for her ballet lesson again this week.' I watched her nod at me in understanding and then stop as my words hit home.

'How do you know I teach ballet?' I could see her face twisting as she tried to decide whether I was some fucking stalker or not.

'Hmmm... look, I know how all of this sounds... But I can assure you that all of this...' I lifted one hand up in the air and moved it around in a circle before carrying on. 'All of this is a complete coincidence. I mean, I could have sworn the woman I saw on the bike had pink hair for a start.'

I watched her touch her black painted fingernails to the pink scarf thing she had around her neck, and I nodded back at her in resignation.

'Nothing more than a coincidence.' I smiled over at her as I spoke. Her eyes opened wider in question at me, and I managed to somehow remove the threatening smirk off my lips. 'Brie and I were already talking to Mrs. Brown when you arrived and listening to her conversation with you out back, it was easy to work out.'

'But you didn't think to apologise then and there?'

'You were changing... I didn't think it would have been my best decision.'

'You could have said something at the end.'

'But I didn't.' I scooped a spoonful of cream off the hot chocolate in front of me and after turning it around, I placed the spoon into my mouth and sucked it clean.

'I see,' she added as her eyes homed in to watch my mouth. 'And you feel that's okay, do you?'

I'd temporarily looked away as I tried to gauge who was still listening to our conversation, but the question she'd just asked of me meant I needed to look at her as I answered. I found her eyes with my own and held them captive.

'No... But then, I'm not known for always doing the correct or appropriate thing.' I quirked my left eyebrow up at her as I let the words filter through to her.

'I see,' she managed to answer.

'So you keep saying, Nikita... But I'm not sure you do.' Again, I paused as I took in the body language of the woman across the table from me. I wanted to reach out to touch her and by the way her chest was rising and falling with the sharp intake of breath she was attempting to drag in over her full, wet lips, I could see she was fighting off the same thing, even if it wasn't something she was yet aware of.

'I'm sorry for soaking you and for nearly running you off the road, but darlin' I feel you need to take some ownership of the situation, too.'

'Thank you.' She nodded. 'Yes, I know I probably do, and I'll wear a helmet in future.'

'Can you drive?' I was thinking back to her very detailed resume, but couldn't remember if she'd said or not.

'I can.'

'Good, then there'll be no need to wear a helmet in future, as I have enough vehicles and I'm sure we can find you one to drive… Right, now, where were we?'

'Errmm…' She floundered for a minute as she tried to work out if she'd heard me correctly. 'So, you're Brie's dad? She's a lovely little girl. I really enjoyed her company on Friday,' she spoke as she tried to take charge of the situation. Her hands stopped fidgeting as I fleetingly moved my eyes to them and then back up to hers.

'Yeah? That's good.' I couldn't help the smile that spread over my face at her shot to control the conversation. 'Now… are you staying or going? And if you're staying, do you want to eat… yes or no, before I eat both of these pastries,' I questioned her, feeling amused by her as she stood there still gawping at me, but more and more irritated that people were beginning to stare at the two of us.

Please stay.

'Staying and yes please.' She smiled her answer to me as she sat down quickly.

Polite and able to make a decision. She was becoming more perfect with every second I spent in her company.

'Shall we start from the top?'

'Yes,' she agreed.

'Tell me about you, Nikita?' I encouraged as I pushed myself further back into the armchair I was sitting on, and trying to look more relaxed than I felt, I awkwardly lifted my foot up off the floor and after lifting it over the table, I repositioned my ankle on top of my knee.

'I'm twenty-six and have been a qualified nanny for nearly five years.' She smiled and I felt my gaze leave her eyes to watch her lips as she spoke. My eye movement was quick, but as I watched her tongue flick out to wet her lips, I knew she'd caught me watching.

'Wentworth House trained, I saw, which is something you should be very proud of.'

My compliment made her smile wider, and my dick twitched inside my jeans as I caught sight of what I knew had to be a diamond stud in her mouth, and I was fucking grateful for the fact I'd lifted my leg up and removed my crotch from her view.

She carried on telling me about her qualifications and in truth I switched off. I'd already vetted the documents she'd sent me. What parent in their right mind wouldn't? I had also read about her passion for dancing, which was right up there on the list Brie had informed me she needed. I was looking forward to finding out some of the more personal stuff about her.

'Does your family live around here?'

'Yes, my mum and sister live a couple of villages away.'

'And I'm sure they'd like you working nearer than London?'

'Yes, they would.' I watched as the thought that it might be possible to stay nearby to her family made her face light up.

Stunning.

'Boyfriend, girlfriend… partner?' I questioned, suddenly and almost obsessively needing to know the answer.

'No,' she replied quickly, and I watched her cheeks heat up a little.

'That's a benefit,' I spoke more to me than her.

'It is?' she questioned.

'Yeah, well, we lost Brie's last nanny, Nancy, when she left to start her own family.'

'Oh, I see.' She smiled over at me.

Picking up the hexagonal glass salt container, I twisted it around by its silver top and as I listened to the rhythmic tap on the table, I thought back to what else I needed to tell her.

'Now, although I'm gonna be building a home somewhere around here for me and Brie, the position of her nanny would require you to travel with me, when DD go on tour or are needed back in the U.S. Do you see that being a problem for you?

'Not at all.'

'Are you a close family?'

'Yes.'

'Good, I want that for Brie.'

In fact, you fucking promised Cherise.

She smiled back at me, unaware of the shit inside my head.

'I'm Brie's only parent. I'm sure you're aware of that as you recognised me. So, you probably know we lost her mom a few years ago?'

'Yes, I'm so sorry you lost her.'

My heart missed a beat and I waited for the normal ache of pain to fill the gap. When it came, I was strangely aware that it was duller than normal and disappeared quicker.

'So, Nikita, what else should I ask you?'

'Please call me Nikki, I have to keep reminding myself you're talking to me when you call me Nikita.' She smiled a little shyly over to me.

I contemplated her for a few seconds, as she ripped her pastry with her fingers and placed a small piece into her mouth.

I leant forward and offered her my hand to shake again. 'Pleased to meet you, Nikki. My name is Luke, or Mac... or most importantly Daddy.'

She wiped her fingers on the nearby napkin and reached out to shake mine. My breathing faltered for a few seconds as our flesh connected. I knew she'd felt it too when she released a soft gasp, before releasing my hand and sitting herself back into her chair.

'Pleased to meet you, Luke,' she offered.

As a waitress passed us, I caught her eye. 'Can I use a pen please?'

I took the offered pen from her outstretched hand and smiled up my thanks, before I grabbed another paper napkin out of its holder. Then I scribbled a figure of eighty thousand on it, and before I pushed it across the table in her direction, I asked her one more question.

'Cats or dogs?'

She let out a small laugh which sounded very much like relief before she answered.

'Dogs of course.'

'Correct answer.' I raised my eyebrows at her and pushed the napkin in her direction.

'Obviously, we'll have a proper contract drawn up. I'm sure you've had to sign them and a NDA before?' Her eyes opened wide at the figure, and I carried on, 'There will be a couple of addendums that will have to be added.'

She smiled her answer across to me.

'The salary is generous.' I leant forward and with my forearms on my legs, I joined my hands together as I continued. 'It also includes your own private room, all of your food, the use of a car and any travel costs will, of course, be paid for by me...' I stared at her more intently, 'And lastly, I'm prepared to pay over the odds because I expect you to stay with us for at least the next five years.' I watched her features grow tense as she thought over what I was asking.

'Five years? What if things in our lives change before then?' she asked as her forehead tightened as she thought over what I just imparted to her.

I let out a long exhale and tried to think how the hell to explain what I was looking for and why. 'Brie has had enough change in her young life, she needs stability.'

She needs a family.

She took a few seconds to contemplate what I'd just said and slowly I saw her start to nod back at me.

'Of course… I think I understand what you're trying to achieve. Children thrive on stability.' I smiled at her as she began to agree with me. 'But it would be a very unorthodox arrangement for me to sign a contract that holds me in a position for five years. So many things can change for either party. In fact, I'm unsure that U.K. employment laws would uphold the arrangement.'

Fuck.

I knew it was a huge goddamn ask, but I'd had to try. So, the question I had to ask myself was whether it was a gamechanger. I wasn't used to not getting what I wanted, but I knew I wanted her as Brie's nanny. So, I understood that I needed to run with it.

'I hadn't even considered U.K. employment laws,' I offered as an excuse. 'As long as you understand what I'm trying to give my daughter, I'll leave the salary the same and that stipulation out.'

'I understand, Luke, and please be assured that's exactly what I want to offer my young charges too.' She offered a smile that made my relaxed posture suddenly tense up.

'Good … so if that's an agreeable figure to you,' I began, as I shifted myself around as I tried to relax again, 'and if Brie likes you when you meet her, which I'm sure she will as you're already one of her dance teachers… how soon can you start?'

I watched her long lashes open and close as she glanced down again at the white paper, and I was there to meet her eyes when they finally came back up to mine.

'Is today too soon?' She smiled over her answer to me.

'Today is perfect.' I raised my hot chocolate up to her in agreement. 'In fact, it could be better than perfect, as I've got the opening of The Manor to attend to this afternoon and a gig to play this evening.'

I lifted my left arm and turned over my wrist to check the time, when in truth I'd only just seen it on my phone as the screen lit up briefly with an incoming message. But I needed to unconsciously draw a line under our meeting.

A fatalistic meeting.

Wasn't that what Brody had called it?

Nikki was perfect for Brie. I could tell that in the twenty minutes we'd been in each other's company.

And the problem was?

Well, there's no problem as such.

All I had to do was to keep my hands to my fucking self, as somewhere inside I had a feeling she was also perfect for me.

Eleven

Nikki

I'VE BEEN OFFERED THE job, Lou, subject to meeting his daughter.
Please let mum know I won't be home until later tonight.
My new employer is Luke McKenzie.
Yes, you read that right!
Yes… DD's *Luke McKenzie.*
I'm off to Falham Manor now to meet his daughter Brie.
Keep your fingers crossed for me.

I watched the three dots wiggling as my sister started to reply to the text. I'd sent it less than a minute ago and after turning my mobile over in my hand to face downwards on my lap, I looked back over to the male subject matter sitting next to me, the one that seemed to have made every single cell in my body go on to high alert. My eyes were once again drawn to his well-defined muscles and prominent veins on his forearm. The sleeves of his red-checked shirt were rolled up, and not only gave me a glimpse of the many tattoos I knew were on his body, from the posters all over my walls back at home, but also the said muscles and veins I was staring with very obvious intent.

The view that met my eyes could only have been described as "arm porn".

What the hell is wrong with me?

Was it possible to find a man's hand and arm a complete and utter turn on? I didn't think it had ever happened to me before, but then I had never been in a small enclosed space with the man I'd been convinced I was in love with since my teens.

Things like this never happened to me.

Don't keep looking and don't breathe in the smell of him.

Stop it! After rolling my eyes up high at myself, I blinked quickly and cleared my throat, trying to draw a line under my ridiculous behaviour.

I felt my phone vibrate with Lou's reply. Without even looking at her words, I could feel her excitement and disbelief as it seeped through my jeans. I could see in my mind's eye the look on her face as she'd read my words over and over. I imagined her jumping up and down on the spot while she screamed as she clutched her phone and knew she would have had to sit down before formulating her answer back to me.

Her enthusiasm was feeding my own. I felt almost dizzy with excitement.

I was quickly understanding that posters only went so far into giving you an insight of how a person looked and that only real life could do justice to someone as captivatingly beautiful as my new employer.

Oh fuck! New employer. *Be professional.*

In that second, I had never wanted to be so very much closer to someone but also further away at the same time. Inhaling slowly, I turned my head to the left and looked out of the window as I attempted to yet again compose myself. The first wafts of his expensive cologne filtered enticingly into my nostrils and needing even more of the scent that was so fitting for the man sat next to me, I inhaled deeply as I committed it to memory. I knew it wasn't a cologne I'd ever smelt before, but I also knew it was a fragrance I would never smell again without conjuring up a vision of Luke in my head.

I had no idea how I should be reacting, but I was sure I shouldn't be feeling this way!

Once again, my gaze drifted back from the safety of the window and rested on Luke's arm. I wrenched my eyes away after spending the next couple of seconds watching Luke's hand as he expertly clasped the chrome gearstick and changed down another gear, before he very competently pulled out onto the main road connecting the two villages we were travelling between.

There was something about a man expertly controlling a fast, powerful car, or perhaps that was also down to me being a complete and utter crazy person where he was concerned.

'Ahem.' I cleared the tight constriction in my throat.

My right cheek started to burn, and I quickly worked out that the cause was his eyes on the side of my face. He was probably trying hard to work out just what he was doing with a starstruck idiot in his car. Although my sudden cough had for a few seconds at least allowed me to pull myself together, I refused to turn my head to look back at him, as I was absolutely convinced that my face would reveal to him everything that was mounting up inside of me.

So, I concentrated instead on the lesser of two evils, my mobile in my lap.

Luke McKenzie?
The **Luke McKenzie?**
No, way!

Yes, way!

But you love him!

Why was it the screen seemed to light up even brighter with that reply? I tilted it slightly more towards the window, desperate not to give Luke anymore of an insight into just how big a crush I had on him... *NO! I used to have a crush on him*

OMG! Lou replied immediately after receiving nothing back from me.

I'll see you tonight. I tried to pacify her.

You bet your life you will.
I'll be the one waiting up for all the details.

Smiling to myself, I turned my phone off and leaning forward, I dropped it into my bag between my feet, glad of having something else to do other than fixating on the man beside me.

This had to stop. I needed this job. I needed it for my mum, my sister and foremost to keep my brother in the facility that provided him with the excellent care we all wanted him to have. But, most of all, I wanted this job for me, and I was convinced that if Luke knew just how much of a teenage infatuation I'd had over him, he'd be wheel spinning in the icy lane to turn the car around and dropping me back straight back at my house.

'One village here looks just like the other.' His deep voice washed over me as he slowed the car slightly, crossed his arms over on top of the wheel and leant closer to the road ahead of us.

'Not when you're from around here,' I replied, as I smiled my answer over to him and his eyes, which were now sparkling with amusement, met my own. 'Carry on the way you're going; I won't let you make a wrong turn,' I offered.

'Yeah? That's good to know.' He raised his eyebrow at me and after pulling his mouth to one side, he made a click sound in his cheek, and I knew he was questioning my turn of phrase and teasing me. But whatever it was, it broke down the defensive barricade I had placed between us, and I smiled back at him. He grinned back and offered me a quick wink before directing his eyes back on the road ahead, leaving me to stare at the side of his face.

A flood of wetness hit my inner thighs as my core tightened and all my previous reprimands to myself flew right out of the window.

'You've been quiet since we got in the car, I was afraid you were having second thoughts about working for me?' I watched his lips move, completely and utterly mesmerised.

'No.' I over enthusiastically shook my head and abruptly stopped myself as I contemplated what I must look like.

'That's good to know… 'cause Cade, Raff and Brody would never let me live it down if they found out I'd frightened you away in one day.'

'Look… I'm sorry. I realise I'm acting strangely.' I decided that perhaps honesty might be the best idea. 'But this is a weird situation for me. I've met celebrities before and as you know I've even worked for a couple of them, but as a teenager Default Distraction were… and still are, my favourite band and I never thought I'd end up even meeting you, let alone working for one of you. So, if you can just allow me this one day of being totally starstruck, I promise that tomorrow I will turn back into the very epitome of professionalism and be everything you're looking for in a nanny for Brielle.'

Luke nodded slowly at the explanation that had made me blush profusely, but the same one that I knew I owed him, to clarify the situation between us.

'Sure thing… although don't totally lose the weird because you'll need it being around us all,' he replied and laughed gently. For the first time since entering his vehicle earlier, I felt my body sag a little as I relaxed.

We'd travelled from the tearooms to my house. Once there, I'd run around the house opening up everyone's wardrobes as I looked for a dress. One I could wear to the party Default Distraction were throwing this evening after their official opening of The Manor. After folding up my sister's silver grey, lace-covered skater dress and placing it into a carrier bag with a few toiletries, I'd allowed myself to turn around on the spot and look at all the various poses I knew I would find Luke in, on the tattered looking posters on my walls. The same pictures I knew off by heart.

In a bid to say goodbye to my childish dreams, I'd jumped up onto my bed and after pressing my fingers to my lips, I'd hurriedly placed a kiss on every single pair of Luke's lips on the walls around me. I'd then gone downstairs and allowed myself one glance through the horizontal blinds that gave our living room privacy, to look at the man who was sitting patiently outside for me, as I promised myself I could do this.

But it hadn't worked.

When I needed it to work.

'Now all you need to admit, is which one of us you thought yourself to be in love with.' Luke's deep American accent penetrated my brain.

'I'm sorry,' I exclaimed as my body tensed in panic.

'You heard me.'

'I'm… well, I'm…' I floundered momentarily as I looked for an answer.

'It's best you tell me now… the others will prise it out of you sooner or later anyway. If I know, I can protect you a little.' A smile stretched across his face in what had to be amusement.

No way.

'I've always loved Brody. I mean who doesn't love a lead singer,' I managed to reply as quick as a flash as I attempted to cover up the truth.

Luke smacked his hands hard down onto the wheel as he abruptly grabbed it and turned the car to the right. The car changed direction and started up The Manor's long, sweeping driveway.

An uncomfortable silence seemed to envelope us all over again.

It was my turn to watch him as I witnessed what I was sure was the disappearance of his earlier amusement due to my answer, and then almost under his breath I was even more convinced he muttered, 'Of course… it had to be the fucking lead singer.'

Twelve

Nikki

'DO YOU LIKE IT?' Brie's voice filled the quietness inside her cream tepee, which apparently Luke and Cade had erected in her large bedroom.

'It's beautiful, Brie.' And it really was. It was decorated with pink and yellow bunting and adorned with various fairy lights. We had a soft, circular mattress beneath us, fluffy cushions underneath our heads and fleece blankets over our bodies.

'It's my special place, Daddy says. When I get sad, I can come in here and it will help me feel happy.'

A wave of melancholy swept over me and as her tiny hand slipped into my own as we both lay there staring up into the lights above us, I offered her fingers a small squeeze of reassurance.

'That's a really good idea, Brie... we could all do with a place that helps us to feel happy again.'

'Daddy said that too.'

I might not have known how to take the man, as he'd been blowing hot and cold since I'd met him this afternoon, but he really did seem to understand his daughter and that thrilled me.

'Is Biscuit allowed in here?' I questioned, and grinned as I remembered him greeting us after we'd climbed the stairs and rounded the corner to the wing that Luke had been in the middle of explaining was the one that DD had made their own for the time being.

'Yes, but don't tell Daddy,' she whispered as she turned her head to look at me and giggle, as we'd both thought back to half an hour earlier.

I thought back to my very first meeting with Default Distraction, something I'd been dreaming of for as long as I could remember. It had been nothing like I'd always imagined, but I was at least mature enough to realise that not much was.

In fact, it had been so very much better, as I'd got to see some of the real men behind the DD image.

The small puppy had met us with one of Luke's tan coloured, lace-up brogues in his mouth. As drool poured off the shoelace that hung limply from one side of his mouth to the thick carpet in the hallway, it became apparent that he'd been using it as a teething implement. Luke had shouted out to Brie to come and meet me as he'd taken off, running and shouting out loud for help, trying to swear under his breath. Something, I was quickly understanding, he was pretty competent at.

I'd found some green eyes peering at me with interest as Luke had rushed off after the extremely delighted puppy, who of course was enjoying every single second of the game he'd created. Then three grown men, in various states of dress and undress, had appeared from different doors and two of them had started charging about with Luke as they chased the puppy from room to room, and as they did so, they'd shouted out a quick greeting at me.

I'd watched on as what looked like an episode of a comedy unfolded in front of me, and as Cade fell over not ten feet away from me, I'd burst out laughing. As first meetings went, it had to right up there with the best of them.

Brie had taken hold of Brody as she moved further out of the room and as she wrapped her arms around the top of his thigh for reassurance, Brody was more relaxed than I'd ever imagined he would be. The front man of the group, who normally appeared pensive and serious unless he was on stage and singing, started laughing at the others as he stood next to Brie and offered her his support.

I'd looked quickly up and down DD's lead singer as I'd discovered that he had what looked like flour in various patches on his jeans and wondered if he'd been baking. Then, not wanting to be caught by Luke looking at Brody after my lie in the car earlier, I glanced quickly at the open book in his hand and worked out that he'd been reading to her as well.

Feeling Brielle's eyes on me again, I gave her a small wave. I saw the moment that recognition flashed through her eyes. She unwrapped her arms from Brody's upper thigh, released his leg and left his side.

'Miss Nikki?'

'Hi, Brielle.'

All at once her legs were moving quickly as she left Brody and moved down the hallway towards me.

'You're my new nanny?' she questioned disbelievingly.

'I'd like to be,' I offered, crouching down to her level to give her a smile.

'Daddy you did it!' Her excitement had been evident.

A loud shout had gone up behind her as Luke finally caught up with Biscuit. 'Gotcha, you thieving animal. I swear you're more fucking goat than dog.'

'Daddy,' Brie reprimanded him as she spun around in front of me and crossed her arms over her chest.

'Sorry, Shorty… Now, I see you've met Nikki. Would you like to spend some time with her this afternoon while we're doing the boring stuff downstairs?'

'Yes!' Brie had looked up at me adoringly and I'd found yet another pair of green eyes that made me melt just a little inside. I took hold of her offered hand and moved her in front of me, as I'd silently encouraged her to lead the way to her room.

'Introduce us properly, Mac.' Cade had reappeared and was zipping up a pair of smart suit trousers, while he stomped his boot-covered feet to get the trousers to fall where he wanted them.

Dear God!

I fought hard to keep my eyes up on his face and not to watch his fingers or to stare at his completely tattoo covered torso.

'This is Nikki,' Luke offered.

'Hey.' Cade had smiled and nodded at me, before disappearing into what I could only presume was his room.

'Nice to meet you.' Raff walked towards me with an outstretched hand and shook mine briefly, before going back to fasten up his white, button-down shirt.

'And you.'

'And you've already met Brody,' Luke growled out before disappearing into another room.

Brody's laughter filled up the hallway as he looked between me and the space Luke had vacated. Then he turned back to me grinning, 'Good to meet you, Nikki… ignore him. You know the saying about green eyes…'

I wasn't sure I did, because the only one I knew was green eyed jealousy, and Brody surely couldn't mean that, but I nodded back at him anyway.

'Come and see my room, Miss Nikki.' Brie pulled me along with her.

'Just Nikki, Brielle. Because if we're going to be friends, friends use each other's first names, don't they?'

'Yes, and I'm Brie.' She turned and smiled up at me.

And now, here we were, in her special, happy place, feeling the peace and quiet in our companionship, while four stunning men tore around outside her room trying to make themselves presentable for their flagship hotel's opening. Their laughter and constant ribbing of each other was addictive and I longed to peek at what exactly was going on, but I was here to meet Brie, so I put my adolescent fantasies to one side and concentrated on her.

'Okay, so which one of you ladies are gonna fix my tie?'

I removed my eyes from the twinkling fairy lights on the roof of Brie's tepee and looked down the length of my body to the small opening. To the side of my pink fluffy socks, I saw a pair of tan coloured brogues and my excitement mounted, but not wanting to appear too eager to see all four of them in the suits I'd guessed they'd be in, I stayed stock still.

'He must mean you, Brie.'

I felt my left foot being tapped by the tan brogue and looked over at Brie as I gave her a quick conspirator's grin.

My foot was tapped again, a little harder this time.

'Little piggies, shall I blow your house down with a huff and a puff…'

Brie squealed and sitting up quickly she flew out of the tent.

'Uncle Brody… no don't.'

Oh. With the sight of the tan brogues, I'd assumed it was Luke outside the tent.

'I won't if you straighten my tie,' Brody teased her.

I could hear Brie's excitable voice as she got to attend to her "uncle" and smiled to myself at the way they all seemed to treat her as their own.

Slowly, I began to manoeuvre myself forward to the gap. It wasn't a pretty sight as I thrust my hips up into the air and inched myself, like an upside-down caterpillar, towards the small V-shaped opening. At last, after rolling over and going onto all fours, I managed, in a rather unladylike fashion, to reverse out bum first and prepared myself to stand up.

I think I smelt Luke's cologne, before I realised that he was now also in the room.

'Brie, can you check my tie?' His warm voice filled me up.

'No, Daddy... I'm doing Uncle Brody's.'

I turned my head around at the sound of his voice and looking over my shoulder, I found his eyes focussed on my arse. I watched the corners of his mouth twitch in amusement at my predicament and decided to use the opportunity to do what my head was screaming at me to.

Still on all fours, I looked him up and down appreciatively. He was immaculate, his brown hair was blended short up his neck, with the longer lengths on the top usually falling untidily somewhere over his face, but today it had been brushed backwards and was tidier than I'd ever seen it. He was a gorgeous looking man, but seeing all his face, without his hair covering some part of it, was a first for me and he took my breath away, as he was simply stunning. Tearing my eyes away from his face, I let them roam down his tall, muscular frame. The three-piece suit he was wearing fitted him to perfection. The charcoal grey material was set off with a fine, tan coloured stripe, creating a subtle check pattern. I could immediately see why he had wanted to wear the shoes Biscuit had chewed, but instead he was wearing brown Chelsea boots, making him look less like the seasoned rocker I knew him to be and more like a gentleman. I forced my eyes to travel over him faster, knowing I would be running out of time to peruse my potential new boss at my leisure. A white button-down, collared shirt and tan coloured knitted tie met my eyes, and my gaze found his fingers as he pulled on a rose gold chain and flipped open a matching Albert pocket watch.

'How long we got?' enquired Brody as Brie shifted his tie, slightly to the left and then back again.

'Five minutes.'

'Yo,' came a shout from Cade outside the door. 'You guys ready?'

'Yeah, just coming... as Brie's otherwise engaged, can you check my tie please, Nikki?'

It wasn't until that minute, I understood Brody had played a blinder. Picking up on what he had thought was jealousy earlier, he'd made sure he made it into Brie's room before Luke.

'Yes, sure. No problem,' I answered.

Liar.

As I attempted to look like this was an everyday situation, I began to make a move to stand up. Cramp suddenly got the better of me and I failed miserably. Now on my knees in front of Luke, who had crossed the room towards me, I stared hard at his muscular legs encased in the expensive material of his suit trousers. Making sure my mouth didn't fall open and embarrass me further, I momentarily stopped my attempt to stand and nursed the back of my thigh.

'You, okay?' Luke asked.

But before I had chance to answer, Brody interrupted, 'What are you waiting for, Mac? Help her up, unless of course you like her on her knees.'

'Stop talking, Uncle Brody. Your throat keeps moving and I can't put your tie straight,' Brie reprimanded him.

Luke's head shot around to fix Brody with a stare, before his hand found mine and he pulled on it brusquely. 'Yes, Daniels, it would be a good idea if you chose now to shut the fuck up.'

The room was quiet apart from Brody's laughter.

I stood up onto my feet quickly. I could feel Luke watching me, but without looking up and into his eyes, I focussed my sole attention on quickly checking his tie. Every movement of mine was deliberate and although I could see the slight tremble of my fingers, I took the time to remind myself exactly what my family needed from me. Even if I had the green light from the man that I'd lusted after for years, I couldn't let him fuck me and risk the job I needed and wanted.

Letting out a slow sigh, I managed to adjust his tie to absolute perfection without touching any part of him, while my heart pounded in my chest and I held my breath, so his cologne couldn't capture my senses any more than it had already.

In the belief that we'd been set up by Brody, I finally allowed my eyes to focus onto Luke's face to try to find the affirmation and amusement I was convinced I'd find there. But instead, I found his face was stretched tight and what looked like confused panic had firmly fixed itself in place. Then slowly, his face relaxed under my scrutiny and his eyes brightened. I offered him a small smile and watched his eyes crinkle at the corners as he began to reciprocate.

'I think we're good to go, bro.' Brody's voice entered my ears and I let my hands drop away like I'd been burnt. My fingertips immediately mourned the warmth of Luke's body.

'Eskimo kisses.' I heard Brie giggle and in my peripheral view saw her place her hands either side of Brody's face and rub her nose on his.

My eyes remained fixed to the spot, as I watched Luke follow my hands with his gaze as they fell away and then as his eyes came back up quickly to capture mine.

'Yeah, we are,' he replied. 'Thanks,' he offered me and then directed a question to his daughter. 'Brie, will you be okay with Nikki for a few hours?' He asked the question of his daughter, but his eyes remained focussed on mine.

'Yes. We're going to do girl things.' I felt Brie arrive at my side as she informed him of what we'd already decided as we'd lay side by side in her tepee. 'Give Nikki an Eskimo kiss goodbye, Daddy.'

Luke's brow furrowed with what appeared to be perplexity.

'Yeah, come on, Mac, you know the rules … give her an Eskimo kiss.' Amusement was interlaced through Brody's words.

'I don't think…' Luke started to speak as his eyebrows raised in response to the fact that my eyes had opened wide, like a deer startled by the headlights of a car.

'You must!' I felt Brie stand taller to the side of me, as a flash of stubbornness swept through her. 'You said it's our family kiss… our family always does it.' Her voice was tinged with slight sadness.

'It's fine,' I encouraged, still staring at him.

Fine? You're mad.

Needing no further encouragement to do his daughter's bidding, Luke's large hands gently cupped my cheeks and with his eyes still firmly on mine as he appeared to be waiting for me to cut and run, his face came slowly towards mine. His nose gently brushed over mine a couple of times, leaving me frozen to the spot. His mouth must have opened as he Eskimo kissed me, as I felt the warm air leave his body and tantalisingly skirt over the wet, sensitive flesh of my lips, and my knees began to buckle.

'She seems to have accepted you already... welcome to the family.' The expression on his face was teasing, although his eyes looked full of pain.

'And when we're doing our girl stuff, boys aren't going to be allowed in here.' Brie spoke again and Luke lifted his face away from mine and removed his hands. The moment between us was over as he very deliberately moved away from me, leaving me quaking in his wake.

'Good... That's really good,' he replied to her, but as I heard each word, I wondered why they sounded so unconvincing.

Thirteen

Nikki

'... AND THE NUT WAS good. The end.' I finished the book and after closing it, I placed it down on my lap.

'I like that story, it's one of Daddy's favourites too,' Brie offered me thoughtfully. I heard her voice and smiling to myself, I rolled my eyes up high into my head. I had hoped she'd fall asleep, knowing we were going to be having such a late evening tonight at the party, but it appeared not. Nothing but her strong will had kept her awake this afternoon, even though I read through at least six books.

I'd learnt many things about my new charge this afternoon. One was that she didn't ever close the curtains on her room, even when it was freezing outside, because she liked to feel the moon, which I took to mean she was a little afraid of the dark. She loved to share stories and had bookcases full of all of my favourite children's ones and in complete contrast to how you would imagine a four-year-old child who had lost their mum to be, she was fairly level-headed and mainly unspoilt by all of her uncles' attention. She knew she was loved deeply, and I appreciated that it was the greatest gift you could ever bestow on a child. In return, I identified that without a shadow of a doubt, I would love looking after her. Now, my only worry was being so near to her dad, but I was convinced my infatuation with him would soon wear off once I was living with them full-time.

Simply because it had to.

Brie began to scramble her small body off the bed and finally, once her feet hit the floor, she took off towards the window.

'Nikki, come and see, the people are starting to leave.' The joy in her voice was evident.

'Yeah.' I answered her with more of an acknowledgement than a question and began to move myself off her bed at the same time, desperate to also take a look at what she was watching.

I reached the large window and despite the expensively glazed windows, could instantly feel the cold seeping through from the outside. I pushed the thick curtain away to the side and leant forward to peer though the large circle Brie had created with her hand in the condensation. The two of us stared through the circle to get a better view of the hordes of reporters and hotel inspectors as they began to disperse and move towards their own cars or transport arranged to take them home.

I knew the reviews were going to be good, as with just the little I'd seen of The Manor earlier today when we'd arrived here, and my experience of travelling to the best hotels in the world with my previous employers, it was right up there with the six-star ones.

'How long until we can go down now, Nikki?'

I didn't want to admit that Luke and I hadn't got around to discussing the specifics of my meeting here today with Brie, as it sounded far less professional than how I normally liked to work, and she might only be a child, but I knew she was close to her "uncles" and they'd have a field day with that information if she shared it.

'I'm sure your daddy will be back up here soon, but there's nothing stopping us starting to get ready if you'd like?'

'Yes, can we get ready together?'

'Of course, Brie. I've brought a dress to wear for this evening. What are you going to wear?'

I turned to watch her as she placed her fingers to her chin as she thought, and I thought how very much the little girl next to me looked like her daddy.

'Can I see your dress?' she asked.

It was at that minute I remembered the carrier bag I'd brought with me earlier and the fact I hadn't even taken the dress out to hang it up. Now, I knew no one would be looking at me this evening and my dress being creased to buggery wouldn't matter to anyone except me. I also knew that I shouldn't care how I looked this evening, but I did, and I was far too scared to contemplate why.

'You can,' I declared, moving suddenly to the reusable grocery bag I'd dropped to one side of Brie's bookcase earlier. I bent to pick up the bag, let its contents drop to the floor and after picking it up and shaking out the fabric in my hands, I lifted the dress up high by its shoulders. The dress was skater style and the underlayer of silver-grey fabric was covered in a heavy lace. The long sleeves were just lace and although the body of the dress wasn't too bad, the sleeves looked awful from my neglect.

'It's very pretty, Nikki.' Still holding my dress up in the air, I was suddenly aware of the small girl on her knees beside me as she examined my sister's dress in my hands and the few things I'd thrust haphazardly into the carrier bag earlier. 'It matches your eyes... you will look *so* pretty.'

I smiled down at her for the compliment and grasped that the only footwear I had with me, were the long, black boots I'd worn to my interview. *Was that only this morning?* They'd have to do. After all, I wasn't here to try to impress anyone with the clothes I wore, and I knew as I conjured up a picture in my head that it would look quite cute.

'If you phone Maria, she could get all the lines out.'

'Maria?' I questioned, understanding that Brie meant the creases in the dress.

'She works behind the desk in reception.'

I smiled at her. 'That's a great idea, Brie, thank you. Now, while I phone her, do you want to take a look at what you would like to wear and think about how you'd like me to do your hair for you?'

I moved myself towards the doorway after noticing that although Brie's room was a hotel room, the phone you'd normally find in place had been removed when they'd decorated it especially for her.

'I'm just going to make a call downstairs.'

'Daddy has a phone in his room, it's through the door over there.'

I looked in the direction she'd pointed and remembered seeing the door earlier, and although I'd already worked out it meant her bedroom was probably interconnected, I hadn't thought any more about it. Now all I could think, as my feet walked eagerly towards his sanctuary, was that I was going to be able to smell the beautiful cologne he wore, and I'd be able to get a little insight into him while I made the call. My heart practically skipped inside my chest in excitement.

'I'll make that call then, Brie and you look in your wardrobe.' Recalling our little bit of conversation earlier from the car, I knew that the event this evening was purely for family and friends, and I was convinced that whatever she chose to wear, Luke would be happy with.

Reaching the door, I took hold of the gold coloured, brushed metal doorhandle, pushed down and walked purposefully into his domain. I took lungs full of the slightly cooler air and found the scent of the cologne that I knew I'd been almost desperate to inhale again. I closed my eyes as I walked in to try to identify what made up his signature smell, and I was certain I found hints of musk and spices. But it also had a smoky undertone, which created a sultry illusion and I understood it suited him to the ground. He was a sexy, sexy man, but I could already sense he had closed himself off a while ago.

Understanding that, I momentarily stopped dead in my tracks, before I made myself hurry towards the phone at the side of Luke's bed. I walked alongside the bed and allowed my fingertips to gently brush over the dark green comforter. In stark contrast to his daughter's feminine room, his was very dark and masculine.

A shiver ran down my spine, but shaking my head and exhaling I got on with what I walked in to do in the first place.

I picked up the receiver and pressed the indicated button to connect to reception, just as I heard Brie speak.

'I can't hear you, Brie… I'll be back in a minute,' I called out.

The tone changed in my ear.

'Good evening, how can I help you, Mr. McKenzie?' The friendly voice of what I assumed to be Maria hit my ear.

'Hello. Yes, this is Mr. McKenzie's room …' I started to explain. 'But this is Nikki, Mr. McKenzie's nanny… I was wondering if there was any way of getting an iron and board sent up to Mr. McKenzie's room please, so I can press an item of clothing?'

Why my heart was beating out of my chest at making the simple request. I had no idea. I soon worked it out though, as I pondered on it for a few seconds more; I knew it was because I was in his room, where I hadn't been invited in the first place and never expected to be invited again.

'That's no problem, I'll send someone up from the valet service,' she answered.

'No… I can do it myself, thank you.' I reacted quickly to her assumption that I wanted to be waited on. 'I definitely don't want to give anyone any more work to do today.'

She began to explain how they offered the service to all their guests and that they didn't have irons and boards in any of the rooms.

'Okay, thank you,' I consented, and was told that someone would be up in five minutes to take my dress from me, just as I heard a man's throat being cleared behind me.

Oh shit.

I knew we hadn't yet got a contract in place, and we'd only gone over a few of the expectations, but I knew without a doubt I was not supposed to be in his bedroom. I replaced the receiver and turned slowly around.

Before my eyes connected with Luke's, I started my apology.

'I'm really sorry. I know you don't want me in here… and I *know* I shouldn't be in here…'

'But you were using the phone. I know… Brie told me.' His tone sounded relaxed and he seemed comfortable with the fact that I was in his private space. In fact, I could even recognise the now familiar thread of amusement around his words.

My gaze had lifted from his ankles, which were crossed over as he leant against the doorframe. He'd discarded his suit jacket somewhere, his shirt was pulled away from his trousers and most of the buttons were undone, revealing some of his chest. And to frame it all, his tie was limply hanging down either side of the open shirt. I could feel his eyes on me as he took all of me in, as he probably tried to work out why the hell he'd ever thought I'd be a decent fit for him and Brie. Instead of the normal ball of worry uncurling itself in my gut, I became very aware of just where his eyes were on me, as each part of me they drifted over caught alight. I was still fully clothed, but I could feel his silent appraisal and even though I knew only a couple of minutes had passed, my body had ignited. I knew it was crazy, but as a flood of wetness hit my knickers, I understood that under his perusal I felt more alive and turned on than I'd ever felt with any man before.

No, no, no.

I attempted to pull myself together and, as I swallowed down the weird compulsion I had to run into his arms, I stood tall and took a shot at making myself look calm and in control. After watching him pull on his beard for a few seconds, obviously deep in thought, I managed to talk myself into lifting my gaze.

With his suit jacket gone, the seasoned rockstar I'd loved and drooled over for nearly as far back as I could remember was firmly back in his rightful place. I thanked God we weren't standing closer together, as I wasn't sure that I would have been able to stop myself reaching out to touch him.

The Luke I'd lusted over for years, was standing at least twenty feet away from me and yet my body was trembling from the weird power the man seemed to have over me. His sheer presence made me feel faint, when I'd never in my life fainted.

You haven't eaten in hours.

That's it!

'So, darlin'.'

I heard him speak and my eyes darted up to find his. Once again, his eyes found mine and somehow, I got lost in the bright sparkling depths of them and the promise they seemed to hold.

He called me darling.

He calls all women darling, doesn't he?

You've honestly lost it.

'So?' I managed to squeak out.

'You look good in here... almost like it's where you belong.' The words left his mouth and his head tipped ever so slightly to the side and his brow furrowed as he appeared to think over just what he'd imparted. Then he shook his head and changed his stance as if he wanted to erase his last statement. 'What I meant to say was, as we won't have a room for you tonight... I'll grab my clothes and you can get ready in here. I'll spend a bit of time with Brie and help her, and you can shower or whatever else you need to do. Does that sound good?'

'That sounds really good,' I offered, stunned that he was willing to give up his personal space for me. 'Does that mean I've got the job then?' I asked, as I tried to inject a bit of humour into the taut atmosphere around us.

'Yeah, for definite... she was singing your praises the minute I arrived back. I don't think she'd ever forgive me if I lost you.'

'Thank you. I think she's wonderful, so the feeling's mutual I can assure you.'

'Nikki, are you staying?' Brie's excited voice sounded as she pushed past Luke and entered the room on a run.

I crouched down to her as she arrived at my legs and took hold of her hands in mine.

'I'd like to, Brie. If that's okay with you?'

'YES!' she shouted out and flung her arms around my neck. I wound my arms around her to hug her in return. Then, in Brie like fashion, she gave me a quick Eskimo kiss. 'And you won't leave me?' she questioned.

My eyes looked over at Luke, who also seemed to be waiting on my answer.

'No, not until you don't need me anymore.'

Her eyes widened in fear and my heart stopped, as I recognised the hurt inside of her. It was almost the same kind that I'd carried within me when I wasn't much older than her.

'When will that be?' Her voice was small and hesitant.

God love children and their bloody awful heartrending questions.

'When you're very big, a famous ballerina and travelling around the world.' For a second, I wondered if what I'd said was enough and then a smile stretched across her face. 'Is that okay?' I tentatively questioned.

'Yes, but you can't go then either, because my daddy will need you.'

I hadn't realised until the final sentence had left Brie's mouth that Luke had moved himself off the doorframe and had begun to pick up the clothing he needed. And I was certain I still wouldn't have known if my ears weren't so attuned already to hearing whatever he muttered under his breath. But I was convinced I heard, 'Ain't that the truth.'

His head turned to look at me as I held his daughter tightly in my arms, our eyes found each other's and I knew then, when I glimpsed fear in his eyes, that without a shadow of a doubt I'd heard him correctly.

Fourteen

LUKE

'SO, THEY'RE DESPERATE TO say something… but as always it comes down to me,' Raff started, as he removed his Gibson from the rack next to Cade.

The minute he spoke, Cade, who'd been gently tapping his snare and flexing his foot on the peddle to create a rhythmic beat on his bass drum, stopped.

Suddenly, the air around the four of us came to life, as it did when we walked on stage together to sell-out crowds. I knew all the guys were pleased with how today had gone. We'd successfully opened the first of many hotels we had planned, and now all we had to do was settle down and grab the life we knew we not only wanted, but needed.

As bandmates we were as close as they came. Over the years we'd watched many others fall apart, as growing resentment towards each other spiralled out of control. But for us, DD was not only the way we made a living, but it was also what had arguably kept all of us alive.

We aired our triumphs, pain and any other shit that needed to be spoken or shouted about, and at times we'd used our fists on each other to drive our point home. I knew we were lucky; the years had brought us so close together that we were brothers in arms.

I could feel they had some shit to air, and I could attempt a guess at what it was about.

Although the ballroom was crowded with friends and Raff's family, they were far enough away from us, that I knew they would have to be able to lip read to make out any of our conversation. But just in case they could lip read, we had long ago worked out to face a different direction after every couple of words we spoke to each other on stage, unless we wanted all our shit aired in public, which we no longer did. Years before, we'd played the media game, but after being fucked dry up the ass when Cherise died, we no longer gave the bastards anything.

'Spit it out then.' I turned my head to look at him and grinned. *Come on fucker. I dare ya.*

'We *really* like the new nanny, Mac,' Cade pushed into the conversation and like he was performing to an audience already, he tapped the crash cymbal smartly and then caught it between his fingers to dull the noise as he turned his head and offered me a shit eating grin.

'That's just fine, Cade… just you make sure you keep your dick inside your jeans where she's concerned.'

'I've enough to keep me busy, don't you worry.'

I raised my eyebrows at him in question and hoped Nikki was as good as Nancy had been at sniffing out his shit. Shaking my head at him, I picked up my Fender bass by its neck and placed the strap over my shoulder. Then I plucked at the strings to check their tone.

'One, two… One, two, buckle your shoe.' I heard Brody testing the mic and laughed out loud, wondering not for the first time what the hell his fascination was with nursery rhymes.

'In that case, fuckwit, make sure you only mess around with those that *want* you to mess around with them.' Raff's voice grew more insistent with every word he directed at Cade.

'Boom.' Cade pressed his boot down on the bass and directed the noise at Raff with one of the drumsticks in his hand. 'I am,' he replied as he grinned at Raff.

So, I'm right. I'd been watching Cade sniff around Raff's sister, Winter, for the past few days. He was interested, when he was never interested in anything more than somewhere wet, warm and willing for a few hours.

I stored the information for later use.

'Fuck off, man... and remember she's my bloody sister.' Raff shook his head at Cade and then turned his attention back to me. 'What I was going to say, Mac, before that fucker jumped the gun on me,' Raff spoke again, jabbing a thumb in Cade's direction. 'She seems really nice. Brielle seems comfortable with her. I looked in on them earlier, when I had a minute and she... well, she seems sort of right... So, good job,' Raff added, slapping me on the back at the same time.

I felt Brody's arm come around my shoulder as he came up behind us both.

'And now, asshat, you can get yourself some skirt.' Brody's hand squeezed my ass cheek as he spoke, just to wind me up.

'Fuck off.'

'Just saying,' he added as he took a step backwards, with his hands in the air like he was surrendering.

'Yeah, Mac... you can now pursue the pink-haired dance teacher,' Cade added.

'You'd think, wouldn't ya.' I shook my head at them all as I thought about how to explain. 'No can do, guys.' I watched as puzzled expressions consumed their features.

'No excuses, man. This is where we start living. You're attracted to the dance teacher, so go and see her, take her out, enjoy some time with her and see where it goes,' Brody added.

'I agree... but will my daughter's uncles agree when they find out that Brie's new nanny and my pink-haired bit of skirt are the same person?'

'Well fuck,' Raff groaned.

'That could be awkward,' Cade admitted, tapping a cymbal again.

'But it's not impossible... you want her and from what I saw when I forced that Eskimo kiss earlier, the feeling's mutual... I'd be trying, that's for sure.'

'Yeah, but you fuck anything, Daniels,' Raff added.

Cade burst out laughing at the revelation that Brody had forced me and Nikki into an Eskimo kiss.

'Nah... ya didn't?' Cade laughed as he questioned Brody.

'Yeah, the fucker did, and I can still smell the scent she wears,' I gave them, without thinking about just what I was admitting.

'Then you're well and truly fucked… I still remember the way Lauren smells after seventeen odd years.'

'You need to go for it. In fact, I dare ya,' Cade encouraged.

I narrowed my eyes at him and then shook my head at myself. I hated not being able to say that I wouldn't because of how I needed to put Brie first, then I remembered that it didn't really matter as she fancied Brody. I bent down to plug my bass in and muttered under my breath about how she preferred him anyway.

'What?' Raff questioned, thinking he'd missed something. Not missing a beat, I stood up and effectively ignored his question.

'But before I do that, you fuckers need to get your own houses in order.' I turned the tide of the conversation and directed it back at them.

Their laughter filled the stage.

'You're back for Lauren, Raff… You've just admitted you still remember how she smells and that's because she's never left your heart. Now all you need to do, is convince yourself and her.'

'You're not the first to say that today and do you know what… I agree,' Raff replied nodding at me.

'Well fuck,' Cade muttered. 'At goddamn last, it's only taken you half your life.'

'And you, Cade… are you just fucking about with Winter to wind Raff up, or God fucking forbid has that delectable looking female crawled so far under your skin you can't or, even worse, don't want to shake her free? Because hell, man, you've been sniffing around her the last few days like she's on fucking heat.'

Cade stared at me and then in answer he went into a drum solo. Knowing him as well as I knew myself, I understood that it was his way of not giving me an answer, because he in all probability didn't have an answer himself.

I moved my gaze to Brody, who was standing there grinning at me, thinking I had no shit on him to have a go with.

Eventually, the drumming behind me faded away, as Cade slowed down to try to hear what I was going to say next. Just to keep them all waiting, I glanced across the top of the crowded room to find Brie and Nikki, and when I caught their eyes, I lifted one hand up to them and blew Brie a kiss, which she pretended to catch.

I didn't miss the blush that hit Nikki's cheeks when some of the people in the room turned to look at her, but she'd have to get used to that if she was going to be around us.

'And you, Brody... I think you're fucking with at least one of the kitchen staff. You were covered in flour earlier. Is that why they've all called in sick, and you keep disappearing and missing meetings that we have to cover for?'

'Maybe.'

Stunned at his admission, I took a better look at him and remembered what he'd said to me a couple of days ago.

'Is she your fatalistic meeting?' I asked.

I watched his shoulders shrug at me. Like me and Cade, he was far too fucked up by life to be able to sort through his own feelings.

'If she is, man, grab her, hold on and don't let go.' I watched as my words hit home.

'I tried to.' Brody spun around on the spot. He grabbed the mic, bowed his head and punched his right fist high up in the air.

'WHO'S READY TO ROCK?'

The lights dimmed on cue and Cade smashed his sticks in the air and started the beat that had everyone in the ballroom stamping their feet on the floor. The four of us began to bleed our souls out on the stage like we did every single time we performed together, and we began with the song we had started with for years, "Something's gotta give."

And just like that we were Default Distraction, on stage and ready to perform.

Brody sang and we played.

I leant into my mic to harmonise with Brody for the first chorus and twisted my head to the side. In between, as one of the few lights we'd set up for our small gig flashed over our very enthusiastic crowd, I caught sight of Nikki. She had Brie in her arms as she danced her around. I saw their lips move to sing every word together and I felt myself grin as their happiness found me.

Entranced by the woman holding my daughter, I leant back to the mic and sang the words, 'Even loving you,' just as her eyes found mine.

In that second, something inside me shifted and, plucking the notes I needed for the riff that followed and feeling more than I had in the last couple of years put together, I stepped backwards and intentionally broke our connection.

I was fucking great at giving counsel to the others, but as I moved around on the small stage, I wondered if I was brave enough to take my own damn advice.

I knew we only had a couple of songs left until we were finished for the night, so when Raff made a move towards Brody and spoke into his ear, I raised my eyebrows at Cade in question. Brody nodded and stood up, offering his stool to Raff, who sat down immediately and after getting comfortable he spoke into the mic.

'Yeah, I know, this is a bit of a surprise to me, too. So, here's hoping I don't damage your eardrums too much. I know my dulcet tones aren't what you're used to, when you normally listen to the golden boy behind me.' He looked back at Brody who was picking up a bottle of water, having been made redundant by Raff's move to the mic.

'Get the fuck on with it,' yelled Brody, as he laughed in response. The crowd reacted to the two of them and an amused murmur went around the audience.

Raff swung around again, bringing his acoustic to his lap and grabbing the mic with his free hand. 'Yeah, okay. It's a long story, which not to worry, I'm going to make short. A long time ago, I made the biggest mistake of my life and I need to say sorry, but she won't listen.' The crowd in unison produced an "Ahhhhh" and Raff acknowledged them by nodding slowly. 'Yeah... Well, I was told this morning, by someone who knows me well, that I need to start communicating differently.'

Oh man, he was really going for it. I nodded with reverence, as I understood that one of us was ready to get their life on the track it should have been on all along. I caught sight of Winter, his sister, who was standing next to Lauren at the very edge of the room.

'I agreed... so, here goes. This song is one that we've never covered before, but the crew behind me have always had my back, and they're talented enough to keep up with me. It's a song that takes me back to when my life was simple. When all that mattered was that she loved me, and I loved her. This song is for my girl, the one that after all these years still makes my heart beat faster. One of these days, I'm going to count all her freckles again.' Raff stopped speaking momentarily and cleared his throat before he spoke again. 'She knows who she is.' A murmur went around the crowd as they started to look around and I made sure my eyes didn't give Lauren away, by looking over at Brody and nodding at him.

Raff strummed the first chord on his acoustic and my ears strained to follow where he was leading us. A few notes in and we fell in behind him as he sung the words to **Ronan Keating's – If Tomorrow Never Comes**.

In my peripheral view, I saw Lauren crying as the words Raff was singing to her prised open her heart once again for him to enter.

I closed my eyes for a few seconds and made a wish, which was something I hadn't done since I was a small boy. I had no fucking idea why, because every wish I'd ever made had failed to materialise. But this was the start of our new life and I wished that the three of us would have enough guts to follow where he'd led.

Fifteen

LUKE

'THANK YOU…THANKS SO much… We've been Default
Distraction, double D's over and out.' Brody spoke into the
mic and, as always, raised his two fingers to his temple and
saluted the crowd. Then he moved quickly off his stool and down onto
the edge of the stage where he picked up a couple of bottles of water
and began to down one of them.

The set had finished with the song we always ended every gig with,
"Regret." None of us had ever had the guts to think too goddamn hard
about why we did, or maybe it was because we all knew already that
that the song summed up our lives more perfectly than anything else
Brody or the rest of us had ever written, or were ever likely to write.
And the words were too painful to overanalyse.

Between us, we often said how we had more baggage than the Titanic had when she'd sunk… but the difference was, we'd refused to go down.

Here we were, still standing, still fighting and trying hard to get our lives on track. It had to be said, I had no fucking clue what my track even looked like, but as long as it contained Brie, in my heart I knew that even if I didn't recognise it, I would categorically be able to feel it.

I'd been watching Brie and Nikki dancing to our songs for the past hour and the urge to now leave my bass guitar on the stage and to rush over to join them was suddenly all consuming. I wanted to be with them, I wanted to dance around with them to our latest album that was now being played in the background. I wanted to sing at the top of my voice and not give a shit at how stupid we might look, and I didn't want to probe too far into those feelings as to why.

Being honest with myself, halfway through our set I'd realised that I was going to enjoy this evening's gig, on the tiny little stage in front of most of the people we cared about, more than any we'd played in the past couple of years in front of thousands of screaming fans, and I'd been right.

It had been a fucking revelation, as I'd been living with the secret knowledge that the thrill of performing had been snatched from me, the second Cherise made her way out of my life.

But having my daughter there, enjoying herself with Nikki, I could have almost convinced myself that maybe there really was a God. At last Brie and I were going to be allowed to move on from the grief and pain.

Who knew, maybe all that praying I'd done to God when I was still in Kindergarten and Junior school had finally paid off. There was no way it would have had anything to do with the later years, when I used to kneel by the side of my bed in the dormitory clasping my hands together. Because although I'd mouthed the words that I'd learnt by rote, I was thinking very impure thoughts of the blow jobs I'd managed to get down the side of the bleachers, or the first time I'd run my tongue between a woman's wet lips and had her sweetness flood over my tastebuds as I made her come.

My thoughts made my eyes dart over instinctively to Nikki and I tore them away quickly as my dick began to flex inside his constraints.

Nikki had twirled Brie around in her arms and like some fucking super fan had stayed at the back of the room the whole time we'd been playing, as she taught Brie how to dance to our songs. I'd looked over numerous times to watch them as they appeared to mouth the words to each other during each chorus and had been caught smiling at them both several times by the guys.

As I lifted my bass off my body, I realised that I had shrugged my shoulders at my thoughts when I saw a very amused Cade raise his eyebrows at me.

'Stop the wheels turning, dude.' He pointed his sticks at me, 'Just act.' I flipped him the bird and looked away.

They all ought to know to mind their own fucking business, I thought laughing. He'd obviously been watching me and thought he could fuck with my business. Well then, I could certainly fuck with his.

I looked around, just in time to see some of the women from the U.K. DD fan club make their move towards the stage.

Shit. I'd forgotten they were even here. It wasn't that they weren't important to us all, because our fans were the fucking best. But right now, we all had other things on our minds than meeting them and answering the same old questions.

As I put my bass back into the rack, I took a quick check around to see where everyone was. Raff had already jumped off and was quickly making his way through the crowd to go and find Lauren. I knew I was prepared to do what was needed to give them the space they obviously fucking needed right then, to air all their shit. Brody was still sitting on the edge of the stage, and I looked on as he tipped the contents of another water bottle over his head. We all knew that Brody always needed time to get himself together after each and every performance, and being able to understand his pain, I knew I'd always cover his back so he could do what he needed to.

I felt a wide grin settle itself on my face when Cade, who was far too fucking slow in moving, became my target, and I knew I had him.

I'll teach you to fuck around with Winter.

Without giving it a second thought, I jumped off the stage with a, 'See ya,' to Cade and over my shoulder I watched as he shook his head slowly from side to side as he caught up quickly, realising that he'd been set up and was now the only one available to chat to the group of women standing to one side of him.

The room of people seemed to part as I walked though. I got the occasional pat on the back, a few compliments on the gig and a few more comments of how much they had enjoyed the day and that The Manor was amazing. I offered a perfunctory thanks to anyone I felt needed to hear it and carried on my path.

I carried on walking, knowing that if I delved too much inside my own head as to why I was so desperate to reach the two girls, I might turn back. I went where I wanted to and walked straight over to Nikki and Brie, who were still dancing. I forced away all the reasons why I shouldn't even contemplate getting to know Nikki, and for what felt like the first time since I'd met Rafferty and Cade back in Vegas, I went with what my heart was demanding of me.

'Hey.' I spoke just before I reached them, and I watched somewhat mesmerised as Nikki continued to twirl around on the spot to the faster beat that was now playing. As the gig had gone on, the more my eyes had been drawn to her. A couple of times early on, our eyes had found each other's when I was singing about loving someone, or about being made fucking hard by a woman. I'd tried hard to fight the growing attraction on my part to the woman who was everything my daughter had asked me to provide, until I wasn't sure I could fight it any longer.

I hadn't made eye contact with anyone else on the ballroom floor, I'd smiled and waved at my daughter whenever she waved at me and then, if I was truthful with myself, I'd let my eyes find Nikki's whenever I was able to.

I'd used the cover of twisting my head into the mic as I'd sung and moved around on the small stage to follow the two spotlights we'd rigged up, until I could time them to perfection and knew exactly when they would light the two of them up and bounce off the silver dress she was wearing.

My eyes had swept up and down her figure, several times over. She'd put her hair up into some sort of bun thing at the base of neck, which meant I could see her pale flesh through the silver lace which covered her shoulders. The dress fitted her to perfection, and I could only imagine her small pert tits were braless, given the design. It was tight all the way to the hips, where it then flared out into a fuller skirt that lifted higher, giving me the glimpses that I knew were destined to kill me, of her bare thighs above the long black boots she'd worn to our earlier meeting in the tearoom.

At first, it had been hard to watch her because she had the same tall and willowy dancer's figure as Cherise. But after taking the time to blatantly admire her from a safe distance, I saw that was where their similarities ended.

Ever the ultimate professional, I played on through the first few songs, refusing to listen to any of the words I was singing, as grief hit me first and then coming up fast on its ass, was my old demon; guilt.

I'd even closed my eyes a few times and replaced her with Cherise in my mind. But no matter how hard I tried, I could only see Cherise dancing with Brie as a baby in her embrace.

Something happened up there on the small stage we'd erected to celebrate the start of our new venture, and I knew without even asking that all four of us had experienced something similar. The emotions we were all accepting or still fighting against, meant we probably played one of the best gigs of our lives. On a personal note, I think I made some headway through the emotions that had effectively fucked me up for the past few years and with each and every song we played, I allowed myself to bleed some of that emotion out through my music and into the words I was singing, knowing the guys around me had my back.

Finally, I think I got it. All the things everyone had been saying to me over the previous three years had at last carved a thin fissure through to my heart. I tentatively accepted that although Cherise would always live on in our hearts, she'd existed in a time when Brielle was small. She was no longer here, and we needed to live life to the fullest without her.

Several times, tears had built up behind my eyes and accepting their presence I'd closed them and listened to the words Brody had written about "needing the strength to let love go." When I opened my eyes at the end of the song, I had a renewed vision to find that Cherise was gone and that Nikki, the woman I had only met a few days before, had taken her place, and it was okay. It was okay that Nikki was in our lives. Even if all she became, was the best nanny Brie could ask for, or if added to that she and I could build up a friendship, whatever it was destined to be, it was okay to try to move forward.

For several seconds, my greeting just hung in the air around us. But I knew Nikki had heard me by the way she tensed and then relaxed. I'd been around enough to know I affected her, just by watching the way her body reacted to the knowledge I was close by, even if I wasn't the fucking lead singer.

Fucking Brody.

Nikki spun around, so that Brie and her were now facing me. I swept my hair off my face using one hand and raised my eyebrows at them both, before breaking out into a smile.

'Daddy,' Brie squealed as she lifted her arms up to me. 'Can we dance?' Brie questioned.

'Yes, Shorty.'

With my eyes still on Nikki's, I took Brie from her arms. I felt Brie wrap her arms around my neck and I cuddled her tightly to me. Then after watching Nikki wrap her empty arms around herself as she attempted to fill the void of Brie escaping them, with absolutely no thought whatsoever, I held my hand out to her.

'I'd love to dance with you both,' I offered.

'With me?' she questioned, looking completely stunned.

'I don't see any other beautiful girls around here, other than you two.'

I looked on as although initially hesitant, Nikki looked between my proffered hand and the seriousness in my eyes. Then her small hand slipped into mine and I took a gentle, but firm and encouraging hold, before pulling her to me. I released her hand and quickly wrapped my arm around her tiny waist to hold her as close to me as I dared.

Sixteen

Nikki

THE FEELING OF BEING exactly where I was meant to be swept through me the minute Luke's hand let go of mine and after grabbing my hip, he pulled me to him. Silently, knowing no one could see me enclosed within his arms, I rolled my eyes up high into my head at being so bloody stupid. Then, as his arm wrapped even tighter around me as he very deliberately pulled me in closer to the side of his body and held me there, I caught my breath.

You are so reading this wrong.

So why the hell did it feel so right?

'Relax.' He bent his head down to mine and I gasped as the warm flesh of his lips found the shell of my ear.

Relax he says.

For the first time in my life, I had no idea what music was playing. He began to move the three of us around and I instinctively knew that we would have caught the eyes of a few of the people still left in the ballroom. Not wanting to look stupid and uncomfortable in his arms, but wanting our impromptu dance to look friendly and fun so as not to give people the wrong impression, I placed one arm around his waist and rested it on top of the belt he was wearing, and the other I put just above his on Brie's back.

Her joy at being twirled around with her daddy was evident. Her smile and happy squeals of laughter helped me to relax. I only hoped my complete surprise at being in one of the many places I'd dreamt about being for many years, wasn't written all over my face. My heart was beating out of my chest at his proximity, and as he skilfully moved us around to the music, the T-shirt he'd been wearing on stage lifted up and away from his jeans with every second beat. Each time my thumb and forefinger came into contact with his hot, sweaty flesh, I had to stop myself from lifting my hand to possessively place it under his T-shirt.

Nikki, get a grip.

I fought down the crazy notion of wanting to feel even more of the man I had only ever felt in my dreams. I hadn't even signed my contract yet and I was sure he'd change his mind about hiring me if he could read the dirty thoughts that were beginning to consume me as he held me so close.

I smiled up at Brie, loving her happiness and seeing her as the one hope I had of disguising the way he made me feel.

The ballroom was starting to empty of the invited guests and on cue the music volume began to decrease. At last, our dance was over, and I was too scared to work out if I was happy or sad at the fact.

Brie yawned and I used that to move myself away from Luke.

'I think Brie needs to go up to bed.' I smiled the most professional smile I could muster up in the situation that was totally out of my comfort zone.

'I agree. But first we need to get you back home. Is that okay?' Luke questioned, as he grinned back at me.

'That's fine.'

'No, I want *Nikki* to take me to bed,' Brie added as she tried to stifle yet another yawn.

'I can stay to do that, I don't mind.' The ballroom was becoming emptier with every second that passed, and the room was starting to cool. So, why the hell was I beginning to struggle to take in the deep breath I felt I needed? I was inwardly fighting against losing myself to the almost claustrophobic atmosphere that appeared to have settled around the three of us.

Luke smiled at me; the very same smile that always made the back of my knees feel just that little bit weaker. I knew from earlier pictures of him, that beneath his well-kept beard he had dimples. My fingers twitched, and I fought hard to keep my arm still as the crazy notion of reaching out to run my hand over his beard swept over me.

'I want you both to put me to bed,' Brie asked again as she snuggled further into her daddy's shoulder.

I took hold of her hand and gently stroked the back of her fingers, before touching her nose with my forefinger. *God, I love her...* I'd always loved children, but none more than in that very minute, when her voice effectively popped the bubble around us all and finally, I managed to think with my professional head and not with the sexual need inside of me that was fighting to be unleashed.

'I think we should check with Daddy if that's okay?' I couldn't have been more pleased that when I spoke, my voice sounded normal.

'Yeah, but only if you read the story.' He grinned and then winked at me.

I was absolutely sure that the sudden contraction of the muscles down low in my stomach was my ovaries spontaneously combusting.

'I just need to do something before we go up, it'll only take a minute.'

Luke passed Brie back to me and then taking me by the elbow, he steered us to where Cade was standing nearby looking pissed off.

'Go left.' Luke grabbed Cade by the shoulder and grinned at him.

'What?' He looked back at him puzzled.

'Let me spell it the fuck out for you, arsehole. Winter... you know... Winter, the woman that's got your guts all twisted up inside. Well, when she stormed out of here and away from you, yet again, she turned left... Now, follow her, and this time don't open your mouth and fuck it up.'

Momentarily they man hugged it out.

'Thanks, dude. I owe ya,' Cade offered.

'Get the fuck out of here.'

'And you, Mac.' Cade winked at him and looked between us both. 'You have a good night now, won't ya.'

I had no idea how the three of us had even managed to fit in Brie's tepee. But Brie had insisted that's where we read her books she'd chosen, and eager to settle her for the night after the bath she'd insisted on having before she went to bed, I'd encouraged Luke to go with her wishes. I needed this, what appeared to be a very extended bedtime routine, to come to an end, so I could then get back to my own small childhood bedroom to try to gather my thoughts and feelings over the day. Luckily, Brie was lying in between us both, as I was sure that if I'd been able to feel his body against mine, I might have been rendered speechless and unable to read the stories she'd requested.

'He leaned over and kissed him goodnight.' I spoke the words from the fourth children's book and Luke, who was lying on his side with his head resting on his hand, leant down to rub his nose against Brie's, and I did what I'd been fighting against for the past thirty minutes and took in the man. He was tall and muscular, but luckily not as wide across the shoulders as Cade and Brody, otherwise I wasn't sure he would have been able to fit his upper body in the tepee with Brie and me. His rich brown hair was showing all the effects of a long day, and where it had been swept back this afternoon with some product or another, when he'd made his way downstairs for The Manor's opening, tonight it was falling over the right side of his face, leaving him looking more like the Luke I knew from the posters on my walls and the many concerts and performances I'd seen on various media. I wasn't sure which I preferred, in fact they both had their bonuses. Here on stage tonight and reading his daughter a bedtime story, I felt I was getting to see the man behind the public persona, but earlier today his eyes had been exposed to me and I got to see them both in all their emerald green beauty.

I was completely mixed up inside and was no longer sure which was the most dominant thought or feeling inside of me. My heart ached to be witnessing the love between Luke and Brie, and I understood just how lucky I was to have gained this new job ... then there were the other parts of me that fluttered and ached traitorously with the lust I felt for my new employer. The feelings that most definitely needed placing on the side lines and forgetting about for at least the next few years, so I could do my job, and provide what I needed to support my family.

His head lifted and his smiling eyes caught mine. I watched as he raised both of his eyebrows in question at me and I mumbled something silly about nearly reading myself to sleep with the book, then released a small laugh that I desperately hoped covered up the thoughts and feelings I knew were undoubtedly showing on my face. I turned my head sharply back to the book in my hands and focussed hard on the last page of words about a little nut-brown hare.

Finally, I read the last line and closed the book.

'I love that story,' I whispered to no one in particular.

'Why?' Luke whispered back to me over the now totally relaxed figure of his small daughter.

I shrugged my shoulders as I thought about the right words to say. 'I think because sometimes the strength of feeling you have for someone in your life can be so completely overwhelming it's hard to put it effectively into words. It shows children that in a non-patronising way.'

I wrapped my arms around the book and hugged it to my chest as I stared up into the twinkling fairy lights above us. I could feel Luke's eyes boring into my cheek and my face flushed with embarrassment.

This was why I worked with children; they just got you, without questioning why you were who you were.

In my peripheral view I watched him nod as he digested what I'd just said.

'Have you ever felt like that, Nikki?'

'Like what?' I made the mistake of turning my head to look at him and as they had been doing all day, his eyes captured mine and held them fast.

'Like you feel so much… but can't explain how or why?'

'No.' I shook my head at him. 'I love my mum and siblings with everything I am, that's a given. I would do and have done anything and everything they needed, to show them my love. They know how I feel and vice versa… But…'

'But?' he pushed.

'I haven't experienced it personally… You know, between a man and a woman.' I rolled my eyes at myself and told myself to shut up, but I didn't and carried on. 'Although I'm convinced that sort of thing exists, I'm just not sure all of us get to live it.'

I watched him shrug in thought at my answer. 'So, that's what you're looking for?'

Looking for? I suppose I was in a way.

'Yes, one day, I would love to feel that way… I want to be lucky enough to experience that sudden and blinding sensation, when one day you meet someone and life as you know it transforms into something so perfect you couldn't have imagined it, even in your wildest dreams.'

Oh my God! What the hell is wrong with you? A simple yes would have been more than adequate.

The pause in the conversation was so pointed, that I had to clear my throat to try to break free. Luke stretched out his hand and his fingertips caressed down the side of my face, from my cheek bone and in a circular movement all the way to my jaw and I jumped in response to his touch. In that simple and gentle touch, the whole of my being awakened, like I'd been effectively sleep walking for the whole of my life up until then.

Seventeen

Nikki

'HEY, DUDE… YOU IN there?' Cade's voice filtered through to us.

'Yeah,' Luke replied as he pulled his hand away from my face and after a not-so-subtle shake of his head at me, he began to manoeuvre his body out of the tepee.

'This better be good.'

I heard the amusement thread itself through Cade's voice as he replied, 'Yeah?'

'Yeah,' Luke insisted.

'It is… Amy, Lauren's cousin who was helping out this evening with the food, has gone missing.'

'Missing?' I could hear the disbelief in Luke's voice. 'How the fuck does someone just go missing?'

'I've no fucking idea… we've searched everywhere.'

'We?' Luke asked.

'Me, Winter and now Raff and Lauren.'

'Raff? I can't imagine he was too fucking made up to be interrupted.'

'It's all good... it was a post coitus phone call.' Even in the given situation Cade laughed. 'And no Brody again. Just where the fuck does he keep disappearing to?'

I looked over at Brie, whose breathing had now evened out, and started to try to get myself out from the contraption my new charge seemed to love, but I knew it would result in the men in the room seeing more of me than I wanted them to, yet again.

I held my skirt with one hand, flattening it against the top of my thighs to make sure it covered up my arse and then crawled out backwards. Finally, I stood up.

'That's not good,' I voiced and suddenly their eyes were on me.

'No, I agree. Winter is chewing my fucking ear off about how her and Lauren shouldn't have left her in the room next to the ballroom by herself, because of how drunk she was.'

'The room next to the ballroom?' I questioned, as I went through something in my head that I'd seen earlier.

'Yeah,' Cade replied.

'The double doors to the left of the stage?' I enquired.

Luke turned his head to look at Cade as he waited for the answer.

'Yes,' Cade replied, nodding his head at me.

'That's where Brody went after you finished your set.'

'You saw him?' Luke asked, as looking suddenly pissed off he crossed his arms over his chest.

'Yes, when we were dancing...' No one said a word to me, so I attempted to explain further. 'When you, Brie and I were dancing, I saw him get up off the edge of the stage and disappear inside the room.'

'You did, huh?' Luke's eyes narrowed as he nodded at me. I was sure he muttered something under his breath about "fucking Brody" but couldn't quite make it out. I wasn't sure just what the hell was going through his head, but I started to gingerly shake my head at him anyway.

'That makes perfect fucking sense... Winter's convinced he's been seeing Amy.'

'Well fuck, that'll piss the fans right off if Brody the main man is seeing someone, won't it?'

Luke was speaking to Cade, but directing the words he was saying intentionally at me. All of a sudden, I remembered why. *So, this is what happens when you lie.* All I could do was to look back at him and offer him a small smile.

At that moment, the others arrived at the doorway to Brie's bedroom. Cade explained what I'd just said and what he thought might have happened. I followed behind them both, as they joined the others and the group of five made their way along the corridor to what I now assumed was Brody's room. Then, holding onto the doorframe with one hand, I leant forward and peered down the corridor.

Luke knocked and after a few minutes Brody opened the door to his room. Then after opening his door up wide enough, Luke stepped inside to witness exactly what Brody had already told him and the others, the fact that Amy was safe and sound asleep on his bed. Then I winced as I heard him categorically state that he thought that her *friends'* concerns were misplaced. And if the girls cared about her enough in the first place, they wouldn't have let her get so drunk. The corridor grew quiet and although I didn't know Lauren or Winter, their obvious unease at his words was evident and when they had nothing to say in reply, their guilt was palpable.

I physically cringed for them.

Brody informed Lauren and Winter how he'd been the one who'd held her hair out of the toilet when she'd subsequently been sick earlier, while they were engaged elsewhere, and they both blushed. He ended the conversation by saying she was asleep and would be staying there with him for the night, unless *she* told him otherwise. I could see Luke, Cade and Raff nodding at him. They explained to Winter and Lauren how they knew there was going to be no persuading him differently and convinced them that she was safe with him and then Brody slammed the door shut on them all.

Just as Luke spun around to walk back to Brie's room and his eyes found mine, I took a step backwards and hurriedly moved back into the little girl's space. I'd left the few bits and pieces I'd brought with me earlier that day next to her bookcase, after using Luke's room earlier. Now, feeling uncomfortable at the bizarre feelings his eyes on any single part of me seemed to extract from my body, I squatted down with my back to the doorway. Then twisting my body around, I stared at my belongings, in a bid to focus on them and attempt to distance myself from the man who I knew had now appeared back into the room and pushed the door shut behind him. Trying to remain calm and to not act like an adolescent schoolgirl, I began to busy myself, picking up my things and one by one shoving them into the carrier bag I'd brought them in. For the minutes it took, I cursed myself for not bringing a bag that would have been easier to pack in a hurry.

As the sound of silence met my ears, I all too quickly became aware of the tight, oxygen devouring atmosphere that had settled around us, until I couldn't ignore the impulse to find Luke with my own eyes to see if he was experiencing the same.

'Now, where were we?' Luke spoke in that deep, soulful tone of his.

Unable to answer his question, I righted myself to stand back up and found him standing close beside me. Apprehension streaked through me as I slowly stood up and found his eyes with my own. In one swift movement he stepped closer, until I was able to feel the warmth radiating off his body. Mesmerised, I watched as he lifted his hand and placed his thumb and forefinger on my chin as he tilted my head slightly backwards. I drew in a quick half breath as the tiny connection of his flesh on mine sparked off a chain reaction inside me. My heartbeat began to race and every single cell in my body became aware of every single part of him. The soft, sensitive area at the back of my knees began to tremble and as the crazy fear that they might buckle beneath me took over, I reached out to take hold of his forearm.

Please kiss me. What the hell was I wishing? *Don't kiss me. This is far too complicated already.*

I couldn't imagine how my face must have looked as he looked intently at me. One minute I must have looked like putty in his hands and the next with my eyes wide open in terror, in case he answered my prayers.

Unhurriedly, Luke's face gently lowered to mine. His green orbs held on to mine as he stared attentively into what felt like the very depths of my soul. His thumb lifted and gently brushed over my bottom lip, and I was so poised and ready for the millisecond his flesh touched mine, that with that tiniest of connections I felt my nipples harden beneath my dress. With our eyes still wide open, his warm lips gently brushed against mine and his beard gently grazed my ridiculously sensitive flesh, as the man I had fantasised over for years seemed to discover the real me, the one I'd kept hidden from all others, in that singular moment. I dropped the hairbrush I was still holding in my other hand and as it hit the thick carpet under my feet with a dull thud, my now empty hand came up to hold on to the bare flesh of his forearm.

I became conscious, as his lips found my mine over and over again as he gently coaxed me into opening up for him, that my life had been a life in waiting. My lips instinctively parted, and his tongue swept into my mouth to caress every single nerve ending. His warm tongue gently connected with the diamond stud in my tongue and waves of pure pleasure rippled throughout my body. His hand left my chin and moved to the back of my neck as he took further charge of the way our mouths moved intuitively against each other's. His other hand found my hip and he pulled me into him, until each part of me was melded against his firm, muscular body and for the first time since I'd walked into the tearoom this morning, I truly relaxed. I had read in books how slow and tantalising first kisses could be, but I'd never experienced one before. The whole of my body was on fire, and I couldn't help the soft moan that escaped my lips as we kissed.

I want to be lucky enough to experience that sudden and blinding sensation, when one day you meet someone and life as you know it transforms into something so perfect you couldn't have imagined it, even in your wildest dreams.

And now I have.

The thought had no sooner swept through my head, than our kiss was over.

Swiftly, as my need for him found his ears, he moved away and rested his forehead against mine. Far too quickly, the dilation of his pupils was replaced with a look of confused pain, and then my heart ached as disenchantment spread over his beautiful features.

'What the actual fuck…' I knew the question wasn't for me to answer.

Luke's hands dropped away from my body, like I'd burnt him. I wrapped my arms around myself in protection from his rejection and watched as he took two steps backwards. The air around me suddenly dropped by a couple of degrees and an involuntary shiver ran down my spine.

I watched him slowly shake his head, more at himself than me, and then grimace painfully as something swept through his head.

'FUCK! No, no, no… I'm sorry, Nikki, I shouldn't have done that.'

'Kissed me?' I stupidly questioned.

'I'm sorry.'

'Sorry?' I repeated a little sarcastically as confusion spread through me. Had he not felt what I did? Perhaps I was so inexperienced, I'd got it completely wrong?

After swallowing down the pain he'd created inside me, I raised my eyes to his just as my pain was replaced with anger. He lifted his left hand and swept his hair back off his face and our eyes connected briefly, before he tore them away. The playful amusement I'd found inside his eyes on more than one occasion that day, had been replaced with fear, and understanding just a little of what he might be going through, I took a deep breath and tried to give him the compassion I felt he needed.

'I don't make a move on employees, ever,' he added.

'That's good to know... at least I know now that I'm the only mistake.' Even after what had just happened to me, at the hands of Haydon Millar, inside I already knew Luke wasn't like that. He was a rockstar for God's sake, and I knew that women threw themselves at him. He certainly didn't need to subject himself on his employees.

'You're not a mistake, Nikki ... Fuck!' He propelled himself further away from where I was still standing. 'I'm the fucking mistake ...' He jabbed his index finger sharply into his chest, and although I could hear there was more to that statement than he was prepared to tell me, he moved swiftly on. 'I'm attracted to you... *but* you need to understand... Brie needs you; she needs you so much. You've only been here one day and it's already that fucking obvious.'

One day. That in itself was ridiculous, as I felt like I'd been with them for so very much longer.

'I can see that in the way she responds to you. Brie needs love, she's lost so much in her four years. I know enough about you already to see how you are with the children you look after, to know that you more than look after them; you love them like your own. And while she needs that from you and you're willing to give it, I can't have you. I'm not prepared to fuck this up, for her sake.' Shaking his head vehemently he carried on, 'I won't let myself have you.'

I shook my head at him, mirroring his body language, understanding what he was saying but not wanting to believe it at the same time.

'So, if I don't sign the contract and refuse to become Brie's nanny, you'll be with me?'

I knew the question I'd asked him was completely superfluous. I wasn't going to refuse the job my family needed me to have, nor would

I deny a small child what I knew they also needed, but I wanted the answer for my own selfish reasons.

'Goddamn it, Nikki… don't do that, please don't do that.' The pain laced through his voice was evident. I shook my head and raised my hand at him to placate him and hoped he understood that I would never put my needs above hers.

'You're perfect for her, and I don't deserve fucking perfect.' Then he went through a list. 'You're too young for me.'

'Eight years isn't a lifetime,' I contradicted.

'Maybe not, but you're innocent, in a way I'm not sure I ever was and you're whole when I've been broken for the entirety of my life… Tell me you understand that?' he asked as both of his hands flew through his hair, and I watched as with his hands on his head he dug his fingers deep into his scalp in exasperation.

So, his answer was no, plain and simple.

Pain wracked through me.

'Yes, you've made yourself very clear.'

'Thank you,' he conceded. Then, grimacing again and chewing nervously on his bottom lip at the weird situation between us, he pleaded, 'Please say you'll be back tomorrow. Don't punish my daughter for the sins of her father?'

'My only concern is for Brielle.' I said the words knowing they were a half-truth. I was equally concerned for me, too. In my heart I was terrified that this, whatever it was between us, meant that the new job I so desperately needed wasn't going to work. *Nikki, sort yourself out. For everyone's sake, it has to.* 'And I still want the job, if that's what you're asking,' I stated quickly, before I thought too much more about it.

Luke nodded at me and crossed his arms tightly over his chest, before letting a long exhale leave the same lips that he'd kissed me with so passionately less than five minutes before.

'I'm gonna get security to give you a ride home. Thanks so much for staying on tonight and for helping me get Brie to sleep,' he spoke as he walked away from me, and it was all I could do to fight the inclination to stare at the way his jeans fit over his arse.

But he wasn't mine to stare at. He was my fantasy only and that's where it would have to stay.

'Okay.' I spoke as I pulled myself to stand up taller at his obvious brush off.

Luke walked into his bedroom. I heard him use the phone to request that security be ready to take me home, then the man strode back into his daughter's bedroom looking pissed.

'I'll have your contract of employment ready for tomorrow,' he added very matter of a fact. 'What time do you think you can be packed and ready to be picked up tomorrow?'

Taking his cue, I made myself continue in the professional vein I now knew was needed, when really, I wanted to scream at him for blowing so fucking hot and cold.

'I'll be ready by two tomorrow afternoon, Mr. McKenzie.' I graced him with a half-smile and took in the look of surprise on his face as he heard what I deemed to call him. Because... well, two could play at the hot and cold game... couldn't they? 'Good night.'

And with that I turned and walked out of the room.

Eighteen

Nikki

'FUCKING MEN.'

I leant against the door to my home as I used my backside to drive the wooden door back into its swollen frame and braced myself as the catch clicked into place.

When no further sound came, I released the breath I was holding and walked carefully along the hallway on the left-hand side, trying to avoid the creaky floorboards. At last, I reached the back room that we used as a dining room, pushed open the door and after closing it behind me, I switched on the main light.

'Urghhhh turn it off.' Lou's voice sounded out from the small two-seater she was curled up on and as soon as she'd pulled the chain on the reading lamp beside her, I switched off the main overhead light.

'I can't believe you waited up.'

'I told you I would… now go and get us both a drink and then you can tell me all about your day.' She rubbed at her tired looking eyes as she spoke.

I still can't believe it's only been a day.

I nodded at her, knowing there was no putting her off and stepped down into our tiny kitchen. Spying an already opened bottle of wine on the side, I grabbed it and a couple of clean tumblers off the draining board. I knew Lou wouldn't care that they weren't wine glasses and given that this was probably my last night off for a week, I thought a couple of drinks definitely wouldn't hurt, in fact it might help me sleep.

Liar. I knew I wasn't going to sleep tonight.

I stepped back into our back room and pushed the door shut with my foot behind me. I could feel Louise's eyes on me waiting for me to speak, the only trouble was I didn't know where to start. I plonked myself down beside her and adjusted myself, after feeling the broken spring underneath me flick into my bum cheek.

'So?'

'Luke kissed me,' I blurted out.

'WHAT?' Her voice rose in tone almost becoming shrill in her disbelief. 'No bloody way!'

'Shhhh.' I turned towards her and met her stare with my own, before pointing up at the ceiling at what was our mum's bedroom. She nodded and with wide eyes cupped her mouth. I grimaced at her and holding out the two tumblers in my hand, I gesticulated she needed to take one. In silence, I filled up both of our glasses and drank down two mouthfuls, hoping the liquid would ease the constriction at the back of my throat enough to allow me to answer the many questions I knew were now stacking up inside her mind.

'I think you need to start at the beginning,' she offered.

'I was shocked to find it was him at the tearoom this morning, but he was much nicer than I think, even in my wildest dreams, I expected.' *Wildest dreams.* I remembered what I'd said to him today and shook my head at myself. Glancing down at the phone on my lap I clocked that it was now past midnight. *Okay then… yesterday.*

'Go on,' Lou encouraged.

'And the salary and package are really, really good.'

'Good.' She said the word, but I didn't feel her normal enthusiasm behind it.

'So, I spent the afternoon and evening at The Manor. It's breathtaking.' I nodded at her frozen expression as she tentatively sipped at the wine in her hand, wishing it would change to something else soon. 'Brie, his daughter, is wonderful, and she has a puppy called Biscuit. And did I mention that I saw Default Distraction play last night?' I questioned, hoping my passion would rub off on her.

'No, but you did mention Luke McKenzie, and that he, *the* Luke McKenzie, kissed you.'

My stomach turned over as I remembered our kiss, but I managed to plaster a smile on my face while I tutted at her. 'It was nothing.' I shook my head at her, grinning as I dragged down another large gulp of the wine. 'We've both agreed that it was a mistake that shouldn't have happened.'

'He didn't force himself on you?'

'No.' I shook my head remembering how I'd felt in his arms dancing and then being held as he'd tentatively kissed me at first. 'Oh God, no… this was definitely *not* a Haydon Millar moment, it was just one of those weird, spur of the moment, got carried away sort of things. Which we discussed afterwards… like adults.' I nodded at her and smiled as I understood inside of me that I wanted nothing more than to be Brie's nanny. Selfishly, I wanted to spend more time with her and Luke, even if the whole scenario left me broken hearted and that the feeling was even stronger than my usual desire to do the right thing for my family. It would be fine, as I was always a little broken hearted each and every time I said goodbye to a family and their children. It was the nature of the beast, and this job would be no different. I knew I was attempting to convince myself and stopped over thinking it when I realised it didn't quite ring true.

'You don't have to take this job, Nikki. You're highly qualified and bound to be snapped up soon,' she offered, shaking her head from side to side as she tried hard to get her point across to me.

'Oh, but I do…' I nodded at her. 'We're both adults and after we'd discussed that it wasn't the professional thing to take our mutual attraction further, I said I would still be happy to take on the role of Brie's nanny. I leave to start work and live at The Manor tomorrow, subject to my contract being agreeable of course.'

I added in the last bit and grabbed hold of my sister's hand before squeezing it lightly as I looked eagerly on, wanting to see that my last comment had at least appeased her.

'You're sure?'

'Never been surer.' I smiled at her, hopefully disguising the strange ache in my heart.

'Okay.' She picked up our conjoined hands and pressed them to her cheek. 'Then, now we've been adults… can we please be teenagers again? I need all the details on how *the* Luke McKenzie kisses…'

Knowing I couldn't have the conversation face to face, I slugged back the rest of my wine and after wrapping my arm over her shoulders, I pulled us both back into the worn-out piece of furniture we'd been sitting on all our lives. Then I thought hard on just how I was going to explain how his kiss had felt, without sounding sad or so into it that she would see right through me.

'Luke McKenzie kisses like a rockstar…' I started and added in a sigh for extra emphasis. 'And, Lou, in all seriousness you need to think about getting your tongue pierced… they act like a slut button all the way down to your ...'

'Whaaaat!'

I moved quickly when I heard the noise Lou made and after she spat out the wine she'd just sipped, I covered her mouth with my hand before she woke our mum up. As she turned to face me, and her eyes found mine, I knew I'd succeeded in convincing her when she burst out laughing.

It was just a shame I couldn't convince myself.

Nineteen

LUKE

'THE BOTTOM LINE IS far better than we could have hoped for, and the management team have received the first lot of reviews. Apparently, it looks as though asshats like us can put a plan together, throw enough greenbacks at it and make it a success... even without Lawson's fucking input.' Cade laughed out loud as he brought up DD's manager, who we all thought was more fucking machine than human.

I looked back at the screen in my hand and along with the other two voiced back at him how pleased we were.

'You're quiet, Luke,' Raff questioned and I lifted my gaze from watching Cade rolling his dice over in his hands and passing them in between his fingers without looking, like he did with his drumsticks.

'Yeah, tired I guess,' I answered, hoping he'd shut the fuck up and not pursue the question. I wasn't lying; I had spent most of the night on Brie's bed, waiting for her to stir enough to move her out of her beloved tepee and back into her bed. But if I was truthful, that wasn't the only thing that had kept me tossing and turning all night.

'Yeah?' He nodded at me grinning. 'You sure?' The asshat grinned wider at me, and I lifted my middle finger and aimed it in his direction.

Cade moved again and leant back into the leather sofa behind him. I watched, grateful of the distraction as a broad grin settled itself on his face.

'What the hell have we come to?' he questioned. 'Tell me if I'm wrong, but we are all within the same couple of miles, aren't we? Maybe even in the same building. So, why the hell am I having to Facetime you all, to catch you up on a meeting that we *all* should have been at this morning?'

'Unlike the rest of you excuses for a wank stain, I have a daughter to look after,' I answered knowing that my words had probably been drowned out due to everyone talking at the same time.

Cade shook his head and laughed.

'Because you're a doll, Cade, and I don't know what we'd do without ya,' Brody pushed in and Cade lifted his hand to give Brody the finger, which made Brody laugh louder.

'Where's ya clothes, Daniels, and just where the fucking hell are you?'

I knew Cade was referring to the fact that he appeared to be lying on the floor with a green pillow behind him, in front of a large window. The view behind him was picturesque and filled with the snowy view of the countryside.

'I'm otherwise engaged, but yeah, I'm nearby.' He grinned back and I could see he wasn't willing to give us all any more information. I knew I wasn't the only one who could make a guess that his other hand was holding on to the lovely Amy.

'It's a stunning view,' I added.

'I wanna see where the fuck his other hand is,' Cade added.

'Hey, Mac… I always knew you had the hots for me, man,' Brody replied, laughing at his own joke, and pretending to blow me a kiss. 'And no way, Morello. She's mine and I ain't sharing.'

'Yeah, I've got it now… Women, that's the answer, isn't it? They'd better be worth it, because staring at my phone right now, I have to tell ya that I've never seen three more pussy whipped bastards, than you fucking lot,' Cade shouted out.

The sudden noise erupting from them all made me laugh, even though in my case he couldn't have been more wrong.

'Right, now I've got your attention, there's one more thing.' My eyes refocused on Cade, who was looking more uncomfortable than I thought I'd ever seen him. I tilted my head to one side in question, as I waited to hear what the fuck he was about to say. 'I want a vote on offering Winter the job of opening our next three hotels. I think she's done a fantastic job here… and Nico has discussed with me that he would at least like her for the Vegas opening.'

'Oh yeah?' Brody replied and I moved my eyes off Cade and refocussed on Brody. *I know that look.* I could see he had started to add two and two together and was rapidly coming up with six. When Cade refused to look Brody in the eye and instead looked directly at Raff, who was also surprisingly quiet today, I knew he was waiting for some sort of response.

Before Cade could answer I pushed into the conversation.

'I bet ya fucking do… are you thinking with your ballsack now, Cade? Instead of using that *amazing* brain you keep telling us the drugs haven't fucked up?'

His eyes darted to me and he raised his eyebrows, and for the first time since last night I felt like laughing and started busting a gut at his so fucking obvious reaction.

I had no idea where we all were on Cade's device, but when his eyes shot down to the bottom corner of his screen and guilt filtered into his eyes, I just knew he was staring at Raff and waiting for him to react.

When Raff stared back emotionless, I thought for the second time about just how quiet he was.

Mmmm, that doesn't look good.

Brody speaking up, made my eyes dart over to him.

'She has my vote…'

'And mine too.' I'd stopped laughing after clocking Raff.

'And she, of course, has mine… family first. That's what we all agreed on, wasn't it? She's proved she's more than capable, hasn't she?' Raff finalised the vote.

'Yes, she has.'

'Then you can offer her the job, Cade,' Raff added. 'I'm sure you'll be the one to see her first.'

'He might be… But will there be time for any conversation before he fucks…' I just couldn't help but fuck with them both just a little bit more, as I attempted to work out just what the hell was going on with them all.

'SHUT. IT. LUKE.' Raff shouted into the phone. 'Remember whose little sister she is and which one of us has the daughter… and imagine just how much I'm going to enjoy rubbing your nose in it when some arsehole starts sniffing around her.'

No way was I letting him go there, not when I was trying to work him and Cade out.

'Is it bad that I've got a hard-on just thinking about your little sister in the tight skirts she wears, Raff?' I added, waiting for the sparks to fly on the fuse I'd just lit.

I heard Raff release another tirade of abuse at me, as I let my gaze drift slowly back to Cade as I raised both of my eyebrows, offered him a very knowing grin and a quick wink.

I'd got him.

It was there, written all over his face, just how much Winter meant to him. I could see the jealousy, anger, and possessiveness he felt towards her in the flare of his nostrils, the pointed stare he was giving me and the way his mouth was spread across his face in a tight-lipped grimace. In fact, watching him, I thought that he'd probably experienced jealousy for what was the first time ever.

He moved back away from his device and spoke for the last time.

'I'll tell her. Ciao.'

Then he was gone, leaving the three of us looking at each other in question.

'Interesting,' Brody added as Cade departed.

'Very,' I agreed.

'If he fucks about with her, I'll damn well kill him.'

'He ain't sharing her around, Raff…' I was alluding to the way Cade normally went through women, then after he'd got what he wanted from them he passed them on to someone else, only if they were willing, obviously. We all knew it was his inbuilt defence mechanism that he'd fine-tuned over the years, to prevent himself growing too close to anyone.

'I agree with Mac, Raff. I don't think you've got any concerns over Winter. He might not know it yet, but I think he's in for the long haul.'

'Maybe,' Raff spoke, still staring at the screen.

'On that note, I have another engagement. Catch you on the flipside.' Brody two finger saluted us both and his screen also went blank.

'Wanna talk about it, Raff?' I offered.

'Nah... thanks anyway.' He shook his head at me. 'I wouldn't know where the fuck to start.'

Suddenly, the screen in front of me went black and I was left on my own. I put down my iPad and picked up my phone, turning it over in my hand as I tried to summon up the courage to make the call I needed to. Giving it no more thought I pressed the button and put the phone to my ear.

'Hi,' she answered and instinctively I smiled back, even though I knew she couldn't see me.

'Nikki.' I said her name, unable to deny myself any longer.

'Yes, hello, Mr. McKenzie.'

Inwardly, I cringed, as by saying my full name she once again put me in my place, the one I knew I deserved to be in.

'I just wanted to let you know that the driver will be with you at three, is that okay?'

'And my contract?' she questioned.

'That will be here for you to check over just as soon as you arrive.'

'That won't work, I'm afraid,' she replied and my heart sank, for my daughter and for me. 'I want my lawyer to read it over before I come back to The Manor.'

Lawyer?

'It's all above board, I can assure you.'

'I'm sure it is, Mr. McKenzie, but I want our professional relationship on a firm footing, so I will want to see it before I come back.'

'I'll send it over by email,' I agreed as I let go of a long sigh.

'Thank you. Please tell Brie, I look forward to seeing her this afternoon.'

'I will.'

'Goodbye.' And just like that she was also gone, and I was suddenly very aware that, just like Raff, I had well and truly fucked up too.

Twenty

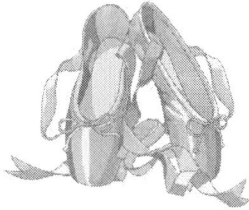

Nikki

'BRIE,' I CALLED OUT, as I hit the length of corridor that led to the wing where all our bedrooms were situated and heard the security door close gently behind me.

'She's in here with me,' Flint shouted back. I smiled to myself as I shook my head, because I wasn't surprised. I knew that when she could, Brie nearly always gravitated towards wherever he was.

After seeing the snow coming down once again after lunch, a flash of inspiration had hit me of what we could do to make the day just a little bit more special. I'd headed outside for a few minutes to make a private phone call. Luckily, the response had been good, and I'd managed to source something to get us out of The Manor for some exercise and fun. While I'd been speaking to Lou's friend Emma, I'd left Brie with Maria downstairs on reception. But when I came back inside, she'd gone and I knew that when Maria smiled and pointed towards the stairs, in all probability I would end up finding her with

Flint. They were ten years apart in age, but as the only children DD had between them, the two of them shared a bond, a beautiful caring bond that was heart-warming to witness.

It was Christmas Eve, and knowing that I was finishing later this afternoon until boxing day, so I could attend a friend's wedding reception tonight and spend Christmas day with my mum and sister, I wanted to do something fun with Brie, and Flint if he'd come too.

I'd been brought up by my mum with very little money, and in my heart I knew that it was always the things that didn't cost very much, but meant we spent quality time together, that were forever seared into my heart. I'd thought over what we could do, because no matter how beautifully The Manor had been decorated, and however many presents there were for Brie and Flint around the real Norwegian blue fir in the large sitting room DD had commandeered for their Christmas celebrations, you couldn't get over the fact that they were all spending their time in a large hotel and not in their own homes.

As I walked past Luke's room, then Brie's and my own, I finally came to the open door of Flint's. I poked my head around the corner, eager to see what I already knew was happening. Finally, my eyes met those of the fourteen-year-old boy who had taken Brie to his heart as he smiled his welcome to me. He was a tall, slim-built lad, with dark brown almost black hair, which was long and nearly always worn covering his grey eyes, which were only slightly lighter than my own. I understood it was an attempt to hide himself away from the world in a very normal teenage way. But today, he'd tied it back and I was greeted with a broad grin that was all his own.

He was the spitting image of Rafferty and I knew, like his dad, it wouldn't be long before the boy in front of me, crouching over Brie as he showed her how to tap out a basic rhythm on his drums, would soon be out breaking hearts all over the world.

He'd had a bad day on Monday and had reminded his dad and his uncles just how difficult navigating the teenage years could be. He'd shown them and me just how young and immature he really was, trapped inside the body of an almost man. I had stood very much on the sidelines, as at first Raff had locked himself away with his son, and then as the whole of the band had taken the time to sit in there with him to share cookies and milk and to "shoot the breeze" as they called it. I knew they weren't a regular two-point-four family, but they left me with no doubt in my mind that the four men and the two children they had fathered, were indeed one of the strongest family units I had ever come across.

His life, after the break-up of his parents' marriage I presumed, had taught him not to trust easily. Luckily for me, I believed the moment Flint had caught a glimpse of a few of my tattoos, and the diamond stud pierced through my tongue, he seemed to have concluded that I wasn't an adult he needed to distance himself from. Brie's second favourite person in the world was happy to be around me and that made me happy.

I leant myself against the doorframe to watch the two of them together. Brie caught sight of me and lifted a hand to wave, resulting in dropping the stick from her hand.

'Shorty, if you're going to play in the band, you need to concentrate on what you're doing. You can't wave at everyone in the crowd,' Flint teased her.

'But, Flint, Nikki isn't everyone, she's my Nikki.' Brie smiled back as she took the proffered drumstick from Flint's hand and began to tap at the drum again. 'Anyway, I'm going to be a dancer, you can play in the band.'

With that she jumped down, leaving Flint by himself. He adjusted the stool, sat down, and went into a quick and gentle drum solo by himself. By the time Brie had reached me he'd caught the cymbal and stopped.

'Nikki, did you get what you said you were going to get?' she asked.

'I did... so, now we need to find some warm clothes and that includes gloves and hats.' I bent down to her level to share my excitement with her. As I watched her eyes open wider, I knew I'd succeeded. 'And if we're going, we need to go now.'

'Can Flint come?'

I looked up and over the top of Brie's head, to see a fleeting look of curiosity fly over Flint's features.

'I was hoping he would. You're more than welcome... it'll be fun,' I encouraged.

'Where are you going?' he questioned, with a well-practised, uninterested shrug of his shoulders, but with a glint of interest showing in his eyes.

'Mmmm, well... you see, it's a surprise. But it's something I always did with friends when there was enough snow around here.'

I watched him grimace as he contemplated coming out of his self-built comfort zone of being a teenager and going back to actually enjoying being a kid again.

'Plleeeaaassseeeee,' Brie pleaded.

'Yeah, okay, Shorty, I'll come,' Flint offered, and in that minute I saw right through his brash mantle. I was certain that's why he loved being with Brie so much, she was his perfect excuse to be a child.

'That's great… My friend Emma will be here in a minute to drop some things off and I need to meet her. Do you think you two can grab your warm coats and boots etc?' I watched as Flint nodded and added, 'I laid Brie's out in her room.'

'No problem,' he replied before he added, 'is Biscuit coming too?'

For a few minutes, Brie jumped up and down on the spot, shouting and chanting, 'Yes,' over and over again, with the dog jumping enthusiastically around her.

'It looks that way.'

He grinned back at me as we both watched my small charge haring around the room at break-neck speed in her excitement.

'Hey, hey, hey, what's all the noise?' A deep voice found my sensitive ears. I knew, as the skin on the back of my neck prickled when I felt his breath caress it, that I wasn't mistaken in instinctively knowing it was Luke.

My body tensed as his voice wound itself around every coherent thought in my head. Then I had to stop breathing momentarily to interrupt the unmistakable smell of his cologne, before it swaddled me in its smoky illusion. Frozen against the doorframe, I focussed my eyes on watching Brie dance around Flint's room and kept a grin plastered to my face as I attempted to effectively zone him out, which shouldn't have been too hard as I'd been doing it since the minute I'd walked back into The Manor a whole four days before, on Monday afternoon. But I'd never had such an intuitive audience before and as I cast my eyes back over Flint, I understood that for a teenager who was struggling with being stuck in between child and adulthood, he had an amazing perception of other people's feelings. I could see by the way his eyes reacted to me that he had seen right through me.

Shit.

'Daddy.' Brie sped past me and straight into Luke's legs with a thump. 'Nikki is taking us on a surprise.'

'On a surprise, huh?' Luke copied her word for word, and I heard the amusement in his tone.

'Yes, and you can come too, Daddy,' she added.

A few seconds passed between us all, and just as I summoned up the strength to turn around and to face Luke behind me, we all heard "Ba, doom, crash" as Flint made the recognisable sound on his drums that signified the punchline had just been spoken and my eyes darted up to Luke's amused ones.

'Cheers, Flint,' Luke offered over the top of my head.

'Welcome… Come on, Shorty, let's grab my gear and then we can go and get yours, while the *adults* sort themselves out.'

Within a couple of minutes, they'd moved past us and had disappeared into Brie's room.

Now, with only the two of us left in the space, I had to talk to the man I knew I'd been avoiding since I'd left here on Sunday night.

'Is it okay if I come too?' he questioned.

'Mr. McKenzie, I work for you, so that's completely up to you.'

'Stop already with the Mr. McKenzie. Please, it's Luke or Mac, and that's not what I was asking, and you know it. I don't want the atmosphere between us to ruin the afternoon for the kids.'

I knew it was entirely the wrong thing to do, but not being able to help myself, I crossed my arms over my chest in a pathetic attempt to create some sort of barrier between me and the man who was stood less than two feet away from me. I knew it gave him an insight into how I felt, and as his eyes followed my movement, I knew I would look even more stupid if I then uncrossed them.

I took a deep breath and accepted the white flag of truce he was offering me with his words. 'If you want to come sledging with us, you'd be more than welcome, Mr. Mc …' His eyebrow raised in question at me, and I corrected myself. 'Luke.'

'Sledging?' he questioned, 'I've never been before, but always wanted to.'

'You've never been?' I asked, instantly throwing away the promise I'd made to myself after I'd packed up my clothes and lay on my bed not sleeping, in the early hours of Monday morning. With my eyes screwed tight, I'd refused to look at the man whose face covered the four walls around me. I'd sworn to myself that I could take the job and secure Stephen's care and my family home, by being completely professional and only taking part in the necessary conversations with Luke to do with Brie's care. And all it had taken was four bloody days for me to destroy that promise.

But I was far too intrigued to stop now.

'Nah… we've travelled the world, but not managed to do half the things that should come with that due to tight schedules, or simply because of who we are and not being able to take part like regular Joes.'

'But surely when you were a child?'

'I grew up in an orphanage in New York. Sledging wasn't part of the curriculum.'

Really?

'An orphanage?' The question slipped out of my mouth before I'd had time to engage my brain. I was convinced that I'd read more than once, how he'd been born to Irish parents and spent time in Ireland before moving to New York. Pain filtered over his features and was immediately wiped away as he smiled and directed that smile straight back at me.

'Yeah.' He nodded resolutely.

'But… I've seen pictures of your home in Ireland.'

'I'm sure you have, because I have a home there. But I wasn't born there.' Luke's smile disintegrated and I could feel the pain once again falling away from him.

'But I read…' I started shaking my head in confusion.

'I know what you read.' He shrugged his shoulders quickly. 'All I can say is, it's surprising what you can fabricate when you have enough money. I mean, sometimes I almost believe it myself.'

'And no reporters ever delved deeper?' I asked in disbelief.

'Nope, not yet.' He shook his head. 'No one's ever been that interested. I have the house for photoshoots, as you've seen… But I've never been there. Although I'd like to go one day.' Luke gave a small laugh of acceptance and amusement. 'Now, had I been Brody, you know, the *lead singer*…' he winked at me as he got his point across, 'well, perhaps they would have looked a bit deeper. But no one is that interested in me… well, if you don't count when my wife overdosed and died in the same hotel room that I was sleeping in, so fucked up I couldn't help her.'

I could feel myself shaking my head at him, then I surrendered to the need to reach out and touch him. The instant connection between us, caused both of us to move our eyes from each other's to fleetingly look to the place where my fingertips touched the bare skin of his forearm.

Luke exhaled a breath and spoke for both of us when he muttered, 'Holy fucking hell.'

He shifted his stance, and I pulled my hand away quickly, stunned at the reaction that I'd apparently released inside both of us.

'I was born in what I can only imagine was some filthy, freezing cold place, before being bundled up in rags and dumped on some church steps,' he carried on, seemingly reluctant to let the newly formed bond between us fragment.

So that's why he called himself a mistake.

'Sorry,' I offered, feeling the pressure of building tears behind my eyes. I sniffed loudly, sorting myself out before I cried in front of him.

'Don't be, we all have our crosses... And now you feel sorry for me, you might just let me come along.' His hands went into praying stance the minute he stopped speaking. I couldn't help the smile that blossomed over my face, but I withdrew it as quickly as I could.

'You look like you've practised that a lot,' I added.

His head cocked over to the side as he spoke again and this time with an Irish inflection. 'Ahh, to be sure... It was a Catholic orphanage. Brown, reddish hair and green eyes,' he pointed to his head, 'and Catholic dumping ground. So, I have to be from Irish descent... And now I've said enough to *really* make you feel sorry for me, you're gonna have to let me come.'

More of our previous conversations seemed to make sense.

'You can come along.' I smiled back at him as I absorbed the truth that he'd been willing to share with me. Although I felt for him, I needed to protect myself, and in defence of my heart I tried to make him understand that the way he'd walked away from me the other night after kissing me hadn't been forgotten, so I added.

'If you *want* to...' I shrugged, 'but this time, if you decide you *want* something, have the guts to admit that you want it and work out how to live with it.'

I knew my words had hit home when he shifted around, looking uncomfortable, and shoved his hands into the back pockets of his jeans.

'Yeah, about that,' he started, and I held my hand up to him and shook my head. 'For what it's worth, I'm sorry.'

I nodded at him quickly and moved past it.

'Right, I've only got two sledges being dropped off, so you'll have to share,' I offered, eager to lift the atmosphere around us.

'Share... yuck,' he grimaced, following my lead.

I watched on, shaking my head at his childishness, and trying desperately hard to work out how we'd managed to be so completely professional with each other for four whole days and yet we'd still come back to this. This... whatever it was between us. This comfortable air of camaraderie and fun, with that unspoken element of attraction thrown in for good measure.

My heart felt the lightest it had for days, and I couldn't help but grin widely back at him.

'There she is, I thought I'd frightened you away,' he admitted, with a look of concern.

'Stupidly enough, no.' I didn't think through my words before I carried on speaking, 'No matter how hard you try.'

Luke clasped both hands to his chest over his heart and pretended to stagger backwards. 'You wound me.'

I walked away and down the corridor to go and meet Emma, laughing all the way as I heard him enter Brie's bedroom, shouting out how he was going sledging with them and then Flint shouting back at him that he'd ruined their surprise.

Twenty-One

LUKE

WHAT THE FUCK ARE you playing at?
The question went around and around my head on fucking repeat, until I wanted to smack my hand hard into the side of my temple to dislodge it.

Trying to live. I finally answered my own question. Although, I couldn't work out how the fuck I was going to put one foot in front of the other when it came to being around Nikki.

I pulled sharply on the wheel in front of me to steer us in between the tall trees to the left-hand side of us, as I followed the wave of the hand of my very reluctant co-pilot. The same one who'd attempted to get into the back seat with my daughter not five minutes before, in what I knew was a bid to try not to sit next to me. I'd stifled a laugh when her face showed she understood that she hadn't moved fast enough, when Flint had jumped in before she had a chance to. I'd nodded at him to show my appreciation at the return of his manners, as he'd opened the passenger door wide from the inside and waved her in, like it was something he did every day. Yet the rest of us knew his decent upbringing had deserted him about two years ago when his hormones had kicked in.

I cleared my throat loudly and stared ahead at the snow-covered lane in front of us, which seemed to be getting narrower by the second, and made sure the tyres followed the two tracks left by someone else that day as they'd passed by the same way. The snow was still coming down as it had been on and off for the previous week. The world around us looked like the picture on the top of the tin of Irish Christmas cookies I remembered from my childhood. Tall evergreen trees, covered in a blanket of crystal clean white flakes, which was so bright in places it was dazzling. I'd always looked forward to looking at the image on the outside of the tin, more than I had to eating the actual things. So, when the tin had arrived in my lap and it had been my turn to take two, I'd taken as long as possible to choose, while I stared at the perfect Christmas scene and wished myself there.

And now, here I was. I knew that England wasn't Ireland, but I felt at home here anyway.

My first white Christmas.

I heard Cherise answering me in my head, telling me it was also one of her bucket-list dreams to see snow on Christmas day and briefly I closed my eyes to silence her voice, which was the same shit I'd been pulling for the past few years.

It's beautiful... You should have stuck around, Cher... If only we'd been enough for you to stay.

When as usual no answer came, I accepted and welcomed the silence in my head. Exhaling quietly, I opened my eyes and stared pointedly in front of the vehicle to the track I was following, which ran down the west side of The Manor. All I really wanted to do was to turn my head to the left to take in the woman who had almost been my sole focus for a week, even when she'd been doing her level best to ignore and keep away from me. I allowed myself a quick look at her as I leant over the wheel, pretending I needed to get a better view of the road ahead and I let my eyes sweep over her.

Her long, black hair was tied up, that much I'd noticed earlier, but now it was covered by the pink thing she wore that seemed to do the job of both a hat and a scarf. Her grey eyes were, to my disappointment, only just visible, as she stared purposefully ahead of the car. Quickly, I swept my eyes over her slender frame, and I understood what she wasn't prepared to say with words. Even though we'd shared a few minutes earlier, when she'd almost spoken to me properly, her whole body was now once again tense, and she seemed to be resting on one ass cheek only. It was obvious, as I took her in, that she was doing her very best to keep herself as close as humanly possible to the passenger door, just so I wouldn't accidentally have an excuse to touch her or brush past her in any way. She was holding on so tightly to the door handle, I was fucking certain that had I been able to see though the pink gloves she was wearing, I'd be able to see her knuckles were white with the strain.

Fuck.

You see, this was what I did to women. It was what I'd been doing to all the women who were stupid enough to be attracted to me since Cherise. I tempted them in and then pushed them away as fast as I could. The fact that Brie's former nanny had already been married when we'd met, and to another woman, had been a huge fucking bonus. It had meant she was off limits to me and the games I seemed to play with everyone, including myself.

The shrill voice of my daughter singing in the back seat and her happy laughter caught my ears and took me out of my own head. I raised my eyes to look in the mirror and offered her a grin. In return, she scrunched up her nose and offered me an air Eskimo kiss.

For her sake, it needed to stop. I needed to stop whatever the fuck it was I was playing at; I just wasn't sure how. But in my heart, I was convinced that I had the chance to move on with Nikki.

The atmosphere in the Land Rover we'd taken from the fleet of cars The Manor held in its extensive garages to travel in, was happy. The children were behind us, singing along to Christmas songs that were playing on the radio and it was the day that Nikki had given a little and let me in to join in with her plans.

This time, I was determined not to fuck it up.

Twenty-Two

LUKE

'YOU WAIT UNTIL WE get to the top,' Nikki shouted to Flint, as he trudged up the hill behind her.

'Is the sledging fast?' I heard him question.

'Yes, fast enough, and the view will take your breath away,' she replied.

'I've been to the top of the Eiffel Tower, is it that good?' I knew he was goading her and watched as she turned again to look at him next to her.

'Well, I'm not sure… I've not been, although I'd like to go to Paris one day.' She nodded slightly, and I watched mesmerised as her face broke out into a wide grin when she worked him out too. Nikki began to half-heartedly reprimand him, but I was already far too lost in my own fucking thoughts to register the retort she was giving him over her shoulder as she continued on her set path to the top of the hill.

Brie's arms wrapped even tighter around my forehead, making it a more uncomfortable journey up the side of the hill than was necessary. But I was goddamn grateful that my young daughter was up high on my shoulders. After finding that the snow was too deep in places for her to walk through, I'd enthusiastically picked her up to help her. Little did she know she was helping me too, with her yellow snowsuit covering over half my eyes, I was able to sneakily watch the woman who had ridden into my life only a week before and taken over most of my thoughts ever since.

It had been a long four fucking days, as I tried to work out what to do about my undeniable attraction to her, and four even longer sleepless nights when I'd tried and failed to come up with reason upon fucking reason as to why I should leave her the hell alone. Every early morning as sleep finally found me, I'd just about managed to convince myself to stay the fuck away. Then my good intentions had been blown out of the fucking water when the cold light of day hit, and I felt her nearby or heard her laughter.

I wanted her in my life and worst of all, I was strangely convinced I needed her in it.

No sooner had I acknowledged that fact in my head, than the urge to be nearer to her consumed me. I took larger strides as I tried to eat up the distance between where I was and where she was dragging a sledge, which was made that much harder with Biscuit going around my legs in circles.

Happier once I'd closed the distance between us, I looked forwards again and up to the top of what I was convinced had to be Summerhouse Hill. The very same place I'd last cried over losing Cherise, while holding our daughter in my arms.

Holy fucking hell.

Summerhouse Hill, the place I'd taken my first look at where our future lay. And now, here I was again, trudging up to the exact same place. I really fucking hoped that the view from the top would be as enlightening as the first time I'd stood up there.

Nikki stopped suddenly and following her lead, I stopped too. She turned to look in the direction of Brie and me, as if she was checking where we were, but couldn't look at me square on. Her cheeks were flushed from her exertion, and I knew I'd not seen her looking more fucking beautiful since I'd very nearly run her off the road the first day we'd met.

Whoa! I don't need to reach the top. The view is just as fucking good from here.

As our eyes met for the first time since she'd agreed to let me come out with them, I physically reeled at the power trapped between us. I could no longer hold back and I offered her what I'd been told was a sure-fire panty-dropping smile, then I grabbed Brie's hands in my own to give me a better view of her reaction.

I watched the corners of her beautiful mouth begin to twitch as she fought hard not to smile back at me in response.

You're fucking beautiful.

'Does this place have a name?' I questioned, already convinced I knew the answer but needing to engage her in conversation, as desperation and reluctance to let her turn away from me hit me like a sledgehammer.

'Well, us locals call it Elephant Hill,' she offered as she looked down to the floor shyly, digging the toe of her boot into some deeper snow. Somewhere in the back of my mind I remembered Raff telling us the same thing, although for the life of me I couldn't remember the explanation he'd given as to why, because I probably hadn't been fucking listening.

I watched as the red blush to her cheeks spread further when she looked back up at me. My eyes took her prisoner and I refused to let her look away.

You can pretend you want to steer clear of me, darlin'. But your reactions say different.

I knew we were with the kids, but for the first time since I'd kissed her last weekend, she was finally looking straight at me, talking to me and not doing whatever the fuck it was she'd been busying herself with all damn week. With the taste of her lips still on mine, I was reluctant to lose her just yet.

My body had gone into overdrive. My dick was rock hard in my pants, and I was shifting from one foot to the other as I fought to stay in one place and not let go of Brie so I could reach out to touch her. I knew I'd never felt such a strong magnetic attraction to anyone else I'd met.

'Are there elephants here, then?' I quirked my eyebrows at her as I smirked.

'No,' she replied, shaking her head and sighing at the ridiculousness of my question.

'Elephants?' Brie moved on my shoulders and sitting up straighter she suddenly entered the conversation. 'I *love* elephants.'

Nikki pulled her eyes from mine and my heartrate accelerated when, for the first time, I thought I saw reluctance in her eyes that she couldn't let me have control over her for just a few seconds longer.

'I'm sorry, Brie... There's no *real* elephants here.' She shook her head gently at my daughter who let out a disappointed sigh. 'Just a chalk marking on one side that looks like a picture of an elephant.'

'A chalk elephant?' Brie sighed, sounding confused.

'Well, it's a chalk picture of an elephant,' Nikki tried again.

Brie moved on my shoulders and turned her head around as she searched for pictures. I couldn't help the wide smile that developed over my face as I watched the woman stood in front of me trying to work out what the hell to say next.

'Brie, it's a hill that was built from chalky soil for the rich person who built Falham Manor. That's why you can see chalk patterns sometimes in the grass that look like pictures on the side of it.'

'That's silly... I don't understand. Why would he build a hill?' Brie questioned.

I struggled to contain the laughter in me.

'The rich man loved Falham Manor,' Nikki started.

'I love it too,' Brie interrupted.

'I'm pleased.' Nikki smiled at her, and my heart somersaulted inside my chest. 'The rich man also wanted a view of the sea, so he had this hill made and on the very top of it he placed a large summerhouse, which gave him the view he was looking for.'

Nikki instinctively took the couple of steps needed to bring her back to my side and although I knew it was all for Brie's sake, I couldn't help being pleased at our close proximity. Dropping the rope, she reached out to take Brie's hand from mine and into her own and my body stirred as the fragrance of flowers and summer grass on a warm breeze, drifted up and into my nostrils from her exposed wrist. In my peripheral view, I watched as she rubbed Brie's hand with her gloved fingers, and I committed to memory the scent that I could only liken to the way this hill had smelt in the summertime three years before, when I witnessed my future. Now, I knew I would always associate it with Nikki and this beautiful place.

My future?

'In the Spring, when the snow has gone, I'll bring you back and show you it and hopefully that will help you to understand what I mean.'

Another smile developed quickly on my face, and I saw Nikki look at it in question. Her words had appeased Brie, but the fact she was making plans for the Spring made me feel optimistic and that shit spread quickly over my face.

'COME ON,' Flint shouted from the top, waving his arm around at us all. 'I can see the sea … it's fantastic.'

'Coming,' Nikki shouted back.

'I'll race ya,' I shouted out to her, and without thinking I moved my other hand to make damn sure I had a firm grasp of Brie on my shoulders. Then I took off, running uphill with the dog barking at my ankles in the direction of where Flint was standing.

'That's cheating!' I heard Nikki shout out from behind me and then the sudden sound of her snow boots compressing the snow underneath them found me, and I knew she'd taken up my challenge.

'Daddy, Nikki's coming… go faster.' Brie's encouragement hit my ears as she began to squirm around in excitement and attempt at the same time to turn to see where Nikki was.

'Keep still, Brie,' I encouraged.

Feeling Nikki close by, I turned my head and witnessed the split-second she came alongside us. Amusement flashed through her pupils and then uneasiness as she realised it was too late for me and possibly too late for Brie. Her eyes opened wider, and she silently mouthed, "oh no," when she saw our fate.

'Luke!' I heard Flint's shout of concern just before I reached the summit, when another shift of Brie's weight on my shoulders, coupled with the unsteady ground, had me mis-calculating my last couple of steps. Knowing what was coming next and understanding I had to save my daughter over myself, I lifted her off my shoulders and prepared to place her feet to the floor, just before I fell down heavily into the snow in a tangled heap of limbs and winded myself in the process.

The laughter that went up around me was life enhancing.

I lifted my face from the snow, spitting out a mouthful for effect, and checked on my daughter who had, thank God, landed on her feet and was completely unharmed.

'Well, shit…' Flint added and for once my daughter didn't reprimand him on his language.

When a hastily formed snowball pelted me straight in the mouth my eyes instinctively darted to Nikki. Slowly, I focussed on the owner of the loud belly laugh as, with her eyes firmly fixed on mine, I watched as Nikki struggled to breathe.

'That's for cheating,' she offered, and the kids roared in response.

'Not sure it was that fucking funny,' I muttered under my breath.

I might have muttered the words, but Nikki obviously heard them, as she started laughing even louder than before.

All my comment had done was to fuel her hysterics and as I watched from behind my veil of hair with clumps of snow attached, I saw tears roll down her face. And from my prone position on the freezing ground, I understood exactly why. For days, we'd been living in close proximity to each other, trying to maintain a professional relationship and it had been tense, really fucking tense. Me falling face first had unceremoniously smashed that pretence to pieces, and I had never been more fucking grateful for falling on my ass before. In all honesty, I was so appreciative of the break in the atmosphere between us, I was even prepared to let the snowball in the face thing go too.

Or am I?

I leant up on my elbows and after shaking my head to rid myself of the snow stuck to my hair and beard, I looked over at the kids who were still laughing and gave them both a quick look that I knew they'd recognise.

In one movement, I pushed my hands to the ground and used the motion to jump up and onto my feet. I ran my hand through my hair and narrowed my eyes on my victim.

'I'm sure that was an accident, wasn't it?' I took a step towards her as I spoke and raised my eyebrows in question to drive my point home.

Nikki had the sense to look panicked and took a step backwards. 'No, it wasn't an accident, you deserved it,' she answered defiantly as she lifted her chin a little higher.

'Oh, darlin',' I shook my head at her for effect. 'I suggest you start running. I'll give ya to the count of ten.'

'What?' She looked over at the kids and then back at me, just in time to see me bend down to scoop up a handful of the white stuff. 'You're joking?' she questioned.

'Nope.' I shook my head again slowly and started to mould the snow between both of my hands. '1, 2, 3…' I hit the count of three and saw the flight response spark inside her pupils and swallowed down a laugh. As I whispered four, she took off running and in reaction I counted from five to ten as fast as the words could trip off my tongue.

'Look after Brie, Flint,' I shouted, as I ran past the kids to chase after her.

She might have been a young, fit dance teacher, but I'd been a runner since kindergarten, and I was on her heels in no time.

'No, Luke, stop… please.' She looked behind her just the once as she begged me to leave her alone, but it was too late. I'd already released the ball from my hand, and it hit her smack bang between the fine globes of her sweet ass.

'Owww!' she screeched as she jumped in response and then slowed to rub at the area.

Seizing the moment, I went to ground behind her and reached out with one hand to grab at her ankle. It had the desired effect and with a small girlish scream she fell exactly where I wanted her. Moving quickly, I covered Nikki with my own body and after wrapping my arms tightly around her, I deliberately started us rolling.

'LUKE. No, you can't,' I heard her shout out, before she started laughing again.

But it was far too late to stop.

I was fucking freezing, but inside my heart felt warmer than it had in forever and holding her tightly in my arms we rolled slowly down the hill while we laughed. To add to it, I quickly worked out that she was making absolutely no attempt to free herself from my hold and in that second, I understood that she was everything I wanted and needed.

Her words ran back through my head as I let her happiness seep into my broken shell.

I want to be lucky enough to experience that sudden and blinding sensation, when one day you meet someone and life as you know it transforms into something so perfect you couldn't have imagined it, even in your wildest dreams.

Realisation hit me like a fucking freight train.

Here she was, *my* wildest dream. I hadn't done anything to deserve her, but I made a pledge there and then, in my heart and head, to do everything I could to convince her she needed to be with me and not just for Brielle's sake.

Finally, we came to a stop, as our conjoined bodies found a levelled area and some bushes. I quickly comprehended that I couldn't have found a better place, we were slightly concealed with half of our bodies underneath some rough shrubbery, which meant it would take the kids slightly longer to find us and that was an added bonus.

The additional noises we'd been making as we rolled and laughed suddenly stopped as we came to a halt. Our breathing was ragged, from the exertion of first running, then rolling and clinging on to each other. The snow-filled sky and the blanket of the white stuff covering everything around us, meant the breath from our bodies seemed to escape more noisily in the silence, until all I could focus on was the small puffs of warm air being released from her deep red lips.

Holy fucking hell.

I wanted to kiss her again.

Fuck, I had more needs than I knew I should have, but before I took whatever the hell I had to have from her, I needed to see that she wanted the exact same thing.

Reluctantly, I moved one hand from her back and lifted it to gently sweep her thick hair away from her face. She was exposed to me, and I fell into her grey eyes. As I watched, her pupils began to dilate, and the black edge around the grey of her eyes enlarged. Her breathing stuttered and her hold on me strengthened.

'Luke.' My name escaped her mouth on a small puff of warm air.

I looked between her eyes and her mouth. God help me, I knew I'd hijacked their afternoon out for my own purposes, but I wished the children were much further away. So, right at that minute in time, I could give in to the urges that were beginning to fucking consume me where this woman was concerned.

I just couldn't help myself. I'd been trying to deny this attraction between us since the minute she walked into the tearoom, and I couldn't do it any fucking longer. She not only made my daughter happy, but she also made every second of every day that I knew she was nearby, exciting and brand new, when all I'd been accepting, for as many years as I could remember, was bearable. Even the lines of charlie I'd inhaled and the smack I'd injected had only just made my life tolerable, but one smile from this woman underneath me, made me want to experience more, and I hadn't wanted more of anything in a long fucking time.

With only seconds of our solitude left, my eyes focussed on her lips. I watched them part and I understood I'd never desired anything as much as the kiss I wanted in that second. The tension between us was palpable and as the voices of Flint and Brie and the barking of Biscuit grew ever nearer, I knew our time was fast running out.

'I'm gonna kiss you, Nikki. Because, goddamn it, I'm not strong enough to fight this need any longer. I heard you earlier… And, just so you know, I recognise that *want*, and I'm working damn hard on learning how to live with it.'

I watched as her lips parted further, small breaths of air escaping them as she began to struggle to breathe with any normal rhythm, and I could feel the tension between us as she waited for me to act out my warning.

'Then kiss me,' the words left her on a whisper.

In that millisecond, I accepted our fate and with my eyes wide open, as I watched her long eyelashes flicker over her soft looking eyes and then close in acceptance, I continued our fleeting kiss more chastely than I've ever kissed a woman in my life as I pressed my mouth down onto hers.

'There you are, are you both alright?' I felt my leg being kicked by Flint. 'Brie and me thought you'd rolled all the way down to the bottom.'

I lifted my mouth away from Nikki's grudgingly and after watching a blush develop over her face at our kiss and us being found, I offered her a wink.

'Shit, why the hell didn't I think of that,' I whispered to her, making sure my beard gently abraded the bare shell of her ear as I spoke.

'Shall we?' I asked her as I moved myself reluctantly off her.

She nodded in answer and after offering her my hand, I stood and pulled her with me from out from the shrubbery and up to meet the very amused faces of the kids.

'Ooooo, you were kissing,' Brie stated.

Well, fuck.

For a minute, I had no answer. I looked quickly at Flint, who shrugged his shoulders.

'Brie.' I crouched down and held out my arms to her, hoping she'd walk into them.

When she did, I picked up my little girl to hold her close to me, unsure how what she'd seen would make her feel.

'You'll always be my best girl, Brie,' I offered, feeling my normal guilt career straight through me. In response, she snuggled herself into my hold and with relief rushing through me, I wrapped my arms tighter around her.

'I know, Daddy… but you need Nikki too, just like me.'

'And you're happy to share, aren't you, Shorty?' Flint asked.

I raised my eyes to silently thank him for his support.

'Yes, because you should always share.' She lifted her head and holding onto either side of my face as she pushed her fingers into my beard, she gave me an Eskimo kiss.

'You're right, Brie… Now, shall we go and share those sledges?' Nikki asked enthusiastically.

The kids let out unanimous yells of 'Yes,' and I released Brie to run ahead with Flint. Then I gave myself a pat on the back for doing something right. It was obvious to the rest of us, in the snow on this man-made hill, that Brie had managed to attain a higher level of maturity in her four years, than I probably ever would.

Letting my arm hang down by my side, I reached out to find Nikki's covered hand with my own. I lifted it up to place a quick kiss on the pink wool and then using my hold on her to pull her with me, I took off running after them, happy in the knowledge that for once in a very long time, I hadn't fucked up.

Twenty-Three

Nikki

'TWO VODKA AND LEMONADES please, and two bottles of water,' I shouted over the temporary bar and offered the barman a quick smile as he wordlessly nodded that he'd heard me.

'Have you ordered?' My sister's voice found me as she pushed her way between the wedding guests to stand next to me.

'Yes, finally.' I turned my head to look at her.

Her face looked as flushed as mine felt, from all the dancing we'd been doing since the speeches had finished and the marquee with the dance floor had been revealed. It was just the sort of night I knew we both needed. It was a shame our mum hadn't felt she was able to come with us, but she had insisted on going to spend Christmas Eve with our brother Stephen. It was something she'd been doing since Lou and I had been adults and I knew that, like always, she would be at home late tomorrow morning to cook up our full English breakfast, or at least I hoped she would, as the snow was still coming down fast and with his facility being a distance away, I wasn't sure that travel would still be an option tomorrow morning.

'Eight pounds please.' The sudden shout of the barman across from me had me turning back to face him. I handed over my bank card and smiled my thanks.

'I never thought I'd be saying this, but I think I need that water a whole lot more than the vodka.'

I laughed at my sister as she twisted the top off the bottle and as ladylike as possible swigged at the cooling liquid to quench her thirst. Taking back my bank card, I lifted my drink to my lips and turned to lean my back on the bar ledge behind me. I took a minute to take a look around the space we were stood in.

For an outside celebration in Winter, with snow on the ground, the Carpenters had thought of everything, as always. Rather than being a stuffy affair, which so many weddings I'd been to over the years had turned into, this one was truly a celebration of the two people getting married and I knew that if I ever married, I'd want mine to be exactly the same. They'd had a small service earlier today and had then invited everyone they knew from the surrounding villages to come and celebrate with them this evening. Having been lucky enough to go to school with the groom Jack, I'd sealed our invitation.

In my mind, I couldn't imagine anything more perfect, except maybe to marry in Paris in the springtime. That was the one place I'd always wanted to go, to soak up the culture and the romance I'd seen in films and read about.

Dear God, stop it.

Suddenly, the music the DJ was playing filtered into my ears once again and I became aware that I was now grinning and shaking my head at myself, and it needed to stop before the very perceptive villagers started to spread rumours that I'd lost the plot and was now one sandwich short of a picnic.

My hand lifted instinctively to touch my lips, as my thoughts once again went back to Luke and the wonderful afternoon we'd shared earlier, with each other and the children. A feeling of giddy excitement began to build up inside of me as I ran through our kiss again. It had been nothing like the first one, there had been no built-up passion behind it like last time... No, this one had been all about acceptance and held the promise of tomorrow.

'You've gone again.' Lou nudged me with her elbow to get my attention. 'What the hell is going on with you?'

'Nothing.' I shook my head at her, 'I'm just enjoying being here.'

'Hi.' A voice I recognised sounded from the other side of me and I turned my head to find Lauren, the owner of The Fairy Garden and the woman Rafferty had been spending a lot of time with.

'Lauren,' I replied. 'Nice to see you, are you enjoying yourselves?' I asked her, implying her, Amy, and Winter, who I had only managed to wave hello to from the other side of the marquee.

'Yes, a girls' night out was just what we needed.'

'This is Lou.' I pulled on Louise's elbow to get her to step forward slightly so I could introduce her properly.

'Nice to meet you, Lou.' Lauren smiled as she narrowed her eyes on Louise. 'Although, I think I recognise you from the rainbow centre, don't I?'

'Possibly,' Lou offered her. 'I help out for free when I'm back from university to give legal advice to anyone in need.'

Lauren nodded her head at us both and we waited for a few seconds as she finally got her order in at the bar.

'I thought so, good for you. I take any food we haven't used over there, because I hate to see waste,' she added as she handed over a twenty pound note for the three tumblers full of what looked like some sort of Whisky being given to her.

'How's it going with Brielle, Nikki?'

'She's fantastic, I'm really enjoying looking after her.'

'I'm pleased. She seems really sweet, and I know they all think the world of her.' She rearranged the tumblers on the bar to ready them all to be picked up together, then she carried on. 'I met her the other day when both of the children turned up at my tearoom. I was lucky enough to spend some time with her and Flint while we baked some cookies.' I looked at her in question. 'They'd taken Biscuit out for a walk and lost him.' She rolled her eyes up into her head, but I could see by the look on her face it had been one of the highlights of her week. 'They're a good couple of kids, which is surprising when you get to know their dads.' Lauren laughed and picked up the three glasses by using both of her hands, before she seemed to think better of it and placed them back down on the bar. 'Talking of dads... how are you getting along with Luke?'

I could feel Louise's eyes on me as she and Lauren waited for my answer, with what appeared to be bated breath.

'Well, thanks,' I answered, smiling at her.

'Good.' She nodded at me. 'I think you're a great fit for them both and having known Cherise for a short while a long time ago, I think she would have loved you too.' The conversation faltered for a few seconds. 'Anyway, nice to see you, Nikki, and to meet you, Lou.' She smiled at us both, 'I'd better be taking these back to the girls before they send out another search party.'

She grimaced at me, and I knew she was remembering the other night, when they'd searched for Amy back at The Manor.

'Bye,' I replied, still thinking about her comment about Cherise.

'Well, that was a well-practised answer if ever I've heard one, now give us the one from your heart.' Lou spoke as we watched Lauren make her way back into the other marquee that contained the DJ and the dance floor, and I understood by her tone that she wasn't going to be fobbed off any longer.

'Oh, Lou, I don't know how to explain how I feel. I've fantasised like most women I know, including you and your lust for Tom Hardy, on the same man for half of my life. Now, in the space of a week, I'm working for my said fantasy.'

The music in the marquee quietened and I sighed in understanding that I was speaking too loudly, and that half of the bar were now looking at me after hearing the word fantasy.

'Shit,' I mumbled as I grabbed Lou's arm. 'Can we move this conversation to elsewhere?' I questioned, as I picked up my water by its neck and downed the rest of my vodka in one hit.

'Sure.' Lou copied my actions. We started walking, following in Lauren's footsteps.

At the end of the next song, the DJ, for the first time that evening, didn't blend straight into another one. Instead, he took his mic in his hand and made an announcement.

'Okay, everybody, that's me for about an hour.' He grinned at the resounding cries of disappointment. 'Awwww.'

'You were saying,' Lou pushed, as I felt her stand closer to me as we watched what was happening on the stage.

Knowing it was noisy enough in here to carry on, I said what I'd been thinking and keeping to myself for the past few days. 'Well, it appears that, the very same fantasy man, the one I've been dreaming of and lusting over for as long as I can remember, the same one who could have his pick of probably millions of women around the world, seems to want me in return. How would you feel if we were talking about you and Tom Hardy?'

'Well, shit,' she replied.

'Yeah, I only left there three hours ago and I miss knowing he's around, even though I've been trying to avoid him for most of the week.' I watched her eyebrows raise. 'I think I need this day and a bit away from him just to catch my breath.'

'You probably do,' she agreed. Then as she barged her body into the side of mine, she teased, 'And you should also probably get all those posters off your walls while you're back. Just imagine how bloody embarrassing it would be if he ever ended up in your bedroom and saw them.'

Her laughter at her own joke broke the moment and sipping at our bottles of water we watched the sudden influx of bodies carrying amps, microphones, and drums on stands onto the large stage behind the DJ. In a matter of a few minutes, he'd finished telling us what an awesome audience we were and how much we were going to enjoy the surprise set up by the best man Charlie and the groomsmen. Charlie, who I'd attended primary school with for a few years, before his parents had pulled him out as was the travelling family way, was stood in the middle of the dance floor, with his pint glass raised high in his hand, turning around full circle absorbing everyone's cheers.

'Mr and Mrs. Jack Carpenter, ladies and gentlemen, I give you… the one… the only… DEFAULT DISTRACTION!' The DJ stepped back at the same time as his desk was lifted away to reveal the bands instruments set up behind him.

In silence, we watched Cade, with his sticks raised high in acknowledgement, enter onto the stage first. The attitude that just exuded from his body was completely captivating. I didn't think I had ever seen a drummer with so much stage presence.

And so, here I was again. I'd only ever dreamed of seeing DD play and now I was going to watch them for the second time in one week. With my empty hand, I gripped hold of my sister's arm in disbelief and excitement.

'Evening.' Cade bent to speak into a mic, placed to one side of the drum kit. He raised a green glass beer bottle up to the happy couple and pointed the neck at them. 'Congratulations to the mad couple.' The crowd cheered and laughed at his words. He then took a swig and placed his beer on the floor.

'Bloody hell,' Lou shouted next to me. 'Did you know they were playing tonight?'

'No.' I shook my head.

'So much for catching your breath.'

I heard her speak, but my eyes were already glued to the stage in front of us.

While he was still standing, Cade began to start to tap out a beat on one drum. It was a beat that I instantly recognised, and I grabbed hold of Lou's water with the same hand mine was in and stretched to put them down on the nearest table. I was pleased that although I'd worn a dress to the wedding reception, it was a short one and looked fantastic teemed with my purple Dr Martens and the thick tights I'd worn, because I knew I was comfortable enough to be dancing for the rest of the night.

Cade flung his leg high over the stool already in position and sat down, his other hand then entered the beat with a flourish. I watched as he closed his eyes and lost himself to his passion. The floor beneath my feet began to pulse as the crowd around me started to jump up and down to the rhythm and I pulled Lou with me and right into the centre of the floor.

I needed to be there when Luke walked out, and I knew he would be coming out next.

The crowd grew louder as he emerged carrying his bass in one hand, and as he pushed it higher to show his appreciation to the excited crowd, I started screaming with the rest of them. He quietly took his place and started strumming the chords in time with Cade. With my arms up in the air I gyrated and twisted my body to the beat, but I held my eyes firmly on Luke, while I took the time to admire him.

His hair had fallen over his face in his trademark way, and I knew he wouldn't look back up again for a while. He was concentrating on the bass in his hands as he made it come alive, so I let my eyes move away from his face and down his body. I grinned to myself when I saw he was wearing a similar checked shirt to the one he'd worn to the tearoom to meet me. But this one was green and black, and I knew that when he eventually lifted his gaze, it would make his eyes pop. The sleeves of the shirt were rolled up to above his elbows, showing off his many tattoos and the various leather and silver chains and bands he wore on both arms. Underneath the open shirt, I could see a thin, grey, grandad collar T-shirt which he'd worn unbuttoned, and I couldn't help but take note of how it stretched across his muscular frame, the same hard body that I had felt wrapped around mine only a few hours before. Team that with the ripped, faded grey jeans he was wearing and the heavy black boots on his feet and I was practically ready to throw myself at him.

Tonight, there were no children involved, and no professional contract to be adhered to. The beat was intoxicating. I'd not drunk a lot, but I knew the alcohol in my blood stream was relieving me of all my inhibitions. After our kiss earlier, I wanted more. I wanted something for me, and I knew I was willing to work to get it.

I continued moving to the beat they were playing, feeling more confident by the minute. At last, I was as near as I could get to Luke. I'd stopped dancing to watch when I understood he could feel me nearby. Slowly, he lifted his eyes from the neck he'd been caressing with his long fingers and his eyes found mine.

Everything I ever thought I knew about attraction and finding someone you wanted to be with, reconfigured inside my head. His beautiful green eyes found mine and he held my gaze as he always did, while his expression changed from one of complete seriousness to one of unexpected awe and I knew his night had been improved by finding me in the audience. I offered him a knowing but shy smile, because I was unsure I'd ever affected anyone in the same way he seemed to be affected by my presence, and the strength of that knowledge totally floored me.

He placed his plectrum in between his lips and gesticulated with one finger held up high that he wanted me to turn around for him, and I did so without thinking and added a little swish of the slightly fuller skirt of my short dress as I came back around to face him.

A look of possession came over his features as he raised his eyebrows and nodded at me in appreciation, and I had never felt more beautiful in my life.

'Christ, no wonder you can't explain it,' Lou shouted in my ear. 'He looks like he wants to devour you.'

As a feeling of total happiness rushed over me, I grabbed both of her hands and lifting our arms up together I began to lead her into a dance I knew we'd practised many times in our living room.

The atmosphere in the marquee grew to a frenzy as off stage the lead guitar started playing a well-known riff that sent the people around me wild. I watched in pride as our local boy Rafferty walked out in his trademark leathers. He blew a kiss out into the crowd as his eyes wandered over the top of us all. I knew right at that minute he was searching for Lauren and when his eyes remained stuck fast on the doorway behind where we were, I knew he'd found her.

I hadn't thought the crowd around me could get any louder, but the excitement in the air ramped up as Brody entered the stage. Hearing the screams, I turned around to watch as he entered from the right and walked onto the stage with his normal swagger.

Brody took his place behind the mic that had been centralised at the front of the stage. He had a leather hat on his head and was looking down, and I couldn't see his features around the brim. I continued dancing with Lou as the claps and cheers increased around us now the band were stood complete on the stage and waited for Brody's voice to add its richness to the song I knew they were playing. Fleetingly, my gaze left Luke to look at Brody's hands which were cupping his mic, and then to his ring-covered fingers.

The crowd was already singing the words to the song that Default Distraction were playing and when Brody finally lifted his head, two-finger saluted us, and joined his amazing voice with ours, the marquee erupted, and we were all projected into a frenzy of excitement.

Still dancing, I moved my gaze back to Luke and offered him a smile and a shake of my head when I saw his lips spread into a broad grin as he mouthed, 'Fucking Brody.'

Twenty-Four

LUKE

IT WAS IN THE second that her eyes came back to mine after watching Brody walk onto the stage, that I dared to hope. When her eyes remained firmly fixed on mine, and a beautiful smile started to caress her lips, the same lips I'd been daydreaming about all fucking week, and she still concentrated solely on me, I was nearly floored by the strength of feeling between us. And after Brody had started singing and she still continued to look at only me while she danced, I thought, just maybe, I understood. Then, as a powerful sensation of warmth flooded my heart, I worked out I'd never felt anything like it before. Realisation hit me with a powerful thud, and I comprehended just what a fantastic fucking liar Nikki was.

'Fucking Brody,' I mouthed to her, shaking my head at her and the pathetic jealousy I'd been carrying around with me for days.

Not caring that for a few seconds my bass would be nowhere to be found in the song we were playing; I lifted my hand up and away from the strings, pointed at her and then back to my chest, to the place I had a Claddagh tattooed over my heart.

'It was never him; it was always me.' I spoke the words this time, not audibly for anyone else, but enough I hoped, for her to at the very least feel them.

I couldn't hope to hear an answer in the noise around us, even if she gave me one. But as I stared at her with my hand still holding my chest, I watched her face heat up with a blush as my statement filtered through. With more optimism in my heart than I knew I'd ever felt before, I took in the slight nod of her head as she agreed with me.

Holy fucking hell.

Complete…was the single word that flew around my head for the next few minutes. The song we were playing had a strong and very recognisable beat and I cast my eyes out to the crowd of possibly two hundred people as they jumped up and down in time with Raff and me. I even leant into the mic when required and stomped on my compression peddle when needed. I was as usual lost to the music we were playing, but it quickly became apparent that after years of playing, in hundreds of different countries, to thousands of die-hard fans, I had *never* felt as validated as a man as I did when I knew Nikki was breathing the same air and had her eyes solely focussed on me.

I was thirty-four years old; I had more money than I knew what to do with and the love of a little girl who I would kill for, but the connection I felt to the young woman in the crowd gave me the feeling of being whole, for the first time in my life.

I'd always understood that I was, without a doubt, the fragmented, malfunctioning version of the person I probably could have been, had my birth and upbringing been different. Together with the rest of DD, we had for years acted out the "rock 'n' roll" life as we attempted to try to dull the pain and to cement the cracks together with the drinks and drugs we'd consumed, and the faceless women we'd fucked. Yet somehow, we'd still always given our manager Lawson and the world just what they'd demanded of us. Even now, and with the many regrets I had inside my head about the path I knew I'd led us down, I understood that those bad choices had helped us all to blur the fucking edges of our lives and made it liveable.

We'd had to live through those years. We'd had to exist in order to be here now and ready to go forward, and fuck was I ready.

As we went into the next song and Nikki began to sing the words back to me about acceptance and moving on, I knew I wanted to do that with her. Cherise and I had clung to each other for so very long, too fucking long, because we were all the other had. We'd worked through the initial lust, our very fragile connection, me helping her to try to beat her addiction and the birth of our amazing daughter. When really, I understood now that we should have let each other go years before. I could see it so clearly stood up here surrounded by my family of brothers and with my eyes on the breath of fresh air that had entered my life that was Nikki.

Cherise had been my mirror image, another lonely orphan who danced to make a living and she had later told me that she had even prostituted herself to eat. I hadn't judged her, how could I? I'd witnessed first-hand the desperation that causes you to sell yourself so you could survive and knew that I was more than likely the result of my birth mom having to do the exact same thing.

The trouble was, with a mirror image of yourself, you stood no fucking chance of filling in all of your broken parts and becoming whole. With Nikki, I knew I stood a chance of gluing all those shattered parts back together.

I could see the concern spreading over Nikki's face as she watched me go through the motions of performing and at the same time sieve through the crap inside my head. As soon as I saw the concern reach her eyes, I gave her my best fucking grin, the one that used to show my dimples before I had a beard. It was also the same one I'd been able to see for days affected her, even when she was trying to ignore me. I also proffered her a quick wink as I convinced her I was okay.

Because with her in my life, I was.

We were such a well-oiled machine as a band, that we'd played through four or five songs without me having to think about what I was doing and without missing a beat. The whole time my eyes had been on Nikki as I watched her dancing. I'd been so fucking busy fighting the building need I had for her and my urge to jump off the stage and take her into my arms, I'd switched off to everything else in the space around me. But when Brody's voice filled with even more emotion than normal and he faltered in the middle of a song, I reluctantly ripped my eyes away from her and moved myself instinctively closer to my brother's side.

Following his eyes out into the crowd on the dance floor, I saw Amy throw herself at some asshat standing next to her, she kissed him and then running, she disappeared through the parting crowd.

'Well, fuck,' I let out softly, but being too close to the mic, I heard my voice travel around the marquee. Brody dropped his mic, our instruments stilled, and I heard Raff saying we'd all be back in a few minutes time. Thank fuck for the DJ, who must have been waiting in the wings, as I heard his voice speak from behind us to the crowd on the dance floor as he got some tracks together.

I took a few minutes before I followed the others. One of us needed to stay back to unplug the amps and switch off the mics we were using, before the feedback I knew was sure to happen, with our equipment being unceremoniously dumped on stage, deafened the people on the dance floor. Eventually, I lifted my bass off my neck and placed it in the rack next to Cade's kit, then after acknowledging the DJ with a nod of my head, I jumped off the stage. As my boots hit the floor, I grabbed hold of Nikki's hand, because whatever the hell was now going on, I'd only just found her and I wasn't letting her go anytime soon.

Eventually, I caught up with Cade, Raff and the girls and I looked questioningly at them all. They were standing close to the closed doors that led from the inside of the marquee to the outside decking. The doors might have been shut, but we could all hear the conversation that was going on outside. My newly pieced together heart broke for Brody, as standing behind the translucent panels of the door, we all heard him speak; and he could have been speaking for each one of us.

'If being a former addict wasn't enough, I'm a member of a band, and in that band we've all learnt the hard way how much people want to be with us for what they can get out of it. Then I came across you. You're the most beautiful woman I have ever laid eyes on. Added to all of that, I could feel a chemistry between us that felt like it was off the charts... You saw me, not my addictions, not what I could buy you or the money you could make by selling your story to the highest bidder and not all the mistakes I'd made... you just saw me.'

It was too fucking personal to stand there any longer, listening to their emotional conversation. I wasn't sure what the fuck he'd done, but I prayed for his sake she'd forgive him. Winter and Lauren were stood crying and holding each other tightly as Raff and Cade looked impotently on. I shook my head at Cade and clapped Raff on the shoulder as I offered them all my support, and with my hand still holding onto Nikki's, I pulled her against me.

'Life's too fucking short.' I spoke out loud to no one in particular and watched as five pairs of eyes acknowledged my statement.

Her body collided with mine and a small gasp left her mouth. I released her hand and after placing my hands on her hips, I pulled her further into me and exhaled in relief as her hands came over my shoulders and she clasped her fingers behind my neck to pull me down to her.

With my forehead resting on hers, standing there with the swirling emotions of the others around us and breathing in the air that had just left each other's bodies, I brushed my lips over hers. I was restrained, very fucking restrained, as I refused to give into the inclination to consume her with the deep-seated need I had for her. Because the next time I kissed her with the passion that had built up inside of me, I was going all the fucking way, and I wanted no one else present. Too much of my life had been spent in the view of others. Nikki and this thing that was growing rapidly between us, was for our eyes only.

Reluctantly, I lifted my mouth away and rubbed my nose gently against hers. I watched transfixed as her beautiful lips spread into a smile. In the background I could hear **Eric Clapton** singing **Wonderful Tonight**.

'Come and dance with me, darlin'.'

Twenty-Five

Nikki

WE'D STAYED ON THE dance floor, holding each other tightly, as we danced to all the slow songs the DJ had played during the unscheduled break. Although I was enjoying every single second of the way Luke was holding me close, the dance floor had been very nearly empty, and I knew a lot of the locals had clocked the two of us together as they'd walked past the open doors. If I wasn't careful, my mum would hear about it before I'd had the chance to tell her, and given that I'd only just told her about my new job and the fact she didn't need to put the house on the market anymore, I didn't want her to worry.

Luke's eyes had mainly rested on mine as I felt him trying to convey silently how he was feeling. But I knew as much as he wanted to be with me, his mind was also elsewhere. Every now and again, his eyes were drawn back to where we'd left the others while we waited for them to reappear.

Eventually, they strode back in… well, the guys did. I wasn't sure where the girls had gone, but I knew it wasn't a good sign that they'd failed to all come back together, and the pain showing on Brody's face made him look like he'd been to hell and back. Reluctantly, Luke released me from his arms just as **Make You Feel My Love** by **Adele** started to fade, and the song came to an end.

'Let's welcome back DEFAULT DISTRACTION to the stage!' The DJ shouted out as soon as he spotted the three of them coming back and I watched as people started to appear from all the doors that led into the marquee.

I didn't know what I was expecting, but I think I had assumed Luke would distance himself just as soon as the audience around us grew. But to my relief and happiness, he held onto my hand until he had moved me back into the place I'd been dancing earlier.

'We'll be about thirty minutes. Last song will be…' He looked at me to check I was listening.

'I know,' I nodded at him smiling. 'Your last song will be "Regret," it's one of my favourites.' I looked up at him.

'Yeah, of course you'd know. I'd forgotten you were a super-fan.' He winked at me and laughed loudly. The sound that rumbled through his chest made me feel warm inside.

I grabbed hold of the front of his shirt and narrowed my eyes on him, before I jokingly pushed him away. Luke leant down and placed his mouth to my ear to whisper the words that he didn't want everyone else to hear and my core ached with the implication behind them. 'Don't go anywhere, darlin', 'cause I'm the one who's gonna be taking you home.'

I knew it was deliberate that his beard brushed against the shell of my ear again before he lifted his head away, and finding my eyes with his he gave me the grin that made the back of my knees feel weak.

After twirling me around slowly for his own perusal, he kissed my hand and with one leap, he jumped back up onto the stage.

Within seconds, all four of them were back on the stage together in work mode. Throughout the first song they played, I only swayed to the music as I watched each of them and came to understand how wholly professional they were as a unit. Brody had looked as though his heart had been ripped out of his chest and pierced with a stiletto heel as he'd walked back. But as soon as the music started, and the first verse of the song had given way to the chorus, he was back, and he managed to give off the impression that he was perfectly fine.

As a fan of theirs for many years, I understood as I stood there just how easily they managed to slip the facade back on, no matter what was going on in their lives, and my heart broke just a little for them all. My dad walking out and leaving us had meant money had always been a problem for my small family. But stood there swaying to the music, as my sister's arm wrapped around my waist when she came up next to me, I contemplated that Default Distraction had everything money could buy, but without love, it undoubtedly wasn't enough.

'What on earth has gotten into you? I've never seen you stand still at a gig before,' she shouted into my ear. I nodded at her observation and leant over to her.

'Just thinking,' I shouted back, cupping my hand over her ear to make sure she heard me.

She looked at me with wide eyes, laughed and shook her head before she grimaced. 'Well, just stop, will you!' she berated me and smiled, before taking my hand in hers and after pushing me a little to get me to step backwards, she twirled me around under her arm. I did the same to her and just like that we were back dancing.

The endorphins were flowing quickly around my body as I truly relaxed for the first time since Haydon Millar had laid his sweaty hands on my body. It had been an emotional few weeks, and an even more emotional evening in more ways than one, but it was one I knew I would remember forever.

Dancing on, lost in the music I had loved for forever, I sung all the words at the top of my lungs as Lou joined in with me. The dance floor was packed around us, making it harder to see clearly on to the stage, but whenever I managed it, I found him looking back at me. Several times, I'd smiled at him and had even blown him a kiss fuelled by the earlier vodka I'd been drinking. In return, Luke's eyes had never seemed to leave me. He'd leant into the mic to harmonise, and transfixed I'd watched him caress the words he was singing with his very talented mouth. I'd listened to the same songs over and over before, but I'd never felt them the way I felt them when his eyes opened wide and he directed them straight at me.

I knew that they were nearly at the end of their set, but after I'd lifted away one of the pieces of my hair that had fallen from the loose bun I'd created earlier and was stuck to my face, I grasped the situation I was in.

You must look bloody awful.

More hair had plastered itself to the back of my neck, and my dress was sticking to my back in places. Realisation hit and hit fast; Luke could probably have his pick of nearly any one of the hundred or so women invited to the wedding reception. I didn't want him getting off the stage and finding me looking a sweaty mess. I checked him out again and watched him travelling around the stage with Raff. His shirt had already been chucked to the back of the stage and I could see sweat soaking through the back of his t-shirt from his spine. His hair was wet at the back of his neck, but hot and sweaty definitely looked better on him than I knew it would on me.

After putting his plectrum between his teeth, I watched him sweep his hair back with one hand and tilt his chin in the air. Knowing my eyes were firmly fixed on him and him alone, he removed the plectrum from his lips and blew me an air kiss, and I practically swooned

God, he's hot.

Suddenly, I felt the need to get out to find some cooler air.

'Lou, come to the toilet with me?' I grabbed her arm as I spoke and pointed in the direction I needed to go.

I watched her nod at me and looked up to find Luke still watching my every move. I lifted my hand and gesticulated I was going out for five minutes and then I'd be back.

I took exactly four minutes in the loo, tidying my hair with my fingers and having the wee I was desperate for. Then just before I left the room, I dabbed at my face with some cold, wet tissue paper and peered closer into the mirror to check my mascara hadn't run down beneath my eyes.

Definitely not perfect, but I'll do.

The door to the toilet banged shut behind me as I heard the first chords of "Regret" start and I momentarily froze as I decided which way to turn. Usually, I'd have rushed back in to watch at least the first verse being sung, but I knew that tonight I couldn't cope with watching Brody sing, knowing his heart was breaking. So, I crossed the open deck back to the marquee that contained the bar, and to where I knew my sister was waiting.

Excitement was mounting inside of me with each step I took. I knew Luke would soon be off the stage and, understanding that, I hoped I would be back in his arms before long. My body trembled as I remembered what that felt like, and I unconsciously rubbed my arms with my hands in anticipation.

I carried on walking towards where I could see Lou standing with her back to me as she chatted to some friends. With every step I took as I crossed the mainly empty space, my eyes wandered up and down the few people left in there. I raised my hand to one or two and smiled at a few others as I made my way past them and continued on my set path.

'Excuse me please.' I touched the shoulders of what I knew was Mrs. Carpenter, the groom's mother.

Her head turned to look at me. 'Hello, Nikki, how are you?'

'Hi,' I smiled back. 'I'm well, thanks,' I offered. 'Thank you for the invitation, it's been a fantastic evening.'

'Oh, you're welcome. I'll let Jack and Lily know you've had fun.'

'Thanks, see you soon.'

She tapped her hand on mine and went back to her previous conversation and I took the final few steps towards Louise. Once there, I wrapped my arms around her waist. She felt stiff like a statue. I laid my head on her back and hugged her happily to me, before lifting my head and taking a look over her shoulder at just who she was talking to.

All the previous happiness and joy I'd been carrying for the previous few hours, drained quickly from my body and I felt my mouth open in shock.

Oh God! What the hell!

I understood exactly why Lou had felt so tense in my arms.

'There she is, talk... talk of the devil.' I could hear the slur and condemnation contained in Lewis's voice, which told me he'd had a skinful and I cringed just a little inside. I glanced quickly around us to see who was in ear shot, and comprehended that the bar area had continued to empty out as more people had left to go back and watch the band's final song. I swallowed down my nervousness as awareness swept through me, as now there were less than ten people anywhere near us, which could either be a very good or a very bad thing, dependant on how his alcohol-fuelled mood took him.

I had known the minute he'd set foot into the pub for a drink a few weeks before, that he felt we still had unfinished business. In truth, I'd been looking out for him everywhere I'd gone, in order to take him to one side and have the talk I felt was way overdue.

But not here, not at Jack and Lily's wedding and not with Luke nearby.

'Like I said, Lewis,' my sister over emphasised his name for effect, 'she's here tonight, but what you think that has to do with you, I've no bloody idea.'

I'm not hiding, I have nothing to feel ashamed of.

I watched as he raised his finger to his lips and "shhhushed" at her. I let go of my hold on Lou and stepped around her to face him.

'I see you've moved on, bitch!' he directed straight at me.

Until that second, although I'd been looking at him, he hadn't got my sole focus, because I hadn't felt he deserved that sort of commitment from me. But the instant I saw his spittle leave his mouth and heard the violence in his tone, my eyes leapt up to find his.

'How dare you.' I stopped short at shouting the words at him, as I comprehended that the room had fallen quiet, and the word "bitch" felt as though it was ricocheting off the plastic and aluminium walls.

'Lewis, I have absolutely no inkling why you still seem to think that four years on, whatever I'm doing with my life has anything to do with you?' I shook my head at him.

'*You* told me you loved *me*.' I stood my ground as he took a step nearer to where I was. In my peripheral view, I could see Lou looking around as she tried to silently ask for help, as the situation started to move fast out of our control.

'I was seventeen and at the time I thought you were the man I was looking for. At twenty-two I found out differently, didn't I?'

My heart was beginning to race, and I felt the cold sheen of panic break out over my skin. I'd been in this situation with him three times before, and it had been on the very last time, when he'd raised his hand to me and slapped me to the ground, that I'd finally summoned up the courage and walked away from what I knew was fast developing into an abusive relationship.

'Why... didn't I match up to Daddy's high standards?' His face took on a disparaging look as he brought up my family's history.

'You know why I left.'

Somewhere in the back of my head, I was aware that inside the other marquee loud cheers and whistles had just started ringing out. DD must have finished singing Regret and I knew Luke would be searching me out in a few minutes.

Regret, how apt. Here I was, stood in front of the biggest one of mine.

'I was watching you... you loved his hands on you... so, why not mine?' He haphazardly pointed to where I had been dancing with Luke earlier, making it look like in his drunken stupor he was going to overbalance and fall over. But no matter how hard I wished for it to happen, he managed to stay upright.

'Enough, Lewis, you're embarrassing yourself,' Louise pushed into the conversation on a sigh. 'Can't you take him away?' She spoke over Lewis's head to one of his friends who was nonchalantly pouring the rest of his bottle of beer down his neck, as he went into competition with Lewis to see who could be the first to pass out from alcohol poisoning.

I didn't see his hand lift, as I'd been concentrating so hard on staring him out as I tried my hardest to stay assertive and face him down in a bid to extinguish his anger. But I felt it just as soon as his hand grabbed at the front of my square-necked dress, scratching across my chest in the process. Holding a fist full of the flimsy fabric he pulled me nearer to him and I was forced to step forward and into his personal space. The force of the connection and the bite of his fingers into my skin, made my hands instantaneously fly up to his arm and I latched both of my hands onto his wrist, as I attempted to pull his hand away.

The smell of beer was trickling out of every sweaty pore of his, and while I might have been stood in a completely different place and time, I relived the feeling of having unwanted hands on me once again. My stomach revolted as I reluctantly inhaled the fumes and the fear of feeling his hands on my body. But, holding onto his wrist tightly with both hands, I did what I hadn't been able to last time; I lifted my knee up fast and connected with his groin and what felt like a semi-erect cock. Bile rose to the back of my throat as I understood he was getting his rocks off as he threatened me.

'Ommph.' The sound left him, and I expected his arm to fall away with the sudden pain. But to my dismay, I worked out that I hadn't done it hard enough, or the alcohol in his system had made him numb, when his hand stayed firmly in place. Apprehension swept through me when he crunched over slightly and stood back upright in a matter of seconds. As his eyes came back into focus, I watched the cruelty I knew he had in him flood his pupils.

Bastard.

'CHARLIE!' I heard my sister's voice shouting at Jack's best man to get his attention.

'This is why I didn't want to be with you, because you're not a man, no *man* treats a woman like this.' I answered his question, as I smacked his arm with both of my hands. I knew my words had hit home when I watched his nostrils flare and a sneer spread over his mouth.

'Does he know you're fucking using him.'

'Who?' I almost screamed back at him, desperate for the conversation to be over.

'The fucking pin-up prick… the one that's always made your pussy flood.'

'LET GO OF ME,' I screamed back at him, 'you're disgusting and deranged.' I pulled on his hand again trying to get him to release his hold.

'You fucking heard her!' I heard Luke's accented voice fill the void around me, and my body sagged in relief when I comprehended that whatever this was would be over soon. Heavy boots thudded on the wooden decking underneath me, sending welcome vibrations throughout my body. Charlie answered Louise's shout and appeared like magic behind Lewis. The former bare-knuckle fighter grabbed him from behind and quickly put him into a hold I knew he wouldn't get free from, just as a fist came flying passed my right eye and connected hard into the side of Lewis's jaw.

In slow motion, my dress was released, and Lewis's eyes rolled high up into his head with the impact, just as Luke's arms came around me from behind and he pulled me into the safety and shelter of his hard body.

'You okay, darlin'?' he asked, as he turned me gently around in his hold. He shook out his right hand as he bent his knees, so he was now level with me to look into my eyes.

'I am now.'

I could hear behind me, that Jack was now involved and between him and Charlie they escorted Lewis away.

'I'm sorry, Jack,' I called out to the groom and shook my head at him as I tried to convey just how upset I was that this had spilt over into his wedding.

'Nothing to be sorry for, Nik… All the best fucking weddings have a fight in 'em, ain't that so, Charch?' He laughed loudly as he and Charlie manhandled Lewis between them.

'Hey, arsehole… heads up,' Lewis aimed at Luke. 'She'd sell herself for that bloodsucking family of hers and make you promises she never intends to keep… *You* have been warned.'

'What... by you?' Luke shouted back, laughing loudly. 'You're steaming drunk, man, and you've pissed your pants... your warnings mean jack shit.'

'She belongs to me,' Lewis called out, reaching the ears of the growing audience.

'No woman belongs to anyone, especially someone she fucking obviously doesn't want to be with... Now shut the fuck up.' Jack hit Lewis again and I looked on as Lewis's head lolled forward as he passed out. Laughing between the two of them Jack and Charlie lifted his motionless frame and with his shiny shoes being dragged over the wooden boards they removed him.

'Thanks, I owe ya,' Luke shouted out.

'Nah, no problem, mate... we fucking *love* taking out the rubbish,' Jack shouted back.

Twenty-Six

Nikki

W E TRAVELLED SLOWLY BACK through the snowy lanes to my family home. It appeared that Luke had commandeered the white Land Rover we'd used earlier to take the kids sledging. The car was comfortable and warm, and Luke and Lou had chatted about this and that. Although I'd joined in occasionally, most of the time my eyes were drawn to the fields and trees around us as I gathered my thoughts. I knew my earlier happy mood had been affected by the stunt Lewis had pulled and that Luke had witnessed it.

At last, we pulled up outside and as I looked at our pillar-box red coloured door with a wreath hanging by a small piece of twisted wire on the knocker, I understood that I'd been so lost in my own head as we'd travelled, that I didn't remember our journey at all.

'Ah, so you're the lawyer,' Luke laughed as he spoke. I worked out that his statement had been fed from something Lou, who was sitting behind us, had said. 'It all makes sense now.' He squeezed my thigh, which he'd rested his hand on the minute we'd pulled away from Jack and Lily's farm.

'Not quite, but nearly... I'm in my last year at university, so in another three and a half years... after my final year, my assessments and work experience... I will be,' she replied.

'I'm impressed,' he offered.

'Thank you. And now, I'm about to show you one of the main qualities needed to be a lawyer... diplomacy.'

I turned around in the heated seat I was sitting on to look at Louise, as I tried to work out what she was going to say.

'If you look along the lane, you'll see Emma waving.'

I did exactly what she'd said and found Emma holding her dressing gown tightly around herself to keep out the cold with one hand and waving frantically with the other.

'So?' I interrogated, as I looked to where she was now leaning forward between the two front seats. Fleetingly, I caught sight of questioning look on Luke's face.

'I'm staying with them tonight and you know where I am if you need me, Nik. But for once, big sis, I think you need to act your age and be responsible for yourself only and this is me giving you the space to do just that.' With that, she moved nearer to the door and opened it, letting a freezing draft of air enter the car. 'One last thing, I need you to remember *this*. Because in four years' time, when I'm Tom Hardy's lawyer and he leaves his wife for me, I will need you to be equally as discreet, Nik,' she winked at me. I shook my head at her comment, and as butterflies took flight inside me with my nervousness, I managed a small laugh at her.

'You're so far away from discreet, you can't even see it.'

She grinned her response and waggled her eyebrows.

'Night, to you both. Happy Christmas, Luke.'

'Yeah, and a Happy Christmas to you too, Lou.' My body responded to his deep, soulful voice as he spoke, and I appreciated that we were about to be left alone, when we'd never really been alone before. The car door slammed shut and I watched her walk away from us both, and with a last wave she disappeared into the warmth of Emma's house.

'Why do I feel like a teenager, who's just been given permission to fuck you?' Luke questioned, breaking the silence between us. I turned to look at him, just as he swept the hair off his face and turned his head towards me.

'I'm sorry... my family.' I shook my head at him, screwing up my face at the weirdness of it all. 'What can I say?'

Luke shifted his body to turn completely sideways. With his right arm now resting on top of the wheel, his left reached out until his thumb and forefinger were on my chin and gently, he held my gaze still.

'Don't be, it's good to have family.'

'I'm Brie's nanny.' I said the words that I knew would bring us back to reality with a bump. 'And you're... well, you're you.'

'Yep.' He grinned at me. 'For over a week, since I met you in the tearoom, I've been thinking along the same lines.' I watched as for a second or two he chewed his bottom lip.

'You have?' My voice sounded smaller, and I knew my body had sagged in resignation. 'Look, it's been a fantastic day, that's been topped off with a totally weird, but very wonderful evening. Thank you for the lift, but I understand you have Brie to get home to. It's Christmas tomorrow and I don't need...' I shrugged my shoulders.

My voice broke off, as I tried to comprehend exactly what I did or didn't need.

'What?' he questioned. 'What don't you need?'

'I don't need to have my hand held tonight.'

'Need and want are entirely different things, Nikki.'

'I know.' My voice lifted as I tried to convince him.

'I don't have to be home until early tomorrow morning. Brie is having a sleepover with Flint, and Raff's mom who's arrived for Christmas. I want to be there when she wakes up, but that's...' He twisted his right arm over to expose the large watch face on the inside of his wrist. 'That's five hours away and I *want* to spend those with you,' he finished.

'She is? It is, and you do?' I was beginning to fidget with my hands on my lap, as the strength of the pull from the strongest sexual tension I'd ever felt, held me in its clutches.

'Yes,' he laughed. 'And you didn't let me finish.'

Luke's eyes focussed intently on mine, he moved his body towards me and brushed his mouth against mine. Once, twice, his warm flesh connected against mine. Desperate to keep the connection between us, I reached out to take a hold of his checked shirt, and caressed the material I held in my hand, hoping he could feel how much I wanted to touch him. His hand left my chin and he moved it to connect with the bare skin at the back of my neck, holding me exactly where he wanted me. The intensity created from that single, innocuous touch travelled to all my extremities and as his mouth continued to implore mine to open to him, my toes curled inside my boots.

My lips parted and his tongue swept in, and as it did, every single nerve ending I hadn't even known existed sparked to life. My body went on high alert at understanding just what this man could do to me.

At his encouragement, I kissed him back, mirroring in my naivety his exact movements. Where he teased, so did I; where he caressed, I followed. Reluctantly, with my body primed to straddle him where he sat, I felt him pulling away, until he'd created a small fissure between our mouths.

With his forehead resting on mine, his breath skimmed over my swollen lips.

'I'm a thirty-four-year-old jaded musician, who has more baggage, guilt and grief than some days I know what to do with. I'm also a former drug user... so why the actual fuck would a stunningly attractive twenty-six-year-old, want anything to do with me? Why the hell should she when she's fucking perfect?'

'I'm not perfect and I also have baggage, too much of it for my liking. You witnessed some of that tonight,' I answered back. 'I still need to thank you for helping me tonight... Lewis is an ex, I caught him shagging someone else, but he won't, or can't, let go...'

'Forget it. I'm not interested in your past, darlin'... just your future.' His lips came back to mine as he deliberately took away my ability to carry on talking. I lost myself into the moment with him, because boy, could the man kiss. Until all my senses were focussed on him and that single moment in time. The smell of his cologne, the heat permeating from his hand into my skin and his quiet commanding control.

Once again, he pulled away a millimetre or two from me.

'And did I mention I have a young daughter,' he carried on.

'You might have.' I smiled at him as I inhaled deeply to catch my breath.

'Nikki... *this* between us is so damn deep. I can't fight it any longer and I'm sorta hoping you can't either, because I want you with a need I know I've never felt before...' He shrugged his shoulders at me. 'So, now it's down to what you want.'

Not once did my heart beat before I answered him.

'I want you; it's always been you.'

I grabbed the front of his shirt and pulled his mouth back to mine.

Twenty-Seven

LUKE

MOVE FUCKER.

I was struggling to do the right thing, but eventually I managed to shift myself away from her. Even though my instinct was to lift her up to straddle my lap, so I could sink my dick, balls deep inside of her, right here in the car. But she deserved more, my heart understood it, even though my body was at the minute refusing point blank to recognise it.

With one hand, I pulled savagely at the lever to open the door and relief washed through me as soon as I felt my boots connect with the snow-covered ground. With testosterone ruling every single cell I owned, I shoved my hand at the car door and heard it slam loudly behind me. I winced at the sudden loud noise reverberating off the row of small houses and took a couple of seconds to calm myself the hell down.

The need to have her back in my arms as quickly as possible had fuelled my every movement and I'd given no thought to anyone else around us. That need deepened inside my gut and I jogged the few paces around the front of the car and within seconds, I was looking at her through the glass. I grabbed at the handle and ripped open the door, sending a cold draft of cold air across her.

'Darlin'.' I raised both of my hands up to her. It was only a few steps to her front door, but missing her touch already, I was adamant that we were going to cross them together. 'I'm ready to accept whatever this is between us, are you?'

'Luke.' It was one word, one single fucking syllable, but her voice sounded breathless as she spoke my name. 'If we do this, if we take this step, we're risking so much.'

'I know,' I admitted and fleetingly my head pictured the little girl that until now had been my entire world.

Am I wrong to want more? I fucking hoped not.

But one thing I knew for sure was I needed to take the chance, and to trust that just maybe this time things would work out.

'Nikki, life's a risk and there's no guarantees. But I can guarantee you this, if you're never prepared to take a risk… then, darlin', you're never gonna live. Question is, are you willing to take that risk with me?'

'Yes,' she replied breathlessly as she toyed with her bottom lip.

'Arms around my neck,' I demanded.

She did what she was told, after moving her ass to the edge of the seat and, in response, I lifted her up and away from the car and held her tightly against my body.

'Legs around my waist,' I insisted and she immediately complied with my wishes.

I'd been sporting a semi since I'd danced with her earlier, but as her damp heat collided with the head of my dick and her toned dancer's legs engulfed me, she nearly unmanned me, right there in the fucking street.

'Holy fucking hell, woman.' I groaned into her ear as every litre of blood in the rest of my body travelled to my crotch. My balls hitched up tightly and my dick filled the entirety of the crotch of my jeans. 'Do you have any idea what you're doing to me?'

'I hope so,' she whispered.

My body ignited at the words and the way she said them.

'Allow me to show you.' Grinning at her, I snatched the keys from her hand and after securing her in my hold, we were moving. A few strides later, we were stood outside her home.

Reluctantly, I took my hand away from her ass, so I could drive the single key she had on a fluffy keyring, home. Instinctively her thighs tightened their hold on my waist, and I sucked in a breath as my mind imagined them tightening around my hips as I fucked her. To my relief and sanity, the key found its place on the first go and from the light of the Christmas tree glowing through the side window of her home, I grabbed at the handle and twisted it clockwise. With a hasty tap from my boot, the door opened and hit the wall behind it with a resounding crash, which sounded out like a starting gun inside my head.

I took the couple of steps needed to take us away from the world and crossed over the threshold. Then I caught the edge of the doorjamb with the toe of my boot and after kicking my foot backwards, it closed with a velocity that rattled the loose doorhandle.

She jumped in my arms at the sound, and then as reality hit, she slowly exhaled and relaxed again, and just like that we were alone.

Turning us both around hurriedly, I pushed her back into the glass on the top half of the door, knowing the temperature difference between it and me would heighten her senses. Using her back on the door to my advantage, I changed my hold over her. The necessity to have her feel just how she was driving me fucking crazy, had consumed me. Quickly, my eyes got used to the much dimmer light and I found her watching me intently. I trailed my forefinger over her cheek bone and down to her jaw, before letting it dip down lower where I traced over her collarbone.

Holding her tightly, with my body pressed into hers, I felt her breathing change at just those few touches on her body. Her silver-grey eyes began to darken as I trailed my fingertips lightly down the side of her body, and with her held tightly between me and the door, I felt as she began to take small breaths in an attempt to quell her body's sudden need for air.

Taking hold of her thigh as my arm finally dropped lower, I lifted her leg up and over my hip and held her toned leg exactly where it needed to be. I rolled my hips into her a few times and watched as she began to fall apart in my arms.

'Ohhh.' Her plump, blood-filled lips let go of a moan and her eyes grew wider. Her need and receptiveness fed the soul that I had been convinced the devil had owned for longer than I could remember.

I'd felt her warm hands as they came up to clutch my head and her fingers pushed their way through the longer strands of my hair. I'd heard her silent plea as she took a firm hold and attempted to bring my mouth back down to hers.

'I hear ya, darlin'… but I need to watch you. I've been dreaming about this and I'm gonna watch you fall apart for me.' I let her pull me in so far and then I took back the control, so I could keep my eyes firmly focussed on hers, as I rolled my hips back into the molten heat of her core.

'Luke,' she moaned and it travelled down though me until I felt the sticky wet heat of my pre-cum ooze out and onto the head of my dick.

'Ah, fuck,' I answered, feeling my earlier strength and control ebb in response.

A trace of her floral perfume rose from in between our bodies, feeding the frenzy that I was trying to regulate inside of me. I'd just about managed to shelve that, when a different aroma hit me, one that was all her. She was sweet and musky, and my mouth salivated in response to the need to run my tongue through her slit, to taste her.

Holy fucking hell.

I'd experienced many fucking highs in my life, but the scent that was drifting into my nostrils was driving me wild with need and catapulting me faster into oblivion than any shit I'd paid for. I hadn't figured on my reaction to her being like this… whatever the hell this was.

This gorgeous woman, this fucking beautiful woman, who had happily put her trust in me, was taking me to places I knew I'd never even dreamt existed.

I swallowed hard as I fought the urge to fuck her hard against the door. Her eyes darted to my throat as she watched my Adam's apple move and as her mouth found the protruding bump, she enclosed it within her lips and I felt her tongue lick over the area, before her teeth nipped a small piece of skin.

Well fuck, Nikki, you learn quick.

'Hell.' The word came out on a groan. My balls hitched up higher in response and I gripped her thigh tighter. I had to close my eyes temporarily, as I struggled with just how much I wanted her.

'I'm hungry, darlin', I've been craving you since I saw your ass rising up and down off that bike saddle. I hope to hell you're ready for me?'

'I am… I'm wet, so very wet,' she whispered shyly into my neck. The connection of her warm breath on the skin she'd recently let her mouth vacate, caused my breathing to halt.

Lifting my hand quickly, I found the back of her head and threaded my fingers into any loose hair I could find. I used the hold I had on her and pulled her out of her hiding place, to where my eyes could once again take her in. My mouth captured hers as I rewarded her for her brutal honesty. Her lips, already plump from our earlier kiss, were already open in her desperation to feel the connection between us. My tongue darted in, in a frantic bid to caress each sensitive part of her. The noises that she'd started to make at the back of her throat, nearly drove me fucking insane.

I released her hair and captured the back of her neck, as the craving to touch her skin consumed me. As I felt the heat of her feverish skin underneath my fingers, I rolled my hips back into her core. But instead of continuing the roll, I left my dick pulsing against her.

The mewl that left her mouth and travelled into mine let me know I had, without a fucking doubt, caught her engorged clit between my dick and her pelvic bone and, spurred on by her need, I rocked myself against her over and over, needing to drive her as fucking wild as she was driving me.

The hands that were still caught in my hair, released me suddenly and snaked their way around my torso. One grabbed hold of my shirt in between my shoulder blades and the other found its way to my belt, as they worked together to pull me further into her body. I couldn't remember having ever been as hard as I was in that moment.

Spurred on by her need to keep me moving against her clit, I turned our caressing and teasing kiss into one that was unbending and merciless. I licked, bit and tasted any available part of her mouth until she was so far gone that she exploded in my arms, as her first orgasm of the night wracked through her body.

'Oh, God, Luke. Oh… yes,' she cried into and against my mouth.

I tensed my body against her soft one as she instinctively rode out her orgasm.

Slowly, she came back down to earth until she'd relaxed in my hold, and I eased my dick marginally away from her heat, knowing I was one false fucking move away from blowing my load.

With as much restraint as I could find, I removed my throbbing lips from hers and rested my forehead against her as we both took in fast gulps of air. Looking down at her, I ran my tongue fleetingly once again over her lips, needing to feel the swelling I'd put there.

A few seconds of reprieve later, I bent my head down to her neck. The moment my mouth, tongue and teeth did their best against the sensitive skin, she once again started taking incomplete breaths. Smiling into her, at the way she was responding to me, I deliberately used my beard over the vulnerable area I'd created.

'Now I understand why you grew the beard,' she whispered and then gasped, as in response to her sarcasm I allowed my teeth to graze her collarbone.

'Only for you, darlin'... you seem to enjoy it so fucking much,' I whispered to her with a smile, as my mouth found hers fleetingly again before I licked my way down the other side of her neck.

I pulled her dress off one shoulder and sucked her flesh into my mouth.

'Oh, dear God, Luke.' She spoke out loud, and like the God she seemed to think I was, I answered her prayers by rolling my hips just the once against what I knew was now her soaking wet pussy. But it backfired and set off a reaction of need throughout my entire body. I couldn't fight against what I wanted any longer.

'Where we going?' I released the skin on her shoulder and spoke, making sure my warm breath connected with the wet, sensitive area my mouth had left behind. 'Bedroom?'

Holding her closer to me, I turned us both around and looked down the narrow entryway.

'No...' she managed to answer. 'No, not there.'

'Then where, darlin'?' My voice was coarse and ragged, and sounded out my own desperate need. 'I don't care if it's here against the outside door, in the kitchen, or back in the car. But at some point tonight, I'm gonna feel your pussy milking my cock when I make you come.'

'Front room, first door behind you,' she breathlessly replied.

It took me three long strides to reach the front room.

The door was closed over, but there was no way I was letting go of the hold I had on her, so I used my elbow to push the door open wide.

The room felt warm and seeking the source, my eyes found a small open fire, covered by a guard. The lights on the Christmas tree made the room glow softly.

I fell to my knees in front of the fire, still holding her to me, but loosening my unrelenting hold on her, I positioned her to straddle my thighs. Already missing her gasps of need, I grabbed hold of the fine globes of her ass and pulled her onto my cock.

Her body jerked awake, and I grinned my approval at her response to me. I'd been with many, many faceless women, but I understood already that I'd never been with anyone like her. I knew, without a doubt, that I would always remember how she smelt and how she reacted to me. The way she gasped each shuddering breath and how her eyes rolled high into her head as pleasure consumed her.

'You're wearing too many clothes.' As I spoke, my hands found the bottom of her dress. In one quick movement I lifted it up, took it over her head and threw it to the side. Keeping my eyes firmly on hers, I brushed my thumb across her bottom lip and trailed my fingers.

Finally, I allowed my eyes to run down over her body.

'You're gorgeous.'

My fingers made quick work of her front fastening bra and with my eyes back on hers I skimmed my hands over her shoulders, taking her straps away from her flushed looking skin, until they fell to her forearms, trapping her arms impotently to her sides.

My mouth fell to her hard, extended nipples and with my mouth salivating to take her in, I gripped hold of her tiny waist and brought her body to mine. My tongue licked in circular movements around both of her areola as I teased her.

Her back arched in response and my self-restraint snapped.

Taking one of her heavy tits in one hand, I allowed myself to draw the other into my mouth. As I sucked, kneaded, and teased, her hips unconsciously began to flex into my groin, as she sought out a way to quell the fire that was once again building inside of her.

I lifted my mouth to find the hollow of her throat and lowered her to the thick carpet on the floor.

'Oh, Luke, please...' She half spoke and half groaned.

Hearing her plea and completely going against the need I had to keep her restrained and under my control, as desperation to feel her hands on me rose quickly to the surface, I pulled her bra strap off one wrist to release her.

Another time, darlin'.

Twenty-Eight

Nikki

A S MY BARE BACK found the thick, shaggy rug underneath me, I watched as Luke swept his eyes over my exposed body, and saw a fire ignite inside his eyes.

He moved so quickly, I hardly had time to keep up with him. His hands found my hair and running his long fingers through the loose and errant strands that dancing had created, he effectively pulled apart the bun I'd been wearing. With one hand now wrapped around my long hair, his mouth crashed down to mine.

And every coherent thought I had in that minute, disintegrated to dust around me.

His mouth consumed mine with a desperation that only matched my own.

I didn't have a lot of experience, but where this man was concerned, I was convinced I didn't need it. I felt like I'd been awakened from a long sleep, and taking his lead I kissed him back, matching every single stroke of his tongue with my own.

My hands, which had found the back of his head and tugged and pulled on the shorter strands at the top of his neck, began to find their way down his back. Without thinking about what I was doing, but going with what my body was screaming out for, I started to tug at the bottom of his shirt.

I needed to feel him all over me.

Answering my unspoken prayers, Luke lifted his mouth off mine and releasing his hold on my hair, he sat back up on his haunches and blew out a long exhale.

'Fuck, darlin'... you kiss like I was already fucking you.'

In my innocence, I had no idea what to make of his dirty mouth, all I knew was it was helping to stoke the fire inside of me. But I was so well primed already, that every time he spoke, I thought I would spontaneously combust.

'I want your clothes off,' I voiced and felt heat consume my cheeks.

In the light of the fire, I watched as my words permeated his brain and he gave me a slow and very deliberate smile as my reward for being honest and telling him just what I wanted. He took hold of my hand to sit me up, before placing my hand on his chest for me to undress him.

'I don't...' I started, before Luke pressed one finger to my lips.

'You want me undressed... So, undress me.' His eyebrows raised as he gently commanded.

With hands that were shaking, I took on each button he'd done up on his shirt as we'd left the wedding to travel home. I pushed the fabric over his shoulders and down his arms, then he took over, pulling it off and throwing it down to one side. He lifted his T-shirt, holding on to it at the back of his neck and pulling it over his head and his body was, at last, exposed to me. Tentatively, I reached out to touch his chest and he inhaled a breath, like my touch had scolded him. Feeling bold, as I recognised how I affected him, I brushed my fingers over him again and watched as his muscles tensed. His tattoos met my eyes, and I took in just how stunning his body was. His muscles were well-developed, but not overly so and his tattoo artist was an absolute genius, as the two things combined to make his body a work of art.

Of course, I'd seen them before, in the many pictures from photo shoots I'd looked at. But in reality, they were so very much more.

'Nikki.' His voice caressed my name and my eyes darted up to his. 'I've been hard since we danced and God fucking help me, I can't wait much longer to be inside you.'

'Then don't,' I whispered back as my hands reached out to the large, eagle-shaped buckle of his belt. Somehow, with his eyes on mine, I managed to release the metal prong and a couple of the buttons on his fly. Feeling bold, I reached inside with one hand and wrapped my fingers around his cock. His cock was beautifully smooth, almost unbearably hot to touch and so rock-hard I inhaled quickly at the thought of him inside me.

Impulsively, I strengthened my hold on him.

Luke's eyes rolled high into his head and a groan that fed the need inside me escaped from his mouth. With a feeling of power like I'd never known before travelling through me, I did what I was desperate to do, and after taking an even firmer hold of him inside his jeans, I swept my thumb over the pre-cum that was leaking onto the head of his cock.

Once, twice, three times, I swept my thumb over his glans in a circular movement, completely mesmerised as I watched him come undone.

'Fuck.' He expelled the word on a groan.

I observed as every ounce of his self-control evaporated around us and as it finally disappeared, I knew my time to explore was at an end, for now.

Then, we were moving. Somehow, Luke pulled us both up to standing and his mouth descended onto mine with a force that left me reeling. Everything around me was a sudden flurry of motion. His hands were on me, strong and demanding, and no matter what had happened to me tonight with Lewis and weeks before back at the Millars' house, I wasn't scared, because it was so very different. Luke pulled his mouth from mine and with his hands holding my hips, he moved it to suck and tease at each of my nipples, until I was struggling to stop my knees from giving way and collapsing underneath me.

Then, with a firm hold on my hips, he lowered himself in front of me, tasting and savouring the skin between my breasts until he reached my still-covered abdomen. I heard my tights ripping and recognised the warm air from the fire as it found my uncovered flesh.

His hold on me changed again and he gently lowered me backwards. In a matter of minutes, my tights, knickers, and boots had been removed and I was undressed, laid back out on the rug and completely exposed to him. While the man I'd been having wet dreams about since my early teens, stood before me in only his jeans and boots, with his cock in one hand. The whole time, his eyes studied me closely as he moved his hand up and down his shaft. I was certain that if anyone else looked at me the same way that he was, devouring each inch of me with his eyes, I would have attempted to cover myself up, but under his perusal I felt empowered.

Another whimper left my lips.

Then he was on me, tasting and touching every single part of me, as he made his way up my needy body, until he was lying between my legs that he'd spread out wide and kissing my inner thighs.

It was too much.

I couldn't think.

I was lost.

His arms moved to pin down my thighs and his hands came up to rest over my stomach, as he held me right where he wanted me to be. With our eyes connecting as he looked up and over my body to where I had lifted my head to watch him, he teasingly ran the tip of his tongue over my engorged lips in a circular movement. Each and every nerve ending I possessed went on high alert, goosebumps broke out over my skin and a moan left my mouth. Every coherent thought left me, until my mind and body were consumed with the impulse to feel his warm tongue just where I needed it to be. In answer, my hips started to try to flex, but Luke held on to me tightly, as he forced me to accept only what he was willing to give. My body rose higher on each sweep around his tongue made. As his fingertips parted my swollen lips and the cool air found my engorged clit, I knew I was balancing precariously on top of the highest precipice I'd ever been on. With the very first sweep of his tongue inside my soaking wet folds, he connected for the first time with the vertical piercing I'd had in the hood of my clitoris for the past few years, and my brain imploded. Wave upon wave travelled up and down my body. White light exploded behind my closed eyes, and I heard screaming in the distance that I intuitively knew was my own, as my body convulsed again and again in his hold.

The groan that escaped him was primeval.

'Take it all, Nikki… ride it out, darlin'.'

Luke's tongue continued to press down onto the double bar of pearl beads, and I was forced to ride out every aftershock with his eyes watching me as he looked up the length of my body, until finally I was replete, and struggling to keep my eyes open.

I felt him move and heard the unmistakable sound of a condom being ripped open.

'You're making me unhinged, darlin'. Your tits are gorgeous and that fucking piercing... well, fuck. Just the scent of your pussy is wrecking me. I need to be balls deep inside you... I need to fuck you hard, so hard, I'm worried I'm gonna break you apart.'

He climbed up me, to settle himself between my legs and I felt the heat of his cock pressing impatiently against my entrance. My hands reached around his back, and I stroked my fingertips across his hot and feverish skin, before I grazed one long fingernail down his spine and gripped his arse cheek. Releasing a groan, he leant down to reclaim my mouth with his own and in one swift movement he flexed his hips and entered me.

'Fuck, Nikki,' he groaned into my mouth.

Intuitively, I wrapped my legs around him to hold him to me. Every rock-hard inch of him filled me and his cock stretched me to absolute capacity. The second he started rocking his hips into me, I understood I was a lost cause. My body was still convulsing with the odd aftershock from my last orgasm and all too soon, I was riding the precipice to another. With every thrust he made inside me, pleasure travelled faster and faster throughout me.

'Luke, oh, Luke.' My eyes closed and his name fell away from my mouth as I worshipped the man, and just what he could do to me.

'Nikki. Nikki... look at me,' he demanded.

My eyes found his just as the feeling of him pulsing inside me started. His hair fell over his eyes and his back arched as he accepted his fate and with our eyes firmly fixed on each other's, we rode out our mutual orgasm together.

Coming back down to earth, he gently lowered his body weight onto mine and I cradled his head into the hollow of my neck.

'Merry Christmas, darlin',' I heard him whisper, just before I succumbed to the sleep my body was demanding.

Twenty-Nine

Nikki

'COME ON, YOU TWO, it's ready.' I heard my mum's voice travel up the stairs and as she held onto the note of the last word in the sentence, I carefully opened one eye and started to stretch out my deliciously aching body.

Just like any other morning that I woke up in my childhood bedroom, I found myself gazing at what had to be said was my absolute favourite poster of Luke McKenzie. I lifted my hand and smiling to myself, I stroked my fingertips over his beard, as I took in the realisation that this wasn't the same as any other morning. The man I was staring at was no longer a part of my dreams, but I hoped was part of my reality.

'Note to self, take down the posters,' I spoke on a whisper to myself.

'Girls… the bacon is getting cold.'

'Coming, Mum,' I shouted back, without removing my fingers from the delicate paper I was gently caressing.

Then my own insecurities hit. I pulled out my phone from under my pillow, and found it was ten o'clock. Luke had only left me five hours ago, but what if last night had been a one-time thing, or even worse, what if because I'd given in to what he wanted, I'd consequently lost my job.

As worry released itself in my gut, I twisted my body quickly and sat up to see my door opening a little. I hastily grabbed at the quilt to pull it around me, not wanting my mum to see I'd fallen into bed naked.

My eyes found Lou's and my body sagged in relief.

'Well, good morning,' she offered, smiling at me and then after taking in my expression she added, 'stop worrying.'

I shook my head at her.

'Unless it was *that* bad.'

I laughed at her. 'What do you think?'

She tilted her head from side to side as she pretended to mull over my question. 'I think, big sister, that he rocked your world and now you're panicking.'

'Mmmm,' I answered.

'Okay,' came another shout up the stairs. 'I'll eat it all myself.'

'We're just coming, Mum.' Lou moved her head to shout back down the stairs and then her eyes came back to find mine. 'And you can tell me later, when Mum falls asleep after the Queen's speech.'

We ate our breakfast standing in the small kitchen, as was our family tradition. With the turkey already cooking, we prepared the vegetables while Mum laid the table in the back room we used as our dining room.

'I've put Stephen's presents to you both under the tree,' our mum called out, in between polishing the sterling silver cutlery.

'How was he?' I asked and moved to the doorway between the two rooms to witness her answer.

I watched, as not realising my eyes were on her, she instantly stopped what she was doing and with her hands frozen in mid-air, she thought over her words. What she was unaware of, was the fact she'd already answered me.

'That good, huh?'

Her eyes found mine and instantly filled with tears. In response, I dropped the knife I was holding and after walking over to her, I wrapped my arms around her tightly.

'He was as well as can be expected.' She nodded to me.

Louise came up behind us and wrapped her arms around us both. 'But?'

'But it's Christmas day and I need to get the roast potatoes in.' She hugged us both back momentarily and then removed herself from our hold and walked back to the kitchen.

The doorbell sounding, had us all freezing in the tracks of pretending that all in our world was fine and getting on with the chores.

'Well, I can't go.' Mum shook her head at us both, with tears still very evidently captured in her eyes.

'And I'm in my pyjamas,' Lou pushed in and fled to the kitchen to give her words more punch.

I looked down at myself. I had only cleaned my teeth, shoved my hair up into an extremely messy bun and pulled on an old, faded, Wentworth House sweatshirt and grey leggings which I'd tucked into thick socks.

'I suppose it's down to me, then.' I shrugged and moved out into the much cooler hallway, pulling the door behind me to keep the heat in the room.

'When will it warm up a bit?' I asked myself quietly, as a shiver made its way down my spine.

The doorbell sounding again pulled me out of my own thoughts and after making the final couple of steps, I lifted my hand to turn the handle and pulled the door open.

'Merry Christmas, Nikki.'

I cast my eyes down to the voice and smiled as I found Brie standing on our front doormat. She was wearing the complete pink ballet outfit I had managed to buy from Betty a few days before, and holding on to the edge of her tutu she turned around in a circle for me to see her ensemble. I looked her up and down as a smile developed on my face at her obvious excitement. It had to be said that the best part was the handknitted crossover cardigan I knew Mrs. Harper from "A stitch in time" had made. I appreciated then, as I watched her little face glow, that I might not have spent a lot of money, but somehow, I'd managed to find the perfect gift for my small charge.

'Thank you for my presents.'

I bent down to gather her into my arms. 'You're very welcome, Brie,' I replied, as I cuddled her to me and inhaled the coconut shampoo she always insisted on using.

A deep voice had my eyes lifting to find Luke, who was leaning against the very dirty, white Land Rover.

Feeling like a woman starved of nourishment, I fought hard to make my eyes move slowly over his tall frame. As usual, a well-worn pair of boots covered his feet and tucked just inside were the bottoms of a black pair of jeans. I continued to raise my eyes higher as I took in every tantalising piece of him. Surprisingly, my eyes found a dark green, knitted cable jumper on his body and knowing just what the colour must be doing to his eyes, I couldn't resist any longer and lifted my eyes quickly to find his.

The involuntary reaction inside of me, at finding his eyes with my own, would have been enough to make my knees weak and I thanked my lucky stars I was crouched down holding on to Brie.

I watched mesmerised, as he released the side of his bottom lip from his teeth and uncrossed his arms. After stepping a couple of paces towards me, he swept his hand through his hair, lifting it away from his face and ruffled it with his fingers.

'Hi.' He carried on walking as he spoke.

'Good morning, Merry Christmas.'

'Brie wanted to come and see you.' The words left his mouth and then I watched as he mouthed, "And so did I," and my heart galloped as I gave him a smile over her shoulder. 'She wanted to thank you for her presents. But I know it's your day off.'

'It's more than fine. It's lovely to see you both.'

There was so much waiting to be said and it swirled in the air around us as a gust of wind lifted up some snow and carried it away.

Slowly, I released Brie and stood up. All the while, I was fighting the urge to step into his hold after finding his hands clenching and releasing again as he fought with what seemed to be the urge to reach out to me.

'How's your Christmas going?' I shifted to lean against the doorframe as I asked the question. I hoped he couldn't see right through me. I knew I'd asked the question to keep him standing in front of me for longer and in doing so, I hoped I could work out where we'd taken this thing between us to, last night.

Luke looked down as he shrugged his shoulders and then let go of a long exhale. I followed his gaze with my own and saw him take the couple of steps needed to come alongside Brie. His hand lifted and I jumped at the sudden connection of his finger and thumb as they gently caught hold of my chin and he lifted my eyes to meet his. My heart leapt, as I realised that he was still willing to touch me in front of Brie.

'Not so good.' He shook his head.

'No?' I questioned, almost afraid to ask why.

'No… It started off with a fantastic bang and then went downhill fast.' The grin on his face was infectious.

I smiled back at him.

'But I thought you all had company?' I enquired.

'Yeah, we have, I suppose they still do. But it's not the company I wanted.'

'No?' My voice sounded hesitant as I asked the question.

'No.'

'Oh.'

'So, it's been total shit,' he whispered as his mouth came down to meet mine and he gently brushed his lips to mine a couple of times, '…but suddenly it's looking up.' He continued with his eyes firmly on mine as he drove his words home.

'Happy Christmas, Luke.' My sister's voice sounded behind me. 'Mum wanted me to ask if you and Brie would like to stay to dinner?'

'Yes, please.' Brie rushed past my legs and into the hallway behind me. I heard her talking to Lou as they disappeared into the back room and once again, we were alone.

'Is that okay?' Luke quietly questioned as he furrowed his brow.

'It's more than okay,' I whispered back as I stood on tiptoe to brush my lips against his to seal my decision.

After taking his hand in mine, I turned to lead the way. As I felt that simple connection between us, it appeared that my earlier worries of what we now were to each other no longer mattered.

Thirty

Nikki

I KNEW, AS I cast my eyes around the table, that this Christmas dinner would forever remain in my head as one of my absolute favourites. Even beating the last one I remember spending with my dad, because it was obvious to me as an adult, that he already had plans in place to leave us. Knowing the raw pain I still occasionally felt, even after all these years of him abandoning us, would soon be showing on my face, I discarded my thoughts and took in the happy faces that surrounded me. Everyone, including Luke, had a paper hat sitting crookedly on their heads, although not surprisingly, on him, it looked like one of the latest fashion accessories.

'Read mine, Daddy, please.' Brie pushed a small rectangular piece of paper under Luke's nose. Suddenly, she was desperate to join in with the rest of us and to add to the laughter. Almost acknowledging what I had just thought, she turned her gaze to us one by one and aimed a beautiful smile to each of us.

'Okay, Shorty,' he agreed as he unravelled the curled up, cream paper in his fingertips. He released an unexpected laugh, when uncharacteristically for a joke from a cracker, it seemed to amuse him. 'Yeah, right... I think you've set me up, Mrs. O.' Luke lifted his eyes fleetingly off the paper and grinned straight over at my mum, who openly swooned.

'I keep saying, Luke, my name is Tina. You make me feel old calling me Mrs. O, I feel like I was married to JFK.'

'What?' Lou questioned, looking bemused.

'Don't worry.' Our mum waved her hand at Lou and laughed as she shook her head.

Luke nodded and although he'd obviously already read the words on the tiny piece of paper, he read them out loud to us all. 'Who's Rudolph's favourite pop star?'

I released a small laugh.

Briefly he lifted his eyes and looked around at us all waiting for an answer. When his eyes fell on mine, my breathing momentarily faltered as I comprehended that my favourite was sitting at my family's table, sharing Christmas with me.

Completely surreal. I managed to stop myself from shaking my head at my thoughts.

'Come on, ladies,' he encouraged. When we all shook our heads at him, he carried on. 'Beyon-sleigh!'

Our table was once again the focal point for family laughter, and I wasn't sure, glancing at the five of us, which one of us appreciated it the most.

After Luke had arrived earlier and been encouraged to spend Christmas day with us, he'd explained that we'd saved him and Brie. Apparently, the atmosphere between Raff and his stepfather was ruining the day. Brody was in an unreachable place after his heartrending fall out with Amy at last night's wedding, and so far, Winter and Lauren had yet to show up. Cade had started drinking early, and him and Flint had disappeared to get in some drum practice, leaving Raff to face his parents. The less than jovial Christmas feeling back at The Manor, had been one of the reasons he'd given in to Brie and brought her over to mine. I think my face must have shown my slight disappointment, so he'd grabbed my hand and after bringing my fingers up to his lips fleetingly, he'd explained that the predominant reason for interrupting my day off was he wanted to see me too.

'Oh, look at the time. The Queen will be on in a few minutes. Leave the plates we can do them later.' My mum pushed her chair backwards after glancing at the wall clock.

'I'm happy to clean up,' Luke offered as he followed my mum's move and stood.

'No, I couldn't let you.' A look of absolute horror consumed my mum's face.

'Why?' Luke grinned at her knowing exactly why. 'You've been good enough to allow me and Brie to crash your Christmas, it's the least I can do.'

'But you're...' Mum began.

'Mrs. O.' Mum lifted her hand at Luke to stop him. 'Sorry... Tina,' he carried on. 'It's just that I remember having this exact conversation with your daughter over a week ago... I might be in a band, but that's just the way I earn my living. It doesn't make me a better or worse person than anyone else. You made the dinner, *so* I can clean up.'

Mum started nodding in acceptance at his words.

'There's not much I can say to that, is there? A point well made, Luke... Just so you understand, you and Brie are always welcome here. Especially after your offer of cleaning up.' Mum smiled at them both. 'I have to warn you, though, we don't have a dishwasher. Washing up is done by hand in this house.'

Standing, I started to collect the plates together as I watched on, amused at the conversation between them.

'I'm sure I'll manage,' Luke added, as he took a stack of plates from in front of me. 'My job back in the orphanage was to scrape and wash the plates. So, it might have been a while, but I'm an expert.'

'Oh.' I had known instantly that Mum had liked what she'd found in Luke when they'd met earlier that day, but the added information he'd just given her, gave her expression a further softness. 'I'm sure you are.' She pushed her chair into the table and walked towards the door that led out into our hallway, so she could watch the Queen on TV in the living room. Just as her hand reached the doorhandle, she turned back. 'It's been a pleasure having your company today, Luke and Brielle... And lovely getting to know you, Luke especially, when it feels like you've been living in this house with us for years.'

He glanced over at me and rolled his eyes up high into his forehead. 'Sorry, if Nikki played us all the time,' he laughed.

'No, I didn't mean the music.' She smiled at him before continuing. 'It's your face, it's plastered all over her bedroom walls. It's as though you've always belonged here.'

Way to go, Mum.

Mum disappeared, and the remaining adult eyes left in the room fell on me. It was my turn to roll my eyes and let out a long sigh, before I felt my shoulders slump in resignation. I wasn't sure what happened first. I heard the plates Luke was holding connect once again with the table and at the same time I noticed him moving quickly towards the door my mum had just gone out of.

'No!' left my mouth, as the realisation of just what he was about to do washed over me.

'I think perhaps we should play a game. What do you think, Brie?' Lou asked with a hint of laughter in her tone. Brie excitedly replied, but I was too focussed on stopping Luke to concentrate on her words.

Suddenly, we were both scrambling to see who would make it to the door handle first. Of course, Luke made it and before I knew it, he was flying up the steep, narrow staircase in our end of terrace home. The reverberations our feet made banging on the stairs shook through the house.

'Please don't,' I shouted out, as I heard the television in the living room coming to life.

He turned his head backwards just the once and winked at me. I knew I had seen most of his many looks, but as the playful sparkle in his eyes hit me, I understood I'd only ever seen this one once before; on the snow-covered hill we'd rolled down together. Although my worst nightmare was just about to unfold before my eyes, somehow, I knew that if this was what I had to relinquish to be the person he was prepared to direct his unfiltered joy at, I couldn't have cared less.

Lost in my thoughts and not concentrating fully on the job in hand, I slipped on a couple of the stairs. Laughing at my predicament as I lay out prone on the carpet, I smacked out at the back of his legs to get him to stop.

'A gentleman would stop and help a lady up.'

'I'm no fucking gentleman, darlin'.' Although I couldn't see his expression, I could imagine the wicked gleam in his eyes as his words came back at me. All the while, I could hear him laughing. The awareness that I was getting to see a part of his personality that I knew for certain only a few others would have ever seen before, was heart-warming.

'No, Luke. Stop!' I shouted out, already knowing it was in vain.

'The Queen is talking. Please quieten it down out there to a dull roar,' my mum screamed out.

'Yeah, ssshhh.' Luke disappeared from my view as he reached the top of the stairs and disappeared around the corner.

By the time I got back up on my feet and reached the corner, he'd already vanished into a room. I made it to mine and after seeing he wasn't inside, I closed the door. I'd only just managed to grip on to either side of the doorframe, when he slowly appeared from Lou's room.

The landing at the top of our stairs was only a small space which led to four doors, but with Luke now standing in it and making small steps to where he knew I was blocking him from, all the air seemed to have dissipated.

'Please don't do this,' I begged.

'Nikki,' he laughed. 'I love to hear you begging.' His arms, which were hanging down either side of his body, opened, effectively caging me in. In those few seconds, I recognised his demeanour had completely changed and in that small space he made me feel like I was being pursued. 'But beg all you like... You *know* I've got to see it.'

'No, you really haven't.'

I watched mesmerised as he brought one hand up to his face, began to stroke his fingers through his beard and leant his head over to one side as he pretended to think things over.

'Now, darlin', we can do this the easy way, or the hard way.' He released his hold on his beard and stepped into my personal space, grabbed my hips, and pulled me to him. The millisecond his hard body collided into mine, my body sagged, relieved to feel him once again against me.

'And if I get to choose... I prefer the hard way.' He rocked his body against mine, making sure I felt the hardness of his erection.

'You don't play fair.' I placed my arms around his shoulders and felt one of his arms come tightly around my waist as he lifted my feet up and away from the floor.

'I never said I did.'

His mouth came down to mine and I was lost, all other thoughts vanished from my head. It was only when I came to again, I became aware of the fact he was moving me backwards. We came to a standstill and gently he lifted his lips away from mine. My eyes sprung open, and

I observed as his began to open, and then as his head lifted to take in my shame.

'Jesus fucking H,' Luke whispered, as with one arm still holding tightly around my waist, he started to turn us both around on the spot.

'Oh no.' I dipped my head to his chest as I attempted to hide.

'I don't think... well...' he offered. 'Well, I thought somewhere in the world this room might exist.' He shook his head as the ghost of a smile moved over his mouth. 'I just never thought I'd damn well see it.'

'It's embarrassing. But in my defence, I haven't lived here for a *very* long time...'

'That's a given, but you must stay here for the odd night.'

'Well, yes.' I was fighting to work out exactly what he was thinking, and I couldn't bear to think how ridiculous he must think I was.

'I'll make you a deal, darlin'.'

I lifted my head away from his chest to look at him properly and felt my brow furrow as I silently questioned his words.

'A deal?

'Yeah.'

He dipped his head until his beard brushed against my ear, deliberately. The connection sent sparks of need exploding throughout my body.

'Now, I'm standing in my idea of hell. But somehow, it's okay, because it's with you.' I felt his shoulders shrug. 'So, back to doing this the hard way... you tell me exactly which picture you masturbated to on those odd nights back home, and I'll *try* to forget what I've seen in this room.'

My traitorous eyes immediately darted to the picture right beside my bed and Luke followed my gaze with his own.

'Well, fuck, there really is one.' He released a small laugh and then his mouth found its way down to my neck, where he began to nibble at my needy flesh. In an obviously planned move, he turned us both around and, in an instant, I was falling backwards onto my single bed closely followed by him. Somehow, he controlled the weight of his body until at last, it collided with mine. Instinctively, I tightened my hold around him.

'What does he do to you when you're lying here in the dark?' Luke questioned, as he shifted his weight onto one elbow and stared purposefully down at me, waiting for me to answer him.

'He touches me,' I whispered back, without any hesitation.

'I can understand why, I love touching you… You're so damn responsive.' Luke used his index finger and drew it gently around my mouth. 'But where does he touch you?' Luke's beautiful green eyes came back from following the path of his finger. As they found mine once again, I saw they had started to darken as they began to dilate. I was hypnotised and knew I would tell him anything he wanted to know.

'His fingers thread in my hair.'

'Yeah.' His fingers touched the hair at the back of my neck and made my breathing falter. 'And?'

'His mouth sucks my nipples. He kisses and bites his way down my body until he's resting between my legs.'

Who the hell am I?

'Mmmm, I can taste you, darlin'… and you're mighty fine…' He ran his tongue around his mouth just the once. 'And?'

'His cock fills me, stretching me until I'm full. Then he rocks in and out of me, until I'm slick with both of our orgasms.'

'Well, fuck…' I saw Luke's eyes open wide and his Adam's apple bob as he swallowed abruptly. He exhaled sharply, trying to force down the lust that had risen quickly between us. A grin finally appeared on his face, and he rocked his erection into my pelvic mound. 'That was the best story… But how's reality?' he questioned, as he deliberately rose onto both of his elbows and moved a piece of hair off my face to get a better look at me.

'Not sure,' I turned my head, and ran one finger down the picture of Luke to the side of me. Then I looked back at him. 'You see he was pretty damn good and I'm still checking out your skills.'

'You wound me,' Luke smirked.

'All I'm saying is, I'll need many more examinations and demonstrations of your skills to make a comparison.' I smiled sweetly at him and pulled his mouth to mine to brush my lips gently over his.

As our lips parted, I watched as a pained expression took over his features.

'Is it bad, Nikki, that I wanna fuck you in this bed?' he rested his forehead to mine and let out a loud exhale.

'Everyone's here,' I managed to whisper back, knowing I wouldn't take much convincing myself. As if he could read my mind, Luke's mouth kissed its way back down to underneath my jawbone. The attention he lavished on the sensitive skin made my eyelids droop and a sigh released from my lips.

'Mmmm.' He raised his head from my neck and lifted his eyebrows at me. 'I think I'm gonna need to find an excuse to get you back to the hotel tonight.'

I studied him closely and shook my head at him.

'I think we need to get back downstairs.' I reluctantly said the words that needed saying.

'Really?' He winced at me.

'Really.'

'Hey, upstairs,' Lou shouted up, as if on cue. 'Mum's ready to make the toast.'

'Okay,' I shouted back. Then I whispered to the man in my arms. 'We need to go back down.'

'Very reluctantly, I agree… I'm just not sure I can face being in your living room with your mom, knowing what I did to you in there only last night… I'm gonna be getting flashbacks.'

Grinning at the look of total horror covering my face, he stood up and pulled me up into his arms.

'Behave, that's all I ask.' I smacked a reprimanding hand against his chest.

'Everyone got a glass?' My mum questioned.

'I have,' Brie answered, holding her glass full of elderflower and pear sparkling water.

'Then let's raise our glasses… to family.'

Mum deliberately looked at Luke and Brie before lifting her glass to sip at the Prosecco inside.

'To family,' Lou and I repeated.

Luke silently sipped from his glass, and I noticed his posture was slightly stiffer, before he mumbled under his breath, 'To family.'

'And to those we love who aren't lucky enough to be with us celebrating here today.' Mum added.

'To Mummy. She isn't here.' Brie spoke out loud and clear and after a couple of seconds of stunned silence we joined in her toast.

'And to Stephen.' My mum toasted again as tears formed in her eyes. We followed her lead and then made to move over to hug her, but she shook her head at both Lou and I and after clearing her throat, she placed her glass back down and looked at Brie.

'So, come on then… what game are we playing, Brie?'

Thirty-One

LUKE

'THANKS AGAIN.' I WOUND my arms around Nikki and after placing my hands on the round globes of her ass, I pulled her against me, shifting my feet in the couple of inches of snow beneath my boots. Then I leant my back against the Land Rover that I'd just placed my sleeping daughter into.

'I've just spent the best Christmas day I can remember for a long time, with most of the people who mean anything to me.' Nikki looked up at me, as she wound her arms around my neck and linked her fingers together. 'And you and Brie made my mum's day by turning up today. So seriously, no thanks are needed.'

I smiled down at her and kissed the tip of her nose.

'That's a headline I've never read before... Jaded, ex-addict, asshat of a Rockstar makes someone's day.' I lifted one hand, as I pretended to light up the words between my thumb and forefinger in the cold wintery looking sky, which for the first time ever I noticed was dotted with thousands of bright stars. Replacing my hand, I squeezed the globes of her fine ass, trying to ground myself with something I fully understood; lust. My nostrils flared as I inhaled quickly, as the virtually unrecognisable feeling continued to rush through me and I struggled to cope with the sensation.

Resting my chin on the top of Nikki's head, I held on to her tightly and hoped to give myself a few minutes reprieve.

What the fuck? Whatever this was, I knew it was about so much more than sex.

Cade and the others had often, in the past couple of years, talked about how brilliant and equally how fucking dire coming back to life had felt. The years we'd spent since battling our addictions to various fucking shit we'd been into. The same shit we'd used to blur the edges of our lives and to try to forget our histories that we weren't ready to, or still weren't able to, cope with. I'd even taken in how hard it had been for the three of them to face the pain of their pasts once again, as their emotions, no longer muted by the lines of charlie, smack and bottles of bourbon, once again took a firm fucking grip over them.

Some days had been so torturous, that they'd struggled to shake themselves free, and in others they'd experienced such extreme highs, they'd grappled inside themselves to deal with their consciousness.

But I was different. Mainly, I'd just been undeservedly numb.

I'd recognised the torture. I'd even embraced the goddamn pain and let the ugly fucking bitch sink her sharp, scarring talons deep into my flesh, where she had taken a permanent hold. My own punishment had been the acceptance that I needed a constant reminder of what it felt like to have had a hand in being the catalyst of someone else's demise. I didn't deserve to feel anything other than the anguish and subsequent numbness that came with a heavy burden of guilt. Sure, I'd also experienced small moments of elation. But I'd only allowed it to come in the achievements of my beautiful daughter, and for a couple of hours here and there with the women I'd fucked. The same ones I hadn't allowed myself to get close to, no matter how hard they'd tried.

I'd had my reasons why.

Number one was Cherise. Two was Cherise. Three was that I didn't deserve to and four... well, four was that Brie wasn't ready for me to.

Or maybe they had all been an excuse; and I hadn't wanted to.

Well, I'm damn well ready now.

I exhaled a sigh and breathed in the warm air coming away from Nikki's comforting body.

I'd been clean for a long time, but my sole focus had been on Brielle and making sure I didn't fuck up her life. Swearing to myself that history wouldn't repeat itself. Promising to make sure she had exactly what she needed. Because there was no way she was going to, somewhere down the line, feel the need to blur the fucking edges of her life.

I'd thought what I'd been doing was the right thing, but after meeting Nikki, things now just didn't add up. I'd always known that Brie needed more, but now, so did I. After far too many years to count, I was going through the elation they'd said came with the experience of living life again. I wasn't experiencing it because my beautiful daughter had accomplished something amazing, but because I was allowing myself to live.

Right here, with this young woman who'd ridden into my life, and it now seemed was cracking the ice around my frozen heart with a sledgehammer, I was goddamn feeling; and I was scared as fuck.

I might have had severe doubts about many of the decisions I'd made in my life. To the point that only moving to Vegas, forming Default Distraction, holding my new-born daughter against my bare chest, and choosing to move to England, made any sense to me at all some days. But I knew, deep in my heart, that I had to have Nikki in my life. Somehow, I had to convince her to stay.

Brie needed her, I wanted her.

But I needed her even more.

She had to stay, I couldn't lose her after only just finding her, but I hadn't got the tools in my arsenal to explain that to her.

So, how the fuck?

I felt my body stiffen in reaction to my thoughts and fears. I was no longer the rich, successful Rockstar woman threw themselves at, I was just a man holding a woman in his arms and literally fighting to work out how I would survive if she too left me.

A fatalistic meeting? Brody's voice sounded inside my head.

'You made my family's Christmas. Having you and Brie here has brightened our day. We always struggle like many families at Christmas time.' Nikki's voice sounded and I watched as her words travelled up and into the night in a cloud of warmth.

I heard her, and intrigued, I tried to shelve my own thoughts and moved my head to look back down into her swirling grey eyes that now seemed to be filled with tears.

'Yeah?'

'Mmmm hmmm,' she admitted as she sucked her bottom lip into her mouth.

'Care to expand?'

I watched her shoulders shrug slightly and as she tore her emotional looking eyes away from mine.

'It's nothing other families don't have to deal with.'

'And?' I persuaded.

'Oh, okay. Long story short, our dad walked out on us when it became apparent that our little brother had something wrong with him and he never came back.'

Fucking asshat. I was too well acquainted with the feeling of being deserted, but to have been left to cope with three young kids, when you'd thought up until then you were part of a solid unit, well my gut burnt with anger for Mrs. O... Tina. I already liked the woman I'd only met that day, but now she'd shot straight to the top of my respect list, and it was a fucking small list.

I understood I was a lot of things, but I knew I'd never stoop that fucking low.

Reluctantly, I released Nikki's ass, as it no longer felt appropriate to still be squeezing it. After wrapping one arm tightly around her waist, I placed my other fingers on her chin and tipped her head back so I could rest my forehead gently against hers, effectively trapping her gaze with my own. With her eyes back on mine I started speaking.

'Everyone has their own hurt to carry, darlin'... You're allowed to feel and acknowledge that emotion.' I could hear my therapist inside my head as I spoke his words to her. It was fucking weird that this was the first time they'd ever really made any sense to me. 'Everyone else having their own history and pasts, doesn't make yours any less.'

'I know, but I hate wallowing in self-pity.' She tried to smile, but I wasn't convinced at her brush off or excuse. 'Anyway, I wanted to let you know that you two, being here today, gave us something else to focus on and that meant a lot...' She began to fidget in my hold. 'Enough about me... I'll see you the day after Boxing Day, I know you need to get Brie home.'

I felt myself grimace as I shook my head slightly at her and then as my arms tightened instinctively around her.

'Nah... you're not getting rid of me that easily.'

Fear sparked in her eyes, and it was one I instantly recognised. It was the same one that I knew if I looked in a mirror, I'd see reflected back at me, when I was challenged about still carrying the hurt and guilt I felt over Cherise. But even though I still struggled with being confronted, I knew I was going to do exactly that to her. I had Nikki tightly in my hold and I wasn't going to be letting her go anytime soon.

'I take it your brother is the Stephen your mum made a toast to?'

'Yes.'

I shifted my feet in the snow, feeling the cold filtering through the thick soles of my boots and the fear enter my system of asking the next question.

'Is he dead?'

I knew the answer before she spoke the words, as her face softened and relief swept through me as she started to shake her head against mine.

'No, he's remarkable. His long-term prognosis isn't great, but each day he battles on to stay here with us and to enjoy the time he has left.'

'What's wrong with him, will you tell me?'

'He has a condition called Duchenne Muscular Dystrophy.'

I knew nothing about the condition her younger brother had, so I quietly stood there holding her tightly as she explained that her little brother had a condition that meant his life would be shortened because of it. 'DMD is something we all know far too much about. It presented itself within the first few years of Stephen's life and he was diagnosed when he was young, after he'd failed to reach some age-appropriate milestones.'

'Does he know?' I reluctantly asked, trying to sift through the stuff in my head to work out what I thought I knew about his illness.

I came up with a big fat nothing.

'He's well aware of his prognosis, and I hate that.' Her hands moved from behind my neck and fixed themselves into position on my shoulders. 'It's bad enough knowing we're going to lose him a lot sooner than we want to, but to see the occasional sadness seep into his eyes and then as he bravely makes it go away so he doesn't upset us, is soul destroying.'

'Shit!' I exhaled loudly. 'I can't even imagine.'

'The place where he lives take great care of him, I really can't fault them. But he is having problems breathing after his last chest infection and we know his time with us is short. He also knows it to; I can see it in his eyes.'

'That's a lot to deal with,' I offered, feeling fucking impotent at her family's situation. The same family who had taken my daughter and me in that day to share their Christmas celebrations with no hesitancy. My history had shown me that these sorts of people, the ones who did something for others with absolutely no agenda, were few and far between.

'I just wish we were rich... if we had enough money, we could build an extension onto the side of our house that could be adapted to have Stephen live with us. As his family, we could offer him so much more and it's my mum's dream to be able to help care for him in our home, with help from carers, of course.'

Instinctively, I looked up at the side of their house. Even I could see that it would be easy to double the size of the place. 'Can't you get help to do that?' I questioned, as my eyes found hers again.

'We could get a small amount from our local authority. It would be enough to buy the equipment Stephen has to have, but there would be nothing left to fund a build with.' I could sense I was pushing her to somewhere uncomfortable, but an idea was beginning to formulate inside my head.

Suddenly, I was the one with a fucking agenda.

'How much would it cost to build?'

'No idea... the last time we looked into it, it was around two hundred thousand.'

'You wouldn't know this, but to offset against tax, me and the guys have a charity running in the U.S. to help out with things like this.'

'Oh my God... I wasn't telling you my life story to get charity.' Reluctantly, I let her move a little away from me as her cheeks heated up and her body language showed she needed the space between us. Slowly, she begun to shake her head at me.

'I know,' I assured her, nodding as I tried to encourage her to keep talking.

'I was telling you... well, because...' She sighed and the blush on her cheeks grew. I knew it was a serious conversation we were having, but I could feel the corners of my mouth twitching as she grew uncomfortable trying to find the words. 'I was telling you because you're my friend.' Her shoulders slumped and I couldn't stop the smile that now stretched across my face due to her embarrassment at not being able to find the words to explain what we were.

We're every fucking thing, darlin'. I heard my thought, and effectively shelved it, because I knew it was too soon to voice it.

'Bloody hell,' she began again, 'that sounds even worse… please, just forget I said anything. My mum would hate for me to be asking for charity.'

She began to try to move from my hold.

'Why be embarrassed? A lot of people need help. My birth mom needed help.' I knew I was an asshole, in using my status as an orphan, but hell, it had to have some fucking advantages.

'Yes, of course they do.' She nodded and I could see in her eyes that hearing my last statement had swayed her thoughts a little. Without giving my head permission, my words backfired on me. I thought back to my birth mom and her leaving me to become a foundling, on a cold step, on a night much like the one we were standing in right now, and I tensed, bracing myself against the pain that began to unravel. When it came, but with a much lesser degree than normal, I knew it was because Nikki was with me.

She has to stay.

'And you should never be afraid to ask… especially from a *friend*.' I grinned as I turned her terminology right back at her.

'My mum would never forgive me.'

I was adamant I was going to get her what her family needed and fuck it, I was going to get what I needed too.

'Then, okay, let's not go down the "charity" route. I have a business proposition for you, instead.' I tilted my head to one side as I captured her eyes with mine and refused to let her tear them away. For my own singular personal gain, I made sure I was using everything I'd spent years refining in front of thousands of generally screaming women. I flashed her the smile I already knew set her body alight and lifted one hand to cup the back of her neck.

'A business proposition?' I saw intrigue as well as desire encapsulated in her eyes as she breathlessly questioned.

'Yeah… you give me what I want, and I'll give you what you say your family need.'

My heart had accelerated and was now thumping in my chest. I knew I was tantalisingly close to having the first thing I'd really wanted in my life for a long fucking time.

I felt her body stiffen in my arms.

'What?'

With a small smile, I started to try to explain something, which I had a feeling the happiness of my mine and Brie's future suddenly depended on.

'Stay... Fuck it, Nikki, tell me you'll stay with *me*.' Without thinking over my body language, I removed my hand from her neck and placed my palm over my heart. After her eyes had followed my movement, I wrapped it back around her waist. 'Stay and be Brie's nanny for the five years I originally asked for, and I'll advance you fifty percent of your five-year salary.'

'You want me to stay for Brie that much, that you'd give me the money early?' I watched as her lips parted a little as she thought over my sudden proposal.

'Yeah, but I also want you to stay for me,' I confided in her, and unable to bare the weight of her eyes on mine any longer, I placed a kiss to the tip of her nose. Then looking up to the stars, I blew out my apprehension that she might refuse into the night sky.

'But, Luke. What if...'

My eyes found hers again quickly. Grudgingly, I released one arm from around her and placed one finger to her lips and shook my head gently at her.

'What if... Darlin', the world is full of what ifs. You said yesterday you trusted me enough to risk everything... so prove it.' I swallowed down just how much her choosing me would mean.

Nikki blinked a few times as she tried to process what I'd offered her.

'But...' she started to protest.

'Question is, Nikki. Do you *really* trust me?' I cocked my head to one side and looked at her questioningly.

'Yes,' she implored.

'Then prove it, let's do this. You give me the five years and the security I need for Brie, and I'll give you the advance of salary you can use to get what you and your family want for Stephen. And the bonus is, we also get each other.'

Her hands tightened around the back of my neck, and I watched her nod her head, slowly at first and then with increasing vigour, until reality swept in, and she froze.

'For how long? And what do we do when...' She voiced her fears.

I placed my finger to her lips to effectively silence her. I knew what she was asking, but hell, as I hadn't got an answer, I couldn't let her finish.

'Life isn't a guarantee, you have to learn to live with the now.'

'I know.' She nodded again; the movement overly exaggerated as she tried hard to convince herself. 'Okay.'

I bent my knees and moved my hands to either side of her face, trapping her gently as I stared pointedly into her eyes.

'Okay?' I checked one last time, 'So, that's a yes?'

Elation built up inside me.

'That's a yes.' She nodded just the once in my hands.

YES!

I moved my mouth back over hers to seal our agreement, but mainly I kissed her because I knew it was exactly what we both needed.

Hell, it was what I needed.

Thirty-Two

Nikki

S
LEEP WASN'T REALLY HAPPENING. I'd tried over and over to get myself comfortable, but however much I'd fidgeted, it had all been in vain.

My head refused to switch off.

I rolled onto my back, pulled my arms out of my quilt and after lifting them up high, I thumped them down on the bed either side of me in exasperation.

For the first time, I allowed my eyes to travel over the many different silhouettes of Luke McKenzie, but it wasn't enough, I needed to see him for real. My heart was pounding as anxiety and excitement rushed around my system.

Lifting one hand, I reached behind me to feel for the switch to my bedside light. I squeezed my eyes tightly shut as my small room was bathed in a bright, yellow light. Then slowly, after taking a deep breath,

I opened my eyes and took in the man who graced my walls and I thought over the previous week of my life.

Just what had I agreed to?

'Enough,' I whispered into the cool night air. 'It's all fine. It will all be fine.'

Reaching to my bedside cabinet beside me, I lifted the small piece of rectangular paper. On one side was Brie's Christmas cracker joke and on the other side, Luke had, after he'd kissed me, written,

I'll advance you two hundred and fifty thousand of your salary if you agree to stay.

We'd both signed it and I'd been left staring at the scrap of paper in my hand as he'd pulled slowly out of our lane. I'd still been staring hard at it after his red taillights had disappeared, and even when Lou had come to the front door to call me back indoors and out of the cold.

As I'd turned and walked towards her, I'd tucked the insignificant looking, but immensely powerful piece of paper inside the cuff of my sweatshirt and had met her smile with my own. I'd even managed to sit through a Christmas special with her and our mum. I'd laughed in all the appropriate places, before feigning a headache and going off to my own room.

I knew the paper wasn't legally binding.

But in my mind, it was no less powerful.

I'd managed to get my family exactly what they needed, and at the same time I'd signed myself up to being with a beautiful little girl that I already adored and the man that, until just over a week before, I could only imagine being with in my dreams.

In my wildest dreams.

An awareness prickled over my skin as realisation became my predominant feeling. Our conversation before he'd departed tonight had been that moment. The one I knew I'd been waiting to happen. That blinding sensation that happens when someone walks into your life and life as you knew it transforms into something so perfect you couldn't have imagined it.

I just wasn't sure how the hell I was going to explain it to my mum.

Suddenly, I sat bolt up.

And at the end of the five years, when he let me go, I wasn't sure how the hell I was going to be able to explain it all to myself.

Thirty-Three

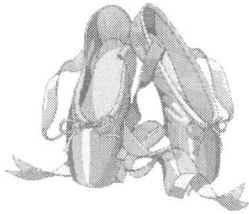

Nikki

'IS THIS GOING TO take very long, Nikki?' My mum dried her hands on the tea towel she was carrying, as I wrung mine with the nerves I was trying so very hard to hide.

Slowly, she took her seat at the table, with only a single glance back at the potatoes she was attempting to mash with cream and butter, ready for our traditional boxing day meal.

'No, it won't,' I answered as assertively as I could without once looking at Louise, who had her eyes firmly fixed on the side of my face. Instead, I looked at Stephen and gave him a broad smile.

His carers had brought him to share our meal with us, but I knew he'd only be here for a couple of hours before they came back to collect him. The conversation we were about to have concerned him more than anyone else in the room.

'Stephen, it's lovely to have you home.' I blew him a kiss and watched as he slowly smiled at me and acknowledged my sentiment.

Then I looked at my sister and mum just the once as I summoned up the courage to start.

'Yesterday evening, as Luke and Brie were leaving, we discussed how important it is to have your family around you.' My mum nodded at what I was saying. 'He, as you know, grew up in an orphanage and Brie's mum died a few years ago.'

'Terrible,' Mum added as she shook her head.

Refusing to be put off from what I'd been practising over and over in my head since I'd sat up in bed in the early hours of the morning, and texted Luke to check I hadn't imagined our conversation, I carried on.

'Luke has offered me a very generous salary and he wants to advance me half, so that we can build onto the house and get you home to be with us, Stephen.' I let out the breath I'd been holding and swallowed down my nerves.

'Half of your salary?' Mum questioned as her eyes widened and she started to dry her already dry hands on the tea towel she was still clutching.

'Yes,' I released more forcefully than I intended.

'I don't know what to say. Your salary is yours.'

That wasn't quite true, but I appreciated the sentiment.

'My new salary is ridiculously high and who better do I have to share it with, than all of you?'

'But one day, you'll want a home of your own, with a family of your own, won't she, Louise?' Mum roped my sister into backing her concerns and arguments up.

'Probably.' Lou spoke one single word and I heard the undisclosed reservation in her voice. I could also tell that Lou was now trying hard to figure out exactly what had happened in my conversation with Luke last night.

'I'm still going to be earning enough money to save for that.' I shrugged as I tried hard to show a relaxed, easy-going posture to my family. Inside, my heart was pounding and blood was whooshing past my eardrums at a ridiculous rate.

'You are?' Happiness shone out of every part of our mum's face as she slowly began to realise that what she wanted more than anything else, could be within her reach. Mum looked at both of us girls, before looking over at our younger brother. He was sat in the only place he could be when he spent time at home. His large, electric wheelchair, which only just fitted down our narrow hallway had been manually backed into the corner of our back room, next to the window which looked out onto the garden.

'Stephen… what do you think?' I couldn't see my mum's face, but I could hear she was fighting back tears.

Suddenly, our room was filled with emotion as we watched and waited for Stephen to reply. He understood us perfectly, but his condition meant his ability to speak easily had been affected.

'I'd—like—to—come—home.' Each word he spoke was slow and very deliberate.

I stood, suddenly eager to put a line under the decision. Moving around the furniture, I hugged Mum on the way past her. 'That's decided then. Now, it's probably best if you get on with finishing the mash, Mum,' I encouraged, before bending over to place a kiss my brother's cheek.

'After dinner, Stephen, you need to help me kick Lou's arse at chess… you up for it.'

'Yes.' Stephen grinned at me in reply.

'Great, okay. I'm just going upstairs for five minutes, I need to check I've packed up everything I need.' The lie came tumbling with ease from my mouth.

I moved quickly, trying to get the hell out of there and had made it halfway up the stairs when I heard Louise's voice behind me.

'Wait up.'

Without turning, I carried on towards my bedroom, needing to get out of the hallway, which was within Mum's earshot, before she started questioning me. I walked into my room and heard the click as Lou closed the door behind her.

'So, Luke has decided to give you half your salary upfront?'

'Yes.' I patted at my bed, in a bid to make it look like I was tidying it but stopped and released a small sigh when I knew I wouldn't fool her. All I was doing was wasting our precious time with Stephen. With that thought in my head, I pulled the scrap of paper out of my jeans pocket and after turning around to face her I offered it to her to read.

Her baby pink-coloured fingernails took what I was offering. I watched her eyes run over the few words a couple of times before her eyes lifted to find mine.

'How long do you have to stay?'

'Five years.' I said it fast.

'You've sold yourself,' she accused.

'I have not!' I said the words with as much vehemence as I could attach to them without, I hoped, being so loud I'd alert Mum.

'Sorry,' she offered, shaking her head and folding her arms over her chest. 'At the very least though, you've signed your life away,' she softly accused.

'Many jobs require you to sign-up for a designated tenure.' I carried on with the arguments I already had in place inside my head.

'Really?' she questioned, with a hint of exasperation escaping in her tone

'Yes, and it would be for much longer if I was going into the military.' I nodded at her enthusiastically.

'But this isn't the military, Nik... you've effectively signed up to look after a little girl and live in the home of a man you've only just recently met.'

'Lou, I appreciate your concern,' I shrugged at her, 'but as a nanny, that is generally how my job works. Only this time we get the bonus of having the money to get Stephen home, which will make Mum happier than I think either of us remember her being.'

'But what about you? You do remember what happened only a few weeks ago in your last placement, don't you?' Her voice had taken on a quiet sort of complacency.

'God, Lou, *this* isn't the same. It's so very different with Luke and I know it's going to be fine.'

'I know, I know.' She threw her hands up in the air, which if she'd been a poker player would be her tell that she was resigned to losing. 'I'm sorry I lumped Luke as another Millar.' She started to nod as she carried on. 'I've seen the way he looks at you, Nikki. He wants you even more than he needs a nanny for Brie... But what I'm really worried about is... well, have you thought about what happens when it's over?'

I shook my head at her, before walking towards her and taking her in my arms. Postponing the fear that was already in the forefront of my mind, I wrapped my arms tightly around her and spoke over her shoulder, the words Luke had spoken to me.

'Life is a risk, there are no guarantees with anything, are there? I was with Lewis for years, but that didn't stop him shagging that skank, did it? And I want to live, Nikki. I want to take the chance... Please don't tell Mum, don't spoil it, you know she'll refuse it if she finds out. Let me get this for Mum and Stephen and let me do this for me...

because if Tom Hardy came calling for you with a similar proposition, I'm convinced you'd want to do the same thing.'

'Probably,' she whispered on a sigh.

'Definitely.' I smiled as I replied, knowing I'd won her over.

'Although, I'd demand a penthouse in London and annual income.' Her hands strengthened their hold on my back, before she moved herself to look at me once again. 'I could get you more you know... This isn't worth the paper it's written on,' she carried on, resigned to my decision.

'I know, but I don't want anymore. I've always wanted him; it's always been him and for however long it lasts, it seems he also wants me.'

Thirty-Four

LUKE

'FIVE... SIX... SEVEN... EIGHT... nine... ten... sssshhhhh.'
I let out the last count as my chin touched the bar I was
holding tightly in my grip. Then, watching myself in the
floor to ceiling mirror, I used the negative repetition and lowered
myself slowly to the sprung flooring we'd had laid in the hotel's gym.
My biceps were burning, and I slowed the movement down to virtually
nothing, making my arms begin to shake with the exertion of holding
my own weight. I felt the rivers of sweat careering down my back and
watched my nostrils flare as I exhaled. And all the while, I absorbed the
numbness, the control it gave me, and I savoured the feeling.

Finally, my bare feet touched the cool floor. I bent at the waist and
shook out my arms in front of me to remove the lactic acid I knew was
building up inside my tired muscles. Then I retrieved the towel I'd

brought with me off the floor and after wiping over my face, I threw it back down and walked over to the leg press.

Standing next to the machine, I took a quick look at my watch and worked out I had roughly thirty minutes left before Brie woke up, if she stuck to her normal schedule. I wasn't worried about her. I knew if she woke up early and couldn't find me in my bed, she'd make her way into one of the other's rooms to find an uncle to fix her some breakfast, and this morning I knew she'd have a choice, because at least two of them hadn't had a woman sharing their beds last night, so it was all good. Or not, depending on how you looked at it.

I released a small laugh into the large, mainly empty space.

But Brody and Raff's loss, meant I was able to make the most of getting a little downtime to myself.

Truth was I hadn't slept much last night, and I'd woken up early with a hard-on that I knew wasn't going to subside anytime fucking soon. I'd been dreaming I had Nikki in my bed. Hell, I could still smell her sweet pussy, and taste her skin on my tongue long after I'd opened my eyes. I'd lay there in the darkness and working my hand up and down the length of my shaft, I'd tried to get some relief before I made my way to the shower. In my head, I'd replayed Christmas Eve, and it was one hell of a mistake. I imagined I heard her cry out as her orgasm convulsed through her beautiful body and suddenly, I couldn't hold out any longer. I blew my load into my other hand like some fucking teenager. After getting out of bed and cleaning up, my erection had appeared again as thoughts of Nikki came rushing back. The way she responded to me, and how good it felt being inside her, and I'd decided my only option was to try to work her out of my system in the gym.

So far, it wasn't fucking working. My head was consumed with thoughts of her, and I'd been sporting a fucking semi for the duration of my workout.

I couldn't wait to see her. It had been less than thirty-six hours since I'd pulled away from her home on Christmas evening and it felt like a year.

I missed her, simple as.

Her contract stated that after any day off she'd be back with us around breakfast time the next morning. I knew that whatever happened today, she was going to spend tonight in my bed. I'd been so fucking caught up in imagining how it would feel to savour every delectable part of her, as I cleaned my teeth, that I had to rub another one out in a freezing cold shower before I even made it downstairs to the gym.

Lifting my water bottle, I drank down a few mouthfuls to rehydrate before I started on the next piece of equipment and thought back to the day before.

I'd caught up with Brody and Raff, as we'd spent time together with the kids on our first Boxing Day in England. We'd played games in the morning, on Flint's new X-Box and even a couple of traditional board games Raff's parents had bought for Brie for Christmas. Then, trying to avoid the company of Raff's stepfather, we'd taken the kids and dog out after lunch for a snowball fight.

We'd had a good time, just messing about in the snow. Raff and Brody had even laughed a few times as they managed for a few hours to forget how their lives had turned to shit over the previous few days. I was riding a huge fucking high, and after getting a text from Nikki that afternoon, saying her family wanted to accept what I was offering, I'd felt like I'd put in a nickel, pulled the lever, and won the fucking jackpot.

Cade had turned up later in the afternoon, while we were all being subjected to watching Brie's favourite film yet again, wearing a smug ass grin. I'd watched him closely as I cuddled my daughter to my chest. At first, he'd cooked s'mores on the open fire in the room we'd commandeered for our Christmas celebrations. He'd then sat quietly staring into space, rolling his dice around in his hand as he thought. He was playing his cards close to his chest, but I could tell he had made better progress with Winter than he was prepared to share, probably because Raff and Brody were so fucking pissed with their own lives.

I was happy for him, but jealous as fuck because I'd have given anything to have spent the day with Nikki.

Jealousy? It was a new one on me, like every other thing Nikki seemed to bring into my life. My own reflection, in one of the mirrors that covered the gym walls, caught my eye. I grinned and shook my head at myself

'Get on with it, Mac.' I spoke the words quietly to myself.

I pulled out the pin on the leg press and after moving it down a few weights, I pushed it home at the four hundred kilograms.

'Paul, can you put on **Radioactive** by **Imagine Dragons?'** I shouted out to the manager; the only other person in the gym. I watched his reflection give me the thumbs up, before he wandered into the office. The system that was quietly playing in the background increased in sound. 'Volume, please,' I shouted.

As the music filled the room, I let the bass fill me up inside, and losing myself to the stress of the music, I jumped up on the machine and followed the distinct beat I knew the album offered and began to use it to do my reps.

With my eyes closed, I pushed out my first set and after slugging back some more water from my bottle beside me, I began to push out my next as I sung loudly along.

'Hey, dude.' I heard Cade's voice, but knowing he'd make his way over to where I was, I stayed in the zone and continued to focus on the job in hand. Carrying on, I drove my legs forward as I gripped tightly to the bars either side of me.

'You're a fucking beast... four hundred?'

I heard the asshat and after lowering the weights, with a resounding clank of the heavy metal plates closing together, I opened my eyes and turned to fix him with a look.

'Whatdaya want?' I couldn't help a grin forming.

'I came to bow down to your strength, man... I mean that weight is almost half what I can press.'

'Fuck off, Morello. What are you now, goddamn Thor?'

'That's one of the many things the ladies call me as they *love* my large hammer.' He flexed his hips forward. In response, I stuck two fingers to the back of my throat and pretended to gag.

I shook my head at him as I laughed. 'You look like shit, you smell like shit and you're still wearing yesterday's clothes, so which member of the fan club's bed did you just roll out of?'

'Bed? Who said anything about a fucking bed?' He grinned at me.

'How's Winter?' I questioned, raising my eyebrows at him.

I watched as he touched his nose, telling me to mind my own business. Cade sounded a click in his mouth as he sucked in his cheek and unknowingly acknowledged that I'd hit the nail on the head. Then he shook his head at me, refusing to put what I'd already guessed into words.

'In your own time, man.' I nodded at him and pushing my back flat against the support behind me, I started on my third set. 'So, you still haven't said what you want?'

'The reason I'm down here, according to you, smelling and looking like shit.' I looked at him out of the corner of my eyes, as I pushed my legs out straight and expelled a lungful of air through my clenched teeth on a sharp hiss. 'Is because, as I arrived back here about twenty minutes ago, Raff was talking to Lawson. And Lawson wants to talk to us all.'

I shook my head at the mention of our manager and let out an over exaggerated sigh. We all knew he was the best in the business, but that didn't stop the bile rising to the back of my throat when I heard his name, or had to have any dealings with him. In fact, most of the time I was surprised we still employed the fucker. We were as solid as bands went and loved each other like brothers, but none of us had anything less than an irritated annoyance at the man who had been with us since the beginning, and most of the time we held an intense hatred of him. But somehow, the intense hatred we had for the guy seemed to work for us all. We recognised he worked hard, because the asshat coveted money more than anything else in his life. We also appreciated that we probably wouldn't be anywhere near as successful without his input. He was the one who had made things happen for us. We'd joked for years that he was more fucking machine than man and he'd certainly made us work for everything we had, and at times too fucking hard.

Somehow the love-hate relationship we'd had for as far back as I remembered, had driven us to be one of the best-selling bands in the world. He was a cat with nine lives, and we knew he'd used most of them on the fucking shit he'd pulled from time to time to gain more publicity, or to talk us into a deal we weren't happy about. But somehow his plans had always got the desired results and I'm sure that's why he still had his job. He was yet another toxic relationship in my life, but one I had more control over than the one I'd had with Cherise.

I'd made peace with the fact that we didn't need to like him, we just had to put up with him.

'Yeah, how the hell did he get him to answer? I thought we were effectively ignoring him for at least the rest of the holidays.'

'The cunt called Flint's cell, knowing the kid would pick up to his grandfather and obviously he also knew when he asked to speak to Raff, Flint would find him.'

I was the one who held the biggest fucking grudge. I had a memory like an elephant. I was convinced that even though I'd been in a drug induced fog for a few years, that he'd been the one to out Cherise, when we'd found the paparazzi waiting for us as I'd picked her up from her second stint in rehab. The photo of the two us leaving the back entrance of the building, had found its way to the front of every single paper in the US, just as our thirteenth single "Going Nuclear" released, driving it straight to the top of the charts. Since that sort of thing was just his style.

'Asshat... what's he after?'

'No idea. He's calling back in thirty.'

The cell started vibrating and travelling across the glass top of the table. One by one we all grinned at each other childishly, as Lawson's face lit up the screen. We let it ring until it rung off, knowing we would be annoying the hell out of him by not immediately jumping when he clicked his fingers.

When it started again, Raff placed his finger to the screen, refused the video call and slid his finger over the bar to accept the audio.

'Yo,' Brody shouted.

'Daniels,' Lawson replied, 'are all four of you there?'

One by one we all replied.

'Had you accepted the video, I wouldn't have to ask...'

'Apparently, I look like shit...' Cade laughed, 'and we didn't want to upset your delicate stomach.'

'Morello, I've seen your tongue in more than one groupie's asshole, you should have thought about what you censored from me years ago.'

Ain't that the fucking truth.

None of us verbally replied, but I knew the same thought was inside all our heads as we looked up from the cell and at each other.

'Hope you all had a good Christmas?'

'We did,' Brody offered, even though it was more or less a lie, as far as he was concerned. The years had taught us to only let Lawson have necessary information.

'I've got good news... Congratulations, Default Distraction has just been confirmed as the winners of best all-time single with "Regret," in the US Rock Ballad Nominations.'

We looked up from the cell and at each other, as we silently congratulated each other with a smile and a nod of appreciation. I reached out and slapped Brody on the back.

'They'd like you to attend the awards in LA just after New Year.'

'And you told them we would?' Raff asked, looking resigned to the fact we were going to have to return to the US.

'Yes... You need to be there.'

'When do we fly back?' I questioned, knowing Lawson would have already arranged it.

'I've scheduled the plane from Heathrow to LA for the second of January, the awards are on the fourth. You're all booked into the Wilshire for a couple of weeks. I also wanna discuss some business while you're out here and there will of course be some further interviews you'll be expected to attend. Who knows, you may love being back so much, you'll stay for a while.'

'Fuck off, man... and we can tell you resolutely, right fucking now, that won't be happening,' Cade added as the rest of us laughed at his comment.

'That ain't gonna be happening, Lawson. We work better with you on one side of the Atlantic and us on the other,' Raff spoke quietly.

'My daughter would like to see her son sometime, Rafferty.' I could almost see the supercilious smile on the bastard's face and shook my head at his stupidity. The asshat was riding so fucking close to the edge of the rug, he couldn't see we were all within inches of pulling it out from under his feet.

I watched as Raff moved closer to the cell. 'That's between Ashley and me. I suggest you just do your job and piss off, before we relieve you of the job you love more than that daughter of yours.'

Feeling the tension ramping up fast in the room, due to the threat Raff had made, I spoke. 'How long?' I questioned, knowing it was the one question we all wanted an answer to.

'How long?' Lawson repeated.

'You know what I'm asking, Lawson... don't come the fucking innocent with me. Just how long have you signed our souls away for?'

I heard him clear his throat before he answered and looked at the other three as they tensed, waiting on his answer.

'How long?' I questioned again with more forcefulness than I wanted to. I'd decided a few years before, to never allow the asshat any insight into how I felt. But I knew we all had varying reasons for not being out of England for too long and needed to know.

'Until the end of January,' he reluctantly replied.

'Well, fuck.' Raff expelled, propelling himself backwards into his seat.

'That's total shit, man!' Brody shouted, before he smashed his ring covered fist into the table, making the solid piece of glass shatter into hundreds of pieces, as he showed his anger at yet another decision Lawson had made without discussing it with us first. Then standing abruptly, he spun around and walked over to the window, swearing under his breath.

This stops here!

'When we get back to the U.S., we'll give you a date of a meeting you need to attend,' I spoke quietly as a feeling of resignation came over me.

'What?' Lawson questioned.

Brody came back to the table, suddenly interested by what he'd just heard me say.

'Your contract is up for renewal, Lawson.'

Cade raised his arms up high into the air and slapped one hand over his other that was clenched into a fist, like he needed a substitute for a cymbal.

A stressed-filled laugh filtered from the cell, as I cast my eyes back over the three of them in the room with me.

'Well, well, well... fuck, Mac... I preferred it when you were constantly fucking high and on the verge of killing yourself.'

'Yeah, I'm sure you did, but imagine how much money you'd have lost.' I responded sarcastically.

'What's going on, boys? You know I've always done the best for you...'

'That's it, right there... we're no longer boys. It's nearly twenty years since we started this goddamned rollercoaster and we're fucking sick of your stunts,' Cade added.

'Think on how you need to change, Lawson... if, of course, you still want a job at the end of January.'

'I work hard for Default Distraction.'

'We ain't arguing,' Raff agreed.

'But as far as we're concerned, you need to up your fucking game and remember we're human, not just a money-making scheme.' Brody backed up Raff's statement.

'English pussy must sure be...' Lawson started.

'It's every fucking thing,' I pushed in, interrupting the dickwad and watched as all the heads in the room turned towards me.

'You know it's a given that we'll commit to what the fans need from us... Thanks for calling, we'll see you on the fourth.' Raff finished the conversation and disconnected the call.

Cade started clapping as he nodded his respect over to me.

'I'm the numbers man, Mac. How the fuck didn't I know his contract was up for renewal?' he asked with his hands waving in the air and showing his Italian heritage.

'It wasn't until Brody obliterated the glass on the table, that I remembered seeing the date on something a few months ago and you've been busy with this and the Vegas hotel.' I shrugged at him.

'We owe ya, dude,' Brody added.

'Yeah, yeah.'

'Now, all I *really* need to know about is the "every fucking thing" English pussy.' Raff laughed loudly and just like that the previous tension that had filled the room evaporated.

'Fuck right off,' I laughed. 'But back to owing me... I could definitely do with a couple of favours.'

I told them exactly what I needed and watched as they nodded, grinning back at me.

Thirty-Five

Nikki

'THAT'S WONDERFUL, BRIE.' I clapped my hands together lightly and smiled at her as I mirrored her pose. 'Make sure your heels are together, toes pointing out and legs straight. That's it… and now let's hold on to the barre. We are now in first position.'

'I'm doing it.' The excitement in her voice was heart-warming.

'You are, you look so beautiful… Hold the position for a count of three, stand up nice and tall. Brilliant, Brie, well done. Now we're going to practise plié.'

I bent my knees and held my right arm in front of me. I saw as her eyes followed my movement and then as she copied my pose.

'Am I right?'

'You're doing wonderfully. Now, we're going to let go of the barre and listening to the music we're playing, I think it would be fun to glide around your bedroom.' I was already playing the music to Swan Lake for our ballet lesson and knew the piece I was looking for was just about to start.

'How?' I saw Brie's face scrunch up as the fear of getting it wrong showed in her expression. It was something I'd already seen a few times in her and especially when she was dancing. In a child so young, it was not only rare and inspiring, but it was also equally worrying that she was so hard on herself.

'Any way you like... watch me and see how I feel the music. The piece that's just about to start, is one of my favourites. It's called the dance of the cygnets. Cygnets are baby swans and swans are large birds. So, how do you think they would move to the music?'

I watched her pout slightly and narrow her eyes on me as she worked out just what I was asking from her, afraid of getting it wrong. It was hard to explain to her that nothing she did would be wrong. All I was asking her to do was to move however she liked to the music she could hear.

I knew I had to show her instead.

The dance of the cygnets had already started to play, so I released the barre. I started by moving across the carpet away from her in a traditional ballet movement and then for fun, and to encourage her, I began wiggling my bum and flapping my elbows as I pretended to be a bird.

A giggle met my ears and I spun around, excited to see I'd finally convinced her to have a little fun. Soon she was right next to me as we wiggled and flapped our way around the room, laughing together.

'This is fun, Nikki,' she shouted out to me above the sound of Biscuit, who had been woken by the laughter in the room and was now following us both, wagging his tail ecstatically and going around us both in circles.

'Dancing is meant to be fun, Brie,' I called out.

Losing myself into creating locomotion with my small charge around the room, I couldn't say quite when the atmosphere had changed around us, but changed it had. My skin prickled with an awareness just as I deliberately put extra effort into wiggling my bum so much that I could bump into Brie. The bump caused her to laugh all the more as she tried to keep up with me.

'Daddy,' she shrieked and suddenly the small body next to mine moved quickly and tore off behind me.

I stopped wiggling my bum and flapping my arms the second she took off running and then took my time before turning to follow where she'd gone.

Trying to regain some composure in front of Luke, I turned gracefully around and demurely lifted my eyes up to find him. I found him with his back leant against the wall just inside Brie's bedroom door, with his bare feet crossed at the ankles and a small towel draped around his shoulders. His arms were folded over his chest, and underneath his tattooed arms, I could just make out a sweat stained T-shirt. Brie arrived at his legs and wrapped her body around them tightly. He reciprocated and held her to him tightly, rubbing one hand gently through her hair.

'Morning, Shorty.'

Luke's eyes lifted away from Brie and found mine. I saw the instant his face lit up and he smiled his pleasure at discovering me.

'Hey, welcome home... I was loving the interpretation.' His soulful, melodic tone washed over me as he voiced his welcome. He then smiled as he supressed a laugh.

Home?

I smiled back at him, as I thought over his greeting and found that inside it did feel sort of true. Being with Luke and Brie in the same room felt as it should be. They made me feel like I was home.

'Hi,' I whispered back, as I concentrated hard on slowing my unexpectedly erratic breathing and swept my grateful eyes over the man I had missed more than I could, in that minute, put into words.

I hadn't seen Luke since he'd pulled away from our house on Christmas Day and I'd only spoken to him twice by text, between then and Boxing Day. The first text had been to clarify that he'd really meant what he'd offered, and the second time was to tell him my family were excited to go ahead and therefore, so was I.

I'd walked out of the front door of my home at eight that morning to get in the car Luke had sent for me, just as the main contractor they'd employed at The Manor to oversee the renovations and building work, had pulled up. I knew money talked, but I hadn't until that very minute comprehended just how much. I'd shaken Gordon's hand and called out for my mum to come back outside, as she'd already departed the cold winter morning and gone back indoors. I'd then climbed into the waiting car. Half an hour before, I'd received a message from Lou to say that our mum couldn't be happier. In that short space of time, Gordon had listened to what she wanted for Stephen, surveyed the area and had shown her a few rough pencil drawings of his ideas. He left, telling her he'd have the plans drawn up quickly and would make sure she had the final say on them, before he put them in front of the local authority as soon as they reopened in the New Year.

When I'd arrived early that morning and had made my way up to Brie's bedroom, I'd found Raff's mum reading Brie a story. I'd said a polite hello, hugged Brie briefly to me, before going to my room to unpack, while I tried hard to shelve the disappointment at not finding Luke there too.

I'd quickly unpacked and taken over to relieve Raff's mum of my small charge. We'd shared breakfast together and Brie had decided we needed to dance. I'd gratefully agreed, eager to have something else to do other than to fantasise about her father.

And here we were.

In the space of the few seconds that we stood still and took each other in, the room filled with an electrical charge. I had to quell the urge to move towards him, knowing Brielle would always have to take precedence. But there and then, as the butterflies took flight inside my stomach and chills sped over my warm skin, instantly putting my body on high alert, I made a pact with myself. A pact to always, for whatever time we had together, appreciate how he made me feel just by entering the same room and capturing my eyes with his own.

'Daddy, lift me up, we need an Eskimo kiss.'

Laughing softly at me, as his daughter broke through the sexual connection that had developed promptly between us, Luke changed his hold on her and slowly lifted her up until her arms wrapped tightly around his neck and she pressed her nose against his.

'I love you, Brielle Cherise McKenzie.'

A giggle left her, and my heart swelled slightly at watching the moment between the two of them as she rubbed her nose on his.

'I love you too, Daddy, but I need to get down now, because you're all sweaty.'

'Ohhhh, Shorty, that I can't do... because now you're asking for THIS!' Luke started to rub his face all over hers and she squealed in response. With my eyes still focussed on the two of them and the love they shared, my feet instinctively moved nearer as I stopped fighting against what I really wanted.

'No, Daddy, you're too spiky.' Her voice rose in volume as she voiced her protest.

I clamped my thighs together tighter as I reminisced just what his beard felt like between my thighs.

'Too smelly and too bristly. That's a shame, 'cause I thought you loved me,' he teased.

Brie moved her face away from Luke's and as quick as a flash she retorted, 'I do... and I'll love you more when you're clean.' She laughed at the look on his face and stared back at him, smiling.

'For you, Brie... I'd do anything.'

'I know, Daddy,' she whispered, as she moved her hands to either side of his face to give him a quick peck on the lips, before she grimaced once again.

'Hey, Brielle,' Flint shouted, trying hard to control his voice as it struggled to stay in one place between the lightness of boyhood and the deeper voice he normally spoke with. Hearing him call her, instantly made Brie wriggle to free herself from Luke's arms.

'Yes,' she shouted out in reply.

'Wanna come for a swim?' Flint's head appeared around the open door.

'Yes.' Brie's excitement was palpable.

Luke released her from his hold and let her feet find the floor. After pushing himself off the wall he'd been leaning on, he turned towards Flint.

'You going with your dad?'

'Yep, weirdly enough, he asked me,' Flint answered, as a look of disbelief swept across his face.

'Good.' Luke nodded as if he already knew the answer to his question.

Brie rushed to the large, white tallboy in the corner of her room. Looking first at the drawers, she then turned to face me as she silently questioned exactly where she would find her costume.

'The top left one.' I nodded at her.

She stood for a few seconds as she tried to work out her left from her right.

'Next to the curtain,' I offered as I made my way over to help her.

'I'll be back in five, Brie,' Flint called out.

I helped Brie pull out the drawer she needed and knowing precisely where I'd find what she was looking for, I grabbed her Elsa swimsuit.

'Take it into the bathroom, Brie, and I'll be in soon to help you get into it.'

Grabbing the item from my hand, she sped off to her bathroom and not being able to help myself any longer, I turned back around to find Luke watching me with interest.

'Loving my view, Nikki.' As he spoke his eyes travelled over me once again, as if he was trying to commit the scene to memory. 'Not sure if I prefer it with or without the boots and stripey socks.' His eyes sparkled with amusement as he teased me about the very first time he'd seen me, cycling in front of his car.

'Neither were needed today, it's warm enough in here.'

'You can say that again.' Luke's tone became deeper, letting me know exactly what was on his mind. Like a rabbit caught in the headlights all I could do was to stare back at him and wait.

Slowly, Luke walked towards where I was standing frozen to the spot. He wrapped both of his hands around the ends of the towel and understanding that he had my undivided attention, he held both ends up in the air. Abruptly, he released one end, whipped the towel from his neck and dropped it to the floor. My breathing faltered fleetingly, as he then pulled his T-shirt up and away from his body. Without removing his eyes from mine he released it, only for it to fall on top of the towel he'd just discarded. Briefly, my eyes were drawn to the Claddagh he had tattooed over his heart, as still shining with sweat it attracted my attention.

'It's almost as if you knew they were going to invite Brie swimming,' I questioned, having already worked out the answer.

He swept his damp hair off his face and after raising his left eyebrow at me, he stroked one hand through his beard as he pretended to think, before allowing a smirk to capture the lips I was desperate to once again feel against mine.

'I can see how you might think that,' he offered, as he continued to close the distance between us.

'I bet.'

Luke finally arrived in my personal space, and I waited impatiently in my thin ballet attire for our bodies to collide, as I willed him to pull me against his hard body. The air around us crackled, with anticipation and the knowledge and expectancy of just what was to come.

Removing his eyes from mine, he looked down between the two of us. I felt my body's instant response to his perusal, my nipples promptly pebbled as his gaze brushed over my breasts, and the ballet tights I had put on earlier for Brie's dance lesson felt wet at the apex of my thighs, as my need for the man that all my senses were drowning in, left my body.

'I missed you.' The words left his mouth, as his hands found my hips and finally, he did what I had been screaming out in my head for him to do. My body relaxed into his hold as the softness of my breasts and stomach found the hardness of his muscles as he pulled me suddenly to him.

'I've missed you too.'

Luke inhaled as if he was trying to absorb what I'd imparted and the moment we were stood in.

'Do you know, you're the first person apart from Brie to *ever* say that to me.'

I shook my head before he leant closer to me and rested his forehead on mine.

'Nikki,' Brie's voice called out from the bathroom, 'I can't do my straps.'

I turned my head slightly to answer her, as he lifted his head away. 'I'm coming.'

'Not yet, darlin'. But I'll be happy to help you out with that very soon.'

Looking back at him, I smiled, before desperation took hold of me, and after rapidly pushing up onto my tiptoes, I fleetingly put my lips to his and in that simple, chaste expression of my affection, my soul breathed easier for the first time since he'd driven away from me on Christmas evening.

'Nikki,' Brie called again, with impatience very evident in her tone. Reluctantly, I made myself remove my lips away from his and opened my eyes. After creating a small fissure between us and inhaling the warm air that had just left his body, I let him in to the fear that seemed to be a constant in my mind whenever I wasn't in his arms.

'How do we do this, Luke?'

'It's real easy, darlin', just let me in and I'll take care of the rest.'

'Is it?'

'Yeah, if you want to be with me, it is… Do you want to be with me?'

'More than anything,' I nodded slowly at him, 'but it can't be that simple… my life has *never* been that simple.' I wound my arms around his neck, knowing I needed to help Brie, but reluctant to lose this moment in his arms.

'Here's how it goes.' He smiled down at me. 'In the daytime, you take care of Brie and at night, you let me take care of you.' The happiness that radiated off him was addictive.

'That sounds simple enough,' I admitted, as I returned his smile with one of my own. 'But what about my days off?'

'I'll think of something.' He bent his knees and winked at me, before placing a quick kiss on my nose.

Thirty-Six

Nikki

'AFTER WE'VE HAD A swim, I'm treating the kids to lunch at the tearooms, we'll be back in a couple of hours,' Raff shouted over his shoulder, after swinging a very excited Brie up high and into his arms. Once there, she waved her goodbyes to us both.

'Yes!' Flint punched his fist high up in the air. 'I love Lauren's food.'

'Is that a good idea?' Luke questioned Raff as the two of us watched him and the children walk down the corridor towards the first landing.

'It's the only one I've got…' Raff turned just the once to fix Luke with a look, 'but if you have any better suggestions, let me know. All I know is I need to see her and to let her know I'm still here.'

Beside me, Luke grabbed my hand and after bringing my fingers up to his lips to kiss them, he nodded at the situation Raff was now in.

'Good luck, man,' Luke offered.

'Cheers, I'm gonna need it.' My heart fell as I witnessed pain etch itself onto Rafferty's handsome features.

The party of three disappeared from view and we were alone.

'Now, where were we?' Still holding my hand, Luke turned towards me and closed the small distance between us. I took three steps backwards, until my shoulders collided with the expensive, flocked wallpaper behind me.

'I think you need to tell me,' I managed to whisper.

'Mmmm, I'd prefer to show you,' he teased.

'I think I'd like that.'

'I know you would.' Luke's eyes darkened as his pupils dilated. The green in his eyes lessened, but surprisingly they became no less brilliant.

And I fell in, head-first.

My heart already loved him and somehow the stupid bloody organ had managed to convince my normally steadfast head.

I knew I was in trouble, but I no longer had the strength or care to fight it.

In those few seconds, the teasing atmosphere between us evaporated, as did any ideas I had about keeping something back for myself. Something I could attempt to draw strength from when my contract of employment was over.

'Like I also know… I'm falling hard for you, Nikki.'

I heard myself draw in a shaky breath at his admission and watched transfixed as I became the sole focus of his attention. Luke was a gorgeous looking man. One who had been created by his past, like so many of us. I already understood that he had, without a doubt, developed many masking and coping mechanisms, in order to function in the world he frequented in the eye of the media. But when his eyes focussed solely on mine, it gave me the rare opportunity to see into his soul, and in doing so I allowed him in to touch mine.

Holding my hand tightly against my side, he lifted the other and caressed my cheekbone with his thumb, before allowing his fingers to travel down over my jaw and down my neck.

His mouth came to meet mine with such passion, my body instantly reeled from the connection between us. There was no give and take, because the need we had for each other was far too great. Our tongues began their dance as we both teased and caressed each other's, in an effort to sate, or was it to stoke, the assembling inferno we were caught up in the middle of? As soon as Luke's tongue sought out my piercing, sparks of need set sail to all four corners of my body. My knees felt weak, and my body unsteady, my hand threaded around his waist and my fingernails gripped tightly to his flesh. As he circled the diamond with his tongue, refusing to give in just yet to what he knew I wanted, a primeval moan left me. Finally, in response to my audible encouragement, he flicked the diamond and ignited my body. My arms lifted and after lacing my fingers through his hair, I held his head in my grasp, unwilling or unable to let him go.

I wasn't sure how, but with his mouth still on mine he lifted me up and began to walk. When his cologne hit my nostrils, it left me in no doubt as to where he'd taken me. As our mouths continued to give and take exactly what we both needed from each other, for a few seconds I felt the two of us become unbalanced. A loud bang rang out as he kicked the door closed behind us, shutting us in his private space.

Then his strides lengthened, until I was gently lowered onto the soft Chenille of the dark coloured comforter, I knew was placed at the bottom of his bed.

Still in my hold, his head lifted away from mine, separating our lips, and I took some deep, cleansing lungfuls of air. For a few seconds, we breathed each other in, before he knelt down in between my open thighs.

I comprehended in those few, all-too-short seconds, that I wasn't afraid anymore.

This man had me. I couldn't hide or hold back from the way he made me feel when he was around. And the way he touched me, made me feel like no one had ever touched me before.

I was his, the contract of employment between us was superfluous.

I moved my hands to cup his face.

'You've touched my soul, Luke, and no one has ever done that before.'

He inhaled sharply as the words I'd spoken resonated around him. He nodded just the once, allowing me to see that my words had affected him and that he accepted them, but that they were almost too much for him to deal with.

Unexpectedly, his hold on me changed and I was swung precipitously up and into his arms.

'Where are you taking me?'

'Somewhere I can take my sweet time worshipping you, like the Goddess you are.'

Luke

I held her tightly to me as I carried her into the large, luxurious bathroom I'd had installed. Then slowly, knowing I needed to feel all of her incredible, lithe figure against mine, I lowered her slowly down the front of my body. As her toned stomach stroked over the top of my rock-hard dick, I released a groan.

'You're fucking magnificent.'

With one arm around her waist, supporting her against the side of me, I reached in and switched on the large, central shower head and the four smaller ones that were placed around it. Then walking backwards into the open space, I guided her in with me until we were both under the spray of the main head.

As the water massaged her, Nikki tilted her head backwards, giggling with acceptance. Listening to her happiness and understanding I was the cause; I knew I couldn't hold back any longer. I brought myself down to her level and allowed my mouth to fall onto the exposed skin of her neck. I ran my tongue up her fevered flesh, gathering in the water that was running in fast rivulets over her pale skin, and savoured the salty flavour on my tongue.

'I'm addicted to the way you taste, darlin'.'

The mewl that left her mouth fed my debauched soul. And I was too far gone to worry about whether I was good enough for her anymore. She wanted me, like no one had ever wanted me before, and I was too much of a selfish asshole to deny myself the pleasure I knew we'd find in each other, the same pleasure I knew that as long as we stayed together, we would always find with and in each other.

Reluctantly, I released my hold on her but was encouraged when she placed her hands on the sides of my body to steady herself. Removing the pins from her hair, I started to turn the prim ballet teacher she was dressed up as, into the woman I knew she was underneath. The same one who had claimed and possessed me. Her long, dark hair fell from its confines, until it was one long mane down her spine. Nikki tipped her head back, as she recognised its weight and closed her eyes to the inflexible downpour of the water.

Moving my hands down over her shoulders I pushed off the pink, side-tie wrap thing she was wearing and after untying the ribbon at the side of her body, I pulled the soaking wet fabric away from her body and dropped it to the floor, before kicking it to the side with my foot.

Casting my eyes downward, I found her small, perfect tits encased in a light looking sports bra. With her head still leant backwards and the water still caressing her face, I wrapped one arm around her tightly and used the other with my fingertips outstretched, to draw down over her slight, dancer's frame. My fingers continued to travel slowly over her neck, as I watched her skin react to my touch. Before undoing the front fastening bra, I skirted my fingers over both of her protruding nipples, before giving in to what I knew she was unconsciously pushing her body nearer to me for and pinched them between my finger and thumb.

'You're a masterpiece… my beautiful masterpiece.'

'Yes, yours.' Her voice was barely audible above the sound of the water, but I heard it and so did my blackened, scarred heart.

Unzipping the bra quickly, I let it hang open, while I feasted my eyes on her beautiful skin as the water touched her tits for the first time. Her chest rose and fell as she struggled to contain the way her body was beginning to make her feel.

Unable to hold back any longer, I bent my knees and took one of her rose-bud pink nipples into my mouth and as it closed around her sensitive skin, my abdominals clenched tight, and my dick pushed itself out of the top of my running shorts. The water cascading down my chest met with the head of my dick and I released a groan of pure pleasure against her sensitive flesh and knew I'd sparked a chain reaction.

Her head fell forward to watch.

I claimed her mouth with my own and after pushing the bra down her arms, I wrapped the material around her wrists a second time to constrain her arms behind her back. Then, with my tongue tangled up with hers as I toyed with her piercing, and with our mutual moans of pleasure captured inside our mouths, I pushed her gently backwards until she was touching the granite walls of my shower.

My mouth left hers, needing to hear her cries of pleasure, allowing my mouth and teeth to explore her neck. I heard the little skirt she was wearing rip as my fingers tore the flimsy fabric away from her body and as my mouth gathered up her neglected nipple, I pushed the damaged skirt and her tights down over her hips.

Releasing her elongated flesh from my mouth, I instructed her, 'Step out.'

I helped her with one hand, while I pushed my shorts down with my other. Desperation to feel the walls of her pussy clamped around my dick as she rode out her orgasm was fuelling my every thought and action.

Finally, she was naked, and my mouth was back feasting between her nipples, and by the sounds she was making and the way her hips were flexing towards me trying to find leverage, I guessed that if I carried on, I'd be able to make her come concentrating on her nipples alone.

I inhaled sharply as the scent of her wet pussy floated up on the steam of the shower. I needed to taste her, I needed to see the pearls I'd dreamt about for the previous few fucking days, in the light, but for now I knew it would have to wait until tonight.

Fuck.

I tapped her ankles with one foot, silently asking her to widen her stance. As soon as she complied, I moved into her and rolled my hips over her pubic mound just the once.

'Holy fucking hell, woman. You better not be counting on getting any sleep tonight.'

'I don't need sleep, all I need is you.'

'You better fucking believe it... eyes on mine, darlin'. Don't close them and don't look away.'

I swept my hair off my face, captured her grey orbs with my own and took hold of her hips. Then I lifted her up the wall.

'Legs around my waist.'

The strong, lithe woman I had secured in my arms, conformed to my demands instinctively, and after lining myself up against her entrance, with my eyes focussed solely on the beautiful creature in my hold, I lowered her slowly down the full length of my shaft.

'Jesus Christ, woman, you feel so fucking good.'

She made no reply, other than to tighten the walls of her pussy in response.

'I'm gonna fuck you so hard.'

'Yes,' was all that escaped her beautiful bee stung lips.

Mesmerised with what our mutual passion had done, I skimmed my thumb over her mouth and then pushed it inside.

'Suck,' I demanded. When she fastened her teeth on to it and lathed at the tip, my balls hitched, and I started to fuck her.

There was no going slow.

I wanted her too much and I knew intuitively that she needed me just as much. In an almost animalistic frenzy, I moved fast in and out of her, as we chased the release we both so desperately needed. As her legs locked behind my back holding me in place and her body stiffened, I felt her pussy convulse and knew she was close. My toes curled on the granite beneath my feet, and I rejoiced at the start of my own impending orgasm. Her back arched, and her cries sounded in my ears, and I knew I could let go.

We came minutes later, crying out each other's names. As cum left my balls in long never-ending streams to coat the walls of her pussy, I grasped the fact I hadn't worn a condom and worst of all—that I didn't give a fuck.

Thirty-Seven

Nikki

TOO HOT.

Coming to in the large bed and finding myself lying on my back, I stretched my legs out wide as I attempted, in vain it appeared, to find a cooler area to place my feet.

As my brain very leisurely and reluctantly began to wake up, the first thing I became aware of, was that my core was aching. Slowly, as I came back to complete consciousness, I realised that my clit was throbbing in need, and I was soaking wet between my legs.

No way. I smiled to the empty room.

I'd had three more orgasms the previous evening, after our shower sex. How the hell could I still be dreaming about and wanting more?

Just what exactly had I been dreaming about?

Luke.

The answer was simple.

We'd put Brie to bed the previous night after hearing about the fun she'd had swimming with Flint and how much she'd enjoyed seeing Lauren. She'd repeated herself several times as she described the treats Lauren had packed up for her and Flint to take away. Finally, after allowing herself to lie back against her pillow, she'd very seriously told us in between yawns, how her Uncle Riff Raff had seemed very sad but happy all at the same time, when Lauren had come over to speak to her and Flint.

We'd then read a book I'd recently bought for her about an invisible string of love that existed even when the person you loved was out of sight, thinking it would help her with the loss of her mum and Nancy, her former nanny. The intuitive four-year-old child declared she would let Rafferty borrow it, so he would know that love never really went away. Then she'd looked at me and her dad. After grabbing both of our hands and placing them over her heart, she'd squealed in excitement and told us both with a huge smile that the three of us now had our very own invisible string.

In total awe of the beautiful little girl she was, we'd watched her drift off to sleep, not leaving until we were sure she no longer needed either of us. Luke had then silently, and with his eyes never leaving mine, walked around her bed and had taken me into his arms. Then making very determined strides, he'd taken us back to my room.

Where, through the late evening and into the early hours of the morning, he'd lavished me with attention, until I had fallen asleep in his arms. I'd only come to for a few seconds, when I'd felt him release his hold on me and my door clicked back into place when he went back to his room.

Opening one eye, I peered into the bleakness of my surroundings and glanced quickly to the clock beside me. It was just after five and I knew I possibly had an hour before I had to get ready for my day.

Leisurely, I let one hand drift down my naked body. My nipples were hard and needy, just as I knew they would be. I continued to let my hand move down on instinct and inhaled sharply as my body reacted to my touch. Clenching my eyes shut tight, I pictured the scene that had only happened a few hours previously, when I'd watched as Luke had come undone thanks to my, it seemed, diamond stud and very clever mouth. I knew that whatever I'd been dreaming about had already taken me over halfway there and all I probably needed to do was to touch the bar of pearls in the hood of my clit for me to fall over the edge. My fingers brushed over my pubic mound, and I held my breath waiting for the contact.

In that split second, between acceptance of what I needed to do and feeling the release I understood I was so desperately craving, my hand was stopped from progressing further. A large hand had unceremoniously seized mine and the fingers from the same hand were now wrapped tightly around my wrist.

'Morning, darlin'.' Luke's amused tone washed over me and unexpectedly he lifted the duvet up and away from our bodies. 'Uh-uh. This, from now on, is mine.' He blew a warm draft of air onto my pussy, leaving me in no doubt of what *this* was.

Completely awake, I lifted my head off the pillow and looked down between my legs to find the man I knew I had been dreaming about. Luke swept his hair off his face with one hand and in the light of just my bedside clock, I saw pleasure encapsulated in his eyes before a grin formed over his mouth. He quickly moved and releasing my wrist, pushed his hands under each of my thighs.

His hands jerked my body inches down the bed and his warm mouth greedily fell on my pussy.

'Ahhhh.' The sensation was instantly far too much. His determined tongue encircled my clit in the same way he'd teased the stud in my mouth the day before and my body climbed irreversibly higher. My arms fell to the sheet either side of my body as I effectively surrendered to the man between my legs.

'Please, Luke… please.'

As soon as my pleading met his ears, Luke lifted himself away. His calloused fingers opened my soaking wet lips wide, and he began to use his beard on my delicate flesh instead.

'Oh, my God.' My body tensed in surprise.

Pain took over where only warm, wet pleasure had been seconds before and not quite trusting myself with the strange feelings the dull pain was beginning to chase from a hiding place inside of me, I lifted myself up to look down at the man who somehow knew me better than I understood myself. With a small amount of light now filtering through the chink at the top of my drawn curtains, his eyes captured mine, as using the bristles of his beard again he chafed over my swollen clit.

'Too much,' I cried out, as a cataclysmic sensation hurried around my body and my moans filled the space around us.

'No… it'll never be too much, Nikki. Take it, take it all.' His warm breath soothed my hypersensitive skin, driving me higher in my need to reach the ending.

His tongue pressed down once onto my piercing, and his lips fixed onto the silver bar and quickly he sucked it into his waiting mouth. Pain returned to pleasure; a pleasure only heightened by the little bit of pain he'd created. My head fell back onto the mattress, my back arched, and my fingers dug deep into the bedding beneath me as I attempted to gain a foothold on the height Luke was taking me to.

'Luke, Luke… Ohhhh. Yes! Luke!' My cries of pleasure appeared to fuel his need to feel and to taste each and every single part of me. I rode out my extended orgasm on his face as my body convulsed time after time in his hold.

'Hey.'

The sound of Luke's voice brought me around as the smell of coffee hit my nostrils. Moving slightly, I saw him place a mug beside me on the bedside table.

'Thank you,' I managed to whisper. Then as worry unfurled itself inside of me and on impulse, I sat up quickly, grabbing the cover to me. 'Have I overslept?'

'Mmmmm, just a bit.' Luke looked down at me, grinning as he answered.

'Brie?' I questioned, feeling my eyes open wide as I looked past the delicious, obviously just showered man stood next to me and around the room in panic.

'She's dressed and downstairs having breakfast with Brody.'

'Oh.' I fell back on the bed in relief. 'I'm sorry.'

Shaking his head as he let out a low laugh, he leant forward. After connecting his fisted hands to the mattress beneath me, Luke leant forward to brush his mouth against mine.

'Good morning.' He spoke into the small gap he'd created, and his warm, minty breath washed over me. 'You have nothing to be sorry for. It was already organised, they're off to the local vet to get a certificate of health for Biscuit, after eating.'

'They are?' Just how long had I slept for? I looked once again at the clock beside me for reassurance to find it was a little after eight.

'Yeah, Biscuit needs one to travel.'

'Travel?' I questioned, suddenly feeling like I had slept a day away and had missed a lot.

'Yeah, I forgot to say yesterday, 'cause we were otherwise occupied...' He grinned and then carried on, 'Lawson...' He stopped momentarily as he waited to see if I knew who he was talking about. Seeing me nod in recognition, he carried on. 'Lawson told us yesterday that we've just won an award, which we need to turn up to accept in a few day' time, in L.A.'

'L.A.' I repeated.

'You ever been?' His excitement was palpable.

'A few times, it was where one of my previous families had a second home.' I didn't want to tell him that while I loved the US, Los Angeles was one of my least favourite places to visit.

His expression changed to one of disappointment. 'Shame, I was looking forward to showing you something new.'

'I think you did that last night...' I felt a blush beginning to tinge my face red, but determined to lift his mood I carried on, 'and you definitely did this morning.' I winked at him and felt my heart skip a beat as I witnessed one of his beautiful smiles spread over his face.

'Yeah, I had a feeling I did,' he teased me, as he brought one hand up to his beard and began to stroke it while waggling his eyebrows at me. I knew the second he did, I would never be able to watch his mannerism again, without thinking back to the very first night we'd spent together. 'As we're talking about yesterday...' I watched his excitement dissipate. He grimaced and then he released a long, sigh. 'In the shower, I'm ashamed to say I didn't use a condom.'

'I know,' I admitted, 'I could tell by the way you felt... Are you clean?' I asked the only thing that had worried me.

'Yeah... checked monthly... I haven't been bareback, in... well,' he shrugged. 'Since Cherise.'

'Then we're fine. I have an IUD fitted. I'm an independent woman who takes care of her body. I'm also clean, as... well, it's a bit embarrassing, but I haven't had sex in a while.'

'Hadn't had sex,' he corrected and as relief slipped back over his features, I knew he'd never looked so handsome than right at that very minute. 'From now on, you're gonna be having a whole lot of it.'

Luke closed the gap between us and kissed me again.

'We're gonna be gone for a few weeks; L.A. Vegas and New York for definite.' His minty breath caressed my lips.

'Now, I've never been to Vegas.' I smiled shyly back at him.

'Then consider yourself as having a date for sin city, Miss Osbourne.'

'A date?' I couldn't quell the excitement inside me.

A date with Luke McKenzie. Inside, I swooned.

'Also, you'd better let your mom know,' he offered thoughtfully.

'Okay… and, morning.' I wound my arms around Luke's neck as everything sunk in. Relief at not having buggered up what he'd said was going to be so very simple on the very first morning, travelled through me. 'I'll do better tomorrow, I promise.' I smiled up at him.

Slowly, Luke tipped his head from shoulder to shoulder and narrowed his eyes on me as he mulled over my words.

'Don't make a promise, I'm not sure I can let you keep, darlin'.' His mouth came back to find mine.

Thirty-Eight

Nikki

'WHY THE HELL ARE ya wearing that?'

I moved my eyes away from desperately trying to pin my brown, felt hat onto my thick hair, that I'd forced into a neat, low bun, to find Luke staring at me in the full-length mirror. He'd quietly entered my bedroom in the suite of rooms we'd taken as ours in the Wilshire, without me noticing. I could normally sense his presence, but I'd been so preoccupied with trying to work out what the hell I should wear, I must have missed his arrival. Needing to take him in, and to ground my panic at attending the awards with him, my eyes unashamedly rushed over his calm, commanding figure.

His hair was uncharacteristically neat and swept back, making the green of his eyes stand out even more prominently on his face, if that were even possible. His beard had been trimmed and as he caught me admiring him in those few seconds, I appreciated that I could see the indentation of where both of his dimples should be. The man looked

damn fine. Black leather biker jacket over a brilliant white T-shirt, with washed out, torn, black jeans that fitted him in all the right places, which he'd tucked into heavy biker boots.

My core clenched and the very top of my thighs felt instantly damp.

'My uniform,' I whispered in reply. We were due to arrive at the awards ceremony in just over an hour and as Brie and Flint were going to watch, I'd been invited along too. 'I thought it might be appropriate.'

'Appropriate?' Luke smiled at my nervousness, 'You amaze me… I love your English propriety.' He started to cross the floor of the large room and close the distance between us.

'You do?'

'Not really.' Luke smiled, before his arms snaked around my waist, and he pulled me into him. My back to his front. His cologne filled my nostrils, instantly relaxing me with its musk and spices. I sagged against the strength I found in our connection and momentarily closed my eyes as my fears and worries left me.

His lips found my neck as his eyes, filled with amusement at me, found mine in the reflection. In seconds, the heat that was always between us, was reignited and stoked into large, all-consuming flames. The kiss he'd offered had turned into a few more and as I released his name on a moan, his teeth had started to nibble up my neck until he'd sucked my exposed lobe into his ear.

'Ooooo…. No!' Brie's voice found us, making me freeze in Luke's hold, before I tried to break free from his arms. For the few weeks we'd been together, we'd been so careful about what she saw between us. She'd seen him kiss me a few times when we messed around together. But she'd never seen him hold me like he was now, almost as if I was his reason for being, and now here we were.

'Don't,' Luke's strong voice commanded in my ear.

'What's up, Brie?' he questioned without releasing his hold over me and without turning around.

'Tell her, Daddy.'

'Whatdaya want me to say, Shorty?'

My heart flew into my chest. This was going to be the moment. That single defining moment, when his daughter asked him to choose between me and her.

'I don't like that yucky dress… brown doesn't look pretty on you, Nikki. You don't look like you, does she Daddy, and I don't like it.'

'I'd just more or less told her that, Shorty.'

I released the breath I'd been holding on to, when I understood that even though she'd witnessed her daddy holding me to him and probably kissing my neck with passion, that she wasn't fazed and seemed to have no objections to our intimacy at all. Tears pricked the back of my eyes when I comprehended that her objection was to my outfit and nothing more.

'What do you think I should wear then, Brie?' I questioned, as I enclosed Luke's arms with my own. 'You'll have to help me; I've never been to a music award ceremony before.'

'I know!' she declared and quick as a flash she disappeared into my walk-in wardrobe.

'She accepted it?' I managed to utter in disbelief to the man who was still looking at me over my shoulder.

'She did…. Brie is one amazing little girl. She's always been perceptive, and I'm sure she knew I needed you in my life, even before I understood it… and I do need you in my life, darlin'. You know that, don't you?'

'Yes.'

All at once I was turned around in his arms. One hand came up to my hair and my horrible brown hat went spinning off my head to somewhere behind me and after he pulled a few pins from the nape of my neck, my hair uncoiled down my back and Luke's eyes captured mine.

'I need you, too.' Raising my hands, I held on to the sides of his unzipped jacket.

'You're fucking beautiful, what we have together is beautiful and tonight I want the world to see you at my side, and not just as Brie's fucking nanny.'

'But I am…' His forefinger lifted to my lips as he shushed me.

'You're something even more important and I never thought I'd say that.' I could feel his feet shuffling around on the expensive carpet beneath his boots, as he thought over what words to say. 'You're mine and don't ever forget it.'

Luke bent his knees and brushed a kiss against my lips, instantly catapulting the way I felt for him into the stratosphere.

'So, I'm asking you again… Have you ever felt like that, Nikki?' he questioned as I was instantaneously taken back to a few weeks previously.

'Only the once,' I admitted. 'I was lucky enough to meet someone and from the second I sat down at his table for a hot chocolate, I understood that life as I knew it had transformed. I was scared to admit at first that what we had between us, could be so very perfect.'

'Beyond your wildest dreams?' Luke pushed further.

Swallowing down my nervousness, I looked to answer his question. 'This, between us, is so very much more than my wildest dreams.'

His forehead came to rest on mine and for a split second we just breathed each other in.

'No more pretending that we sleep in different beds, tonight and every night going forward from now, you're mine and from this moment, I get to hold you all night long.'

'I'd like that.'

'Too fucking right, you do.' Luke laughed.

'These,' came a shout to the side of us, as Brie rushed out of the closet. She was carrying so much I could hardly see the determined little girl behind the mountain she was holding. My knee-high, black Dr. Martens. A black net tutu, which I'd never worn, and a silver off-the-shoulder, sparkly top. Unceremoniously, she dropped them to the floor and ran back in the wardrobe.

'Looks like my daughter has you all sorted.' Luke kissed the end of my nose as he started to walk away.

'It seems that way.'

'See you both outside in fifteen minutes.' I watched as he made his way to the door that led to the lounge area. As his hand grabbed hold of the frame, he turned to look at me once again. 'Just in case you don't recognise me, I'll be the one holding out my hand.'

'I'm sure I'll recognise you.' I smiled at him and nodded.

'Just checking... you might get me confused with the lead singer.' The laughter that left him, warmed me up.

'I think I know who's who,' I teased as I watched him chew gently on the side of his mouth.

'I'm sure you do.' He grinned and then went back to looking contemplative, 'You need to be aware that when you take a hold, you'll be accepting more than just my hand.'

'I will?'

'Oh, yeah, darlin'... you'll be accepting my love.'

I knew that if I didn't stop soon, the skin on my left arm was going to be sore. I'd pinched myself so many times since walking out into the lounge area, to find the whole of Default Distraction and Flint waiting for Brie and me.

I wasn't sure what Luke had said to them, but they'd all stood when we entered the room and turned to take a look at us both. I'd worn everything Brie had chosen for me, and left my hair long, just how Luke seemed to like it best. I normally wore no make-up when I was working, but as Luke had categorically stated, I was now more than just Brie's nanny, so I'd added some smoky eyes and dark red lips to my ensemble. Although I'd been nervous about showing my tattoos, and truthfully my true colours, the looks and nods of approval from them all had set my mind at rest. Flint had been twirling Brie around on the spot as he told her how pretty she looked, when Luke had stepped forward and uttered, 'Holy fucking hell,' and extended his hand towards me.

I'd placed my hand in his and accepted everything he was offering.

Our hands had remained entwined, the whole time; from our suite, through the screaming fans who'd threatened to engulf us as we stepped outside the limo once we'd reached The Forum, and he'd continued holding it all the time we'd been sitting down at the table reserved for us at the front of the indoor arena. Ten minutes before, as DD had risen to accept their award, Luke had pulled me up with him and released my hand. He'd placed his hands on my hips, pulling me into him and placed a long, lingering kiss to my lips. And just like that, he'd announced to the world that we were together, and the arena around us had gone white with the flashes from hundreds or maybe even thousands of cameras as they'd gone off simultaneously.

Flint, Brie and DD security had instinctively closed ranks around me as Luke and the others had run up and jumped athletically onto the stage. The crowd amassed inside the building had screamed themselves hoarse while watching.

Brie held my hand as she climbed up on the chair next to me to watch her dad and I'd pinched my arm once again, as I tried to make sure I was actually witnessing what was in front of my eyes.

'Good evening, Forum.' Brody spoke into the mic, and the crowd shouted back to him.

'Have you missed us?' he questioned, as he put one hand on his forehead to shield his eyes, as he attempted to see out into the arena.

A frenzy enveloped the thousands of people around us.

'You're too kind.' He held his hand over his heart, then spun around on one foot to face the others. Luke and Raff took their places either side of him and Cade brought his sticks up into the air and after rapping them together twice, the rectangular stage they were on ignited with an explosion of colour and sound. Brody cupped the mic with one ring covered hand and punched one fist into the air.

At the crowd's response, he went into the first line of "Never Die." With their music and the atmosphere around me carrying me away, I jumped up on the chair next to Brie and started to dance alongside her.

Holding her hand in my own, I watched as Default Distraction did what they did best and together the four of them captivated the thousands of people alongside me. Their energy compelled you not to look away, but it was their togetherness and passion that kept you truly hypnotised.

At the end of their second number one in the U.K, they followed straight on with "Nuclear," systematically shutting down my dancing, as I focussed solely on Luke. I watched as he swung his Rickenbacker Fireglo bass guitar around his back, picked up his electric violin and began to play the main riff in the heavy rock anthem, like he did in a few of their other songs.

When a stool was brought out onto the stage, I knew to settle down. Anyone who had ever watched DD play "Regret," understood just by watching Brody, how much it took out of him just singing that one song. He, like Raff and Luke, could jump around on stage, run end to end and cover a walkway in seconds front to back, and not be out of breath. But that was pure physicality. Singing "Regret" left no one in any doubt that it was one of the most emotional rock ballads they had ever heard, and it always left Brody looking completely drained.

'Thank you, to everyone who voted for us. We've been Default Distraction. Leaving you with the song you voted for.' Brody smashed his closed fist over his chest and two finger saluted the crowd with the same arm. 'This is for all the people we've ever loved, for our children, the women in our lives... and for, of course, you... all our fans.'

Just over three minutes later and it was over.

As Brody sung the last few words with his eyes closed, into the mic, I looked over to Luke and watched as he blew me a kiss.

I caught the kiss in the air, Cade's sticks came down, Brody's body fell forwards and the stage fell into darkness. As the crowd went wild, I felt thousands of eyes come to rest on me. Eyes bored into me from every direction, but as a sense of foreboding entered my gut and my stomach twisted, I instinctively turned my head to confront the situation.

My eyes found those of my former employer, Haydon Millar, and as he lifted the glass in his hand to me and sneered, I knew I'd never felt more exposed in my life.

Thirty-Nine

LUKE

'L OOKS LIKE LAWSON MIGHT have actually listened.' Brody leant forward to pick up a bottle of Mountain Dew. After unscrewing the cap, he threw back his head and took a few long gulps, before looking back at us all.

'He just might,' Raff answered, as I nodded my head thinking back to our unplanned meeting as we waited to leave the Forum. After congratulating the four of us on our performance, which was something Lawson had stopped doing years ago, he'd greeted his grandson and Brie, before introducing us to his guest. In a few well-rehearsed sentences, he'd given us a brief outline of what the guy with him, a record company chief exec, was offering. Then our impromptu gathering had been cut short when a few of our fans had managed to make their way behind the main stage. As their screams hit our ears, giving us warning of just what was imminent, we'd shaken their hands, jumped into the awaiting car, and sped away into the darkness.

Shifting in my seat, I adjusted my one-armed hold on my sleeping daughter and lifted Nikki's hand to my lips as I kissed the back of it and then placed it back down. She'd laid her head on my shoulder the minute we'd all clambered into our awaiting stretch limo, showing me just how tired she was. I was sure she was still awake, at least I'd hoped to fuck she was, as I had plans for her that evening. But she'd almost hidden herself into the corner, using my body as protection from the others.

She was possibly coming to terms with just how crazy our lives were.

Even now, after all this time, it still never ceased to surprise me just how unreal and out there our lifestyle seemed to other people.

To us it was the version of normal that we lived in, albeit a bit fucked up.

To others from outside our circle, or new to it, I could see that it would be overwhelming and at times over the fucking top, because it was.

I hoped it hadn't scared her off, because I knew even now, surrounded by the men I thought of as brothers, that I'd jack this shit in tomorrow if I had to choose between her, the family I wanted, and the music industry.

'Lawson, the asshat, seemed fucking made up with himself, didn't he?' Cade flicked the bottle cap he was fidgeting with between his fingers and managed to hit the centre console.

'What do we know about them... anything?' Raff questioned, after nodding a reply.

'They're a major player in the U.K. and European market, and we have enough history and a strong enough foothold in the U.S. to know what we're doing there, so I don't see there's any worries if we decide to move.' Cade answered his question and moved his gaze to look at us all. 'The percentage that Lawson says Windmill is offering, is way better than our current contract.'

'It goes without saying that the percentage increase we receive on our work, is well worth our time looking at... although it's the greater control over when we record/release/tour that really interests me,' Brody added. 'I think we've worked out that we want a U.K. base going forward... hell, I know I have.'

I thought over what he was saying.

'Fuck, yeah.' I nodded and squeezed Nikki's hand again, more gently this time in case she really was asleep. 'Family is without a doubt where it's at from now on and we've got our new venture with the hotels to think about as well.'

Cade moved his head from side to side showing he wasn't entirely convinced either way. 'Hotels, yeah… not sure about a permanent base in England for me as yet.'

'Depends on the woman warming your bed, man… I get it.' I grinned over at him as he showed me the finger.

'Agreed,' Raff spoke up, as pain once again consumed his face and I was convinced he was thinking of Lauren. 'Although, I wanna see what the guy is really offering in black and white, so we'll need to schedule a meeting with, what was he called?' He looked around us all.

'Haydon Millar, CEO of Windmill Records,' Brody answered.

I felt Nikki slump further into the leather upholstery and sighed as I resigned myself to the fact that I was going to be carrying more than just Brie to bed tonight.

'We can see what's in it for us, but what's in it for him?' I asked, as a prickle of uncertainty made the hairs on the back of my neck stand to attention.

'Lawson or Millar?'

Shaking my head, I replied to Raff. 'Nah, I get Lawson… he wants us to know he's finally fucking listening, making sure he doesn't lose his well-paid job and…' I looked quickly over at Flint who was lying with his head on Raff's lap, to check he was asleep. I smiled to myself as I watched Raff stroke his hand over his sleeping son's head and run his fingers lightly through his hair. Because what fourteen-year-old would put up with that shit if he was awake?

'And not be able to support his several fucking mistresses and the various little bastards he's spawned.' I lowered my voice for the last part. I wasn't sure whether Flint knew about his grandfather being more fucking rockstar than the rest of us and wanted to make sure that when he did hear, it wasn't from my mouth.

'Says the biggest bastard of them all,' Brody reprimanded.

'Yeah, I know… it's not their fault their father is a total asshole. Anyway, I meant that Haydon guy. Why the fuck would he offer us more money and greater control, just what's in it for him?'

I watched Cade shrug, 'An opening in the U.S. market?'

'Suppose,' I answered, satisfied for the minute with his answer. Nikki moved again to the side of me and turning my head I placed a kiss on the top of her head. 'I can't think what else he'd be after.'

Forty

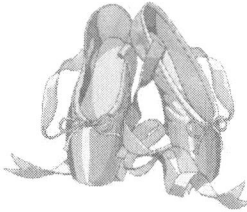

Nikki

I NEVER WANTED PRETENCE to be part of our relationship, but when Luke handed Brie over to Brody and pushed his hands under my body to lift me up and into his arms, in those few seconds, it appeared allowing him to think I was asleep was what I needed.

I couldn't let him in yet. I already understood that although we'd only known each other for a few weeks, he would see right through me. Experiencing the biggest high of my entire life, as Luke had made sure that everyone at the Forum and those watching the televised broadcast around the world, had seen him acknowledge that we were an item, had been fundamentally wrecked a few seconds later, when I'd found Haydon Millar sitting a few feet away from me.

I now needed time to organise my thoughts.

Carefully, Luke had carried me up to his suite and after placing me down on his bed, he'd muttered, 'Night, darlin'. Dream of me, I'll be dreaming of you.' He'd then dropped the blinds and had gone off to put Brie to bed in the next room. All the time he'd been gone, I'd lay with my eyes wide open and stared in the semi-dark at the outline of what I knew was a landscape picture of Malibu.

Why? Was the one thought running over and over in my mind like a broken record. Luke had said everything could be so simple and I'd wanted to believe that finally my life could essentially be just that. In fact, I'd got so caught up in that fact, that perhaps it was my fault. I'd let down my guard.

I felt the bed dip down as Luke got into the other side, and then as he gathered me into his arms and placed a few kisses onto my exposed shoulder and said another whispered goodnight, a tear escaped my eye.

I had no idea how long I'd lay there, unable to move and trying to keep my breathing regular, when all I wanted to do was to scream out in protest and thump my fists into the bedding that Luke had carefully covered me with. At last, I heard Luke's breathing had evened out and hating myself, I lifted his arm and extracted myself from his body. Gently, I lowered his heavy arm to the sheet, wiggled to the edge of the bed and cautiously placed my feet to the floor. Although I was still fully dressed, Luke had at least taken off my boots, so my stocking clad feet made no noise as they found the dark wood flooring. I cast my eyes over his prone figure just the once and feeling more deceitful than I had ever felt before, I picked up my phone from the side table and made my way to the bathroom.

Sitting in the dark, on the cold, tiled floor, I pressed the button I needed and sighed with relief when after a few seconds, I heard the international dialling code sounding in my ear.

'Hi, Nik.' My sister's excited tone filtered through to me.

'Lou.' I spoke her name and relaxed into her voice and pulling myself together I attempted to pull myself out of the shark infested waters I'd landed into and back to reality. 'How's the build?'

'Christ, it's going up so fast. I'll send you some pics later.'

'That's good.' I swallowed down my own fears and tried hard to hang on to her every excited word.

'Mum is so happy. Gordon is consulting her on everything and so far, she's getting the entirety of what she wished for Stephen. I had no idea planning could even go through in a week, and to have them start the day after it was agreed, was miraculous. Mind you, a lot has to be said for the neighbours having no problems with the extension.'

'We knew they wouldn't, it's one of the best things about living in a small village, isn't it? Everyone looks out for everyone else, and they know how much it means to us to have Stephen home... Also, money talks, we both know that already.' Bending my legs, I pulled them in tightly to my body and with one arm, I hugged them to me, as I wished myself back in the small place we called home. Then my eyes wandered over to the door I'd covertly shut behind me to make the call.

He was out there, sleeping in his bed, the one he'd only declared yesterday that we were going to share from now on and here I was sitting in the cold and keeping my distance.

How the hell had it come to this?

'Oh my God. We saw you...' As delight at speaking to me seized hold of Lou, her voice raised in volume. 'Mum and me, we saw you at the awards.' I held my mobile even tighter to my ear, to stop her voice filling the bathroom and giving my precarious position away.

'You did?' I wondered if they'd also seen the guy at the table next to ours.

'Yes. I managed to pick up a U.S. channel on my laptop and we watched it all. Fuck a duck, they were brilliant. All these years of you making my ears bleed and forcing me to listen to them, and until the last couple of months I never appreciated just how good they really are. You know, I did the sisterly thing... you loved them, so I was determined not to.'

'Is that an actual thing?' I laughed slightly.

'Yes, I can assure you it is.' She laughed back.

'They were fantastic, weren't they?' I nodded my head as I thought back to their performance.

'Amazing, and when he blew you a kiss and the camera panned straight over to you... well, Mum and I were crying. It's like a dream come true, isn't it?'

'The wildest.' I spoke the words and allowed my head to loll forwards as pain filled my entirety at the thought of losing the man I knew I loved.

'I've gotta say, I know I've never quite got your sense of dress, tattoos and piercings… they were just you and I loved you for the way you were willing to show yourself to the world. Today though, they made perfect sense to me, seeing you standing up on that chair… You, my beautiful, incredible, caring, one of a kind, big sister, have been a woman in waiting.'

'What?' Despite my turmoil, I couldn't help but feel uplifted by her words and a small smile teased the corners of my mouth.

'You've got to see it… with them, with DD and Luke… Nik, you looked like you'd been a part of them from the very beginning, like you always should have been there.' When I didn't reply, as I let her words sink in, she carried on, 'You slot right in.'

'I love him, Lou.'

'You don't say! Doh!'

A few silent seconds followed, until I summoned up the courage to say the words I needed to voice.

'Did you see who was sitting at the table next to me at the awards?'

'No… and don't you dare bloody tell me it was Tom Hardy, because love you or not, if you didn't get his phone number and his promise to whisk me away to his pleasure palace… I'm disowning you, right now, right this minute.'

'Haydon Millar.' Even saying his name caused my stomach to roll over in revolt and I heard her gasp as I stopped her in her tracks.

'Well shit!'

'Precisely,' I uttered. 'He was there with their manager, Lawson, offering them a new recording contract by the sounds of it.'

'You need to tell Luke who he is, and what he did.' She said just what I'd been dreading hearing her say.

'I can't.'

'Why?' Her voice quietened as she gently questioned me. I could only imagine it would be the same tone she would use on a scared witness when she finally made the courtrooms.

'He appears to be offering them exactly what they all need right now.'

'That's as maybe, but you still need to talk to Luke about it.'

'I know, I'm just not sure that right now is the right time for them. Listening to them all, well… I just want them to make their own minds up about what they need. Not to come to a conclusion about it, after hearing what very nearly happened with me.'

'He'd want to know… I'm sure they all would, after all would you want to get into bed with a snake?'

'No… You're talking sense and I will tell him, after they make their decision as to what's right for them and their futures.'

'You're Luke's future.'

'Only for the next five years. Brie is his future for the rest of his life.'

'Nikki, stop it… you need to tell him and soon.'

I uncoiled my body from my sitting, foetal position and with renewed determination, as I convinced myself I was doing the right thing, I stretched my legs out in front of me.

I will, I promise, but I won't derail what he feels he needs to do for Brie's sake. I'm an adult, I can deal with it for now, as long as I don't have to be anywhere near him.'

'Soon.'

'Yes, I promise, very soon. Thanks for the chat. We travel to Vegas tomorrow and I'll try to call in a couple of days.'

'Love you.' I could hear the resignation in her tone, as she accepted, I wasn't going to be talked around.

'Love you too, give my love to Stephen and Mum.'

I disconnected the call and stood up. I had a wee, washed my hands and stripped, leaving my clothes in a pile on the floor.

Then with a renewed determination, I opened the door to our bedroom and after taking a couple of steps towards the bed, I stopped to let my eyes adjust to the small amount of light filtering into the room, as the cold light of night slowly started to be replaced by the warm rays of the very beginning of sunrise.

Wrapping my arms tightly around my body, effectively hugging myself, I cast my eyes over the man who had started by capturing my imagination, then my admiration, my heart and, to conclude, everything I was or was capable of being. I listened as his chest rose and fell rhythmically as he took breath after breath, and let how I felt just being this close to him steady my nerves.

He was on his back, with one arm bent up and over his face. I noticed that his longer strands of hair were scattered messily around him. His chest was bare, showing all its artistic splendour and as I surveyed him, I instantly looked at the Claddagh tattooed over his heart. With my heart now pounding in my chest, I let my gaze move down his body. He had one of his knees bent and the sheet, I'd noticed, was making a poor show of concealing his abs and the V of muscle he'd developed so magnificently.

So damned magnificently, it made my mouth water and my tongue twitch.

My eyes ran over him of their own accord, like they had been starved. They jumped to his happy trail and to the root of his cock. My body responded. My nipples instantaneously beaded, a flood of wetness hit the apex of my thighs and my skin went on edge as it showed its desperation to feel him against me.

I needed to touch him, to taste him and to feel the way he wanted me in return.

Shelving my previous fears, I crossed the distance between us and lifted the sheet up and away from him. As I revealed his naked body to my eyes, I heard myself gasp as I took in how devastatingly gorgeous he was.

With my mouth practically salivating, I imagined taking his cock into my mouth. Unable to deny myself I crawled on all fours, up in between his legs and gently pushed his bent knee to the side. Sitting back on my haunches, I trailed my fingernails up either side of his inner thighs and watched in awe as his balls tightened and his erection sprung to life, growing to its full glory in a matter of seconds.

In my peripheral view, I saw the second Luke removed his arm from covering his eyes and lifted his head to look down at me.

'Nikki.' Just the way he said my name, in that inexplicable interval in time that is flanked by unconscious and consciousness, had me reeling. My name left his lips as though he couldn't work out if I was a wishful figment of his imagination or not. Allowing myself to be fuelled by that, I gathered my hair behind me with one hand and bent my head downwards. After blowing warm air onto the slick wetness that I could already see glistening enticingly on the head of his cock, I waited for his erection to flex upwards in response and sucked him quickly into my mouth.

Savouring the rock-hard, velvet-covered steel and the salty flavour that was all Luke on my tongue, I cupped his balls with one hand as I massaged them and began to move my head up and down his shaft.

'Ahhhh… fuck, Nikki.'

Hearing his groans and feeling his cock swell inside my cheeks, I slowed the pace down and added a circle of my tongue around the head of his cock. I wasn't quite sure what the hell I was doing, but I wanted him to feel indulged like he made me feel. I only knew I didn't want him coming too soon.

'Jesus fucking hell… where the hell did you learn…'

Desperate to drive him to the point where he was experiencing a level of gratification that literally made him incoherent, I once again quickened my pace. Exposing my teeth for a few seconds, I took him to the back of my throat and grazed up his length and then added my tongue stud into the equation. After repeating the action a few times, I knew he was reaching the crest of his orgasm when his legs tensed either side of me. He grabbed my hair and wound it around his fist.

'Fuck.' Luke expelled the single word on a long, drawn-out groan.

I acknowledged in my head that my playtime was over, I was now effectively under his command and I relaxed into his direction. He held my head in the place he needed it to be, as he thrust himself into my mouth.

'Ahhhh, fuck… yes, Nikki…yes.' Listening to him closely as he fucked my mouth and feeling like I was back in control of my life, I ran my tongue over his glans, deliberately connecting with the slit and with a sense of satisfaction I felt him temporarily freeze as he lost all control. In seconds, my mouth was full of his release and feeling elated at where I'd taken him, and how in doing so I quelled my own doubts, I swallowed my prize.

Forty-One

Nikki

'OH, FUCK!' FLINT SHOUTING out behind me, had me turning around just in time to see him chasing Biscuit behind the floor to ceiling curtains. For a few seconds, I had visions of him bringing the whole bloody lot down, including the rail. When Biscuit finally appeared again from out of the other side, he was swallowing yet another string of tassels from the curtains and wagging his tail excitedly when he saw that all eyes were on him.

'That's ruined that.' I sighed and rolled my eyes up high in my head, imagining the bill for damages that Luke would be presented with.

'Well, that's total shit.' Brie swearing when she was normally the swear police of the group, had Flint and I bursting into laughter.

'It's not at the minute, Shorty, but very soon your dog will be shitting out tassels for the second time this week,' Flint added.

The three of us laughed at the situation, while Flint picked up Biscuit and put him back into his crate and shot the bolt across. Worn out by his performance, Biscuit curled up instantly and closed his eyes in resignation that for now his fun was over.

Normally, my job would have been to correct Brie's language, but not then. At that very moment in time, the three of us needed the escape. Luke and the rest of DD had left early that morning to catch a flight to New York. They were being interviewed on one of the many channels in the U.S. about their latest award and their future plans. We were going to watch the interview, then I was flying with the children and a security team to Vegas, where Flint would be picked up by his mum. Flint was pleased to be seeing her, but the atmosphere wrapped around us felt sad, as the only two children in the group got to grips with the fact they were going to be separated for a while.

'It's on!' Brie shouted out.

Quickly, I rushed over and settled myself on the settee that hadn't been trashed by the dog, nor covered with his drool. Sitting down in between the children, I held my breath as the interviewers greeted their audience and explained with obvious excitement just how pleased they were to announce who was on their couch. Their next few words were drowned out by screaming and my heart momentarily stopped as I waited with desperation for the camera to pan around, so I could see Luke. The man had only been gone for eight hours, but I felt like a woman denied oxygen.

The blonde haired, stunning looking interviewer placed a finger to her lips and moved her flat hand up and down as she attempted to quieten the crowd.

'Good evening, ladies and gentlemen,' the male host spoke to the audience, 'it is our absolute pleasure here at JXT to have back on our couch... Folks, please welcome DEFAULT DISTRACTION.'

The hosts stood up and started to clap their guests in and finally the camera panned to the right to find the four of them walking onto the stage and stayed on them while they sat down. Briefly, I ran my eyes over them all. Then my eyes settled on Luke and refused to budge.

He greeted the hosts as they welcomed him personally and changed his position a few times on the bright-blue, uncomfortable looking studio couch. He was the only one leaning forward, as if he couldn't get close enough to the camera and he stared with intent into it as he grinned wickedly. As per usual, he looked amazing in dark-blue jeans and a green checked shirt that was left unbuttoned to below his chest, showing an array of chains around his neck. I looked at his hands clasped together and then took in what could only be described as arm porn, at least it was to me. I shook my head slightly at myself, as straightaway my body reacted after seeing he'd rolled up his sleeves to just below his elbows, exposing his tattooed skin.

Unwittingly, but needing to be as close as possible, I mirrored his position.

Could he feel me?

I wasn't sure. But when he lifted his hand to his face and stroked his fingers through his tidy beard, my core tightened, and I clenched the top of my thighs together remembering the other night. Mesmerised by the man, I stared hard at the screen to see him place a hand over the Claddagh tattooed on his heart and I knew his actions were especially for me.

I listened transfixed, as Cade announced he had fallen in love and left his heart back in England. Brody and Luke high fived each other, like they had a bet on this exact piece of news, and Raff shot Cade a questioning look. The audience in the studio seemed to be split into two. There were cries, screams of "no" and also a smattering of clapping as some of their fans celebrated the fact that one of their idols had at last found happiness.

Uncharacteristically, Cade now remained quiet and focussed as he stared hard at the camera, and I knew that Winter must be watching back at home.

'Rafferty, I understand that Flint has been spending time with you over in the U.K.' Trudy the female host questioned.

'Yes, we had a great Christmas over there.'

'Is he still determined to get into the music business?'

'I don't know, love.' Raff's English upbringing crept in momentarily. 'That's up to him, he has my blessing to do whatever makes him happy.' I looked to my left so see Flint nodding in acceptance of his dad's words, and at that minute was beyond proud of Rafferty's parenting skills. 'We were in the U.K. opening our flagship hotel,' he added, trying to steer the conversation.

'Could a permanent move be on the cards?' Trudy pushed and the crowd following her cue let rip with more cries of "no."

'It's possible, depending on where our hearts take us,' Luke answered the question.

Without warning my heart sped up inside my chest, as Trudy seized the moment and with an annoying look of satisfaction on her face, she stared pointedly at Luke.

'Oh no! Ladies, surely this can't be true... have they all lost their hearts?' Bloody annoying Trudy dug deeper and incited the audience to help her. 'So, Luke, do *you* also have an exclusive for us all here at JXT.'

Luke tensed for a millisecond, then like a seasoned performer he laughed and shook his head at her, and the others followed suit. The moment was a dream come true rolled into a nightmare for me. Had Millar not turned up the other night, I would have been wishing that Luke would announce that we were together. Now, I didn't want Millar knowing any more about us than he'd already witnessed.

'I'm only asking what everyone is dying to know, Luke...' She pushed in and I held my breath as I waited for Luke to reply.

Like a well-oiled machine, the guys closed ranks around him.

'I've got an exclusive.' Brody stopped tapping his ankle and raised an eyebrow at her. 'We've just opened a fucking spectacular hotel, if that's what you're asking?'

'Oh, yes... the first of many, I hear?' She carried on unfazed as publicity photos of The Manor filled up the screen behind the four of them.

'Hopefully.' Brody twisted a couple of his rings around his fingers and then carried on. 'The hotel we opened in Kent was well received, and we're looking forward to seeing where that takes us.'

'Yes, and I understand the next will be in Vegas?'

'Yeah,' Cade answered.

'So, Luke...' She started again and I held my breath as I wondered just how close to the wind she was going to fly with her questions. 'We saw some wonderful pictures of Brielle dancing at the music awards the other night. She really is a credit to you and looks so very like her mom.' She looked out to the audience as she offered her explanation, 'Luke's wife, Cherise, who unfortunately is no longer with us.'

A few "Awwws" left the crowd.

'She's a beauty, inside and out. She's kind, funny and accepting of others and I couldn't ask for more from her,' Luke replied and I felt Brie smile into my side.

She carried on and I swallowed, scared at just what was coming next. 'Do you think she'll take after Cherise and take it up professionally?'

'Who knows... as Raff said, our children's happiness matters more than anything.'

'And is she happy now you've found someone special to share your life with?'

Luke looked questioningly at her and I froze, waiting on his reply.

'I think we have a picture of her.' Like a dog with a bone, Trudy pressed Luke further. Then she beamed a wide smile at the audience, making sure they were going along with her for the ride as the pictures of the hotel faded and one appeared in their place of Brie and me instead. 'There we are. Brielle was up dancing on her chair with a beautiful young woman, and our sources tell us that the young woman is Brielle's new English nanny.' Even my breathing halted as every single part of me concentrated on the TV.

Luke nodded at her.

'My heart skipped when I saw you blow her a kiss.' Trudy fleetingly held her hand to her chest. 'Would you like to tell us about the new lady in your life?' Her saccharine smile made my stomach turn over.

'We love and appreciate our fans...' Luke stopped talking as the studio erupted. Cade and Brody raised their hands up to the audience to appreciate. 'But our private life is our own. We will live wherever we're the happiest and love whoever completes us and accepts the crazy in our lives.'

'Consequently, you're announcing to us that you've found love again, Luke?'

'Brie is the only special person in my life, Trudy.' Luke stared at her, like she was a piece of shit he'd just trod in. I knew what he was doing and why he was doing it, but hearing him say the words made my heart hurt, even though I knew it was the right thing to say.

'I wonder if you can tell the fans what they really want to know. When will the next album be out and will you be touring the U.S. in the near future?' The male interviewer pushed in a question of his own, as he tried to cut through the growing tension.

'Yes, we can, Mike... because that's why we're here isn't it, Trudy?' Cade answered.

Trudy at least had the humility to blush and to look down at her notes as her body language effectively told Mike that the interview was now his to complete.

'We're writing this year and plan to hole up in the studio to record the next album. That should mean that a new album releases the end of this year and I'm convinced we will back that up with a tour next year.' Sitting bolt upright as the tense atmosphere engulfed them, Brody answered the question.

'That's good news.' Mike directed his comment to the audience who immediately backed him up. 'I also hear on the grapevine that here has been talk of a new record deal on the table for Default Distraction?'

'Yeah?' Raff questioned, lifting his eyebrows high and looking to his left at the others.

'With Windmill Records?' Mike carried on.

The four of them shook their heads as they looked at each other in disbelief.

'Not sure where you've gotten hold of that info, Mike. We're not in the market for a new contract,' Cade added.

It was Mike's turn to glance down at his notes.

'So, even if that were true, it wouldn't be happening, we'd be staying right where we are... because confidentiality means a lot to us,' Luke answered the unspoken question and my body sagged in relief at the announced decision.

'Thanks for having us.' Raff effectively shut the interview down and the guys stood up from the settee. With their arms over each other's shoulders, like they'd finished a set on stage, they waved to the crowd and shouted out their goodbyes.

Forty-Two

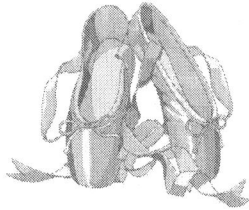

Nikki

THE FLOOR TO CEILING windows and the corner positioning of the two-storey penthouse suite that Luke kept at The Venetian Hotel, meant that my early morning view of Vegas was second to none. Unable to sleep, as Haydon Millar filtered through my mind, I'd resigned myself to getting up. In doing so, I'd managed to convince myself it would all work out and effectively dampened down my concerns, as I replayed the look of disgust and distrust that had penetrated all the guys' faces on the TV the day before.

It was just after six, far too early. But a feeling of eagerness to look at the place I'd only read about or seen in films had engulfed me, so I was up far earlier than was necessary. Knowing that my peace could be shattered at any minute, I'd showered and dressed into denim shorts and an old Bryan Adam's tour T-shirt, before I'd made my way downstairs to have a much needed cup of tea.

Sipping at the mug I was holding with both hands, I watched fully focussed as the world below me sprung to life. The previous day's dust and dirt was cleaned off the famous street and once again the city below me was readied for the thousands of tourists who would walk around its famous sights, just like they did every day of the year.

I'd arrived on an early evening flight with the children the previous night, which had been quick and painless and saw us landing at North Las Vegas airport just as the sun was setting and the normally bright lights of Vegas were beginning to come to life. Butterflies had fluttered around my stomach as, like a child unable to contain its excitement, I'd pressed my nose to the small window on the plane to get the best possible vantage as we flew parallel to the famous strip, before finally touching down.

My mobile vibrating in my back pocket interrupted my thoughts and changing my hold on my mug, I fished it quickly out of my pocket. Seeing Luke's face lighting up my phone, caused a broad smile to attach itself to my face.

'Morning,' I offered as I looked down onto the screen.

'Mornin'.' I watched transfixed as he swept his hair away from his face and then as he placed his arm underneath his head. 'Where are you?'

'I'm downstairs having a peaceful cup of tea, while I people watch.'

'By yourself?'

'For the minute, but who knows when that will change.' I grinned at him, excited to have him all to myself, even if it was only on FaceTime.

I watched as his face lit up mischievously. He pulsed his eyebrows at me, before a smirk lifted the corners of the mouth I so loved to feel anywhere, just so long as it was on me.

'Are you still in bed?' I teased, trying to hide the fact that I knew my face had suddenly coloured under his perusal and that my core had instinctively clenched.

'Yeah, I was dreaming of you.' The wicked glint in his eyes should have prepared me for the very next thing he did. All at once, my view changed as Luke changed the camera angle and slowly showed me down the length of his body. Without proffering his movement any speed at all, I saw in close proximity the familiar tattoos that covered the length of his torso, his muscular chest, prominent abs, until finally I caught sight of his obvious erection, wrapped up in a crisp white sheet and framed by the defined V of his Adonis's belt. Without any warning, he ripped the sheet away and his heavy looking cock was exposed to me.

My mouth watered and a moan escaped my lips.

'You don't play fair, Luke McKenzie.' I shook my head, unable to look away from the picture he was presenting.

'Never said I did, darlin'... You missing me?' His face came back into view as he asked me the question and he chewed on the side of his mouth nervously, as he waited for my reply.

'Yes.'

In the background I heard a loud knock on what I presumed was Luke's door.

'Fuck,' he muttered, before another loud bang sounded out.

'Yes!' he shouted out, and then we were both moving.

'Get your arse outta bed, Mac.' I heard Raff's voice and assumed he'd barged his way into Luke's room, which was probably just as well as having taken in the glint in Luke's eye, I wasn't sure what his next move would have been, having found out that I was alone. 'Car's here in thirty.'

'Yeah, yeah... I'm up.'

'Hi, Nikki,' Raff shouted.

'Hi,' I replied.

'This excuse for a boyfriend has told me you two have a date tomorrow?'

'Fucking boyfriend,' I heard Luke shout out in disgust from somewhere in the room.

'Apparently so.' I smiled back at the phone to no one, as Luke seemed to have put me down somewhere and all I could see was the ceiling.

'I'll be taking Brie off your hands for a few days. '

'You will?'

Raff's face filled the whole of the screen as he picked up the phone and took me with him to sit down. The handsome man smiled at me as he spoke, but in the space of a few seconds, I took in how worn out he looked. The dark lines under his eyes were more prominent and he had extra length to his normally well-kept scruff. Raff very noticeably had a lot on his mind.

'Yeah, I'm going to spend some time out at mine and Ashley's house, we need to sort through some stuff, and although Flint needs to be around for some of it, he doesn't need to be party to it all. Brie and her airy, loving persona will give him the diversion he needs... so it's for selfish reasons, really.'

'That's as maybe, but I'm sure she'd love it. She was so sad going to bed last night at the thought of Flint leaving today.'

Raff spoke again as he told me how much Brie loved spending time at his house, swimming in the large pool and baking with the housekeeper, and I nodded and made listening noises as I tried to justify why I was so excited at the prospect. The words I'd just spoken were absolutely one hundred percent true, but as my heart raced at just the thought of having Luke to myself for a few days, I knew exactly why I was so enthusiastic.

Suddenly, the phone moved again, and I was dropped to the floor before a wet looking Luke appeared back in the screen.

'Shit!... get some fucking duds on man,' Raff shouted out, and a loud bang sounded out as he apparently left the room.

'Sorry about the rude interruption... I'll be back in Vegas in about eight hours.' Luke nodded. 'Enjoy your quiet time before the kids wake up. Ashley will be with you at around ten this morning to pick up Flint.'

'I know.'

'Thanks again for being there to hand him over.'

'It's no problem.' I nodded at him, as I tried in vain to pull my professional self, back together.

'See ya later.'

I blew him a kiss and watched as he winked back, and the phone screen went blank.

'Flint, your mum's here,' I called up the stairs, after being given the nod by phone from security.

'Okay,' he acknowledged, shouting back.

'Will you be much longer?'

'Just packing.'

I released the glass-partitioned banister I'd been holding on to and sighed. I'd been asking the teenager to get out of bed, eat and to pack up the few bits he'd got out the previous night, for over an hour. I wasn't sure if it was the teenager in him that couldn't get his arse into gear, or a reluctance to go home with his mum, and I hoped it was the first reason.

The doorbell sounding to the suite, had me pulling my thick hair up into a ponytail and sweeping my eyes down myself to check I hadn't spilt any of my cereal down my T-shirt. I knew just how glamourous Raff's ex was and was convinced she wouldn't have any interest in me at all, but I at least wanted to be clean and presentable.

'You'll do, Bryan,' I whispered to myself, as I ran my hand over my T-shirt in an attempt to smooth out the creases.

'Hello.' I pulled open the door with a flourish and waved my other hand to offer her entrance to the suite.

'Hi there, it's Nikki, isn't it?' The welcome in her tone was completely unexpected and feeling eager to make her acquaintance, I smiled generously at her before replying.

'Yes, hi… please come in.'

'Of course, over here okay?'

'Absolutely.' Without me leading her any further, and seemingly knowing exactly where to go, Ashley made her way to the furthest seating arrangement in front of the windows and looked out of the same window I'd been staring out of only a few hours before.

'Can I get you a drink?' I questioned, as I swept my eyes up and down her. She had a voluptuous figure and carried more weight than I remembered from previous photographs, but it was weight that appeared to be in all the right places, and it suited her. Casting my eyes down myself, I identified that being in her presence made me question my almost boy-like frame.

Luke likes it, get a grip.

'A Voss if you have one.' Momentarily, Ashley turned her head to look back at me and offered me a smile.

'A Voss,' I repeated. 'Coming up.' At least I hoped it was. Until I opened the fridge and wracked my brain as to what coloured fancy bottle of water I was looking for, I wouldn't know.

Green? Blue?

I swept my eyes over the ridiculous amount on offer in the fridge and finally found the capital letters I was looking for on a clear glass bottle.

'With ice?' I called out over my shoulder.

'No thanks.'

Hurriedly, I poured out the water and walked over to place the glass down on the low table nearest to where she was standing.

'There you go. I'll just give Flint a call. Please take a seat.'

'I'm fine, I'm sure he'll be down soon… thank you for the drink.'

'You're welcome.' I stood in place, wondering how to make small talk with a woman who didn't appear to be anything like I thought she'd be.

'How are you enjoying your new position?' Ashley turned her head around from looking out of the window, flicking her shoulder length, platinum blonde hair as she did so. She faced me properly for the first time since she'd walked in, and I stood stock still as her eyes drifted over me several times.

'I'm loving it.' I relaxed in the knowledge that she was willing to be friendly. 'Brie is a lovely little girl and I've had the pleasure of getting to know Flint, too. He's a real credit to you and his dad.'

When she offered me a smile that didn't quite reach her eyes, I knew in that millisecond that she'd given me a false sense of security in the few minutes we'd been in each other's company. Having her taking all of me in, from the roots of my hair to my bare feet, with their usual black painted toenails as they curled up into the thick, light grey rug beneath my feet, had me running my fingers nervously over the tattered hems of my Denim shorts.

'Thank you… and one day when he's a famous drummer in his own right, he'll be even more of a credit.' Her condescending tone had me physically reeling.

What?

I stopped my eyes from rolling up high into my head and swallowed down what I really wanted to say, as I heard the children's voices getting nearer and watched her half smile at me again.

'I saw you dancing at the awards the other night.'

On instinct, I wrapped my arms around myself as I waited for what I could feel she was gearing up for.

'Yes, we had fun,' I nodded.

'You fit right in; he couldn't have picked anyone better for the role.' She waved her hand at me, and for the second time, I took in how false and seemingly practised most of her expressions were. Although I considered that it could have been down to the Botox or the fillers I hadn't noticed before. The same ones that suddenly appeared so very noticeable.

'Thank you.' My manners got the better of me as I replied warily and waited for her next hit.

'I'm happy for Luke. He needs someone in his life and Brie needs a mom.'

Is that it? Was she worried I was trying to replace Cherise? I felt some of the tension leave my shoulders.

'Brie already has a mom. I'm not trying to take the place of Cherise. I'm happy in my role as her nanny and as her friend.' My voice grew in strength as I tried to convince her and to somehow get her on my side.

'For now,' she sarcastically added.

'For as long as that's what she needs.'

'I was Cherise's friend...'

'I can assure you I'm not trying to take her place,' I interrupted. 'If that's what this little talk is about.'

As she tried once again to raise a supercilious smile at me, my bitch radar rang out its alarm loudly in my ears. Realisation struck, as I comprehended that I didn't want this woman on my side.

What a fucking bitch of a woman. Sorry, Flint.

'No, no.' She picked up her glass and took a sip and all the time her eyes focussed on mine. I was aware that the children's voices hadn't come any closer. I had no idea why, but knowing Flint he was probably keeping Brie clear for a few minutes. 'I just think it's amazing how he's being true to Cherise and keeping the promise he made.'

I couldn't help myself and crossed my arms over my chest as I prepared myself to hear what I knew she was so desperate to get out. So bloody desperate in fact, that a visible sheen of sweat was sitting unattractively on her top lip. It was unsightly. Ashley had unexpectedly become hideous looking in the space of a few seconds, even though she would be deemed an attractive looking woman. It amazed me that someone could look so stunningly beautiful one minute and in the same diminutive amount of time, change to be so completely ugly the next. But then beauty wasn't skin deep, it came from inside out, or so I'd always believed, and here she was proving me correct.

'I bet.' Truthfully, I had no clue just what I was betting on.

'You have no idea, do you? Then allow me to help you.' A condescending expression captured her face, and I could see the enormous amount of pleasure she knew she was going to get by trying to belittle me, as it fuelled her every word. 'Luke promised Cherise that Brie would have what they both didn't have growing up. After she died, he swore he'd create a family for Brie, and I'm *thrilled* he's finally making good on that promise.'

'*Create* a family?' I narrowed my eyebrows at her and watched as she carefully made her way around the pieces of furniture to come closer. I stopped myself from shaking my head in disbelief, as a wave of pain took my breath away.

'Whatever you think is going on between you, is fake. Luke lives in a world of fake, it's sadly all he knows.' She smiled at me like she'd just bestowed a compliment.

All I could do was stare at her, as no suitable come back appeared on my lips.

'It's surprising just how convincing money is, isn't it? And Luke constantly amazes me with just what he's prepared to do and literally put himself through, to manufacture an illusion.' She added a laugh before breezing past me and touching my arm gently with her fingertips in a false attempt to console me with her body language. A picture of his fabricated home in Ireland swept into my mind, followed by a feeling of panic that unfurled inside my gut. I moved in response and shook her poisonous touch away like she'd burnt me.

You've sold yourself. My sister's voice sounded in my head.

No!

I took a deep breath and stood tall, refusing to let what she'd just implied get to me.

'Ashley, I can call you Ashley, can't I… as you're no longer together with Raff?' I didn't wait for her reply before carrying on. 'I have no idea what you're on about. You're obviously a person who, for whatever reasons I'm unsure of, feels they must defend something that isn't, nor ever was, theirs to defend and as for why…' I moved my arms out from my body as I shrugged my shoulders and opened both palms to the ceiling. 'Again, I'm unsure… but I'd hazard a guess at the fact your jealousy knows no bounds, and I'm sure it smarts like hellfire to know that DD have moved on with their lives and left you in their wake. Because now they're creating the rock dynasty you so discernibly wanted to be part of, and it's not the same, is it, when you're on the outside looking in?'

I was grateful for always keeping up to date with the gossip that surrounded DD and it appeared the tabloids had done a fair job on reporting her as a manipulative bitch. Christ only knows why Raff had married her and not Lauren.

She carried on walking away and put the glass in her hand calmly down on a counter, but as her back stiffened I knew my words had the desired effect.

'FLINT!' Ashley shouted upstairs. 'We're going.' There was no motherly tone of love in her voice. No seeming excitement at seeing her son again and I hated her even more.

Movement sounded upstairs, and she spun around to face me, eager to have one last dig.

'I hear you're off out on a "date" tomorrow.'

I knew she was stating a fact and not asking a question. So, I did the same back. 'Do you?'

'Seeing Vegas as a tourist, how sweet... I wonder if he'll take you to all of Cherise's favourite places?'

'I'm sure he won't.'

'Are you?' She took on a sickly-sweet tone to show her sympathy for poor little old me, before carrying on. 'That's as maybe, but I'm sure Luke will do something soon enough, that'll prove to you that all he's doing is smothering his guilt, by playacting with you and then you'll know for certain then, won't you?'

Flint arrived and stood on the very last step, understandably wary on taking the final step to be in the room with us both.

'You'll see then that you've just become part of the story he's invented... all to keep his promise to the only woman he'll ever love.'

With that she was out the door and shouting out again for Flint to follow her.

'Bye, Nikki... Brie's staying upstairs, she hates goodbyes.' I could see the concern on his face as he spoke and looked between me and his mum. I managed to smile at him and effectively throw off, for a few seconds, just how uncertain his mum's words had made me feel. I gathered him up into my arms, whether he wanted a hug or not didn't even cross my mind. The poor kid had that excuse for a mum, and I needed to console him in the only way I knew how. When he hugged me back, I understood how very grown up he really was.

'Bye, Flint... have fun and I *will* see you soon.'

I nodded at him, just the once, to convince him I was fine and compartmentalised her word vomit with my concerns of Haydon Millar.

Forty-Three

LUKE

'WHERE TO?' I PULLED my baseball cap down further over my face, making sure my hair was concealed and that my apparently instantly recognisable eyes could only be seen by Nikki.

The buzz of Vegas unexpectedly hit me, it wasn't something you could normally feel behind the metal and glass of a vehicle and for just for a few seconds, I was completely floored. It was a sucker punch straight in the gut as memories consumed me. I hadn't walked around Vegas for years, because for one thing, it was as difficult as hell to, and reason two, I no longer had any need to. As the memories came back, I remembered that the last time I'd walked anywhere around Vegas had been with Cherise and worst of all, I knew it was written all over my face when Nikki stopped dead in her tracks.

'Is doing this with me too much?' Pain and uncertainty took over her beautiful features.

'No, just… well, fuck… it brings back memories.' I shrugged as I tried to explain.

'Did you come here with Cherise?'

'Here?'

'You know,' she shrugged her shoulders looking embarrassed at what she wanted to know. 'The tourist sights and this hotel.'

'Fuck, no… you don't do the tourist thing when you live somewhere, and I never shared that suite with Cherise if that's what you're asking.'

'Good… I mean, it's okay if you did.' I stepped up closer to her and after placing my thumb and finger to her chin, I tilted her head backwards so her eyes would meet mine.

'Is it?' I questioned, already knowing the answer by the look on her face.

'No, not really.' She fought in my hold to tear her eyes away from mine as she admitted the truth, but I held her there, knowing we needed to go through this together. 'We can go,' she offered, looking sad, as doubt captured her bottomless grey eyes.

'No, I wanna do this with you… we had a date, remember?' I smiled my reassurance over to her. 'And I remember someone telling me that I had to own my wants, not so long ago.'

A small smile captured her bee stung looking lips and then the doubt swept back in.

'I don't want to upset you, you know, remind you of what you've lost.'

'How the hell can you even think that?' I bent my knees to get down to her level and placed the peak of my ball cap against her forehead, effectively enclosing the two of us.

'Cherise and you were together for a long time, and I understand that this must be difficult. I just want you to know that,' she explained as she lifted her hands up to my T-shirt covered chest.

'Define together.'

'You were married… you'd been together since you were young, and you had Brie.' Her fingers tapped lightly on my chest as she spoke.

'No truer words… but slowly, I'm coming to terms with the fact that in all those fucking years, we were only *really* together for a couple of them… and it was never, not in any one of those few years, anything like this feels with you.'

'It wasn't?' Her eyes opened wider at my admission.

'It hurts to say it, and I'm not proud of myself… but, no.'

'Oh.' She couldn't contain the smile that started to make the corners of her mouth begin to lift.

I inhaled quickly, knowing I had to carry on, as I tried to explain myself and I hoped I wouldn't sound like a man who was practically fucking certain he hadn't got a hope in hell of ever fully working out how a relationship worked.

'Look, I'm not used to airing my shit.'

'Talking things out is good… but if it's too hard on you, then forget I asked.' She gently shook her head and offered me a way out. One that I would have normally grabbed with both fucking hands.

'No… This is all new to me, but I know I need to do this with you. No one has ever made me want to attempt to before, darlin'. But with you…' I inhaled sharply and swallowed to clear my throat and with my heart pounding hard in my chest, I carried on. 'Well… I'm gonna make an effort for both our sakes.'

With unshed tears beginning to fill her eyes, she nodded instead of answering me.

'It kills me that she's not here, she's missing out on our beautiful daughter. I miss her, but I don't miss our toxic life together. I don't ache for her. I don't miss touching her. I don't crave her laughter or want to nuzzle into her neck just to breathe her in, like I do with you. I don't miss how we were together, in fact the more time that passes, the more I understand that the overriding emotion I still feel about my dead wife is guilt.'

'Guilt?' Nikki's hands stopped moving.

'She wouldn't let me go and I wasn't strong enough to stay and be there the way she needed me to be. I wish I could turn back the clock and do right by her, but it's too late.'

'Oh.' Her body appeared to sag in relief. 'I'm sorry.'

'Don't be sorry, you're the first person I've *ever* admitted all that to and I'm pretty sure my therapist would be fucking amazed.'

'Thank you for choosing to share it with me… talking things out is therapeutic, and just for the record, you constantly amaze me.' Nikki glanced at my mouth and in reaction I brushed her lips gently with my own.

It was a kiss of acceptance and I hoped that the doubts I'd apparently given her had been erased by our conversation.

As our lips broke apart, she looked at me with an expression that was pure need. It took every fucking thing I was, not to pull her back into the building behind us.

The woman made me fucking insatiable.

Instead, of going with what I really wanted to do, I grabbed at her fingers and entwined them with my own, before taking a step back, lifting our conjoined hands above her head and twirling her around on the spot, just so I could admire what was mine. The short as fuck, flowery printed dress, twirled around the tops of her legs and as I saw more of her exposed flesh than I was expecting to, I thanked fuck that Vegas was warmer than usual for late January.

'I'll ask again, where we going?' I questioned as I grinned at her.

'I have no idea,' she giggled. The lightness that consumed me when she was by my side never ceased to fucking surprise me. 'You promised to show me around and I'm more than happy just being here with you.'

I changed my hold over her and with both hands on her hips I pulled her in closer to my body. Then stooping down, I whispered into her ear, deliberately catching the shell with my beard as I spoke.

'Then we need to make a plan and move, because Jesus fucking H, woman, I'll forget our date and drag you back upstairs given the opportunity.'

The gasps she released, set fire to my soul.

I'd promised her a day showing her all the things that tourists loved to see, but it was nearly eleven in the morning and so far, after making her come all over my face with my tongue and then fucking her from behind, holding on to the ass that regularly made top billing in my dreams, I still wanted her with a need I couldn't fathom.

'You would?' she breathlessly questioned.

'Hell yeah.' I nibbled her lobe after the words left my mouth.

'Whoa.' Nikki gently pushed her palm against my chest and separated us. 'I think we'll need some personal space today.'

'Do ya.' I laughed and adjusted my cap yet again, pulling it back down after catching a look from a passing onlooker.

'Yes.'

'Then I'll step away, darlin', and I won't touch you again until ya *beg* me to.'

I saw what I'd just said flash through her eyes, before she retorted, 'Fine, but that won't stop me touching you, Luke McKenzie...'

Reluctantly, I moved my hands away from her hips and placed a finger from one hand close to her lips without touching them and warned her with a raise of my eyebrows not to say my full name out loud again. It was going to be hard enough to pull off the date without being recognised and if she was going to announce who I was, we might as well give up now.

'Okay, I've got it… I have a list.'

I withdrew my finger and tucked both hands into my jeans, but refused to step away from her.

'Hit me with it.'

'A gondola ride, then up the miniature Eifel tower and I want to see the hotel that's shaped like a pyramid. Do you think we can go inside too?'

I nodded at her.

'Then I'd like to eat at Denny's.'

'Denny's?' I questioned in disbelief.

'Yes.'

'Okay,' I conceded. 'Anything else?'

'The water fountains at the Bellagio.'

'Is that it?'

'Yes.'

'Then let's go.'

I started walking away, without offering her my hand and without checking she was with me. As I reached the walkway that went back inside the hotel, I felt her come alongside me and suppressed the grin that threatened my face.

'You're not even going to hold my hand?'

'Nah, you wanted personal space, darlin', and you got it.'

'I'm not sure I'm going to like this.'

'You might not… but by the time I get you back tonight, you'll be craving my touch.'

'I'm already craving it,' she moaned and pouted as she spoke, making my dick twitch in response.

Walking faster, I stepped in front of her to block her path. There wasn't a hope in hell I was going to let her feel how much I wanted to touch her, but for a second, I allowed myself to breathe in her light, floral scent.

'Then just imagine how you'll feel after several hours of build up, as you anticipate my tongue savouring your skin and my mouth devouring you.' I moved an inch closer until our bodies were only centimetres apart. When I spoke again, I watched her tongue flick out to wet her lips as she inhaled sharply. 'We're gonna watch the fountains from the corner window in the suite. You'll watch them reach their climax, just as I finger fuck you to yours and I won't stop until my hand is soaked in your juices. Then, while your knees are still fucking trembling, I'm gonna sink my dick into your sweet pussy.'

Fleetingly, her eyes flickered closed, and I knew her imagination had carried her away.

'That's hours away and now I'm going to touch you more than ever. In fact...' She stood up on her tiptoes, wrapped her arms around my neck and pushed her body up tightly against mine, making me swallow down a groan. 'Luke, I'm going to do everything possible to tempt you.'

'Oh, darlin', I was hoping you would.'

Forty-Four

LUKE

'Yes, AND TOMORROW FLINT and Uncle Riff Raff are going to teach me to swim without my water wings.'

'That's fantastic, Brie. Sounds like you're having fun.'

'I am.' The giggle she released warmed my insides. 'I practised my dancing today, Nikki.'

The woman who had laid her head down on my lap the minute our plane had taken off for London, shifted slightly. I watched her heavy eyelids open as I ran my fingers through her soft mane of hair, letting the heavy tendrils caress the insides of my fingers and then fall heavily back into place. I grinned, knowing it was down to me having kept her up most of last night as I fucked her, with the view of Vegas as our backdrop, that had her so exhausted.

'That's great, Brie,' Nikki acknowledged, with tiredness enveloping her tone.

'Flint thought it was really funny when I showed him how to dance like a duck.'

How the two of us suppressed the laughter I could feel was bubbling up inside us both at the picture her words conjured up, I'd never understand.

'Did he join in, Shorty?'

'YES!' Her giggling filled the otherwise empty private plane and I laughed right along with her. 'So did Uncle Riff.'

'Well, fuck!'

'Daddy... no swearing.'

'Sorry, Brie.'

'Coming,' Brie called out in an excited voice. 'Daddy, Flint and Uncle Riff are calling me.'

'Is Ashley not there, too?' Nikki unexpectedly questioned. I looked down at the beautiful woman on my lap as I tried to gauge the expression on her face.

'No. Flint says she's staying with her friend, he's called Travis.'

Nikki nodded and smiled a small smile.

Good fucking job!

Hopefully, Raff had managed to get her out of his home and life once and for all.

How, out of the four of us, two had continued with what were malfunctioning relationships, for the length of time we had, was incomprehensible.

Time to move forward, man.

I spoke to Raff in my head and fully focussed on the beautiful woman, who had in turn twisted her head to look up at me, as if she could read the thoughts inside my head.

'Daddy, what are you and Nikki going to do in London?'

I cleared my throat and grinned like an asshat at the dirty thoughts and pictures her question had flicking through my head.

As if she read my filthy mind, Nikki lifted her hand and after finding my nipple, using her finger and thumb she tweaked it hard. Instantaneously, every fucking nerve ending in my body snapped to life. On instinct, my hand raised, and I seized her small wrist in warning.

'Not helping, darlin',' I whispered as my cock flexed against the side of her head and I shook mine at her in caution. A slow and knowing, carnal smile stretched over her gorgeous face.

'London Bridge and Buckingham Palace, before we go back to Falham to see how Stephen's building is coming on,' she answered and then looking mischievous, she carried on. 'Oh, and don't forget Big Ben, I'm really excited to be seeing Big Ben again,' Nikki offered, as a laugh left her mouth and I shook my head at her euphemism.

'Can I see them next time we're in England, Daddy?'

'Sure thing, Shorty,' I agreed still shaking my head at Nikki as I tried to laugh quietly.

'Good. I need to go now. I love you.'

'Love you too, Brie.' I voiced the words I'd only ever spoken and meant to one person before, my daughter, looking straight into Nikki's eyes, and my whole fucking life flashed in front of my eyes.

'Bye, Daddy… bye, Nikki. Eskimo kisses for you both, I'll see you in three days.'

We both answered and the line went dead.

With our eyes still captured in each other's, emotions I knew I'd never felt before unravelled themselves inside my gut, as understanding swept through me and in those few seconds, something completely unrecognisable passed between the two of us.

Love.

It was so goddamn real it hurt.

Out of your fucking depth. The thought went around my head, mirroring a stuck piece of vinyl on a turntable. Slowly, I came to terms with just where I was, caught up in that strange moment in time when everything around the two of us fell to silence. And all I could concentrate on was the person who matched the exact template, I'd been unknowingly searching for my whole fucking life, as she entered my heart. I knew any normal person would clutch hold of her. They'd clasp her tightly as they tried to convey just how they felt… fuck, I'd been singing about this defining moment for fucking years. I knew how it was meant to go. But instead, like the damaged asshole I knew I was, I felt my body stiffen against my will, as I attempted to hold myself together.

Can't cope.

Panic raced through me. My breathing became ragged and eventually stopped. And a pain so fucking vibrant and life affirming took hold of my heart. With a sudden desperation to feel and live life to the full, I demanded of myself, to open my heart and absorb everything Nikki was offering.

Pressure began to build at the back of my eyes, as my mouth formed the three words I knew I wanted to say to her. I tried repeatedly, but it never came. As no words left me, I saw her look of understanding at my struggle, which was eventually replaced with the pain I'd caused her, and I hated myself with everything I was.

'Fuck!' I banged a fist down beside us.

'It's okay...' She reached over and ran one fingertip over my beard.

'It's not FUCKING OKAY... I want to tell you how I feel.' The words left my mouth, hissing through my teeth as anger at myself consumed me.

'You do it in other ways, there's no rush,' she offered.

'I told you I was fucking damaged.'

Nikki moved suddenly; her hand fell away and she turned her body towards mine, as she attempted to control the hurt I knew I'd caused her. After pushing one arm behind my back to hold me, she raised herself up on her elbow and lifted her beautiful face towards mine. My nostrils flared in anger at myself as I saw the unshed tears encapsulated in her eyes.

'That's as maybe, but you're mine... I love you, Luke.' I closed my eyes for a split second and then forced myself to open them, to accept the woman who was holding me like I was her very reason for existing.

'I don't fucking deserve you.'

'Yes, you do. I've told you once before, Luke McKenzie, it's always been you. I'm yours because I was born to be yours. I love you, Luke, and one day in time I hope you'll be able to tell me the same thing. But for now... kiss me.'

I looked deep into her eyes for a few seconds. Then I swept some errant pieces of hair away from her face and behind her ear, and slowly lowered my mouth down to hers, hoping against hell that she'd feel everything I wasn't capable of yet telling her with words.

Exhaling loudly, I looked out to the darkening sky we were flying into, as I struggled not to match my mood to the stormy looking expanse around us.

'You still there?'

'Yep,' I answered, getting more and more uninterested in what he was really trying to tell me.

'If you'd still been here, we could have arranged for a meeting with him.'

'I know... Let me check I've got this right. Even though we told Lawson it wasn't happening at his job review a couple of days ago, this Millar still wants to speak to me?'

'Yep, that's just about it. Raff, Brody and I have heard him out and told him no, now it's your turn.'

'Right.' I sighed out loud and reluctantly accepted the situation.

Nikki shifting around in her sleep, caught my attention.

'Yeah, let's do it... give him my cell and tell him to call within the next twenty minutes. Then I'm outta this for a few days. I've got something else that deserves my attention more.'

Cade's laughter hit my ears, 'Something my fucking ass. That's a someone... and you deserve her, dude.'

'Mmmmm... I'm trying to imagine any sort of world where that was true. Thanks for trying though.'

'Right.' Cade cleared his throat, 'Okay, I'll call and tell him. Have a great time in London, send us pictures of *all* the sights, now, won't ya?'

Catching his obvious insinuation, I laughed. 'Not a fucking hope in hell, dickwad.'

'Ciao.'

'See ya.'

It couldn't have been more than ten minutes since I'd closed my sore eyes and rested my head against the head cushion, when my cell, which I'd switched onto silent, began to vibrate on the armrest next to me.

I shifted myself, trying to bring myself around and while doing so, I checked that Nikki was still asleep. When she moaned and made a soft snoring sound, I answered the call.

'Yes.'

'Hello.' An English accent hit my ears. 'Luke McKenzie?'

'One and the same.' I knew my tone had already given away my feelings at having to take his call and hoped the fucker would take the hint and make what he wanted to say quick. Anger at my earlier fucking performance, had made sure I was sitting right on the edge of craving oblivion. I'd been eyeing up a full bottle of bourbon for at least an hour and it was only because Nikki was asleep with her head on my lap, I hadn't grabbed it, unscrewed the top and swigged down half.

'Haydon Millar here. I'm grateful you took my call, as I know you're going to want to hear what I have to say.'

I laughed at the conviction in his voice.

'Yeah?'

'Lawson has explained that *all* the band have vetoed the offer of a new recording contract with my company, Windmill records?' I thought back to a very grateful Lawson, as he'd accepted the terms he had to adhere to, if he wanted to keep his job. His first task had been to issue a point-blank refusal to Windmill records.

'You heard right... we appreciate the offer, but it's a unanimous and resounding no from us all.'

'That's a shame. I think we could have worked well together.'

'That's a fucking no, right there.' I thought back to the JXT interview. 'This isn't our first rodeo, man. We demand anyone we sign a contract with, to give us unreserved loyalty, respect, and the confidentiality we deserve... In one fucking hit, you blew it, man.'

His laughter came at me down the line, and for a couple of seconds I took the cell away from my ear and looked at it, grimacing.

'The loyalty and respect you say?'

'Yes, that's about it.'

Again, the guy let go of a laugh that sounded almost manic.

'And do you expect all your business transactions to go the same way?'

'Yes... Now, if that's all you've got to say?'

'How about your new nanny. Does her contract demand that she's loyal and respectful?'

My insides bottomed out.

'What the fuck are you getting at, man?' I shook my head at his question and tore my eyes off the bottle of Bourbon, to look down at Nikki.

'I know just how far she gets under your skin, and how the need for her runs hot around your veins.'

Suddenly my body demanded me to move, to distance myself and to get closer to the one thing I knew would take the edge off. Lifting Nikki's head away from my lap, I shifted from underneath her, stood up and laid her head back down to the seat, more brusquely than I wanted to. Then I was striding up the cabin towards the bar.

'What the hell are you on about?' I spat out into my cell as I reached the alcohol.

'I saw you and her at the awards the other night and thought you ought to know, that you're not the first one she's pulled this stunt with.'

I couldn't help but look accusingly over my shoulder at her sleeping figure on the two-seater we'd made our own.

'And just what fucking stunt are you talking about?' I hated hearing the desperation in my tone. I hated being out of control of my life and yet here I was.

'I've got to take my hat off to her. She's moved on from a very married record exec to widowed, single rockstar, and you're a whole new level of minted.'

'Just because we don't want your fucking record deal, you come at me with this… this fucking load of shit! You can sit on your finger and swivel, fucker.' I managed to add a laugh to my words.

I'd been about to end the call when he'd spoken again. 'That family of hers… she'd sell her soul to the devil himself, to get what they need.'

'And you'd know this…' I prompted, sick of listening to the heavily laced, pity-filled silence between his words.

'She was my nanny, too.' My nostrils flared. I blew out an exhale between gritted teeth and raised my eyes to the aircraft ceiling.

'So? *If* she worked for you before, then yours was one of the three glowing references I read. If there was a problem, you wouldn't have given her one,' I questioned, refusing to believe what I knew he was getting at and at the same time hearing that drunken asshole, Lewis, or whatever his fucking name was, accuse her of the same thing back at the wedding we'd played at.

'Met her family, have you?' I could picture the look of satisfaction on his face, as he and I realised he'd got me by the balls, and that I needed to hear him out. 'Her sister is one very persuasive lawyer.'

'Get on with it.'

'I loaned her the money to get her kid brother the wheelchair he needed and in return... well, I'll do the decent thing and leave that to your imagination.' I clenched my other hand into a fist. Making the longer nails I kept for playing my bass dig so far into my palm, I hoped they'd draw blood. 'Now, here I am, wondering just what her family needed next and just how much that beautiful little body of hers was worth to you?'

What the hell would a beautiful, twenty-six-year-old, want with a damaged fucker like me? My own words came back to me, but fighting on like I'd done since the day I'd been born, I made sure he felt he had nothing over me.

'The decent thing. Fucking hell, you're deluded, man. I've listened to what you have to say, and I never wanna talk to you again. If I so much as see you anywhere near me, expect to end up in the nearest emergency room... YOU LISTENING?'

'I was just...'

'Fuck off! That was a rhetorical question...' I heard as he cleared his throat, probably trying to swallow his words. 'I wondered from day fucking one what your angle was, when you offered that generous percentage for the recording contract and now, I know. You're one fucking jealous piece of shit. If I see Nikki's or my name involved with any of this malicious crap, floating anywhere around the media, I'll get our lawyers to talk to your wife and we'll see just how "very married" she thinks she is to you... then I'll suggest to your better half that we rip your goddamn company out from underneath your fat ass.'

I touched the red button and disconnected the call.

Instantly, my breathing felt laboured, and excruciating pain sprinted around my whole body. Having felt rejection many times before, I recognised the sensation. It took only a matter of seconds to understand that this time it had manifested itself ten-fold.

Luke McKenzie you're a stupid bastard.

Closing my eyes in acceptance, I let my head fall forward and waited until the well-practised sense of numbness travelled through me, as I went back into the place I normally resided in. The same place I'd been hiding in until Nikki had ridden into my life. The only place I knew how to really exist in, and where the only person who could reach me was my daughter.

Without lifting my head, I reached out and found what I needed, unscrewed the cap, and swallowed a third of the amber liquid straight down, relishing the numbing burn at the back of my throat.

Then I spun around to face the woman I would have given the world to, until five short painful fucking minutes before.

'You wanted an asshole rockstar, darlin'; then you've fucking got him.'

Forty-Five

Nikki

I WAS CAUGHT BETWEEN that weird place of not asleep, but not awake either.

So very quiet.

Having fallen asleep to the sound of the plane's engines, it only took a second or two to realise they had fallen silent.

Have we landed?

I knew Luke hadn't allowed me to get a lot of sleep the previous night, but I couldn't believe I'd slept through most of the flight and the landing.

'Luke.' Sleepily, I called out his name and stretched my arm out to the side of me to try to find him. But to no avail.

'Luke?' I questioned again.

But still no answer came.

I knew he was somewhere nearby; I could feel him. He just wasn't as close to me as he normally would be. The sense of foreboding that ran through me was strong. Something was wrong. I'd fallen asleep with my head on his lap in the plane, after he'd kissed me with everything he was, as he'd tried hard to convince me that he loved me, and that one day soon he'd be able to say the words. And I'd believed him. I knew I had never felt as close to another person as I did in that very moment with him. But now, he was nowhere to be found and understanding him as I now did, I could only imagine what had gone on inside his head after I'd closed my eyes.

'Yes, I know what the hell I'm doing.' I heard his voice a way off, although it sounded a little off and momentarily relief ran through me.

'Hey, man, I'm only asking... it's unlike you to change your plans,' Mitchell, one of DD's security team, replied.

'What the fuck are you on about, Mitch? We used to do this all the time,' Luke retorted, saying each word slowly and enunciating each syllable.

'Honestly?' The frustration in Mitchell's voice was evident. 'I thought you'd grown out of this shit.'

'Well, you thought fucking wrong... Now, just do whatcha paid for.'

'I'll phone him,' Mitchell conceded. 'But you need to understand that a new flight plan will take time to sort out.'

A pause sounded in the conversation.

'You have however long it takes me to consume what's left in this bottle...'

He's drinking?

Fear became my overriding emotion and when a shiver travelled down my spine, I sat up and began to rub my hands up and down my arms in response. Gradually as my eyes became more useful in the bright, blinding light, I turned my head and looked towards the cabin behind me.

'Luke?' Panic laced through my tone as I directed my voice in his direction.

Why isn't he answering me?

'I've no fucking idea... Here... you talk to him, Seamus.' Mitchell spoke again, sounding more and more pissed off at whatever the situation was. In my head, I could picture him offering the phone to Luke.

'Hey, Shay!' Luke slurred. 'Yeah, dude... it's been a long fucking time. I'm coming over today... What? No, I couldn't give two fucks if the house is clean or not... I wanna throw a party...'

What the hell's going on?

'Fuck no!' Luke's voice rang out again as he almost shouted to the man on the other end. 'The party to end all fucking parties... Yep, pussy and lots of it and make sure there's plenty of dust and smack to go around, won't ya?'

Drugs?

'Fuck, no.' Mitchell disappointingly moaned the words.

'Fuck, yes,' Luke replied. 'And get a car to meet us at Dublin... Nah, I'm not with anyone special, man.'

No one special?

My breath caught as his last few words resonated time and again around my head. Then as the words fell to silence inside my head, anguish moved into the deep chasms the words had fashioned.

What the hell had happened?

'There she is, my little super fan.' Luke spoke, and I heard the ever-increasing slur caught up in his voice. Lost inside my pain-filled thoughts, it took a few seconds for my eyes to focus on him as he reappeared from the cabin. Gradually, through my tear-filled vision, my eyes converged on him.

'What's going on?'

'I'm being what you want me to be, darlin', what everyone always wants me to be... drunk or stoned and fucking ignorant.' He opened his arms wide. His right hand was fixed tightly around a bottle of alcohol, and as he misjudged the seat closest to him, some of the amber coloured liquid spilt over the grey leather.

'Luke, if this is about what happened earlier... I told you it was alright.' I moved myself forward to the very edge of the seat I was on, but remained sitting as I contemplated what to do next.

'You did, didn't ya?' He nodded his head at me to drive his patronising words home. Then ignoring the alcohol covered seat, he sat himself down, possibly before he fell down. 'But, Brie's nanny...' He moved his empty hand down diagonally through the space in front of him to signify a forward slash. 'Nikki, or whoever the fuck you are... I was then given some information about you, that was far from *fucking* alright.' I started when he then shouted out to the crew. 'DIM THE GODDAMN LIGHTS?'

Luke fished around inside the front pocket of the shirt he was wearing and pulled out his sunglasses. For a couple of seconds, he struggled with the frame, before he finally pushed them up the bridge of his nose with one finger and took another drink from the bottle in his hand.

In my peripheral view, I saw the large frame of Mitchell appear to the side of Luke. He crossed his arms over his chest and after glancing quickly at Luke, he shook his head and looked at me sympathetically.

Feeling completely outside of my comfort zone and with several questions threatening to spill from my lips, I contemplated just what to do first.

I watched as in the dimmer light, Luke leant forward and placed his elbows onto his knees. Desperate to discover what had happened while I'd been sleeping, I lifted my eyes up to find his, but unfortunately, they were hidden behind his Aviators. The sound of liquid swilling around a bottle found my ears and as I stared at him, trying to unravel the nightmare I had surely woken up in, he lifted the bottle to his lips again and took another couple of drinks. A satisfied sigh left him and he leant his head back once again into the leather seat.

When his face almost disappeared from view, my heart fell. Even with the space between us, I could feel the pain radiating off his body.

'Talk to me, tell me what's happened,' I implored, as desperation to help the man I loved, and to make things right, became my priority. Standing, I made my way to the seat opposite him, knowing it was as close as I dared get in that moment. I had to give Mitchell his due, he moved past us, and I heard him sit down in the seating area I'd just come from.

'Talk, she says… what fucking good is talking? I told you before I don't like airing my shit.' His face fell forward once again, and I could feel his eyes staring at me accusingly.

'Where are we?' I questioned, knowing the answer but desperate to keep him speaking.

'London, but I'm taking you to my house… Gonna give ya the full fucking rockstar experience.'

'In Ireland?' I asked the question and poised myself as I listened to his answer. Ashley's warning from a few days before ricocheted around my head.

'Yeah… Clontarf.' He held the 'f' for far longer than was necessary as he answered me. I'd read an article in an expensive magazine years ago, that had featured him and his so-called family home just outside of Dublin, and knew that the place he was talking about was one and the same. I couldn't help the instant sag of my shoulders as I submitted to my fears.

'Why, Luke?' I couldn't help my fear coming across in my voice.

''Cause I see you there... yeah, that's it exactly. You and that place were meant to be together.' He leant forward suddenly, and his alcohol smelling breath hit me as he spoke.

'You said it was just for publicity...'

'And you, darlin'... Well, you told me you loved me. It's surprising how well we both lie... isn't it?'

The question was left hanging between us.

'I didn't lie... Luke, I haven't a clue what's happened since I fell asleep, but I've never lied to you.' I shook my head gently at him.

Unceremoniously, he held out his arm over the aisle and dropped the bottle he was holding. The smash of glass rang out as it hit the floor, making me jump. The remainder of the liquid inside splashed everywhere. 'And there's your next fucking lie.'

'No,' I implored.

'This whole fucking thing between us...' I watched him move one finger, slowly between the two of us, 'It seems it was a pretence on both sides.' He leant further forward, and I was shocked to see the depth of his anger stretched over his face. 'Fun while it lasted, though.' His eyebrows raised to me in question.

'I've never pretended anything with you, please believe me.' Not sure where the hell to go with the tension that was building up rapidly between us, I whispered to no one in particular, 'I thought we were going to stay in London for a few days.' I voiced the thought that was inside my head, as I desperately tried to work out what the hell had gone wrong.

'I know ya did... surprising what can happen in the space of a few hours, isn't it?' I could hear laughter in his tone, but instead of filling me with a sense of relief, it filled me with dread, as I recognised it was fake.

Needing to close the gap between us, I began to move forward. I didn't know what was going through his mind, but knowing him, I understood that the distance between us wasn't helping. Then, not thinking twice about what I was about to do, I sat down next to him and wrapped my arm around his waist. I held on tightly as I fought back the tears that were threatening to fall.

His body tensed beneath my touch, but having him in my hold once again, I refused to let go. Reluctantly, I had to let my arm drop away when he pulled himself out of my hold.

'Mac, we've got the clearance, we can leave in fifteen minutes,' Mitchell informed him.

'Luke, please tell me what's going on?' I desperately implored.

Sitting on the edge of the seat, he turned his head and behind his Aviators I felt his eyes observe me properly for the first time since I'd woken up. Relieved, I looked intently back at him as I tried to convey how concerned I was about what was happening. I reached out to try again and placed my hand on his jean-covered thigh, deliberately aiming for an exposed piece of flesh beneath one of the many rips in the material. I hoped that the connection of my skin on his, would bring him back from wherever the hell he'd gone to.

He looked down at my hand and back up to my face.

'Be careful what you wish for, Nikki... You wanted a fucking rockstar and now you've got one.'

'I want you, not whatever the hell's going on right now.'

'Lie number three.' He laughed and at the same time shook my hand off his thigh, unable, it seemed, to feel my touch on him. 'I learnt a long fucking time ago that I wasn't good enough for anyone.'

'YOU ARE GOOD ENOIUGH FOR ME!' My body lurched forwards with the strength of the words that left me.

Luke laughed and shook his head in response. 'Nah... all you wanted was the money... and I stupidly fell for it.' Luke smashed his fist on the centre console, making me jump. 'Fuck, Nikki... I'd have given you the money for Stephen's build. You didn't need to fuck me.' Pain was evident in his voice and the expression on his face changed, when he understood he'd given me a small insight of the pain he was carrying. I readied myself for what was coming next. 'I haven't paid for sex in years, but hell you do it so fucking well... had you told me what game you were playing, I'd have deposited the money each time, for a job well fucking done.'

'STOP IT!' I screamed the words at him, hoping they'd penetrate the mask he was hiding behind. 'I wasn't playing a game and I don't have sex for money!'

'No? I mean that trick with the stud on your tongue placed in my dick slit, sends me to heaven... Hell, you must have practised that goddamn move a few times.'

'I have never... ever done that to anyone else before.'

'Yeah, right. Haydon Millar explained to me just what you were prepared to do for your family.'

Haydon Millar. My head fell forwards into my hands in resignation, although I could envision that in Luke's eyes it would look more like guilt. I could only imagine the crap he'd fed Luke. Lou's voice warning me that I should tell Luke about him the minute he appeared back in my life, reverberated around my head. Hindsight was a wonderful thing, when you had the opportunity to use it, and I was unsure I was going to get that opportunity.

'When did you speak to him?'

'Just after I almost managed to tell you that I loved you... Ironic, huh?'

'I should have told you about him,' I admitted.

'No worries, darlin'... He told me all about you instead.' He dragged his eyes from mine, seemingly unable to look at me any longer and stared straight ahead.

The atmosphere crackled with the tension between us, sending my earlier anxiety levels through the roof and then miraculously my anger arrived, riding in on the pain and accusations of his words.

Just where the hell did he get off, believing Millar over me?

'So, let me get this straight. I know you keep telling me you don't talk, but you and I talked in Vegas, really talked. We got closer, and it scared the fuck out of you. And like it or not, you opened up to me... didn't you?' When he looked back, he stared through me, saying nothing, so I raised my voice. 'DIDN'T YOU?' I accused, jabbing my finger hard into his chest.

'I told ya... one fucked up bastard.' He smacked an open hand on the Claddagh over his heart.

'Stop using that bloody excuse... grow up and grow some balls.'

As hurt devoured me whole, my arm moved on instinct. I followed my accusation and slapped Luke's face so hard that his head turned to the side and although I wasn't prepared to show him, I knew my palm would smart for hours. As his face righted and he turned back to me, I caught a fleeting sight of the Luke I thought I knew, hiding beneath his pain.

'How very fucking dare you believe him over me? I'm not some make-believe woman you've bought with your money. I'm here with you, wanting to be with you, wanting to be allowed to love you. I'm real and not some fake illusion you've created, like this place you want to fly us off to, even if to you, I'm no one special.'

For a brief second, as I repeated his hurtful sentence back to him, I thought briefly that what I'd just said, had gained access to the heart he seemed to have so resolutely shut away and then I watched as he shook his head.

'I've got no idea what you're on about.' I watched his brow furrow as he tried hard to think through his alcohol induced fog. 'Like I've got no idea just who the hell you really are.'

'I'm me, that's it. I have no agenda... but if you can't see that, then I'm unsure what to say to make you change your mind.' I answered his question in a small, but resigned tone.

For a man heavily under the influence, he sure as hell moved fast. His hands came quickly to either side of me as he tried to grab both ends of the safety belt. Knowing there was no way in hell I was leaving England, unless he was prepared to kidnap me, I repositioned my hands to slow down his progress.

His hand tightened around mine in our struggle.

'I'm just giving you what you wanted, darlin'... because you sure as hell never really wanted me.' He snarled back at me as his fingers tightened painfully around my wrist. 'Then you too can sell your story, all about the night you snorted dust and had a threesome with Luke McKenzie.'

'You're hurting me!'

Luke froze as my words hit home and understanding that my time was running out, I took my chance and pulled my hand out of his grasp. Standing up quickly, I looked down at him as I rubbed at the pain with my other hand. The tears I'd fought so hard to keep at bay, fell fast down my cheeks.

'Fuck!' Luke grimaced, as finally he seemed to comprehend just what the actual hell was happening to us.

This wasn't just hurt and anger spewing out -- Luke had really believed Millar. He'd deemed that I was exactly what the lying prick had told him I was, and I was unsure if we would be able to get through it. As my thoughts penetrated my head, my back stiffened in defiance. As a young child, I'd had no say in my dad staying or leaving my life. I knew right then and there, that I was absolutely going to fight with everything I was, to get the only other man I'd ever loved, to want me in his life enough to fight for me to stay.

Forty-Six

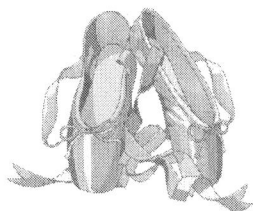

Nikki

'JUST LEAVE.' LUKE SPOKE as he righted his inebriated frame on the seat beneath him. He pointed his finger at me with such vehemence, I saw his hand begin to shake with the effort he was exuding.

'Is that what you really want?' My bottom lip trembled as I asked the question.

'Yes.' His head fell to his hands, and he ran his fingers through his hair in frustration.

'Then understand this, if you let me go, that will prove to me that you really believed the lines of shit Millar fed you about me.' I sniffed up the tears that were falling over my cheeks. 'And I swear if you make me become the very thing Ashley tried so damn hard to convince me I was, a couple of days ago, then I vow that even though I'll continue to look after Brie, because I promised her I'd stay... *you'll* never have me again.'

I spoke the words as evenly as I could, as I tried frantically to diffuse the situation we'd been plunged into. I knew I needed to speak with as much calmness and presence of mind that I could somehow muster, but my body was quaking with emotion. Inside, pain filled my chest, and in the constricted space, my lungs were struggling to take in enough air. But even worse, I could feel his accusations had struck deep into my heart, the same heart that was now fragmenting and I was struggling to work out just how the hell we'd gotten here.

All I knew was, I had to fight with everything I had.

Luke froze as my words hit home. The atmosphere between us was so intense, I was physically shaking. I could feel he was trying to understand just what I'd imparted to him, through the blanket of alcohol he'd swathed around himself for protection.

At last, Luke tore his glasses away from his eyes, making the Aviators spring on their frame between his fingers. The pain was palpable between us as his tortured eyes found mine.

'Everyone always leaves... I can't believe I thought you'd be different?' He shrugged his shoulders and shook his head at me.

'I don't want to leave you... I want to tell you the truth about Haydon Millar and then maybe you can be truthful with me and explain why Ashley seems to think you've bought me, all so you could fulfil a promise you made Cherise.'

At last, his eyes found mine, and as he held them captive in that purposeful way of his, I released the breath I'd been holding. Finally, I knew I had his interest piqued and every single one of his synapses was now focussed on the two of us.

He shook his head fast. 'No,' was the single word that left his mouth in disbelief, and I noticed how he was no longer slurring.

'Then remember this, I'm leaving because you pushed me away... because I refuse to be another victim of you trying to keep everyone at arm's length to protect yourself... If you want me... if you want a chance at a future with me, then this, whatever the bloody hell it is, needs to stop, right here and you need to talk to me.'

'I don't talk... my upbringing didn't teach me how.' My heart bled for him, for the young boy he once was in the orphanage back in New York. But he was an adult now, and he needed to fight for me to stay.

For once, someone needed to want me enough to fight for me.

'Talking always helps... but I can't talk to myself.' I waited a few seconds before carrying on, hoping he'd agree. When he offered nothing, and doubt filtered across his pain-filled eyes, I knew I had to carry on. 'Then, you leave me no choice.' I had to call his bluff, but I also understood I was playing a dangerous game and my tears once again fell faster.

'Mitchell, open the door please,' I called out in resignation.

'You can't leave.' Luke finally spoke. His voice sounded sober, although I could still smell the alcohol prevalent on the air around us.

'No? Then tell me how, now you've effectively shut yourself down, just how the bloody hell can I stay?'

His eyes darted between me and the plane door that Mitchell was preparing to open, but he made no further comment, instead he chewed nervously on the corner of his mouth. Reluctantly, I placed my trembling hand onto the nearest seat. After taking a deep breath, I summoned the strength I'd been relying on since our dad had walked out of our lives, to take the step I never in a million years thought I would ever take.

The one that led me away from him.

Shaking uncontrollably, I turned one last time and took in the damaged man I'd fallen head over heels in love with and took all of him in. I committed him to memory, knowing the next time I saw him, as Brie's nanny, the distance between us that I was prepared to construct to preserve what little I had left of my heart, would be impenetrable.

'Goodbye, Luke.' I caressed his name with my tongue, one more time. 'This evening has been the absolute worst of my life, and I've had a few. But I want you to know that I'll never regret meeting you, the real you, not this person you've become to protect yourself... Because for a very short moment in time; I had it all.'

His eyes widened as my words finally penetrated the mask he was wearing.

Fighting to keep myself together, I turned my head away from him and forcing myself to hold it up high, I walked up the aisle. The emotions running around my body, were making it almost impossible to put one foot in front of the other, but I did, as self-preservation kicked in.

'No, don't,' I was sure I heard him mutter, but it wasn't enough.

I reached out to take hold of the edge of the door.

'NO!' I heard his pain-filled shout and the frantic movement behind me. Then I felt him. Luke had surrounded me. His large hands were placed on the aircraft door and the seat beside me. His closeness flooded all my senses, and instinctively I absorbed everything about him. It was too much, all far too much and I closed my eyes in defence. He spoke gently into my ear and my breath hitched 'I'm sorry... I don't know how the fucking hell to do this... but for you, I want to try.'

'Luke,' I whispered his name, as his warm breath caressed my ear, sending shivers of need for the man, down the length of my body.

'Please stay,' he begged. 'I know I might not be able to change your mind, but please, I want you to stay.'

'I'm not sure.' I spoke the words and watched the warmth of my body leaving me and escaping into the London night air. But one thing I did recognise was that the swirling anger that had enveloped us only minutes before had expired.

'Nikki, darlin', you've touched my soul, and know that no one has *ever* done that before.'

'Close the door please, Mitchell.' I lifted my eyes up to find his concerned face.

'Yeah?' he questioned, looking behind me in question at Luke.

'You heard what Nikki said... and do me a favour and cancel the flight plans,' Luke added.

'Mac, that's the only fucking thing you've said that's made sense in the last few hours.'

Without waiting for Luke's response to his accusation, Mitchell closed the door and shut out the outside world.

Luke moved away from behind me, and I craved our togetherness the minute he'd gone. But then his fingers gently intertwined with mine and a tiny sliver of hope blossomed deep down inside my heart. Slowly, we walked as one towards the original seats we'd taken when our plane had taken off from Vegas, and sat down with our hands still grasping each other's like a lifeline.

'I'm deleting the contract you signed. The fact I coerced you into agreeing to stay for five years was wrong.'

'Why?' The small amount of hope I'd been clinging on to evaporated.

'I need to know you're here because of me and you... no one else, not even Brie. Just you and me.' He lifted my hand up to his mouth and placed a few kisses gently to the wrist he'd hurt earlier.

Then he twisted his body to face mine and lightly his fingers connected with my face as he persuaded me to turn to look at him. I watched as he took in just what he'd done to us, and I was there when regret and sorrow took command of his features.

'I want to talk... I want to listen to you.' I sighed as I swiped the back of my hand over both of my wet cheeks. 'But you need to understand just how much you've hurt me.'

'I'm sorry, Nikki.' His pain was evident, but all I felt was relief. Somehow, my gamble had paid off and I had to hope that it might be able to carry us further.

'You made me feel like my life had changed forever, but in less than an hour you've snatched away everything I thought we were,' I continued, knowing he was with me every step of the way.

'Fuck, you'll never know how much those words hurt to hear and how much remorse I have over my reaction. I should have spoken to you first.'

'You should, because without trust we have nothing.'

Luke moved back in his seat, making the leather underneath him squeak out its protest. He lifted his other hand, and with determination he took hold of mine and using his hold, he pulled me over to sit on his lap. Once I was where he wanted me to be, he wrapped his arms tightly around me and the strength of our connection gave me reason to hope.

'Tell me what you want to say,' I encouraged from my new position. 'Talk to me, Luke.'

'I have regrets... a shit ton of them, and if I never tell you how you make me feel... I won't be able to cope, knowing I didn't do everything in my power to convince you to stay with me.'

'You say you feel something for me, Luke, but today Haydon Millar got to you and by your reaction to his lies, you believed him. Then you had a few drinks and went out of your way to cast me aside. What's even worse is, you wanted to humiliate me doing it.'

Luke looked down to my legs in guilt and then straight back up at me, to meet my accusations. 'That's true... and I'm not proud of any of it.'

'Why didn't you just talk to me about what he'd said, instead of lashing out? That's what I don't understand.'

He changed his hold on my hand and gently caressed the back with his thumb. 'It's not easy to believe you're good enough for anyone, when no one has ever hung around in your life. It's even harder to open up your heart, when you've spent the whole of your life shutting it away to keep it from hurting. Discussing my emotions is not something I've done a hell of a lot of in the past.'

'You spoke to me the other day in Vegas.'

'I know and doing that made me feel more fucking vulnerable than I've felt in goddamn years.'

'I can only imagine what Millar said,' I sighed.

'He said that he wanted to warn me that you'd worked for him before and you were only sleeping with me to get what your family needed.'

'And you doubted me enough, to think that what he was saying about me was true?' I could hear the disbelief in my voice. 'I did work for him and his wife, and they even leant me money to buy Stephen's wheelchair, but I paid it back in full, from the wages I earnt looking after their children.' I blew out a sharp exhale before I carried on. 'I should have left my position the minute he started to make me feel uncomfortable, but I loved the children and for that reason I stayed... Then, one night, he was drunk and tried to rape me.'

I carried on explaining to him what had happened that night and the subsequent days that followed. I felt his body stiffen beneath me as I watched him struggle to contain his anger once again, only this time I knew it wasn't directed at me.

'Hold on... you saw him at the awards that night and told me nothing?' he questioned, raising an eyebrow at me but keeping his voice under control.

'I know... that was the mistake I made. I should have told you straight away.'

'Yeah, you should have, I'd have fucking killed him.' He hissed the words through gritted teeth.

'And would that have helped?' I questioned and offered him a small smile.

'It would have goddamn helped me,' he muttered and then his eyes came back up to meet mine in resignation, 'But this isn't about you and me anymore, is it? It's about us.'

I nodded in reply. 'I didn't tell you about him, because I needed you to make your own minds up about what you needed as a group, what you needed in your future.'

His head shook, as he tried to work out what I was saying. Then his eyes were back on me, looking through a thick curtain of his hair and I knew he'd come up with the answer. 'My future was always going to be with you, did you think I'd get rid of you when the five years were up?'

'I don't know.'

'Tell me the truth?' he asked, sounding more sober by the second, 'And while you're at it, explain what you said, about what Ashley said you were.'

Again, the focus in the aircraft shifted to me and with an embarrassed blush hitting my cheeks, I told him about how in the back of my head I feared I would never be enough for a man like him, and how Ashley had tried to convince me that he'd bought me to create a family for Brie and that it was his way of easing his guilt over Cherise dying.

'Holy fucking hell, woman... how could you believe that?'

'Pot, kettle,' I called him out.

'Yeah, okay,' he conceded. 'I did once promise Cherise that Brie would always have a family around her, but the guys offer that already.' It was my turn to shrug, and I saw the pained expression my doubt gave him, so he tried again. 'It was so hard to let you in, but it was so damned easy to love you and I do love you, Nikki.'

'You love me?' I asked the question as I leant my face into his, needing to be closer to the man.

'Yeah, I love you...' He moved his head from side to side as he mouthed the words over and over. 'It seems I can now say it easily, after being terrified you were going to leave me.' His eyes filled with pain, caused by him remembering just why we were talking, 'Please don't leave. I may be a damaged fucker, but you make me want to be more.'

'I don't want to... but we still need to talk.'

'From the beginning, then...' he proposed and to steady his nerves, he inhaled a deep lungful of air. 'I was left, a foundling on a doorstep. I have no idea what my real name is, my whole fucking life has been a fabrication of some sort. That doesn't set you up real well for trusting anyone.'

I placed my hand on his cheek to hold him closer to me, as I felt the floodgates open on his heart.

'And then there's Cherise. The very worst part about losing Cherise, was that it was only after she'd gone that I comprehended I'd never really told her how much she meant to me.' I prepared myself to hear about how much he loved her and willed myself to accept it. 'We were young when we found each other and after the initial passion left, we needed each other too much to let go... it was us against the world. We both knew we'd fallen out of love, but she was part of my family, and I should have told her how much she still meant to me.'

Rather than feeling the jealously I was dreading, I was pleased to find that I was compassionate enough to feel for them both.

'I wish I'd told her with words instead of getting lost in caring for her and just assuming she knew.' He carried on, seemingly unable to stop the emotions he'd been bottling up for years. 'If only I'd said how much she meant to me, then perhaps she'd still be here. If only I'd had the balls to say the words, I'm sure we both needed to hear, and to walk away from our toxic marriage... then perhaps she would have moved on and found love again, instead of opting out.'

I watched as one huge tear fell over his cheek.

'Oh, Luke.' My heart broke for Brie's mum and the man she'd left behind, confused and hurt at her departure. 'Or perhaps you need to stop blaming yourself for what was a marriage between two people, and understand that she was ill, and however many times you helped, supported and stood by her, it possibly would never have been enough.'

I knew he'd heard me when he tilted his head slightly to the side, as he thought over what I'd said and then nodded with acceptance in my hold. 'It's possible, I suppose.'

'Our mistakes and failures don't define us; they don't hold us back. It's our own fears and regrets that do that...That's some of my mum's wisdom, I know she'd want me to share it with you.'

'Well, I'm frightened right now, and I'm not strong enough to carry around anymore regrets, so I need to tell you.' He cleared his throat. 'Nikki, you're what I've been searching for the whole of my life. The fear of you leaving here today and never being able to be near you again, is scaring the fuck outta me. I love you... you're it for me.'

'I love you too, Luke.' I became aware of the fact my body was trembling with the knowledge of what I now needed to tell him, knowing it could shatter everything we'd already come through. 'But I need to say something... and it's something that could change everything.'

'Then don't do it, whatever it is, don't say it.' He shook his head against mine, as he beseeched me.

'Full disclosure,' I whispered, as his arms tightened their hold around me. 'You opened up and talked to me and I now need to do the same. And if it's something you can't live with... at least we'll be able to console ourselves with the fact that we both tried.'

'If you make me open my arms to let you walk away... then, Nikki, you need to tell me, what do I tell my heart when you've gone?'

'Don't, Luke, I need to say this...' I inhaled quickly and then froze, because everything now hinged on what I was about to admit. Then I pushed out the speech I'd been preparing in my head for the past few years. 'I think you'll eventually want more children, and I can't give you that. I'm a DMD carrier. I *won't* bring a child into this world and subject them to what my brother has to live with.' The secret and pain I'd lived with for so long needed to be aired, and my body wilted in sharing my heartbreak and disappointment.

'Nikki... shit, is that it?' He moved one arm from holding me, so he could place it on the side of my face. He pressed my tear-soaked cheek to his. 'I don't care... fuck... I care, of course I care. But there are other ways to have children. Blood has never meant family to me and there are many children in orphanages and foster homes just waiting to be found, waiting and longing to be loved.'

'There are,' I agreed between sobs, nodding at his words of acceptance.

'All I need is you by my side. I have no parameters on how that has to be, as long as I have you, because I promise you that no one will ever love you like I do.'

'I love you, Luke McKenzie. I've loved you since I was thirteen.'

'Then let's sign a new contract, one that lasts for the rest of our lives.'

'But we've only known each other a few weeks.' I placed my hands on his face and turned his head to face me, needing to see him in all his wonderful, gorgeous entirety. His sparkling, emerald eyes found mine, and like the very first time I ever saw them, they held mine captive. I stroked my fingers down his face and ran them through his beard as I smiled back at him.

'Nikki, life's a risk and there's no guarantees. But I can guarantee you this, if you're never prepared to take a risk... then, darlin', you're never gonna live. Question is, are you willing to take that risk with me?'

'I'm so willing,' I muttered, as his lips came to mine to seal the deal.

Epilogue

LUKE

Four years later

I CLOSED THE HEAVY hotel door behind me as quietly as I could. As I raised the handle slowly to find home, I cursed under my breath when a far too audible click sounded. Instinctively, I made my body still and strained my ears to listen.

When my ears found the soft and gentle breathing of the woman I loved, I took a breath and, relieved, I leant my forehead against the cold, but solid door.

It had been six long fucking hours since she'd holed herself up in here the previous night, on her own. Even after me giving her all my best moves out in the corridor, as I attempted to change her mind. And all night long I'd been awake in the room next door and played back our last few minutes together. How I'd taken hold of her narrow hips to pull her into me, and then I'd let my mouth taste her subtle perfume behind her ears and down the column of her neck, just seeing if I could change her mind. When she'd moaned my name and curved one of those long, bare legs up around my hip and hooked her foot into my ass to have me grind against her, I knew there was no goddamn way she'd deny herself the pleasure of me taking her to bed. Then, right on fucking cue, Lou and the rest of the girls had arrived. They'd shouted out Nikki's name and brought her back to her senses, and she'd pulled away. She'd smiled at them with her swollen and enticingly biteable lips, while shaking her head at me in reprimand, while I'd rather gentlemanly given them all the finger.

I got it; I really did.

She wanted time, space, and a good night's sleep.

Me, on the other hand, I'd been awake all night fucking long, as I saw in each single hour. Not even taking my dick in my hand had been enough to satisfy the need I had for my woman.

But that was last night.

I'd given her what she'd asked for, even though several times over I'd come out of my allocated room and walked straight past hers, arguing in my head as to why the fuck I shouldn't just barge in and take her. But my heart had ruled over the needs of my dick, and I'd strode back again, feeling even more of a surly bastard.

It was now the morning, and I knew all about tradition, but tradition could go fuck itself with a nine-inch fucking nail.

She was mine, and no one, not even her, could demand that we spend any more time apart.

I knew that there was no one in the hotel room but the two of us and I was going to give her the best fucking start to her morning.

Turning around on the spot, I let the small amount of light filtering in either side of the Roman blinds correct my vision. Then I gave myself permission to let them rest on the woman lay out in the middle of the large bed. Standing still, I took the time to admire and appreciate what I owned, body and fucking soul.

Nikki's long, dark hair was fanned out around her nearly naked body, and on her side just above her hip bone, I read the names she had tattooed there, like I had done so many times before. The same ones that always made my throat constrict with emotion.

Brielle.

Aiden.

Cian.

Aoife.

Our lives were full, and more importantly, being the parents of four children, so were our hearts. The young woman I'd first clapped eyes on in a snow-covered lane, had ridden into my life, stolen my heart, taught me how to live and far more importantly, how to love.

And I was going to love her back for the whole of eternity.

I swept my eyes back up and over her body.

She was lying on her front with her face buried into the side of one pillow. My eyes fell to her white, lace panties and my dick, like always, sprung to attention. She took my fucking breath away, and it was all I could do to keep my fucking heart from pounding its way out of my chest.

The way she made me feel was every fucking thing. I'd got better at talking over the years we'd been together, but I still struggled to find the words to let her know just how deeply she made me feel. But now, with the help of all our family, I was going to show her just how much she meant.

But, for the next hour, she was mine and mine alone.

Taking the few steps I needed, I placed both my hands onto the bottom of the mattress. Deliberately, I allowed it to take my weight and watched on as she unconsciously stirred. Then I lowered my face to her feet and brushed my beard over both of her soles, knowing the connection would tickle. Her knees bent on instinct, and she dragged her feet up the bed. Shaking my head as I smirked at her reaction, I walked my hands up either side of her body and took a push-up position over the bottom half of her body. Lowering my face, I inhaled the smell of her floral body lotion on her luminous skin and gently placed my lips on her smooth legs, as I edged my way closer to the nirvana I was practically slavering to taste.

She fidgeted slightly and identifying she was just about to discover me; I lifted my head to watch her emerge from the pillow.

'Mmmmm.' She released one long, drawn out moan and my dick flexed in the confines of the sweats I'd pulled on to walk between our rooms, just as the smell of her arousal reached my nostrils. I'd heard once that the taste of the woman who was meant to be yours, was ambrosia, and I was certainly no fucking God, but I knew enough to know that even the smell of Nikki's arousal was the biggest fucking high I'd ever experienced. I inhaled deeply, knowing that her panties would already be soaked with her need.

'Luke.' My name left her mouth on a half whisper. 'Is that you?'

In years gone by, that question would have struck a nerve, but now it made me smile and I placed my mouth back down onto her needy flesh and moved closer to where I knew we both needed me to be.

'It better be, darlin'... or you're in big fucking trouble, on your wedding day and all.'

She turned over and reached out, and her hands found either side of my head. She pushed my hair off my face, and I found her eyes with my own. The power in the connection between us fucking floored me.

'You'll have to be quick; my bridesmaids will be here soon.' She lifted her head and grinned down at me mischievously.

'And your husband-to-be?' I asked as I blew on the damp patch I knew would be there in her panties.

Her eyes fluttered closed in reaction. 'Oh, you don't have to worry about him. He's under strict orders that he mustn't see me until later.'

'Orders be fucking damned.' I raised my voice and at the same time started moving.

I moved my body up alongside hers and after laying down beside her, I bent my elbow, rested my head on my hand and looked down at her. With our eyes still on each other's, I ran my knuckles over her cheek bone, then my fingertips down the column of her neck. They took the path they knew so well, around her already hardened nipples and down over her flat stomach. At last, I pushed my fingers into the top of her panties.

'Fuck, darlin'. So goddamn responsive... you're fucking soaked.'

'I know, can you tell I've missed you too?'

I grinned back in response.

We'd been apart a week, while DD played a few nights in Europe. Madrid had been followed by Berlin and the night before, we'd played in Paris in front of a jam-packed stadium and everyone who meant anything to us.

Opening her folds with my fingers, I circled the engorged hood of her clit a couple of times and then allowed two of my fingers to sink home. I looked on, as her back arched in response and then her eyes closed, as the fast-flowing ecstasy I'd released filled her veins.

One hand came down to mine and she held my hand in place as she ground her hips against it.

'Oh God, yes... right there.'

'Open your eyes, Nikki.' My voice was heavy with need.

At my demand, her heavy looking eyelids parted, and her dilated grey eyes met mine.

'It's so good, Luke.'

'How bad do you want to come?'

'Badly.' The single word left her lips on a whisper. I pushed my little finger against the tight ring of muscle of her anus and allowed my fingers inside her to work her up into a frenzy. Knowing she was close to falling apart, I dipped my head down and sucked her nearest nipple into my mouth.

Her body froze and then convulsed as she rode to the crescendo of her orgasm and with me directing the pace, she dropped over the edge. A flood of wetness hit my fingers and just as soon as her tight wall of muscles had relaxed enough to release my digits, I removed them from her pussy and like a starving man, I placed them in my mouth to suck them clean.

'Mmmm,' I groaned.

'Open your eyes as you suck them clean. I want to watch you.'

I did as I was told, relishing every single drop of her release, and somehow suppressed the smirk that threatened my face as she told me what to do.

As soon as I was done, I let my hand fall away. Then I was moving, meeting the silent demands in her eyes and those of my balls, which were aching to empty themselves deep inside her. My index finger pushed inside the thin piece of elastic on her hip and with my eyebrows pulsing at her in amusement, I twisted the material around my finger. A snap of elastic found my ears and glancing down at the prize I knew I'd find; I felt a sucker punch in the gut.

Her pussy was bare. That wasn't anything unusual, but the small tattoo I found just above her pubic mound was new. I ran one fingertip over it as I took it in.

A small Claddagh had been tattooed on her skin, and deep set in the middle of the heart the hands were holding, was a small green gem.

'Fuck, Nikki.' I couldn't help but be blown away.

Great fucking minds.

'It's for you… it represents love, loyalty and friendship and the green stone matches your eyes.'

'It sure as hell does.'

'Do you like it? I struggled to find something as a wedding gift for you, Luke.'

'It's incredible, it means you're mine… Although, all you ever had to do was to give yourself to me and that would have been more than enough.'

'I love you, Luke McKenzie.'

'Ditto, darlin'. Now, roll over and let me show you just how much.'

I watched her smile at me before she did as she was told.

'Get on to all fours and raise that beautiful ass into the air.' I slapped one cheek of the beautiful globe of her ass and rejoiced in the red mark it left on her perfect skin.

'Ahhhh, Luke,' she moaned, and then did as she was instructed. I took my position behind her.

'Blinds up.' I spoke loudly, and slowly the hotel room welcomed in the Parisian sunrise as I ran my nails gently down her spine.

'The brass headboard… take a bar in each hand and hold on tightly.'

I pulled her torn panties away from her pussy and let them fall down her leg as I watched her do as I'd asked.

'What can you see out of the window?' I questioned, as I pushed down my sweats with one hand and trailed a finger from the other through her wet, swollen folds, opening her up to my eyes.

'The Eiffel Tower,' she replied with an added gasp, as I swiped the head of my dick through her open lips and placed myself deliberately at her entrance. On impulse, she rocked herself backwards as she attempted to take control.

I flexed my hips fast and entered her in one swift movement. The sensation of being exactly where I was meant to be came over me and, wanting to preserve the feeling, I held her hips with both hands, closed my eyes and stilled.

'Luke.' She released my name on a moan.

Her silent plea was too much. I pulled out of her and then slammed back inside her again and again.

'When I marry you under the Eiffel Tower this afternoon, I intend for you to still be able to feel how well I fucked you this morning.'

'Yes,' she moaned, as she met me thrust for thrust.

'I love you, Nikki Osbourne. This is it… this is what dreams are made of.'

'My wildest dream,' she reiterated, before we came together, always together.

'I hear we have an exclusive for you at JXT.' Trudy, the interviewer, interrupted the conversation she was having with her guest and held her earpiece tighter to her ear. 'WOW! News is just coming in that Luke McKenzie of Default Distraction has just this afternoon, wed his partner, Nikki Osbourne, in a private ceremony, which took place underneath The Eiffel Tower.' She paused to listen further. 'Although the whole area had been sealed off for security reasons, the bright Spring sunshine showed that the bride uncharacteristically wore white, in what I'm hearing was a simple but stunning dress. The wedding was attended by their four children, all her family, Brody, Raff and Cade, with their wives and partners and their five collective children. And we are hearing reports that Luke sealed their love with a Claddagh ring, with an emerald stone. The ring was one he'd designed and had made especially for her.' She looked intently down the camera. 'How romantic is that? We'll come back later, I'm sure, as and when we have further news.'

THE END

Thank you for reading.

We've been Default Distraction.
Double D's, over and out.

Also, by A.S. Roberts

The Fated Series
Fated
Inevitable
Irrevocable
Undeniable

Default Distraction
Brody
Rafferty
Cade
Luke

Brash Boss
(Written in The Cocky Heroes Club)

Galloping Horses MC
Gluttony
(Written in memory of Lavinia Urban)

Written in Kristy Bromberg's Driven World
Deception

About

Andrea S. Roberts is a British author. Her loves include her soulmate, their children and the family dogs. She is the first to admit that she has a quick temper, a sarcastic sense of humour and is a loyal friend. A lover of live music she can sometimes be found in London at the weekend. She loves to create any sort of romance story from suspense to rock stars.

In every novel expect heart stopping moments and plenty of heat. Her eleven published books can all be found on Amazon. Please check out her **website** for more information.

http://asroberts-author.com/

Acknowledgements

Where to start? It's impossible to thank all the people in my life that help to make this dream of mine, a reality.

So, I'll start at the beginning. To my husband and our boys, thank you for putting up with me when I lock myself away and listen to the voices in my head instead of you. I love you all.

To my alpha and beta ladies (Sarah, Kirsty, Debi, Amo, Crystal and Cassandra) who allow me to talk over the stories in my head and subsequently help me to make my books better. I couldn't ride this crazy train without you.

To my long-suffering editor, Karen, thank you. xx

Thanks to my proofreaders, Freda and Kirsty … your eye for detail is amazing.

To my admin, Jo … thank you for running "Andrea's Anomalies" You seriously rock!

Maria MacDonald my sprinting partner, thanks for keeping me going!

The "Anomalies" my safe place and fantastic readers group, I'm in awe and so grateful for your continuous love and support.

https://bit.ly/ASRobertsAnomalies

Printed in Great Britain
by Amazon